Praise for

"Well known for her delightful adventure historicals, Galen raises the bar with *Love and Let Spy*. This is definitely a book you'll read more than once."

—*RT Book Reviews,* 4 1/2 stars, August
Top Pick for Historical Romance

"Ms. Galen gets better all the time... an absolutely sublime love story."

—*Fresh Fiction*

"Gratifyingly fun, ebullient spy-driven plot... while the romantic arc remains authentic and affecting."

—*Kirkus*

"An utterly wonderful historical romance."

—*Books of Love*

"An effortless and enjoyable read. Every aspect was well done—characters, plot, romance, and the right amount of steaminess."

—*Books for Her*

"A Regency story filled with passion, intrigue, and memorable characters."

—*Fresh Fiction*

"From the sweet and hot romance, to the dark secrets and endless thrills, this book was fantastic."

—*Imagine a World*

Also by Shana Galen

Sons of the Revolution
The Making of a Duchess
The Making of a Gentleman
The Rogue Pirate's Bride

Lord and Lady Spy
Lord and Lady Spy
True Spies
The Spy Wore Blue (novella)
Love and Let Spy

Jewels of the Ton
When You Give a Duke a Diamond
If You Give a Rake a Ruby
Sapphires Are an Earl's Best Friend

Covent Garden Cubs
Viscount of Vice (novella)

Earls JUST WANT TO HAVE Fun

SHANA GALEN

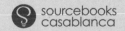
sourcebooks
casablanca

Published by Sourcebooks Casablanca, an imprint of Sourcebooks,
Inc.
P.O. Box 4410, Naperville, Illinois 60567-4410
(630) 961-3900
Fax: (630) 961-2168
www.sourcebooks.com

Printed and bound in Canada.
MBP 10 9 8 7 6 5 4 3 2 1

For Danielle Dresser: stylish woman, hardworking publicist, and all-around awesome human being.

Danger is a most diverting pastime.

One

SHE WAS FIVE. SHE LIKED BEING FIVE BECAUSE IT meant she could hold up every finger on her hand and spread them wide when an adult asked her age. Adults always asked how old she was and her name. Sometimes they asked her favorite color. Those were easy questions. Her name was Elizabeth, and her favorite color was pink.

She liked candied violets and puppies and hated bedtime and her nanny. Nanny always made her stand up straight and keep her dress clean and brush her hair. Elizabeth had long light brown hair, and it tangled. She had to brush it three times a day. *At least*. Nanny asked difficult questions. She asked Elizabeth to spell her name. Elizabeth had once told Mama that she wished she had a name like *Jane*, which was Nanny's name, because Elizabeth was *too long*.

Mama had laughed. Mama was always laughing, and Elizabeth wished she could be with Mama all the time and never have to see Nanny. But Mama and Papa had to go to the Season. That meant they dressed in clothes Elizabeth could not touch unless her hands were scrubbed clean, and they stayed up very late and slept all day. Elizabeth had to be *so* quiet.

She hated being quiet almost as much as she hated bedtime with Nanny, who yelled if Elizabeth didn't stay in bed or if she chattered too much. Elizabeth loved it when Mama tucked her in, because Mama always sang her lullabies. Elizabeth's favorite began "Lavender's blue," but Mama changed the words.

> *Elizabeth's true, dilly, dilly,*
> *Elizabeth's sweet.*
> *A kiss I will give, dilly, dilly,*
> *When next we meet.*

Mama was not with her today. Today was sunny and warm, and Nanny had taken her to the park. Elizabeth was so happy. She could run—if Nanny wasn't looking—and twirl and dance and pick wildflowers for Mama. Nanny had scolded her earlier for muddying her pinafore, but Elizabeth did not see how that could be avoided when everything that was interesting was either beside the mud or in it.

Elizabeth bent over to examine a pretty pink flower and jumped when a ball rolled to a stop at her feet. She looked up, searching for the owner of the ball. A boy, just about her age, waved at her and said, "Kick it back!"

Elizabeth blinked and glanced over her shoulder at Nanny. But Nanny was not watching her. Nanny was speaking to a man Elizabeth did not recognize. Nanny was also smiling and blinking a lot. Elizabeth wondered if her nanny had something in her eyes.

"Kick it!" the boy called again.

Elizabeth wanted to kick the ball, but she was not certain whether Nanny would approve. Of course, Nanny was not watching her at the moment. With a last furtive glance over her shoulder, Elizabeth kicked the ball. It sailed over the grass and down a small hill. The boy let out a *whoop* and chased after it. "Come on!" he called with a wave. He looked like he was having so much fun that Elizabeth followed. He kicked the ball, then let her have another turn. Then it was his turn, then hers again. Elizabeth was laughing and running and wishing the game would never end. She wondered if Nanny saw how much fun she was having, but when she turned, she did not see Nanny. She did not see anything that looked familiar. She was still in the park, but she'd run far away from the path where Nanny and the other people had been enjoying the day.

"Come on!" the boy yelled, kicking the ball again.

Elizabeth shook her head. "I can't. I have to find my nanny." She looked left and then right and frowned. She didn't know which way to go. Her lip trembled, and she felt the sting of tears in her eyes.

Suddenly a man stepped out from behind a tree. The boy seemed to know him and went to him immediately, but the man ignored him. "Don't cry, little girl," he said. "I'll help you find your nanny." He held out his hand, and Elizabeth stepped forward. She looked up at the man and hesitated. His eyes were small and odd—one blue and one green—his teeth were sharp and crooked, and despite his fine clothing, his black hair hung in long and stringy clumps. He smiled, but his eyes did not smile like his mouth. Wordlessly, Elizabeth shook her head and backed away.

"Where are you going, little girl?"

She shook her head and turned to run just as his hands caught her about the waist.

❧

Marlowe watched Gap stroll down Piccadilly as though he hadn't a care in the world. That wasn't as easy as it looked. Piccadilly was so crowded, even the largest of men were likely to be jostled. And the noise. Everyone was talking at once, trying to be heard over the calls of postboys and peddlers of every sort. Gap looked at home, which he was. Hands in his pockets, he whistled a tune through the gap in his teeth and appeared to stroll aimlessly. Men and women kept a watchful eye on him. He looked every inch the pickpocket ready to dive for the first easy bubble he spotted.

That was why Gap didn't dive.

As he neared the corner where she stood, alternately pretending to watch a gentleman have his boots shined and study the printed bills that covered every available wall or scaffold, Marlowe tucked an errant strand of hair into her cap. She'd bound her breasts so tightly she could barely breathe. She had slim hips and legs, but her long hair and her ample bosom would betray her if she were not careful. There was nothing to do about her chest, but she wished Satin would allow her to cut her hair. He wanted her to keep it for some of their better-rackets.

She watched as Gap gave her the signal, tipping his

hat to show her the bubble. Marlowe could dive as well as any of the gang, better than most because she practiced so often. She had the gift of manipulating her speech so she sounded much more cultured than she was. That and her sweet face meant the gentry trusted her. They thought she was one of their own, or not too far beneath them. They never suspected one of their own.

With a tap on the brim of her cap, she indicated she saw the bubble and approved. He was a tall man with broad shoulders and neat blondish-brown hair under his brushed beaver hat. He looked wealthy but not foolish, and she hesitated momentarily, wondering what Gap had been thinking. This was not their usual, easy game. He must have waved some blunt to attract Gap's attention. And if there was blunt to be had, she had better bring it back to the flash ken. She didn't relish another of Satin's punishments.

She turned away from the boot boy and his gentleman, timing her movements perfectly. By the time she stepped into the crowd of people moving alongside Piccadilly, she was almost upon him. His eyes, a sharp, clear blue, met hers, and she had a moment to think *this is a mistake*. But it was too late, because she'd already collided with him, and her nimble hands had done their work.

She had his blunt in her hand by the time she stepped back and bowed to him. "Terribly sorry, sir. Pardon my clumsiness." While one hand stuffed the pounds in her coat pocket, the other tipped her cap genially. Now was his turn to say *think nothing of it, my fine lad*. Then they would both go on their way.

But he didn't say his line. In fact, he didn't even look at her hand tipping her cap. His gaze arrowed directly down to the hand stuffing pounds in her pocket, and his lips curled in a smile. "Good day, Elizabeth. I've been waiting for you."

❧

She ducked into the flash ken with a curse on her lips. She was late, and Satin would have her hide. Strangely enough, that was the least of her worries at the moment. For once, she had bigger problems than Satin, and he was generally a rather substantial problem.

"Ye're late," Satin sneered from the corner of the large room the gang gathered in to eat and socialize. He was gnawing on a greasy chicken leg, his black hair hanging down about his face.

"Sorry."

"Gap said you got nabbed."

She shook her head with a quick look at Gap. Snitch. He'd be sorry later. "No. I took the long way back. I have the blunt." She approached Satin warily and dumped the pile of blunt into the hat between his feet. She felt more than saw the necks of the other boys crane to get a look at her haul. It was impressive, but she didn't pause to bask in Satin's praise. She wanted to escape his attention as quickly as possible. She wanted to be alone, but she couldn't disappear too soon.

Gideon sat to Satin's right, and when she glanced at him, she saw the flicker of a question in his eyes. He knew something was wrong. She prayed Satin didn't.

Satin nodded and grunted then glanced up at her. "That all of it?"

"Yes." She turned out her pockets and dropped her empty purse on the floor. For once she was telling the truth. She hadn't held anything back.

"Good. Go change. You're working the better-racket tonight."

"What? Why?"

His black gaze shot up to her face, and she shut her mouth.

"Because I said so. Need another reason?"

She shook her head.

"Good. I'm sure Gid here will be glad to have you." He nodded at Gideon, whose face remained expressionless.

Marlowe didn't dally. She knew better than that. She went to her room, which was nothing more than a curtained-off space in the room adjoining the main room. It was cold in the back, and she could see through the gaps in the wood to the world outside the building. When it rained, the roof leaked, and everything and everyone got wet. She was the only girl among the group, except for a couple of prostitutes Satin sometimes used for a racket or other. Because she was the only girl, and expected to have some feminine clothing for games like the one tonight, she also had a small trunk. She closed her curtain and opened the trunk, wiping her hands on her trousers to make sure they were clean. She didn't want to soil the muslin of the dress.

Marlowe hated dressing like a girl. She hated it because it was uncomfortable, and she hated it because the other cubs looked at her differently. She worked hard to be one of them. She talked like them, dressed like them, spat like them. She didn't want them to think of her as a girl—not only because it might give them ideas, but because she wanted to fit in. She wanted to be one of the Covent Garden Cubs, as they called their gang. It was the best gang in London, if anyone asked her.

But today had proved she didn't fit in. That bubble had called her *Elizabeth*. She wasn't Elizabeth. She tried to tell him, but he knew she was lying. She was usually a good liar, but she'd been taken off guard. The bubble should have been pleased. She was never taken off guard.

"Marlowe?" a quiet voice asked from the other side of the curtain.

She jumped. "Almost ready." She wasn't almost ready, and she stripped the men's clothing off quickly, pulling on a shift and digging in the chest for a petticoat, stays, and shoes. She was Marlowe, she told herself. That was her name. Not Elizabeth. That was a fantasy she'd conjured to soothe herself after one of Satin's beatings or when she'd been a new cub and was cold and scared.

She wasn't a cub anymore. She was twenty. And she was Marlowe. She shrugged the stays on, struggled with them for a moment, then gave up. "Is Barbara here?" she asked, knowing Gideon was still waiting for her on the other side of the curtain.

"No. She brought dinner and went back. Should I get her?"

Barbara was the wife of the owner of the Rouge Unicorn Cellar, a public house across the street in the cubs' little corner of Seven Dials. Satin had some sort of arrangement with the couple. Marlowe suspected Satin had promised he wouldn't rob the place if Barbara provided a hot meal once a day and cleaned up after the cubs. Barbara also helped Marlowe dress on the rare occasions she needed to look like a lady. But Gideon knew how to dress a woman too. He'd undressed enough of them, she thought.

"No, don't bother," Marlowe said, opening the curtain. She knew Gideon wanted to be on his way. And Marlowe didn't care one way or another whether Gideon fastened her stays. He was more her friend than a man. They'd kissed a few times, when they'd been a bit younger, but neither had felt anything. There was no spark—not that Marlowe knew what a spark felt like, but Gideon said he did, and the two of them didn't have it. That was probably a good thing, since Satin would kill both Marlowe and Gideon if they started sneaking around to make the beast with two backs.

Gideon stepped inside, and she turned. When he didn't begin right away, she looked over her shoulder. He gestured to her chest. "You should probably unbind them first."

She looked down at her all-but-flat chest under the shift. "Right." The shift was loose, and she simply let it drop down to her elbows until she could untie the knot in the bindings. Then she began unwrapping the band of material, which was an arduous task, because there was so much of it. As soon as she'd unwound it a few turns, her breasts began to ache as the blood rushed back into them. She hated their heavy feeling and how they got in the way. She glanced at Gideon and noted he had looked the other way. "Gideon," she said, "you like bubbies well enough."

He laughed and shook his head, still not looking at her. She plucked at one dark nipple. "What makes you so daft over them? I think they're a nuisance."

"Marlowe, I'm not having this conversation with you right now. Pull up your shift and turn around."

She did as he bade her, slipping the stays back on. With deft movements, he laced the back. They pushed her breasts up more than was comfortable, and she sighed, knowing she would be exposed for hours to come.

Interesting that Gideon didn't want to look at her breasts and offer an opinion. She'd seen his noodle. She didn't have much to say about it except that it looked like all the rest she'd seen. She supposed Gideon was trying to act like a gentleman. She didn't know why, when she was no lady.

Gideon finished lacing, and she tied the petticoats on and pulled the dress over her head. Gideon had to help her with the ties and pins on that too. And then there were shoes and her hair, and she'd forgotten to tie her bloody pockets on. She needed them for her knife. Finally, she was ready. What an awful ordeal!

Marlowe stepped out of the curtain and walked back to the main room. Gideon and his cubs were ready—Tiny, Stub, and Joe. Tiny and Stub were young but quick. Joe was fast, and sometimes Satin called him Racer. Joe would stand lookout and race to tell them if they'd been discovered. It was her task to ensure the boys were not discovered.

When she stepped into the common room, every pair of eyes fastened on her. Not on her, exactly, but on her bubbies. This was why she hated dressing like a girl. The boys forgot she could give them a black eye, and started slobbering over her female parts. Marlowe put her hands on her hips. "What are you looking at? Haven't you ever seen bubbies before?"

Some of the boys looked down, but a few grinned at her. One was a cub who'd joined the gang a few years after she had. She didn't know his real name, but he went by Beezle. He was almost as tall as Gideon, and he was strong. Marlowe wasn't certain she could beat him in a brawl. The bawds tended to avoid him, and Marlowe knew he had a reputation for violence. Beezle's gaze stayed on her long after she met his glare straight on. Any other boy would have looked away.

Satin stepped between the two. "Off you go. I want a good haul. I'll meet you at the fencing ken." Gideon handed Marlowe a large burlap sack, and the four cronies stepped outside.

Seven Dials came alive at night. In daylight, it sometimes appeared the sole haunt of the lowest prostitutes and invalids who stooped in every doorway. The bawdy houses and taverns were shuttered and dark, though the gin shops were always open and filled with drunks. In the weak daylight, children and maimed soldiers who were out and about slinked by or crouched in corners, forgotten and forlorn, with their hands out. But darkness had descended now, and with it every man, woman, or child who thrived in the shadows. The streets were crowded, with men and women spilling out of brightly lit public houses. Marlowe watched gentlemen from Mayfair stumble about drunkenly. They would be easy pickings.

"We'll make more on the better-racket," Gideon said, tucking the bess under his coat. He'd use the tool to force the house's door open. He walked beside her, almost protectively. She drew more attention in the dress than she liked. She nodded at the truth of his statement. Besides, she was in no hurry to encounter any more gentlemen tonight. She hadn't forgotten her run-in with the man who called himself Sir Brook. Now she found herself studying every swell they passed, worried it might be he. But he'd said she could come to him. He'd told her where his office was located. Actually, he'd tried to give her his card. Was the man a fool? She couldn't take his card. What if Satin found it?

"You know how this works," Gideon said now as they moved toward the sundial, marking the entrance to Seven Dials. It also marked their exit. Marlowe focused on Gideon's words, rather than think about the events of the afternoon. She couldn't afford to be distracted.

"Marlowe will knock on the door and spill her tale." He handed her a sheet of parchment. She opened it and sighed. She could pick out a few words and saw this was the shipwreck cock-and-bull. She'd used it a hundred times. The paper was a forged passport for Theodosia Buckley. She'd show it to make her story seem more credible. She'd ask for money so she could take the post back home to Shropshire. She probably wouldn't get much blunt, if any, but that wasn't the point. While she detained the owners of the house, Gideon, Stub, and Tiny would gut the place. Joe would stand guard in case the Watch or a carriage passed by. The boys would check all clear before they climbed back out the windows, and when she heard Joe's signal, she'd finish her Banbury tale and meet at the rendezvous.

"Where is the rendezvous?" she asked when Gideon had finished going over the boys' jobs. They all knew what to do, but Gideon liked to make sure everyone was prepared.

"The house is in Cheapside, near a bookstore," Gideon told her. "We meet there. I'll point it out when we pass."

They passed out of Seven Dials, and Gideon suggested they split into two or three groups. A gang of five might look suspicious. Marlowe moved toward Tiny. Usually she walked with the smallest boy because people often thought they were mother and son, but Gideon put his hand on her arm. "Walk with me." He tucked her arm in his, and the two strolled ahead as though they were lovers out for a walk. When they'd left the boys behind, Gideon said, "What's wrong?"

"Nothing," she said quickly.

"Marlowe, I know you. What's wrong?"

She bit the pad of her thumb. Of course she hadn't been able to hide anything from Gideon. "Gap and I were doing a dive on Piccadilly. Gap picked a bubble, and when I bumped into the game, he grabbed me and called me Elizabeth." She whispered the name, though she knew no one could hear her.

"You looked like someone he knows," Gideon suggested.

Marlowe shook her head. "I was dressed like a boy, but even if he'd seen through my disguise, he was looking for me. He told me he'd been waiting."

"But Gap picked him."

"I know." The inspector must have been watching them for several days, noting their movements. It troubled her, but not as much as what he'd said when he'd pulled her into a private doorway. "He said my parents hired him to find me. They want me to come home."

"Satin said—"

"I know what Satin said. He found me lost and abandoned in a park. He saved me." But if that was true, why did she remember being loved, being happy? Satin had said she hadn't known her name, probably hadn't been given one. He claimed she was the daughter of a bunter—a half beggar, half whore. But she remembered a mother who was soft and smelled sweet. She remembered she'd been sung to and cradled and called Elizabeth.

As though he'd read her mind, Gideon said, "Are those memories or…" He trailed off, and she filled in the rest. She'd often wondered herself if her remembrances were just wishful thinking. But if they were just fantasies, how did she know that *dilly, dilly* lullaby? It wasn't as though she'd heard it in St. Giles.

"Sir Brook couldn't have known about any of that," she said finally.

"Sir Brook?"

"He said that was his name. He's an investigator."

"Bow Street? Marlowe, either he's trying to crimp you, or this is some sort of new rig." He sped up. "That's the bookstore."

They ducked into the doorway, and Marlowe realized the conversation was over. Gideon was probably right. After all, how likely was it that she was the daughter of a great rum mort? More likely, she was the by-blow of a bunter. Brook had set up some sort of rig, and she was the bubble. But if it was a game, it was a good one. He'd even known when to walk away. He'd caught her attention and then told her to come to him if she was interested in meeting her parents. And then he'd walked away, leaving her standing on Piccadilly with her mouth hanging open. He hadn't even asked for his blunt back.

"So what are you going to do?" Gideon asked as they waited for the boys to join them.

"Nothing," she said. She hadn't exactly decided, but if she told Gideon she was considering Sir Brook's offer, he'd give her a long lecture about what a bad idea that was. And Gideon would be right. As Satin liked to point out, he spent a lot of time and effort training her and the other cubs. He'd fed them, clothed them, sheltered them. He took it personally when one of his cubs ran away. Few did so more than once. And if a boy did run away again, he was likely to be found floating in the Thames.

Marlowe had only ever tried to run away once, when she was about twelve. For her pains, Satin had beaten her to within an inch of her life. As she'd lain there, bleeding and crying, he'd leaned close to her ear and said, "I will never let you go, Marlowe. You're too valuable to me. I'd rather you were dead than free."

"Satin will never let me go," she said.

"He has plans for you," Gideon said without look-ing at her. He'd shoved his hands in his pockets and looked as if he didn't care what Satin planned, but

Marlowe had a feeling Gideon didn't approve. "A big racket. He'll have to cut line without you, and he's invested too much for that."

Marlowe suspected Satin was saving her for a big racket. She'd seen him whispering with Beezle on several occasions. Once or twice, they'd glanced her way. It was no surprise. She was the best thief the Covent Street Cubs had. But the better the suit, the more likely she'd be caught and thrown in Kings Head Inn. Newgate was not where she wanted to spend the rest of her life.

Neither did she want to spend it bilking for Satin. But what would she say to her parents now? If they had the blunt to hire a nob like Sir Brook, they were rich—by her standards, at any rate. They'd take one look at her and tell her to get out. At least she was wanted and needed by the Covent Garden Cubs.

"Here they come," Gideon said, alerting her to the boys' arrival. "You ready, Marlowe?"

"Always." And she meant it. She put away thoughts of mothers and fathers. She couldn't afford to feel mushy inside or worry whether someone would love her or not. If this racket produced only dead cargo, she'd have a lot more to worry about than whether lovebirds sang in the trees or if Mommy would tuck her in at night.

She straightened her shoulders, gave a nod to Gideon and the boys, then went around the house they'd be robbing. She gave them a moment to get in position before crossing the street and starting up the walk. She heard the clop of horse hooves on the street behind her, but it wasn't unusual for people to be out and about this time of evening. She glanced back at Joe, who stood in the shadows on the corner, and he gave her the all clear. Just a carriage passing by. Nothing to concern her. There was nothing wrong with knocking on someone's door, and that was all the carriage's occupants would see her do.

She started up the steps, and too late spotted a movement from the servants' steps leading to the basement below. Before she could react, a man grabbed her, lifted her as though she were a sack of potatoes, and threw her over his shoulder. She fought and she screamed, but for all her clawing and scratching and punching, he held on. Joe was coming for her, and she screamed for him. He'd save her. If not Joe, Gideon. She would not be spirited away like this. She was certain of that.

And then she was shoved into a carriage, and a sack pulled over her head. Darkness descended.

Two

DANE STARED OUT THE WINDOW OF HIS COACH AND wondered what the hell had possessed him to lend it to Brook. How was staring at a street in Cheapside more interesting than Lady Yorke's soiree?

Oh, very well. Just about anything was more interesting than Lady Yorke's soiree. Watching grass grow was more interesting, and sitting in his carriage for the last hour, circling the same street, was about as interesting as watching grass grow. He sighed and massaged his temples. He might as well sit here. It wasn't as though he had anything better to do, since Parliament did not sit tonight. He smiled, thinking of the speech he'd given at the last session. It had been a rousing denunciation of a proposed bill to allocate more funds to help the poor.

The poor! What about the military or the farmers? What about the deuced Irish problem? Dane had argued quite successfully—as the bill had been defeated—that the poor deserved their fate. They were lazy or preferred sloth to hard work. Dirty, uneducated, and immoral, the lowest classes were barely human. Best the country look to the future—feeding its people and defending them.

As an earl, Dane not only had the responsibilities of a landowner, a peer, and a member of Parliament, he had social duties as well. He was so utterly weary of the same balls, the same insipid debutantes, the same ridiculous conversations about the weather. He hated London during the Season. And this was only the beginning. Duty could be extremely tedious.

He'd thought if he accepted invitations and made appearances, his mother, the Dowager Countess of Dane, would stop haranguing him about finding a wife. If anything, she was worse than she had been before. He should just pick a girl already and be done with it. They were all the same, at any rate.

If Brook had been sitting here, he would have rolled his eyes and said Dane had it *so hard*, being the earl. But not everyone could be a hero like Brook. Not everyone could go about saving people. Someone had to be ordinary.

But devil take him, if this was what Brook's position entailed, then the man was welcome to his heroics. Dane was about to fall asleep from the sheer tedium.

The coach began to move, and Dane frowned. He hadn't ordered his coachman to drive. Were they being waylaid by highwaymen? At least that would make the evening a bit more interesting.

And then he heard the scream.

Dane shot up and opened the curtains just as his brother's voice called out, "Open the door. Open the bloody door!"

Dane threw open the carriage door, even though

the conveyance was still moving. It slowed briefly, and Brook threw a wild animal inside the carriage. Dane jumped back, out of range of the creature's claws, just as Brook dove inside and slammed the carriage door. "Drive!" he yelled.

The carriage lurched forward, racing at a speed that could not be safe, even had they not been on the crowded streets of London. But he had no time to worry about the jehu's dangerous driving. The creature lunged at him, scratching at his leg and managing to get a pretty good bite of his calf. "Ow!" he yelled, shaking it off.

It fell back, and Brook threw a hood over its head. That confused it, and his brother took advantage of its disorientation and bound its hands.

Hands? It was human?

"What the devil is that?" Dane asked.

"It's a who, and her name is Elizabeth," Brook told him, teeth clenched with the effort it took to secure the knot in the rope binding its—her—arms.

"That is a woman?" A woman had just bitten him? Damnation, but his leg hurt like hell. He peered closer and noted the dirty dress she wore. His gaze traveled upward…yes, she was definitely a woman.

"That," Brook said, falling back into the squabs in exhaustion, "is Lady Elizabeth Grafton."

Dane had always thought that when the day came and his brother made a mistake—a monumental mistake, the sort Dane was exceedingly careful never to make—he would be glad. But damn if his leg did not hurt him, and he was too worried for his brother's sanity—and truth be told, his own safety—to be able to say *I told you so.*

Dane glanced at the woman again. He didn't know who she was, but she was not the daughter of the Marquess of Lyndon. She was some sort of street rat. The smell of her alone was enough to prove bathing was not a luxury she frequently, if ever, enjoyed. And her language. No lady knew words like those she'd spewed at Brook. Dane didn't even know some of the curses. And the dirt. He'd have his valet clean these breeches immediately.

"Are you feeling well?" Dane asked. "Have you hit your head recently?"

Brook glared at him. "It's her."

But before Dane could dispute him, the creature—female, if Brook insisted—must have caught her breath, because she began thrashing around again. She couldn't see with the hood over her eyes, and her claws were restrained, but she could still kick. Dane moved from one side of the seat to the other to avoid her quick feet. She would make a fearsome pugilist if her fists were as fast as her feet.

"I can't take her to Lord Lyndon like this," Brook said.

Dane frowned. He didn't like the implications of that statement. When Brook didn't go on, he suggested, "You could toss her back out on the street." He looked out the window and saw they were in Mayfair now. Perhaps they should not unleash such a creature on Mayfair. They might keep driving and leave her somewhere safer. Somewhere like Scotland. Or the Americas.

"I'm not tossing her back on the street."

The woman quieted, as though listening for her fate.

"We could put her on a ship. Australia might be far enough away."

"No!" the wench cried and began thrashing again. Dane held out a hand to protect himself.

Brook rolled his eyes. "Dane."

Dane spread his hands. "You said yourself she was a thief. That's the least of the punishments she might receive."

"True, but I was thinking we might reform her."

Dane narrowed his eyes, and the girl spoke up for the first time. "I don't want no reforming." Her voice was muffled beneath the hood.

Dane pointed an accusatory finger at the woman. "You heard her. She doesn't *want no reforming.*"

"Nevertheless, we take her home—"

"Home!"

"And we clean her up and make her presentable before we give her to Lord and Lady Lyndon."

"No!" This from the creature.

This time Dane didn't avoid her kicks, and his knee suffered the consequences. "Damn it!" Those breeches would be past saving.

"Let me go," she screamed, kicking again. "You bloody cockchafer! Let me out, you bastard boat-licker!" She went on, and Dane glanced at his brother incredulously. He'd never heard a woman speak thus.

"I feel as though I should take notes," he said over the noise. "I might impress the fellows at Gentleman Jackson's."

"You might be thrown out," Brook observed. "In any case, I'm taking her to Derring House."

Now Dane was out of patience. "No, you are not.

Susanna is there, and Mother. We cannot inflict this"—he gestured to her contemptuously—"upon them."

"Nonsense," Brook said, folding his arms across his chest in a gesture Dane knew meant he had made up his mind. "Unlike you, they love a good charitable cause. And it wouldn't kill you to smudge those lily-white hands once in a while."

Dane looked at his spotless gloves. It might not kill him, but it would certainly pain him. "I thought the idea was to keep the rabble and the criminals *out* of Derring House. It's bad enough one can't walk the streets without having one's pocket emptied, or that highwaymen all but own the roads. A man's home should at least be safe."

Brook scowled. "You sound like Father."

"And look what happened to him. The last house-breaking killed him."

"He was already ill and fading."

"The pilfering and ransacking of his home certainly hastened the end."

Brook did not argue, and Dane took his brother's silence as tacit agreement. Dane had lived in London for part of the year all his life, and he was familiar with every sort of crime and criminal. He'd been the target of crime more often than he could count. But Dane carried a heavy walking stick or a pistol when warranted. He could handle himself. The death of his father, though, had angered Dane and fueled his hatred of the lowest class, what he thought of as the criminal class.

When they arrived at the town house near Berkeley Square, Dane stood firm. He was the earl, though his brother often conveniently forgot, and he was not going to allow this wench—that was the only polite word he could think to call her—in his home. Unlike many of the older homes, the kitchen and scullery of Derring House had been situated in the rear yard, which was accessible either through the service rooms or from the outside via a short walkway. The location reduced the risk of the house burning if the kitchen caught fire, and provided for a larger suite of service rooms. His mother and Susanna would still be out, and most of the servants would be in their quarters at this hour. The kitchen should be empty.

Dane instructed the coachman to stop near the servants' stairs before the carriage would be visible to the butler, who was undoubtedly keeping watch for their return.

Dane looked at Brook over the still-fighting woman. Didn't the wench ever tire? "How do we extricate her?"

"We carry her."

That did seem to be the only way, but that didn't mean Dane had to like it.

"If we bring her into the house proper—"

Dane raised a hand, cutting his brother off. With a sigh, he removed his gloves and his coat and showed his brother with hand motions what they would do. If the woman didn't know what was coming, she couldn't plan her attack. Brook nodded, made some of his own hand gestures, which elicited a rather vulgar one from Dane, and then with a sigh, Dane opened the carriage door and hopped out. He nodded, and Brook shoved the woman out the door and into Dane's arms.

He knew better than to hold her too close. As he'd seen Brook do, he tossed her over his shoulder and held her knees close to his chest so she couldn't kick him as hard, or anywhere truly vulnerable. He winced at the stench of her and thought perhaps he would simply burn the shirt after this. Dane looked up at the coachman, who was staring at them open-mouthed.

"Not a word."

"Yes, my lord."

She was lighter than Dane had expected, and he carried her quite easily down the steps and into the kitchen. Brook went ahead of them, opening the door and lighting a lamp so they could see. Adjacent to the kitchen proper was a small common room where the servants ate or sewed or congregated when they had free time. Dane elected to put her in one of the chairs in the common room. It was farther away from knives and other items that might be used as weapons.

He set her down and jumped back. She immediately flailed around and fell off the chair. Brook nodded at her. "You should untie her. She can't use her hands to catch herself."

"*You* untie her," Dane said, but he knew he was going to have to do it. As much as he wanted to, he couldn't leave her tied up. It wasn't humane. Gingerly, he approached her. She seemed to sense where he was, because the hood turned in his direction, and she kicked out at him. He avoided her feet and managed to slide behind her. He grabbed her wrists and attempted to loosen the rope. That wasn't going to work. She'd tightened the knots with all her fighting. Dane went to the kitchen, found a small, sharp knife, and returned.

But he couldn't cut the rope without cutting her if she continued to squirm. "Listen," he said, jumping away when she turned toward his voice and aimed a kick. "I'm going to cut the ropes, but you have to be still, or I'll accidentally cut you." He spoke quietly and calmly, as he might when addressing a skittish mare.

"I'm going to kill you," she screeched.

Brook's brows shot up. Dane tried to keep calm. "That would be much easier to accomplish if your hands were free."

She stopped kicking long enough to consider these words. Finally, she said, "If you try anything—"

"Woman, I assure you, I have no designs on your virtue. *Nothing* you do could tempt me." In the light of the lamp he could see even more clearly the stained dress she wore, the ring of dirt at her wrists, and the half-moons of black under her fingernails. And there was the odor of her unwashed body. He had no desire to move any closer to her. As he watched, she held out her wrists so they were away from her back. Cautiously, Dane stepped beside her and knelt. She didn't move when he slipped the knife under the ropes. He sawed once, and she was free. He jumped back as quickly as she did. Immediately, she pulled off her hood and crouched low, surveying her surroundings.

Dane could only stare at her. "You're just a girl."

Her head whipped in his direction, her dark hair flying in front of her face. "I may be a girl, but I can take you."

Dane held his hands up to ward her off. "I have no doubt you would like to try."

"We will not hurt you," Brook said.

"*You*," she sneered. "You nabbed me. What is this place?" She looked around. "A bawdy house?"

Dane raised a brow. "It's a kitchen."

She did not look as though she believed him, and she continued to jerk her head about, jumping at the slightest sound. Dane was intrigued. He'd judged her thirty or older. She had a woman's body, but her face was still that of a girl's. She couldn't be more than one and twenty, if that. And though her hair was a bit matted, her face had been scrubbed clean—or at least relatively clean. So perhaps she did not relish being dirty. She had large blue eyes that flashed with anger and hatred. This was no simpering miss. The ladies at Almack's would have fainted dead away.

A knock sounded on the door, and she jumped to face it, hands outstretched as though to fight off an attacker. "What is that?"

"We call it knocking," Dane said. "A polite customary way to inform others you would like admittance."

Brook opened the door, and the Derring family jehu stood in the doorway. "Yes, Ezekiel?"

"Note came for you, sir. I thought it best if I brought it." His gaze found the girl, and he seemed relieved she was unharmed. "Wouldn't want the other servants asking questions."

"Thank you." Brook closed the door and broke the seal on the letter. "Damn it."

"What is it?" Dane asked.

"I have to go. Bow Street—"

"No." Dane shook his head. "Absolutely not. I forbid it."

Brook shrugged. "You don't have that sort of authority. I have to go." He started for the door, and Dane moved in front of him, holding the door closed with his hand.

"Now? This moment?"

"It's urgent."

Dane glared at him. "What am I supposed to do with her?" he asked through a clenched jaw.

Brook glanced back as though he'd forgotten her for a moment. "Clean her up. I'll take her to Lord Lyndon tomorrow."

"If you really expect to present that girl to Lord Lyndon as his daughter, you are completely daft."

"We'll see," Brook said. He moved forward then gave Dane a pointed stare when he didn't remove his hand. With a curse, Dane stepped aside, and Brook was gone.

Dane turned and looked at the girl. She looked back at him, a challenge and a threat in her eyes. God save him. He'd only wanted relief from the ennui of the Season. He didn't want a she-devil to contend with. Brook had said to clean her up. Dane supposed that meant clean clothes. But there was no point in putting clean clothes on a dirty body. He'd have to make her wash.

The servants' hip bath was kept in the corner of the room. He'd only need to heat some water over the stove. Not that he knew how to work the stove. That was why he had a cook. He'd have to fetch the cook. And when he returned, the girl would be long gone. Was that such a bad thing? Dane thought not, but his brother would disagree. Dane didn't really care about ruffling Brook's feathers, but he did wonder why his brother thought this girl could be Lady Elizabeth Grafton, daughter of the Marquess of Lyndon. He knew the story of little Lady Elizabeth. She'd disappeared one day in the park, and despite an exhaustive search for her, she'd never been found. The nanny had been blamed and thrown in prison, but Dane suspected the poor woman was innocent. There were men who kidnapped children to send to the colonies, or for darker reasons. Dane tried to remember more details. He'd been about ten at the time, and the little girl perhaps five. So that would make her twenty now. He glanced at the girl before him. She was about the correct age.

"If you would meet your parents, you will have to wash and change."

"I don't have parents," she declared. No surprise there. She was obviously the spawn of Satan.

Still, it was interesting. An enterprising thief, as she seemed to be, might see opportunity in pretending to be the daughter of a marquess. "Then you are not Lady Elizabeth Grafton?" he asked.

"My name is Marlowe."

Dane waited.

"Just Marlowe," she added.

"And you are not the daughter of the Marquess of Lyndon?"

"I don't know the bloody man. Now, if you'll just let me go—" She attempted to push past him, but Dane—setting aside his distaste for the dirt covering her—caught her about the waist. She jumped back, and he stepped to the side before she could hit him. Looked like she had a good right hook too.

"I'm afraid I cannot let you go."

She glared at him. "Why not?"

"So glad you asked. Two reasons, actually. First of all, my brother is a prime investigator. I don't know how he does it, but he knows information. Which leads to the second reason. If he thinks you are Lady Elizabeth Grafton, I must give him the benefit of the doubt."

"That's a fancy way of saying I'm a liar."

Dane spread his hands. "It is nothing of the sort."

She crossed her arms under her ample bosom. "Really? Don't you think I know who I am? I told you my name is Marlowe. I don't know this lady you're talking about. Now, tell me again my name is Elizabeth, and you're calling me a liar."

Dane stared at her for a long moment. Shocking to admit, but the girl had a point. He was, in essence, calling her a liar. "I didn't intend to offend you."

"You can dress a pig up however you want, but it's still a pig."

Now they were speaking of animals? Or was this girl more intelligent than she looked? "Are you using a metaphor?" he asked.

"No more fancy words," she demanded. "Let me go!"

He refused to sink to her level and holler back. "There is no point in allowing you to go. My brother will only find you again." And Dane would have to listen to a lecture for allowing the girl to escape.

"No, he won't. I can hide so I'm never found."

She didn't know Brook. He could find anyone, and he was patient. He could wait years for a man or woman to surface. But Dane wasn't going to argue that point with her. He had others yet to be introduced. "Be that as it may," Dane conceded, "I am not about to let you go. As I see it, you have a choice: either willingly take a bath, don clean clothing, and eat a hot meal..."

"Or?" She tapped her foot rapidly.

"Or do all of that—except perhaps the hot meal—under duress."

"Duress?"

He smiled thinly. "I force you."

"You think you can make me do something I don't want?" She notched her chin up in a challenge.

"Yes."

She looked at him for a long time. He didn't know what she saw in his eyes, but finally she nodded. "All right, but you're not watching the bath."

"Madam, I assure you, I had no intention of doing so. I will stand in the kitchen with my back turned. I give you my word as a gentleman."

She rolled her eyes. "Some gentleman, forcing me to take a bath against my will."

"Yes, I know. The horror."

"And another thing."

He sighed. "What now?"

"I'm not putting on a dress."

He raised his brows.

"I want trousers and a shirt like you have."

"You want to dress as a man? Why?"

"Because I do."

"Strange," he muttered to himself, but at this point he did not care. His mother and sister would be home soon, and he wanted the girl dealt with. Dane went to the door and called, "Ezekiel! Come here."

The jehu must have been loitering nearby, because he appeared within seconds.

"Fetch Crawford."

The words fell like boulders. The coachman twisted his hands together. "Crawford, my lord?" He glanced over Dane's shoulder at the girl. "Are you sure?"

No, Dane wasn't sure. He was relatively certain he'd regret involving Crawford almost immediately, but there was little about this night he did not already regret, and he was at the limit of what he could accomplish without detection. At any rate, he'd probably burn the whole kitchen down if he attempted to use the stove, even to warm water. He might be able to find the chit some food, but he had no idea where he might locate clothing that would fit her, especially if he had to keep watch over her to prevent escape.

Dane sighed and closed his eyes. "Just fetch him, Ezekiel."

"Yes, my lord."

Behind him he heard the girl ask, "Who's Crawford?"

"You'll see."

Five long minutes later, a short man with a balding pate and a crooked nose that made it appear as though he looked down on everyone—although he was generally shorter than everyone—walked ceremoniously through the kitchen door. Dane thought of a king returning to his castle, and in a sense the kitchen and all of the servants' areas were Crawford's castle. "My lord," Crawford said, bowing. His gaze immediately focused on the girl. Crawford missed nothing. "You called?"

"I need your assistance."

"Of course, my lord." The implication in the butler's tone was that no one, ever, accomplished anything without Crawford's assistance.

"I need warm water for a bath, food, and boys' clothing to fit this girl." He gestured to her.

Crawford did not even blink at the odd request. "Of course, my lord. May I ask why we are washing, feeding, and dressing this…street urchin?"

"I'm not an urchin!" the girl yelled.

Crawford's gaze never left Dane's.

"She is one of Brook's projects. That is all you need to know."

"Of course, my lord." He turned, presumably to work his magic and accomplish all of Dane's requests, but then he turned back. "We will not be housing the creature for the night, my lord?"

Dane licked his lips. He could have used a glass of brandy right about then. "I don't know yet, Crawford."

"Of course, my lord. Excuse me, my lord." He made for the door, presumably to carry out Dane's orders.

"Crawford, are my mother and sister home yet?"

"I expect them at any moment, my lord." And Dane knew how Crawford hated to be away from his post when the countess arrived. Crawford had definite opinions as to how Derring House was to be run. Dane might be the captain, but Crawford was the helmsman, and he turned the ship. He had been steering the ship for longer than Dane had been alive. He'd probably still be here when Dane was dead.

Crawford gestured to the girl. "I will not mention…*this* to the countess and Lady Susanna, my lord."

"That would be best," Dane agreed.

"Your father will turn in his grave," Crawford muttered.

"What was that?"

"If that is all, my lord."

Dane nodded. He could hardly chastise the man. His father *would* have turned in his grave. It was rooks like this girl who'd put the late earl in his grave to begin with.

Crawford departed, and Dane knew that within moments footmen and maids would swarm to carry out his orders. He moved away from the door and out of the kitchen proper so as not to be in the way. That put him in the same room with the girl again. She scowled at him, her small face screwed up in an angry snarl. He ignored her. They'd struck a bargain, and he expected her to follow it. There was no honor among thieves, but she was clearly not an idiot. She did not want him holding her down in the bath and scrubbing her.

As predicted, the swarm descended. The servants gave the girl odd looks, a few wrinkled their nose at her stench, but no one spoke any word other than what was required to accomplish his orders. Half of them must have been asleep, but they marshaled as though they'd been standing at attention, awaiting his order. The only clue that he'd interrupted what should have been a restful night were the maids whose caps did not quite cover the rags they'd tied in their hair to produce curls when they woke in the morning.

The housekeeper and Crawford did not get along, she having been in residence only six and ten years and thus still an interloper, and Dane was not surprised to see that Crawford had not roused her. Instead, the cook took charge. She bellowed orders for warm water, and Dane watched as the hip bath was moved into a small room he had not known was there. This must be where the servants bathed. The tantalizing smell of fresh meat and broth made his mouth water, and he noted the girl turned her head in the direction of the kitchen as well.

"The bath is ready, my lord," one of the maids informed him. She held up a boy's clothing. "This was Jimmy's. It's a bit ragged, but it's clean." She handed him the clothing. Jimmy had been a tiger and was now working his way toward becoming an under footman. "Crawford requested extra soap. There's plenty in there, and towels for drying." She bobbed and walked away.

Only Crawford, the kitchen maid, a footman, and the cook were still about.

"Here," Dane said, handing the clothing to the girl. "Put it on after you bathe. And use soap. A lot of soap."

She peered into the room. It was small and dark without a window. He knew she could not escape. It was just big enough to fit the bath and one person. A lamp hung on a peg on the wall, and several towels were stacked beside the bath.

"I'm going to catch my death, sitting in water like that. It's not natural."

"I have survived the ordeal hundreds of times."

She narrowed her eyes at him, as though evaluating his heartiness against her own. "How do I know you won't come in when I'm undressed?"

"I give you my word as a gentleman."

She gave a short laugh. Apparently, she knew the worth of most gentlemen's promises. He gestured to the butler. "Crawford will keep me in check should I be overcome with raging desire at the thought of you without clothing."

"What?"

He shook his head and left her to it. In the kitchen, the cook had set out a bowl filled with some sort of hearty soup, a crust of bread, and a cup of the wine the servants drank. "I did not think it appropriate that she eat at the table, my lord," Crawford informed him. "She may stand in here and eat."

Dane shrugged. He didn't care what she did. "Has my brother returned?"

"No, my lord, but your mother and sister are preparing for bed. Or so I have been informed." His tone held a measure of censure, and Dane realized he would have to make amends for the disruption he'd caused in the nightly ritual. "I only hope Lloyd was able to see all was done correctly."

Lloyd was the head footman.

"I am certain all was done to your specifications, Crawford. Mrs. Worthing, might I trouble you for a measure of that cooking sherry?" He nodded to the bottle on a shelf behind her. It was not brandy, but it would have to suffice for the moment.

"No trouble 'tall, my lord. No, it's no trouble 'tall." She poured him a hearty measure, and he drank it down.

"Is there anything else you require, my lord?" Crawford asked.

Dane ran a hand over his face. If Brook wasn't back yet, he had to do something with the girl. He couldn't put her in one of the house's bedrooms. Even if he hadn't thought she'd rob them blind and run away at the first opportunity, Crawford would never allow it.

She would have to stay where he could keep an eye on her. His dressing room? Dane closed his eyes. He needed to consider that this might turn out to be Lady Elizabeth, however unlikely that seemed at the moment. If rumor that he'd shared the night with her circulated, she would be ruined. Of course, wasn't she already ruined? God knew where she'd lived or what she'd done all these years. Crawford was capable of discretion, even when he ardently disapproved. His loyalties to the family usually outweighed his rigid sense of propriety. Dane, having relied on Crawford's discretion a time or two, knew this firsthand. And Crawford could bully any of the other servants into keeping quiet should they realize the girl had slept in his room.

"Crawford, I shall need your assistance with a delicate task." He pulled the butler aside and explained quietly. The man pursed his lips, but that was the only outward sign that he disapproved.

Dane sent Crawford to do his bidding, then checked his pocket watch. It was late. Very late. He strolled to the door where the girl was bathing. "Are you almost done?"

"Don't you dare come in!"

Dane looked heavenward in silent entreaty and stepped away. He was going to throttle Brook when he saw him. Dane could not believe he was sneaking a girl to his room. He felt like a randy youth again. At least when she emerged, she would not look like a girl anymore.

But then the door opened, and he realized he was very, very wrong.

Three

MARLOWE HAD NEVER LIKED BATHS, BUT SHE HAD NOT realized they could be taken in warm, clean water with fragrant soap. She didn't particularly want to smell like a flower, but it wasn't the worst thing she'd smelled like. The towels she'd dried herself with had been soft and fluffy. She'd never had a towel before. She'd had a small, scratchy cloth she could use for her face, but it rubbed her skin raw with its coarseness. These towels were so soft she wanted to wrap herself in them and wear them all the time.

Instead, she wound one about her dripping wet hair. She would probably die from a chill, but once she'd begun to clean her body, she couldn't stop there. Her hair felt heavy with grime, and she'd washed it until it rinsed clean. The water, when she stepped out, was black. She hadn't realized she had so much dirt on her. As she dressed, she noted her fingernails had white half-moons at the tip, and her skin had a pinkish tinge.

The clothing the bastard had provided her was a bit snug. She didn't have any strips to bind her breasts, and she couldn't put her stays back on by herself, even if she'd wanted to. Looking at them now, all gray with grime, she was not sad to be free of them. But without anything between her skin and the shirt, her breasts stretched the material slightly. The trousers were snug as well, but the shirt was long enough to cover her hips and bottom. She found a cap tucked into the pocket of the trousers, and after drying her hair as best she could, she piled it on her head and set the cap on top.

That was about the time the bastard knocked on the door. She jumped at the sound, and though she was dressed, ordered him not to enter. She needed another moment. She had to don her own shoes again, and took the dagger she had hidden in the pockets of her dress and shoved it in her boot as she usually did. She wouldn't be unprepared for whatever the bastard had in mind.

But the bastard was the least of her worries. Satin was going to kill her. It wouldn't matter if she'd been abducted; she would be to blame for the loss of the cargo Gideon and the boys would have taken in the better-racket. Gideon…what did he think had happened? Had Joe told him she'd been snapped and carried away?

She had to get out of here and get back. She'd take Satin's punishment and promise to make up for tonight next time. Next time she'd make a rum speak. First, she had to escape, but the bastard was proving difficult to evade. He and his brother seemed to think she was the daughter of some swell or other—a Lord Lyndon. The thought made her laugh—and it also made her belly hurt for reasons she did not want to think about too closely. Apparently this swell, Lyndon, was looking for a girl named Elizabeth. It was curious that this girl would have the name Marlowe used in secret, but that did not mean Marlowe was this girl.

She was a bawd's by-blow, not some swell's little princess. And besides, even if her name had once been Elizabeth, that did not mean she was the swell's daughter. It was a common enough name.

So why had Satin given her another?

She shook her head. Better not to question. If Satin gave you a gang name, you used it. Hers was Marlowe, and she'd never told anyone except Gideon that she remembered being called Elizabeth.

She couldn't put off the inevitable much longer. With a deep breath, she opened the door and stepped out of the little bathing room. The bastard was waiting outside. His back was to the door, his shoulders broad and his waist narrow in the tight coat he wore. He was a bang-up cove, that was certain. She'd gotten a close look at his clothing, and it was finer than any she'd ever seen. A knave in grain, as Gideon would have said, as well as a long shanks. She'd known tall men, but they'd always been scraggy. This man had substance.

He turned, and she caught her breath. She didn't like that he could do that to her—make her throat feel tight and her heart race. But he was handsome—far too handsome. He had thick, dark hair that fell to one side of his face and sort of curled about it. His eyebrows were thick slashes over wide brown eyes. She'd seen innumerable people with brown eyes, but no one had eyes like his. She didn't know how to describe them except that they were sort of soft and beautiful. They were almost a woman's eyes—but this man was no woman. He might be clean-shaven, but his jaw was strong, and there was power within him. She'd felt the iron of his strength when he'd carried her. The man did not have a bit of soft flesh about him.

She'd been watching his eyes, so she noticed when his gaze met hers and how his eyes widened. She almost looked down at her clothing, to see what troubled him, but she thought she knew. Men were always interested in bubbies. "I don't have anything to bind them," she said. "If you give me your neckcloth, I could use that."

He stepped back as though he'd been burned. "My cravat stays where it is."

"If you're not going to give me your *cravat*"—she mimicked his pompous way of saying the word— "then I need something else."

He took a deep breath. "This is not a subject I prefer to discuss. You will want to eat?"

She didn't know why he asked the question. Of course she wanted to eat. He could probably hear her stomach rumbling at the smell of the food. She followed him into the kitchen, half perplexed and half amused that he did not want to discuss binding her breasts. These swells had their own rules.

She stepped into the kitchen, and an older woman with her hair in a cap and wearing a clean apron smiled at her. It was a kind smile, but Marlowe didn't smile back. She didn't trust these people. The woman was probably a cook, because she indicated the food on the preparation table near her. Marlowe didn't need it pointed out. She'd spotted it the moment she entered. But she took the gesture as an invitation to begin, and she attacked the meal like a mongrel attacks a bone. She lifted the bowl and drank a hearty measure of the soup, then dipped the hunk of bread in and scooped up the remaining liquid. She shoved the bread in her mouth, chewing quickly and washing it down with a measure of wine. The wine was good, and she drank it all.

She shoved another hunk of bread in her mouth and held the glass out. "More wine?" she said around the bread.

The bastard and the cook stared at her as though they had never seen a person eat. She waved the glass to get the cook's attention, and the woman finally blinked and poured more. "Er…more soup, dear?"

Marlowe nodded. She could have eaten ten bowls of it. It was the best thing she'd had in…well, as long as she could remember. She probably shouldn't be accepting anything from the bastard, but she figured he owed her. She hadn't asked to be nabbed.

She ate two more bowls, and then she was so full she worried she'd have to be rolled out of there. Her stomach, used to being empty, hurt from swelling. But it was a good hurt, and now she felt sleepy. She yawned.

"Let's get you to bed," the bastard said. For some reason, a shiver ran up her spine at his words.

She shook it off. "I'm not sharing a dab with you! If you try and touch me, you'll find your arm missing your hand."

The cook made a strained sound, then pretended to be very busy cleaning up. But she was obviously still listening. The bastard opened his mouth to say something more, and that was when the other servants walked in. They'd been doing something in the other room, and now a mopsqueezer entered, carrying Marlowe's clothing.

"Sorry to interrupt, my lord," the slavey said with a curtsy. Marlowe rolled her eyes. As if the man was worth all that fawning. "What should I do with...these?"

"Burn them."

"Hey!" Marlowe tried to snatch her dress away. "Those are mine!"

The swell stepped in front of her, and the maid shrank back as though Marlowe would attack. "You can go," the bastard told the slaveys. They ran off as though his words came from heaven.

He was still standing in front of her, and she could smell the clean scent of him. He didn't smell like flowers, but like something masculine and fresh. She wanted to move closer and inhale more deeply. Instead, she looked up at him, and for some reason, she felt dizzy. He was looking at her, those brown eyes focused on her face, and she felt too warm and short of breath. Maybe the soup had been poisoned.

"Follow me," he said curtly.

She put her hands on her hips. His eyes followed the movement, and she saw his throat move as he swallowed.

"I'm not going anywhere with you."

He sighed. "Marlowe, there is an easy way to do things and a hard way. I take it you prefer the hard way."

She frowned. When he spoke, she had the feeling

he was saying more than his words would indicate. It was almost as though he was making fun of her. There often seemed no right answer to his questions, so she kept silent.

"In this case, the easy way is for you to follow me to my room."

"No." She said it flatly. She was not going to this man's room.

"The hard way it is." He reached for her, and before she could jump out of the way, he scooped her into his arms. She fought him, more comfortable now in the trousers and man's shirt, but he was prepared. He tossed her over his shoulder and held her legs at the knees to stop her from kicking him. Despite her struggles, she caught the shocked look of the cook, and then they were outside. Marlowe didn't pay much attention to where they were, she just fought and screamed, and finally they stepped in the house and she had to catch her breath.

"You have another choice," he said ominously. "Keep screaming and I bind your mouth, or keep quiet and you remain free."

She took a moment to think about it. Part of her wanted to scream just to spite him, just to wake the whole house up. But another part of her did not relish being gaped at by the family or being bound. He would do it. She knew that much about him now. "Fine," she said quietly.

He set her down, which surprised her.

"Want to try walking?"

But she was speechless now. Before, she'd been staring at the shiny marble floor, now she looked around her and gawked. The entryway was the most gorgeous room she had ever seen. The ceiling soared and seemed to go up and up and then up some more. An enormous column of stairs spread before them, and that too curved gracefully upward. A chandelier with what looked like diamonds glittered above her. It was not lit, but the lamp left burning on an entry table illuminated its glory. What must it look like when lit? It would be as bright as day in here.

A long, wide hallway led to other rooms. She peered down it, but she could not see the end. This house was a castle. She turned her head to stare at the bastard. Who was he? Some sort of king?

He gestured toward the stairs. "This way," he said quietly and began ascending. She followed, pausing when her feet stepped onto the runner. The carpet was so soft and plush, she all but sank into it. Finally, she began walking again, looking around her as she did. Framed paintings of old men and women, as well as country fields, hung on the walls. When she peered over the stone banister, she saw plants and a large wooden door. The butler she had seen earlier was locking it now. He lifted the lamp and followed them at a discreet distance.

She had been in the homes of the wealthy. She could scan this house and know immediately what items would fetch the highest prices—silver glim-sticks, a gilt frame, a marble bust—but she had never been in a home like this one. If she and Gideon could pilfer this house, they would be made for life.

The bastard had reached the landing, and she almost

ran into him. He was obviously waiting for her. Now he gave her a knowing look. "Tallying the value?"

She scowled at him. He had an annoying habit of guessing what she was thinking. "No."

He laughed. "One more flight up."

"How many floors are there?"

"Wouldn't you like to know? Perhaps I should just leave the doors unlocked and give you the house plans."

"That would be helpful," she agreed.

He started up the next set of stairs. "Apparently, today I am nothing if not helpful."

She followed him to another level, but this one did not require ascending quite so many stairs to reach. At the top, he turned right and motioned for her to follow him. These were bedrooms, she assumed. The doors were closed, and it appeared all in the house were sleeping. How many people lived here? Oh, she knew enough to guess that the servants slept on the attic floor. This was clearly not that level. But how many people shared this enormous house? At any given time there were ten to twelve cubs sharing a space not even the size of the entryway to this house. Did this man live here alone? No…he'd mentioned a sister and a mother. And there was his brother. If Sir Brook lived here, that was four people and all of this space.

She was amazed and also a little angry. What made him so special that he got all of this when she had to settle for a cramped corner in a cold, wet, rickety building?

They reached the destination, and he opened the door. It was dark inside, but she went in anyway, not wishing to be carried. The butler, who had been following them, handed him the lamp and murmured something she did not hear.

The bastard declined the butler's offer, then closed the door. He went to a table near the door, slid a drawer open, and took out a key. Inserting the key into the lock, he dubbed up and pocketed the key.

She was alone with him in his bedroom.

Dane put the key in his pocket and watched as her eyes grew wide. Devil take him if she started wailing and screaming again. To stave it off, he said, "I'm not going to touch you. I only want to sleep." He held up his hands as if to show he was harmless and had no interest in anything other than sleeping. The girl was little more than an animal from what he'd seen of her manners. Still...

When the idea of having her in his room came to him, he had no other intentions, but that was before she'd come out of the bath. He'd immediately regretted giving in to her request to wear men's clothing. They clung to her in ways they never would on a man. Her breasts pushed at the fabric of the shirt, stretching it. The outline of her nipples had been visible, and he realized she wasn't wearing any undergarments. That fact was made more obvious when she began to talk about binding her breasts. He had put an immediate stop to that conversation. He did not want to talk about her anatomy, especially not when his body was reacting to it against his will.

He tried looking away from her chest and wished

he had not forced her to bathe. One look at her face made it obvious she was not a boy. The dirt and grime had hid pale, delicate skin, milky white and translucent. She'd stuffed her hair under a cap, but he'd already seen how long it was. Did it fall enticingly about her breasts when she was unclothed?

He'd shaken his head and forced himself to concentrate on the matters at hand. Dane was good at concentrating. He'd been trained to put his own needs and wants second. He was able to ignore her enticing body for several minutes—that was, until she put her hands on her hips, and the material of her shirt rose. Her hips curved the trousers in ways he found incredibly erotic. He could imagine the sweet shape of her bottom, and had the urge to turn her so he could see that part of her as well. Worst of all, one of the buttons on the shirt popped off at her actions, exposing the creamy flesh of her collarbone.

Now she stood before him, looking at him as though he were a wolf and she the sheep. As much as he might reassure her, she was right to distrust him. The entire time he'd carried her in from the kitchen, those soft, full breasts pressing into his shoulder, he had thought of nothing but stripping her naked.

"I'm not going to touch you," he repeated, more for his sake than hers. "We are just going to sleep."

She watched him, warily.

"You can sleep in that chair." He pointed to a comfortable armchair beside his bed.

"Some nob," she said, "giving a lady a chair."

"I don't know you're a lady yet, *Marlowe*," he said. "If it turns out you are Lady Elizabeth, I will apologize profusely." She could say what she wanted. He was not giving up his bed to some street urchin Brook had abducted in Cheapside.

And he was not going to feel guilty about it.

Not very guilty, anyway.

Damn it! The chair was comfortable! He'd fallen asleep in it a time or two when reading. She'd be fine.

But would he? Or would she wait until he fell asleep, steal the key, and escape? Or worse, would she slit his throat?

He didn't have any weapons in his room, but an enterprising girl like her might find something she could use. The letter opener, for example. He swallowed.

With new determination, he went to the drapes and loosed the cords used to hold them back during the day. Thank God he'd given his valet two days off to visit his mother. In the morning, he did not want to have to explain why he had a girl dressed as a boy tied to his chair.

"What are you doing with those?" she asked, backing up. She backed all the way to the door of his dressing room.

"Give me your hands."

She shook her head. "No. I don't want to be tied."

"I can't trust you. I'm only going to tie you to the chair so you cannot escape. I'll give you plenty of slack."

"No!"

He shrugged. "Marlowe, the easy way or the hard way? I believe we've established I have more brute strength than you. One way or another, I will bind you."

He could have sworn a tear glistened in her eyes, but she swiped at her cheek, and then nothing was there. Had he imagined it?

She held out her hands, the expression on her face ugly and stubborn, and he bound them together tightly. Then he pulled her gently to the chair and tied her to the heavy table beside it. She wasn't going anywhere. When he put his hands on her shoulders to sit her in the chair, he felt her trembling.

"Cold?" he asked. "I'll get you a blanket."

"I'm not cold," she spat. But why else would she be shivering? He found a blanket in his clothespress and covered her with it. She kicked it off, and he shrugged and yanked off his coat. Customarily, he would have asked Crawford to serve as valet, but when the butler had inquired as to whether his services would be required, Dane had told him no. Dane reached for his cravat to loosen it, and realized he had an audience. Perhaps he should not undress in front of her. Typically, he slept in the nude, but how was he going to do so with her sitting there?

He decided to sleep in a loose shirt and trousers, and he emerged from his dressing room wearing that. He had no night clothes to speak of. He'd always felt they were more like dresses than something a man would wear.

He extinguished the lamp and climbed into bed, frowning at how cold it was. No bed warmer. He would be glad when this night was over, the girl was gone, and he had his normal life back. He plumped the pillow and settled down.

But he could hear her breathing. He swore he could

hear her shivering, too. "Do you want the blanket back?" he asked, aware she could probably reach it.

"No."

"If you're cold—"

"Stubble it!" she retorted.

He ought to tan her hide for speaking to him thus, but with her tied to the chair, he had the advantage.

He settled down again and pulled the pillow over his head. He felt as though he needed some barrier to keep her at bay. He was beginning to doze when he heard her moving about. He tried to ignore her. She was probably just getting comfortable.

She moved again, and he heard a distinct thud. Dane sat. "What the deuce is going on?"

"Nothing."

But he could see she had toppled the chair and was now lying under it. He should have left her there. Instead, he rose and righted it, then lifted her back into it. He held her in his arms for just a little longer than was necessary. She did feel cold, and he had the impulse to warm her. But more than that, her skin was soft against his fingertips, and her flesh was enticingly round where their bodies brushed together. He had the urge to pass a hand over that roundness, but stifled the urge by saying the first thought that came to mind. "Were you trying to retrieve the blanket?"

No answer.

He wrapped the blanket about her as much to hide her lush figure as to keep her warm. This time she didn't fling it off. He could see her face in the light from the hearth, and the flickering made it look almost tear-stained. He paused to look at her.

"What are you going to do with me?" she asked.

"That's up to my brother." He rose because, even though her body was hidden, her scent teased his senses. She smelled clean and slightly floral, and underneath all of it was a scent that was *woman*. That scent drew him, made him long to bury his face in her hair and put his hands on her body.

"I want to go home," she said.

He opened his mouth to make some retort, and at the last minute changed his mind. "Why?"

"What do you mean, why?"

"I mean, what is waiting for you at home? I imagine it is some sort of hovel you share with a flock of pickpockets and thieves. If you are Lady Elizabeth, why go back?"

She sniffed and looked away from him. The gesture reminded him exactly of something a miffed duchess would do. It made him wonder. But if she didn't want to talk, that was fine with him. He was exhausted. She might be light, but it had been taxing to fight her and then carry her.

Silence descended, and he heard the ticking of the clock. He tried to sleep, even closed his eyes.

"You wouldn't understand," she said finally, breaking the silence.

"Try me."

"My cronies are my family."

"And there's loyalty even among thieves, correct?"

"Loyalty, yes," she said, but he could hear in her voice there was more.

He rose on one elbow, interested now despite his intention of ignoring her and going to sleep.

"Have you considered that if you don't let me go, they might come looking for me?"

"Have you considered they might not care?"

"Oh, they care," she said, her voice strange and flat. "And if you care about your family and your pretty house, you'll let me go before Satin comes for me." He heard the hitch in her voice. "Before it's too late for both of us."

Four

SHE WOKE SUDDENLY AND REACHED FOR HER KNIFE. Something pinned her arm, and it took her a moment to realize she was tied. It took her another moment to remember where she was. Not in the flash ken. Seven Dials was never silent. There was always a baby crying or a bawd arguing with a cove or some ballad-seller screeching about the last confessions of Newgate's condemned. No, this was far too quiet for the flash ken. She was in the bastard's castle. In his bedchamber. The fire in the hearth had burned low, and her body felt heavy and warm. She must have slept for several hours, despite her intention to stay awake and defend herself against the bastard.

She glanced at his bed, staring at it until she could make out his form. He snored softly, and she realized he was also asleep. Maybe he really didn't mean to hurt her. Ha! And once she trusted him, he'd carry out his evil plan. She couldn't afford to trust him. And she couldn't stay in his castle.

It took a bit of doing, because the bastard was better at tying knots than she anticipated, but she managed to free herself from the bindings. She might have pulled her dagger from her boot, but if she cut the cords, he'd know she had it. She might need her secrets. Besides, drapery cords were too silky and thick to be effective. Still, once she was free, something in her chest lifted. The tightness and panic ebbed away.

Silently, she rose from the chair and tiptoed to the bed. In the darkness, it was difficult to discern his features. Finally, she found the spill of his dark hair on his white pillow. His arm was thrown up beside his head, and he did not stir as she stared down at him. His chest rose in a steady rhythm. She couldn't see his face, but she imagined it was slack with sleep. What must it be like to sleep so soundly, so deeply? She always slept with her hand curled about a dagger, her ears listening for any treacherous sound, her eyes ready to pop open. Once again she wondered if the soup had been drugged. She never fell asleep so easily or so completely.

But then her belly was never full, either. Strange to wake and not feel the gnawing hunger in her midsection.

If she were to escape, she needed the key to the bedroom. She tried to remember what he'd done with it after he'd locked the door. He'd been wearing a coat. Maybe he'd stowed it in the coat. He'd taken off the coat before going to bed. She remembered him wearing only shirtsleeves when he'd righted her chair and covered her with the blanket.

She didn't know why he'd done her a kindness. Maybe he felt guilty when he considered what he'd do to her when he'd gained her trust. Would he sell her to a bawdy house? Have her transported? Whatever his plan, she would not wait for it to take shape. Kindness was manipulation, and those who trusted it were the worst sorts of fools.

She looked behind her, at the door he'd gone through after he'd tied her. She had no glim-stick, so she carefully made her way to it and opened the door. It was dark, but she could smell the scent of wool and linen. This was where he stored his clothing. An entire room to store clothes! How would she ever find his coat in here? It was dark, and there were probably dozens of coats.

She bit the pad of her thumb, thinking. It was an old habit and one she felt slightly guilty about, even though neither Satin nor any of the cubs ever said anything. Their bad habits were far worse than hers, at any rate—picking their teeth, farting, blowing snot from their nose. The swell was right that if she'd had a choice, she wouldn't have minded staying here for a few days.

But she didn't have a choice.

She bit her thumb again and then looked back at the bed. If he'd locked the door, he'd want the key close to him. He'd probably stuffed it in the pocket of his... he'd been wearing breeches and a flowing lawn shirt. He wouldn't have pockets. So then he'd put it down on the table beside the bed. She crossed to the table and felt the surface carefully. A book, a glass that had once held what smelled like spirits, and a cold lamp sat there.

Perhaps he held it in his hand or had looped it about his neck. She didn't remember seeing it dangling from his neck, but she hadn't been thinking very clearly when he'd knelt before her.

She'd been thinking about kissing him. Now she bit her thumb hard in punishment. What was wrong with her? She was becoming the sort of silly tib all the cubs made fun of. Of course, she'd noticed bang-up coves before, just as the cubs noticed a rum-duchess. She'd even thought about kissing one or two of the handsome coves. Some of those thoughts had led to her kissing Gideon. But that had been nothing more than idle fantasy, something to pass the time while she waited for a dive or a racket. She hadn't really been near to any of the men she imagined kissing. But this man was different. She'd been very close to him, kissing distance close. And he'd smelled so clean. She'd thought nothing could smell as wonderful as meat and ale, but he came close.

If she kissed him, would they have the spark Gideon had talked about? She feared they would, but she would not ever find out. She would pilfer that key and hide so Sir Brook never found her again. Satin could send her to Bath for a few months. They'd never look for her there.

But if she were to open his hand or remove something from about his neck, she'd better be prepared to defend herself should he wake up. She could pick a pocket, but this was something else entirely. She bent and reached into her boot, extracting her dagger. The familiar weight of it seemed to right the world, and she felt calm again and ready for anything. She'd try his hand first. Clamping the dagger between her teeth, she leaned over the bed. It was a tall bed, and the mattresses had been piled high. She could not manage to achieve a good vantage point for opening his fingers. And those were the fingers beside his head. What if he'd hidden it in the hand beneath the bedclothes?

Clenching her teeth on the blade of the dagger, she gingerly placed her hands on the bedclothes. Instantly, she lifted her hand again. The gold-and-red material was soft and plush. She touched it again, running her hand over it in amazement. She didn't have time to gawk at the finery, so she pushed down, then eased one knee onto the mattress, and carefully hoisted herself up. She brought her other knee up as well, and knelt beside him on the bed. It had to be the softest bed she had ever touched. Of course, she'd never slept in a dab, but she'd been in Barbara's chamber in the back room of the Rouge Unicorn Cellar a few times. She had a wide dab, but it was puny compared to this one. Marlowe slept on a coarse blanket on the floor, and she'd always envied Barbara's bed. But Barbara's mattress was a rock compared to what she knelt on now. Did people really sleep on such softness? She had not even imagined such luxuries might exist.

She leaned toward the pillow and his hand, but she felt herself sinking into the bowl created by his body. He was incredibly warm, the sort of warmth she only felt in a kitchen or during a particularly mild summer. Marlowe wondered what sort of bedclothes covered him, but she could not risk investigating them. She tried to lean close to his hand again and almost fell on top of him. She needed some way to balance herself.

She saw the solution immediately, even if she did not like it. But she was no coward. Carefully, she swung a leg over his body, keeping herself poised precariously over his abdomen. *This is why I don't wear skirts*, she thought as she tested her balance. She'd never be able to do this in a skirt.

Finally, she leaned over him and held her hand above the one resting on his pillow. His fingers curled lightly in sleep. With a sweeping movement, she teased his fingers open. She almost swore when she saw his palm was empty, but she held the curse back. She'd just have to try his other hand. Before she did so, she dipped her head to the side, hoping to shed some light from the hearth on his throat. It was too dark for her to be certain, but she did not think the key was around his neck.

One last hiding place. She knelt on the bedclothes. His hand was underneath, but it jutted at an angle from his body. Her knee rested right below his wrist. Tentatively, she reached under the covers, surprised again at how warm it was beneath them. She touched the sleeve of his shirt and traced the material to his wrist. She touched the warm flesh by accident, then flicked her gaze to his face. His eyes were still closed, and he did not move.

She was about to return to her task when her heart thudded painfully in her chest. She caught her breath and held perfectly still, not certain what had alarmed her. The house was quiet; the bastard beneath her did not move; it was still hours until morning…

She gasped and flicked her gaze to his face. He didn't move! His chest was no longer rising and falling in the steady rhythm of sleep. She no longer heard the soft snores in his throat.

"While I do not usually object to a woman in this position," he said quietly, "I must confess something about the dagger between your lips is less than romantic."

She reached for the dagger, but he was faster, grasping her hands and pinning them at her side. She lost her balance and settled on top of him, and he pushed her down so that she would fall forward if she tried to swing her legs out from under her.

"What, exactly, are you doing?"

She couldn't answer, not with the dagger in her mouth, and she shook her head, shaking her arms to indicate she wanted to be freed from his hold.

"What's the matter? Can't speak with a knife between your lips? Hazard of your profession, I assume." He began to rise, sliding her along his body as he did so. Even beneath the layers of bedclothes, she could feel the strength and power of him. His hands, remarkably strong, held hers at her sides. Nothing she did would free them. He was far too strong. It was times like this she hated being a woman. Gideon would have freed himself easily. He was also tall enough that he wouldn't have needed to climb onto the bed.

When the swell was sitting, with Marlowe conveniently in his lap, he leaned forward so his face was inches from hers. "Drop the knife."

She wanted to tell him it was a dagger, a subtle but important distinction, but she couldn't speak and hold on to her weapon. And she couldn't think very well with her body pressed against his. Something about their positions made her skin tingle and her belly flutter. She should want to pull away. Instead, she fought the urge to push closer, to rock against him. What the bloody hell was *wrong* with her?

"Drop the knife or I'll take it."

She laughed. Just let him try.

"Very well."

To her surprise, he leaned closer, his lips moving so near to hers she could smell his breath. Like the rest of him, it smelled clean. She was so intent upon smelling his breath, so intent upon the heat of his body pulsing against hers, she forgot to move her head back, and she jolted in shock when his lips touched hers. What was he doing? Kissing her?

But then his teeth flashed and closed on the dagger's blade, and she reacted too slowly. He yanked it from her mouth, and she had no choice but to let it go or risk the blade cutting the corners of her sensitive flesh.

"Bastard!" she yelled. He released her hands then, allowing the dagger to drop into one of his. She swung at him, and her fist collided with a satisfying thunk against his cheek. But her satisfaction was short-lived as he recovered easily and flipped her over. Suddenly, she was beneath him on the bed, and all the warmth from the bedclothes and his body were covering her. She bucked immediately, trying to throw him off, but he was solid and heavy, and when his hands grasped her wrists and pinned them to the pillow, she knew she was trapped.

"I'll scream," she threatened.

"Go ahead. The door is locked, and no one will knock it down to save the likes of you."

Save her? Was he going to kill her? A quick peek at his hand told her he still held her dagger. The metal, warmed by her mouth, was pressed against the flesh of her wrist. "What are you going to do to me?"

"It depends. What were you trying to do to me?" He sounded so calm, so utterly unconcerned, that she glanced at his face, even though it was too dark to see his features. She regretted the action immediately. She hadn't realized how close his mouth was to hers. And that led her to notice how his body pressed against hers…in quite a few delicate places. She should hate that his hands imprisoned hers and his body trapped hers. But there was something so deliciously sinful about this position and having him looming over her.

"I was only trying to filch the key. Now get off." If she acted as though she did not enjoy his touch, perhaps he'd move off her. She wouldn't have to feel the heat of his body or the strength in his arms. She wouldn't have to wish he'd lower his mouth to hers and kiss her breathless.

"Key?" He cocked his head. "The key to the room? Are you still trying to escape?"

"Yes! You can't keep me here against my will."

"You weren't trying to slit my throat?" he asked, clearly ignoring her protest about being his prisoner and making no effort at all to let go of her. Which was her goal at the moment. Not kissing him, damn it!

"I'm a thief, not a murderer."

"That's comforting to know." He released his hold on her wrists slightly. "Unfortunately, I cannot release you. You are my guest until Brook returns in the morning."

"You mean prisoner!" She shook her hands to show him how he'd shackled her.

"Quite right," he said, sounding thoughtful. Marlowe held her breath. Did that mean he would release her? Would that he hurried before she made a fool of herself and asked him to kiss her, or something equally mortifying.

"It occurs to me I should probably introduce myself."

Marlowe wanted to cry. She blew out a frustrated breath. These ridiculous swells and all their bloody manners! "I don't care who you are. Just let me—"

"—go. Yes, you keep saying that, and then I have to say, again, that I gave my brother my word I would keep you here. The conversation grows tiresome."

She would have hit him if her hands weren't pinned. She hated him! Her conversation was tiresome? She didn't give a bloody shilling about her conversation. "Then try this *conversation*—let me up or I may have a go at murder."

He chuckled softly, his sweet breath puffing out lightly on her cheek. Bloody hell! Now her skin was tingling. At any moment, she'd do something truly awful and pucker her lips for a kiss.

"Is that a threat?" he asked, sounding amused. No kissing. She would gut the bastard. "Do you even know who it is you're threatening?"

It was on the tip of her tongue to say she did not care, but she bit the retort back because the truth was, she was curious.

"Maxwell Derring, Earl of Dane."

She tried to bite her thumb, but his hand clamped more tightly on her wrist, reminding her he was holding her down. He'd rattled his name so quickly, she was not certain she'd understood. His name was Maxwell, but there was that second part. "Of the what?"

He let out a slow breath. "*Earl of Dane*. Do you know what an earl is?"

Oh, yes. She knew. Satin had schooled all of the cubs in the titles the great rum morts carried. There were the dukes, the barons, the knights, the earls. What were the other two? Marquess, and another... It didn't matter. They all meant the same thing.

Blunt. Lots of blunt.

And power.

This swell certainly had blunt, but it was his power that concerned her. What if he did have the right to imprison her? The rich seemed to have all sorts of privileges she couldn't even imagine. Maybe they had the right to sweep people off the streets and keep them locked up in their homes.

A change in his breathing drew her thoughts back to the present situation, back to the fact that he was pressing his hard body against hers. Every part of his body was hard... She bucked again. "No!"

They wrestled for a moment, and she managed to free one hand. She reached up to claw him, but he feinted to the side and then caught her wrist again. This time his grip was vicious.

"Ow!" she protested.

"Little hellcat! Stop trying to kill me."

"Stop trying to rape me!"

"I'm not—"

"Ha! Your noodle is hard. I'm no bawd, but I know what that means. And I know where to aim my knee."

"I have no doubt of that, but I assure you I have not, nor will I ever, take a woman against her will."

"But your noodle—"

"My noodle. Yes, interesting term. I cannot help that. You see, the thing about noodles is they sometimes act on their own. I'm lying in bed, on top of a beautiful woman with all of the—shall we say—womanly attributes my...noodle appreciates. My body is merely showing its appreciation, even though my brain would prefer I throttle you than make love to you."

"You think I'm beautiful?" She hadn't heard another word after he'd said that. No one had ever called her beautiful. Not even Gideon. In fact, she could count on one hand the number of times any one had ever called her anything other than a mort, a street rat, or a dirty thief. She might have kissed him just for the compliment.

"It's a moot point. If I release you, will you refrain from hitting or kicking me?"

Marlowe didn't know what a *moot* was, but she knew he hadn't answered her question. Perhaps he'd been using one of those metaphors he'd mentioned earlier and did not think she was beautiful at all. Men didn't have to find a woman beautiful to swive her. Marlowe knew dozens of bawds, and they were uglier than sin. At least she had all of her teeth, and her face wasn't marked by the pox. She didn't delude herself into thinking she could compare to the ladies she saw alighting from carriages on Bond Street or at Covent Garden. The Earl of whatever he was probably had one of those ladies in his bed every night. She felt her face flame with embarrassment to think she'd asked if he thought her beautiful. He was too polite to laugh in her face.

"Marlowe?"

"No. I mean, yes. I mean, I don't know what you asked me, but I won't hit you. Just let me up."

"I'm going to count to three."

"Oh, bloody hell! Just let me up!"

"And on that mellifluous note, I release you." As soon as he slid off her, she scrambled up and out from under him. She climbed to the far edge of the bed and sat on her haunches, ready to fight if necessary. The bastard still had her dagger. Now she had two items to filch. But she needn't have prepared for battle. He obviously didn't want her. He rolled off the bed and walked toward the hearth. A moment later, he'd lit two glim-sticks and poured himself a glass of some liquid. "Brandy?" he asked, raising a brow at her.

"Why?"

He looked heavenward. "I feel for your parents, Marlowe. I really do. When she meets you, Lady Lyndon will be so shocked she will no doubt faint dead away."

Marlowe didn't have a response to that, so she merely watched as he poured a second glass of amber liquid and carried it to her. He moved with a grace she could appreciate, having lived with thieves who needed to be quick and agile. But this man was not quick. He moved slowly and with purpose and even beauty. There was something beautiful about the confident way he held himself. "Here." He held one of the glasses out to her. She looked at his hand then back at his face.

"Why are you giving this to me?"

"I don't know. Because it's polite? Because I don't want to drink alone? Because you look like you could use it? Just take it."

She took it and sniffed. It smelled like spirits.

"You've never had brandy, have you?" he asked, swirling his about. "It burns a bit going down, but then it warms you through."

"Like gin?"

"Oh, you've had that, have you? Doesn't surprise me. A bit like gin but much smoother. Try it."

She took a small sip, winced at the taste, and then felt the warmth spread through her. It wasn't bad. Much better than the gin Satin liked to drink.

"The verdict?" he asked.

"What?"

He gave her a half smile. "Do you like it?"

She shrugged. "I've drank worse."

He laughed, and the sound surprised her. "High praise indeed. Now, my girl, I think we had better have a talk."

"I'm not your girl."

"And thank God for small mercies." He took a seat in the chair she'd slept in, leaving her on the bed. "I just thought perhaps we might have a conversation like civilized people. You don't kick me or curse like…well, like yourself, and I will attempt not to throw you over my shoulder or pin you to my bed."

"You like to talk, don't you?"

He grinned at her. "Some women find me charming."

She merely blinked at that. He was handsome

enough, but she had no use for men with charm. They usually wanted to charm guineas out of her pocket.

"Clearly, you don't find me charming." He leaned forward, his elbows resting on his knees. "Be that as it may, I want to propose a compromise."

"Which means I agree to let you have your way and stop fighting."

He opened his mouth to speak, probably to protest, but then he gave a small shrug. "I suppose that is what I mean. But there are benefits to staying the rest of the night."

"What?"

He sat back now. "I can't talk to you when you look like you'll bolt at any moment. Not to mention, your boots are on my counterpane, and it was quite expensive."

She climbed down off the bed and stood, arms crossed, on the other side, so the bed was a barrier between them.

"Thank you."

"You were going to say what I get for staying."

He seemed to consider for a long moment. "A huge breakfast."

Oh, he was cruel, this one. Food was her weakness. She could have fought against anything else he said, but the thought of a full belly in the morning was almost more than she could resist.

"On any given day we sit down to oatmeal with sweet cream, bacon, kippers, cold veal pie, sausage, beef tongue—"

He went on, but she could hardly hear him for the ringing in her ears. Bacon? Sausage? Sweet cream? She could not begin to imagine so much food, much less for only one meal.

"Then there is fresh bread and rolls with butter, honey, marmalade, or jam made from cherries and apples, which we grow on our country estate. Of course, we have tea, coffee, or chocolate to drink."

"Chocolate?"

He finished his brandy and grinned at her. "Have you ever had chocolate?"

"Course." But she hadn't, and from the look on his face, he knew she was lying. When would she have ever had something so decadent as chocolate? Oh, but she'd heard of it. She'd listened to the curtezans talk about it, how they'd spent the night with some great rum duke and had chocolate to drink in the morning. Marlowe had thought they were lying. Apparently, it was true, and if she stayed, *she* could drink it in the morning.

He had her now. He might not know it—she wouldn't have made a very good thief if her every thought appeared on her face—but she could not leave without tasting the chocolate. "If I stay"—she must put up some resistance, mustn't she?—"then after we break our fast, I can go?"

He flicked his wrist, the sleeve of his fine white shirt floating up and back down gracefully. "That is Brook's decision."

"Then where is he? I want to speak with him." She started for the door and had her hand on the latch when she remembered the key. She turned to the earl. "Let me have the key."

"So you can traipse about my house in the middle

of the night, disturbing the servants, not to mention my sister and mother? No. You'll be enough of a shock in the morning."

She put her hands on her hips, and for some reason, his eyes widened slightly. Well, let him see she could be as firm and stubborn as he was. She'd show him that he could not order her around. "Then you go find him and bring him back."

"Eh?" he said.

She huffed out a breath. "I said, you go get him!"

His features, so handsome and genial, darkened then. He rose slowly, unfolding his body gracefully from the chair. Had he been this tall before? She suddenly felt rather scrawny standing in front of his door all alone.

"You, Marlowe, are not giving the orders." He stalked toward her, and she felt like a dog cornered in an alley. Well, she couldn't just roll over and whimper. She'd have to prove she had bite. But she didn't want to make him too angry. There was sausage and bacon and chocolate to think of.

"Apparently, neither are you."

His face hardened, and she knew her punch had hit him in the breadbasket. One thing she knew about men. They did not like their authority challenged. Satin disliked it so much that she'd seen him make some bloody fool choices only to prove he was the undisputed arch rogue.

She'd also seen Satin beat a man to death for a trifle.

She didn't think this earl would hurt her. She winced as his fist collided with the door beside her head. On the other hand, the night was not yet over…

She'd expected an explosion of pain in her jaw,

but he hadn't hit her. She looked left then right, and noted he'd trapped her between his arms. Perhaps he was a bit more violent than she'd thought. "Listen, you little—"

She waited. "Hatchet-face?"

He frowned at her.

"Bundle-tail?" She was short enough that she'd been called that a time or two. "Harridan? Romp?"

"Are you helping me insult you?" Suddenly his face lost that dark, angry look, and the expression that replaced it made her far more nervous. She pushed back against the door.

"You seemed to need help."

The hands that had been beside her head, pressed against the door, moved to her cheeks. She jumped at the unexpected warmth of his flesh and the gentleness that was completely foreign to her. "Who would call you all of those names?"

She couldn't explain why, but tears stung the backs of her eyes. She didn't know the last time she had cried, and it was certainly not over anything so low as being called a harridan. She blinked the tears away and pulled his hands off her cheeks. "Don't touch me," she hissed, though she would have let him touch her more if he'd wanted. No one had ever touched her the way he did. "It's not your business who called me what, but I promise you, he'll do far worse to you if you don't allow me to go."

"And back to this." He sighed. "Marlowe, listen—"

"No, *Maxwell*. You listen."

His face went dark and grim again, and she felt the strange tightness in her chest dissipate. Anger she could understand. That soft, pitying expression was to be avoided. And his touch. She could not allow him to touch her ever again.

"Do not call me that," he ordered.

She frowned at him. He acted as though she'd insulted him. "That's your name, isn't it?"

"You call me Dane or *my lord*."

"I can think of a few other names for you."

"I'm sure you can, and you may use them at your own risk. But do not call me by my Christian name. Ever."

"Why? You call me by mine."

"Because it's my right as your better."

She snorted.

"You and I are not on intimate terms, and we never will be." He said the last with his face so close to hers she could see the dark ring around the brown of his eyes. So that was why they looked so beautiful. The tightness in her chest was back again, and she pushed at him, increasing the distance between them.

"That suits me, cove. But if I have to call you *my lord*, you better call me Miss Marlowe."

He gave her a long look. He stared at her for such a length of time that she thought perhaps he'd had some sort of apoplectic fit and could not move again. "You really have no idea who it is you're dealing with, do you?"

"I—"

He held up a hand, cutting her off. Ha! And the swells were supposed to be well-mannered. He turned away from her and rubbed a hand over his face. "I will murder Brook for this. It is the middle of the night, and I want to sleep." He looked back at her. "What do I need to do to be able to sleep?"

She opened her mouth, and he held up a hand. "Do not say allow you to go. We will discuss it after we break our fast."

This was probably the best offer she would receive. She knew it, and she was clever enough not to argue further. "Fine."

"Fine." He scrubbed his face again. "Now she says fine. Would that we'd saved that hour and a modicum of my sanity. Then let's go to sleep."

"I want the bed," she said. She hadn't even known she would say it. She certainly hadn't expected to say it, but the words seemed to rush forward without her permission. He lowered his hands and raised his eyebrows.

"You want to sleep in my bed."

She did. She'd never slept in a bed, and if he would force her to remain here, the least he could do was give her the bed, not tie her to a chair, although the chair had been more comfortable than her usual sleeping quarters. "I do."

His brow rose again, and when her chest tightened, she quickly added, "Alone."

He stared at her, and she noticed he had a tick in his jaw. He was angry again. Good. That made the strange feeling lessen substantially. He stalked away from her and toward the bed, ripped a pillow off it, and walked back toward the door, muttering something about *gall* and *pummel Brook* and *Gentleman Jackson*. He threw the pillow on the floor in front of the door, and she jumped out of the way. "Are you sleeping there?"

"Correct. Even if you steal the key, you'll still have to move me from the door to escape."

"I could just slit your throat."

"Do you have another dagger?"

He still had hers. What had he done with it? She didn't have another, but she wouldn't reveal that to him.

"Go ahead and slit my throat, but you'll have a difficult time moving my dead body away from the door."

"I could do it."

"And I could wake, take the dagger, and slit *your* throat. Keep that in mind."

Oh, she would. She turned toward the bed and smiled. It was all hers. But before she could climb on top, he said, "Take your dirty boots off, and you might want to fasten that last shirt button. It's gaping, and giving me quite a view."

Five

WITH A VERY MAIDENLY SHRIEK, SHE DID UP THE button again and scrambled under his bedclothes. Thankfully, she'd removed her boots first. Dane looked at the floor and his pillow and tried to make the best of it. He wasn't comfortable on his side or his back, but at least on his back, his view was of the ceiling and not his bed.

He did not know how it had come to this. A chit from the streets was sleeping in his bed, while he slept on the floor. That irked him even more than the fact that he'd woken to find her straddling him with a knife between her lips. The foul-mouthed wench in his bed annoyed him even more than the realization that Brook was probably sleeping soundly and comfortably in some woman's bed while he, the blasted *Earl* of Dane, was sleeping on the cold, hard floor.

And what really rankled was that he wanted to be in the bed with her. In bed. With a street rat! There was something very wrong with him if he had lowered himself to desiring a...what had she called herself? Bundle-tail? Harridan? He had never been in favor of brothels. He didn't like the messiness of mistresses either. He was a man like any other, with needs, which he satisfied when he met an acceptable woman. A young widow or a wife whose husband looked the other way—usually at another woman. He didn't allow his needs to control him, but clearly he needed to meet them more often if he was lowering himself to lusting after criminals.

But what the devil was he supposed to do when she straddled him, all that lovely thick hair falling down around her shoulders, where it had come loose from the ridiculous cap she wore? His body reacted to her warmth and the smell of the clean apricot soap she'd used. She was a woman, even if she was also a thief. It wasn't his fault she had those big blue eyes and that wide mouth, and she stared at him as though in perpetual awe. The look on her face when he'd detailed the food they'd eat at breakfast had been akin to orgasm. He would have to send a note to Cook and ensure she prepared everything he'd promised.

On the other hand, what did he care whether the little thief had bacon or not? He didn't owe her or her kind anything. Let Brook worry about her. It wasn't as if Dane wanted to watch her eat again. Last night in the kitchen had been shocking enough. His hunting dogs had better manners. He couldn't imagine his mother and sister sitting down with her.

But he could imagine that look of pleasure on Marlowe's face again. He did want to see that, and if bacon or chocolate was required, he could provide it. He could imagine her sipping the warm chocolate, her small pink tongue darting out to lick a drop from her chin. She missed it, and the drop fell into that ample cleavage, on display because her damned shirt had come unfastened again.

Dane groaned and shifted uncomfortably.

"What is it?" she asked.

"Nothing," he said, voice clipped and short. "Go to sleep."

"I will."

The damned chit sounded almost gleeful. He'd be gleeful when he finally evicted her from his bed and his life. Just a few more hours…

Dane was awakened from his light sleep by the door to his bedchamber thunking him on the head. It would have been worse if he hadn't heard the handle rattle and then a key in the lock. He moved enough to avoid the worst of the blow. Still, he cursed as he sat, and rubbing his temple, looked up at Crawford. Crawford's face, his thin mouth pursed under his crooked nose, peered back at him through the slit in the door. The butler looked mildly surprised, which was saying something for Crawford, whose range of expressions generally traveled the gamut from grave to somber. "My lord," Crawford said with a nod. "Do you need assistance?"

"No." Dane rose, and immediately his back and neck protested. More good news. He was too old to sleep on the floor without consequences. Crawford pushed the door open and seemed to examine Dane closely. He was probably looking for injuries.

"Did you have a fall, my lord?"

"No. I…" Dane did not want to explain the situation to his butler. How he missed Tibbs, his valet. Tibbs would have screeched to see the state of Dane's clothing, but he would not have expected explanations or remarked on where or how Dane chose to spend the night. "Did you come to help me dress?"

"Yes, my lord."

"Then let's begin."

"If you do not mind my asking, my lord, where is the…ah…"

"Harridan?" came a feminine voice from the other side of the room. "Street wench?"

"Helpful, as usual," Dane muttered.

"In the bed?" Again, Crawford looked mildly shocked, an expression on his face that equated to an eyebrow raised a fraction of an inch. "I shall have the bedclothes burned, my lord," he murmured.

"I can hear you," she said.

As Dane watched, the small mound in the bed moved. The girl was practically dwarfed by the large bed, the bolster, the half-dozen—minus one—pillows, and the bedclothes. She sat, pushing her hair out of her eyes and looking perfectly well-rested. His level of annoyance, which was already rather high, climbed heavenward. She raised her arms and yawned, stretching the fabric of her already too-tight shirt indecently. Dane had the choice to continue watching, and embarrass himself and Crawford with the resulting erection, or look away.

He looked at Crawford. The butler was ugly enough to stem his lust. And there was another surprise. Crawford, the very epitome of etiquette, was watching the girl stretch with undisguised interest. Perhaps Crawford was human after all. He might even be part man underneath all of that marble.

"Crawford," Dane said.

The butler's eyes immediately focused on a point above the bed, and he said, "Yes, my lord?"

"Perhaps we should adjourn to the dressing room and leave the bedchamber to Mar—*Miss* Marlowe."

"Yes, my lord."

Dane started after the butler, toward the dressing room, then turned abruptly, withdrew the key from his pocket, and locked the door again. As he passed the bed, he could have sworn Marlowe hissed, "Bastard."

He had a few choice words for her too—especially when she chose to insult him before he'd had his tea and after spending the night on the floor—but he was too much of a gentleman to use them.

For the moment at least.

An hour later, he emerged from the dressing room, feeling much better. Crawford did not possess Tibbs's finesse, but he was every bit as skilled. Dane was cleanly shaved, washed, and dressed in his favorite breeches, a dark blue coat and matching waistcoat, topped by a stark-white linen shirt and a flawlessly tied cravat in the Horse Collar style, which was all Crawford could seem to manage. Tibbs usually complained the *trone d'Amour* was too austere, but Dane liked austere and liked his usual style.

"There you are!" the street urchin said, moving away from the fire and planting her hands on her hips. Dane clenched his fists. He really wished she would not do that in those clothes. He wished she would not do it at all, as it was not the sort of gesture well-bred ladies would ever affect. But he knew very well she was no lady.

"I thought you'd become lost in that theater you call a dressing room. Bloody hell. What is on your neck?" She approached him, hand outstretched to touch his cravat, but he stepped back.

"It is a cravat. I believe we had this discussion last night."

"Why did you wind it and puff it out like that?"

Dane might have been mistaken—he had better be mistaken—but he thought he heard Crawford chuckle. He looked at the butler with accusation, and Crawford cleared his throat. "If I'm no longer needed, my lord." And away Crawford went, using his key to open the door to the chamber and exiting. The key did not sound in the lock a second time, and Dane reached out and grabbed Marlowe by the elbow just as she bolted.

"You haven't yet broken your fast."

She yanked her arm out of his grip. "After I eat, I'm leaving. Just try and stop me."

"Madam, I will lead the parade to the door."

He escorted her down to the dining room, though one could hardly call it an escort if the so-called lady one was escorting stomped as loudly as a battalion of soldiers behind him. Maids carrying linens hurried by, darting glances their way, while others stood with dusters in hand and mouths agape. Dane hardly took note of them, except that the uncultured urchin could not seem to ignore them.

"What are you looking at?" she challenged one young maid.

The girl clamped her mouth shut and bobbed a curtsy. "Nothing, miss."

Far from appeasing Marlowe, the deference seemed

to anger her. "Are you making sport of me?" she asked, breaking off to corner the girl until she was backed against the wall.

"N-no, miss!"

"Why are you calling me *miss*? What was that little dip you did?"

With a sigh, Dane took Marlowe's elbow. "She is trying to be polite," he said, pulling Marlowe away. "You might take a lesson." The poor maid looked so traumatized, he almost apologized. Instead, he said, "Go back to work, and when I see Mrs. Barstowe, I'll ask her to give you a raise."

"Thank you, my lord." The maid curtsied, and before Marlowe could chastise her again, he dragged Marlowe away. He kept his hand on her elbow as they traversed the long corridor, passing the portraits of the former earls and countesses, his illustrious ancestors. And they thought *they* had reason to frown before.

He and Marlowe arrived at the bottom of the stairs and the entrance to the dining room before he had to intervene again. A footman stood at the door to open it for them, and as Marlowe was preceding him at that point, the footman, in effect, opened the door for her.

"Do you think I can't open the door myself?" she challenged the footman, who had been too well trained by Crawford to respond or even look at the girl. He kept his eyes on the far wall, and merely nodded stiffly at her comment.

"Good morning, Nathaniel," Dane said, pushing Marlowe into the dining room. He didn't usually greet the servants, but everything in his life had been upside down since he'd agreed to loan Brook his carriage.

And now, God willing, all would be put to rights. He stepped into the dining room and immediately searched the table for his brother. He found only his mother, sitting in her usual spot away from the windows, which could be drafty, and sipping her tea. Her cup paused in midair when he entered, the only sign she noticed anything amiss.

His mother had been but a girl herself when she married his father, the earl, who'd been more than twenty years her senior. His father had passed away three years ago after a mild cough turned into pneumonia. Coincidence that the pneumonia had taken hold after the house had been pilfered and ransacked by thieves? Dane thought not. The countess had mourned her husband for the requisite period, but Dane never had the sense that she felt any real loss. Theirs had not been a love match. The earl was probably more of a father to her than a husband, although the couple produced five children, only three of whom survived. Possibly only two, as Brook might not live to see tomorrow.

The countess was a woman in her prime, not yet fifty, and her dark hair was still glossy and free from gray. Her skin was flawless and youthful, and she had a slim, willowy figure, much like his sister, Susanna. In short, she did not look like a mother, particularly a mother of three grown children. That was conceding his younger brother was grown, and Dane had a mind to dispute that. He'd often wondered why his mother did not marry again. She might have had suitors if she'd wanted them, but she seemed utterly uninterested. As much as he respected her, he did not love her. How did one love a marble statue? His mother was as warm and affectionate as the Bandinelli sculpture in the vestibule.

Slowly, and with the grace she was known for, his mother set her teacup on its saucer with nary a clink. "Good morning, Dane. And what is this?"

"This"—Dane said, crossing to the sideboard and lifting a plate for himself and one for Marlowe—"is one of Brook's projects. I have promised her breakfast, and then he will deal with her. Where is he, by the way?"

His mother's gaze never left Marlowe, who was obviously not foolish enough to ask the countess at whom she was looking. In fact, Marlowe still stood just inside the door, her gaze sweeping over the room and her mouth slightly agape. He tried to see it as she might. The room was light blue with white paneling and rather ornate medallions, from which hung two crystal chandeliers. The chandeliers were not lit, as to do so for a simple family breakfast was too extravagant, even for him. The windows faced Berkeley Street, the house being situated very near the square of the same name. The street was quiet at this time of the morning. A footman stood on the opposite side of the room, ready to be of assistance. Dane was certain that though the man pretended not to see, he was secretly committing all to memory so he might tell the rest of the staff later.

His mother had not taken her gaze from Marlowe. "I have not seen your brother since he came to collect you at Lady Yorke's soiree. Shall I assume this…girl was the reason he sought you?"

"You may." He continued piling Marlowe's plate

with food, because he hoped the sooner his mother saw her eat, the sooner she would forget all of her questions. He would prefer not to explain where the girl had slept last night or how she had come to be here.

"And what is your name, girl?" the countess asked.

Dane turned, bringing her heavy plate and his own lighter one to the table and setting them down. He placed hers at the chair Brook usually occupied, which happened to be beside his.

"Marlowe," the girl said, dragging her attention from the room and to the countess.

The countess's eyes widened, and she flicked her gaze to Dane before aiming it back at Marlowe. "Are you always this impertinent?"

Marlowe opened her mouth, but Dane answered before she could speak. "She is usually more so."

Marlowe frowned. "What did I do wrong now?"

"The list is too extensive at this point," Dane said. "Do sit and eat, Miss Marlowe."

The countess's eyebrows rose higher, if that were possible. They would recede into her hairline once she saw the chit eat. "Do you speak to her so familiarly?"

"She has no surname," he said, pulling Marlowe's chair out for her. She sat, and he tried to push it in, but she gave him a potent scowl.

"I can pull my own chair to the table."

"Do not speak to the earl in that tone of voice," his mother said. Dane recognized the tone as the one she typically used to lecture. He and Brook had heard it often enough. Poor Susanna still did. "And when you enter a room, you should curtsy, not stand with your mouth open. And when you address me—"

But Marlowe was not listening. She'd looked down and was now all but drooling at the food he'd heaped on her plate. "Is all of this for me?"

"And there's more if you want it."

Marlowe's blue eyes opened wide, as though she had found a pirate's treasure of precious gems and gold coins.

"I am still speaking!" his mother said, but Marlowe ignored her, lifting a slab of ham and cramming the entire piece into her mouth. His mother let out a small cry of alarm, and even Dane was impressed. She chewed, her cheeks puffed out like a squirrel's, and then she looked about. Dane wondered what she sought, until she grabbed his cup and downed half of his tea.

"This is awful," she said, her mouth still full and her words garbled. "Where's my chocolate?"

Dane signaled to the footman, who came forward with the pot of chocolate. He poured it in the cup before Marlowe, and she lifted it as a man lost in a desert might a cup of water. "It's hot," he warned.

She ignored him, took a large swig, and promptly spit half of it back out. His mother jumped to her feet, threw her napkin down, and said, "Enough! I will not stand for this!" She marched to the exit, the footman opening the door with perfect timing so she might stomp out. She reached the vestibule, then turned on her heel and said, "I want…that…that—"

"Harridan?" Dane supplied at the same time Marlowe said "Bundle-tail?" He shot her a grin, though he knew it would only anger his mother further.

"*Person*," his mother said, her voice high-pitched

with anger, "out of my house before the end of the hour."

The door slammed on her words, and Dane let out a sigh. "You should have eaten with the servants," he said. She crammed a scone into her mouth and then a kipper, all washed down with another healthy swig of chocolate. "But why inflict this punishment on them?" he muttered to himself. Trying to ignore the girl's atrocious eating habits, he ate a few bites of his own breakfast before Crawford entered, carrying a silver tray with a note in the center.

Marlowe barely looked up as she devoured a spoonful of cream, but Dane wiped his mouth with a napkin and took the card. "Thank you, Crawford." He opened it and recognized Brook's hand immediately.

D—

Unavoidably detained. Do not let Lady Elizabeth out of your sight until I return.

Yours,
Brook

Dane swore and, rising, threw his napkin on the chair. "Unbelievable," he muttered, pacing the room behind Marlowe. She'd paid very little attention to anything besides her food for the last several moments, but now she turned slightly to keep a watchful eye on him. She was obviously used to protecting her back and didn't like that he walked behind her. She was going to like being his guest even less.

Dane couldn't say the missive from his brother surprised him. Last summer Brook had used his investigative skills to locate the lost brother of Viscount Chesham. The boy had been missing for a decade or two, and Brook had found him in an opium den in Bath, of all places. The story had been reported in all of the papers, and now Brook had his hands full with requests to locate missing persons. Undoubtedly, that was why Lord and Lady Lyndon had sought him out. Dane cut his eyes to Marlowe, who was watching him, mouth still full to bursting.

He should let the girl go and save her parents the heartache. He did not know the greater tragedy—if she proved to be their daughter or she proved not.

"Wot's it?" she asked before she took another bite. Dane threw the note on the table before her, and she lifted it with her bacon-stained fingers and studied it. Upside down.

"You can't read?" he said, taking it from her.

"Only a little."

"Brook is detained—that means he won't be home—"

"I know what it means," she interrupted.

He gave her a dubious look. "And that means you cannot leave yet."

"Oh, no!" She jumped to her feet, plucking a roll from her plate as she did so. "You promised I could leave after breakfast."

"I made no such promise. I merely implied your departure might be possible."

"Implied? Is that a fancy nob word for lie? You can't keep me here, Lord Dane. I have rights!"

He laughed. "What do you know about rights?"

He waved a hand. "Never mind. You don't even understand that I'm trying to help you. If you are Lady Elizabeth, you'll be rich. You could eat like this every day. You'd have parents, a home, a bed to sleep in. Don't you want that?"

"No!" she said, putting her hands on her hips. Dane exercised extreme willpower and focused his gaze on her face, not the swell of her breasts he knew were now prominently on display. "I am trying to help you. That's what *you* don't understand!"

"Well," a feminine voice interrupted, making them both turn. "This is unexpected."

"Devil take it," Dane muttered.

"Do not allow me to interrupt," Susanna said, her brown eyes wide. "I had not expected to be entertained this morning. I rather thought a lecture waited for me, or I would have come down earlier."

"Mother has retired to her room. You may speak with her there," Dane told his sister.

"Why would I do that?" Her gaze rested firmly on Marlowe. "But I see why she retired. Dane, do not tell me you brought your paramour here."

"No!" he said, sounding as appalled as he felt. How could anyone, even his innocent little sister, think this street urchin was his paramour? Come to think of it, how did his sister even know what a *paramour* was? "This is Brook's project."

"I do wish you'd stop referring to me as a project."

"Oh, how rude of me," Susanna said, coming forward. She gave a curtsy and said, "I am Lady Susanna. A pleasure to meet you."

Marlowe looked at him as if to ask, is this actually

happening? Dane ran a hand through his hair, tousling the careful style Crawford had spent so much time on. "It's customary to introduce yourself," he told the girl.

"I'm Marlowe," she said, "and I'm leaving." She grabbed another roll and stuffed it into her mouth.

"Oh, my, the poor dear is starving!" Susanna remarked. "Didn't Brook feed her?"

"I don't even know where Brook is," Dane said, feeling unaccountably irritated that his sister assumed Marlowe was under Brook's care. God knew he didn't want her, but he should at least receive credit for his part.

"You mustn't leave until after you've finished your breakfast," Susanna said, taking a seat across from Marlowe. Marlowe glanced at him, then sat too. Dane noted her plate was almost empty, a fact which was, in his opinion, quite astounding, as he did not think two men could have finished all of that food so quickly.

"More?" he asked Marlowe.

She nodded, her mouth full and her gaze on Susanna.

The footman poured Susanna her requisite tea while Dane heaped more food on a plate for Marlowe. He set it before her, and Susanna said, "Would you mind making me a plate?"

Dane raised his brows. Susanna never ate breakfast. Correction: she rarely ate in front of their mother. Dane had long suspected the countess made her daughter too nervous to eat. He placed a scone and clotted cream on a plate and delivered it to her, then turned to the footman. "Anything for you, Lloyd?"

Lloyd reddened. "No, my lord."

"Perhaps Crawford or Mrs. Barstowe might like some kippers."

"Do not be ridiculous, Dane," Susanna said. "The servants have already eaten." She turned her attention back to Marlowe. "And so you are Brook's paramour."

"What's a paramour?" Marlowe asked after swallowing. Her hand was beside her plate, and Dane slipped a fork into it. She looked at the implement curiously, then, holding it like a weapon, stabbed another piece of ham. "Is it like a bawd?"

"What is a bawd?"

Dane shook his head. "We are not having this conversation Marlowe, I'd appreciate it if you did not teach my sister anything. Susanna, do cease asking questions."

Susanna frowned at him. "I think I am entitled to ask who it is I am dining with."

"Fine," he said with a heavy sigh. "Brook thinks she's the missing daughter of Lord and Lady Lyndon."

"Really?" Susanna's eyes widened, and she seemed to study Marlowe even more closely. "Hmm. She does have Lady Lyndon's eyes and the Lyndon nose."

Dane looked at Marlowe's nose then closed his eyes. What was he doing? He didn't care if she was Lady Elizabeth or not. He simply wanted her gone.

"Has Brook gone to fetch the Lyndons?"

"I don't know where he is." He tossed the note toward her, and Susanna read it quickly. She looked up at Marlowe. "It appears you are to be our guest for a little while longer."

"Guest!" Marlowe said, almost choking on her third cup of chocolate. "I'm a prisoner. Your brothers abducted me last night and have been holding me here against my will!"

Susanna's eyes widened to the size of saucers. Dane had never seen them so large. She turned to stare at Dane. "Is this true?"

Dane tried to reply, and then sputtered, "When you put it that way, it sounds horrid."

"It *was* horrid!" Marlowe said.

He rounded on her. "I gave you the bed!"

Susanna inhaled sharply. "She slept in your bed?"

Dane held his hands up. "Where else was I to put her? Besides, it was perfectly"—well, somewhat—"innocent. I slept on the floor."

"In front of the door, so I could not escape."

"Dane!"

He crossed his arms over his chest. "I was only doing as Brook asked. He said to keep her here until he returned."

"But you cannot keep a person here against her will."

"Exactly!" Marlowe said, pointing her fork at him. Dane scowled, reached down, and swiped the plate away from her.

"No more for you. Besides, she's not really a person—"

Marlowe jumped to her feet. "Why, you bloody cockchafer! How dare—"

Dane pulled her toward him and covered her mouth. "Ow!" He was bitten for his pains, but at least he stopped the curses. Susanna blinked owlishly at them from across the table.

"Oh my," she said, her face turning red.

"I'm trying to help"—he moved his foot to avoid having his toe smashed and struggled to keep her in his grip—"the girl, but she doesn't think she's really Lady Elizabeth."

"But Brook does?" Susanna asked over the girl's howling.

"Yes. God knows why. I'm putting my money on the spawn of Satan. Ow!" He thrust her away before she could claw him again. He looked down at the scratches on his hand. "I think you drew blood."

"Good."

"That's it!" He grabbed for her, but she jumped out of his reach, and his fist closed on air. "I have endured enough," he said, stalking after her. But she was quick, darting around chairs and even under the table to escape him.

"Dane," Susanna cried. "Dane!" She caught his coat and shook him. "Step away before you do something you will regret."

"The only thing I regret is not having my hands about her throat right now."

"Dane." Susanna pushed him back, and he allowed himself to be thrust against the windows. How he wished he could escape through one of them, but he couldn't leave Marlowe with his sister. He needed Brook to take the little hellion away. Then everything could return to the way it had been.

Dull and tedious—no! Civil. Dignified. Comfortable.

"Will you give me leave to speak to her for a few minutes? Perhaps if we two chat alone—"

"Absolutely not. I will not leave you alone with her. She cannot be trusted."

Susanna sighed. "Very well, but you must promise not to interrupt."

He grunted. That was the best he could do. Susanna gave him a warning look and crossed to Marlowe, who was holding one of the chairs by the back and looking like she might use it as a weapon at the very first opportunity.

"Now, Marlowe," Susanna said, going around the table and approaching her. Susanna was dressed in a blue gown the color of sapphires. Her hair had been pinned up in a thick mass on the back of her head. She was taller than Marlowe, and though she was probably slightly younger, she looked quite a bit older when she stood beside the chit. She looked vastly more feminine and elegant. Susanna was a true lady, possessing beauty and poise and grace. Marlowe was…well, best not to think of what she was. Her boys' clothing should have hidden those lush curves, but they seemed only to accentuate them. Dane turned and looked out the window at the carriages driving by and the flowers blooming in the spring sunshine. A brisk walk would be perfect right now, and he could be at his club in a quarter of an hour. That would be even more perfect.

"Do sit, dear," his sister said. "I promise I will not hurt you."

Dane chuckled. As though anyone would worry his sister might be a danger.

"I'm not your dear," Marlowe said. Dane turned with a warning look and noted she'd taken a seat in the chair she'd been clutching.

"I'm sorry. You said your name was Miss Marlowe."

"I said Marlowe. No *miss*."

Susanna shook her head. "Oh, but I cannot call you Marlowe. That's not proper, as we've only just met."

Marlowe raised a brow. "You think I care about what's proper?"

"I think you should, if you're to meet Lord and Lady Lyndon soon. They are very nice people, but they are also proper people."

"I don't want to meet them rich nobs. I want to go home."

Susanna cocked her head and said simply, "Where is home?"

"Seven Dials. My gang and me live in a flash ken there. Best gang in London, if you ask me."

"And do you have parents there?"

Dane wondered why he had not asked these questions. Did she have parents? What was a flash ken?

Marlowe laughed. "No, I don't have parents. I have Satin. He's the arch rogue. He keeps all the cubs in line, and if I don't get back, he's going to come after me."

"Will you be in trouble for being gone this long?"

Marlowe's expression changed. For the first time, Dane saw fear in her eyes. "I can look out for myself."

"I have no doubt of that, but my point is that if you are already in trouble, why not stay a little longer and meet Lord and Lady Lyndon? Even if this Satin realizes you are here, we won't allow him to see you or speak to you. The footmen can keep him out. Isn't that right, Lloyd?"

"Yes, my lady."

"You see?" Susanna said, gesturing to the head footman. "The servants will protect you. If Satin comes here, Crawford will say he has never heard of you and will not allow this Satin inside."

Dane looked at Marlowe for an argument, but for once she was silent. She looked as though she might be considering. Dane would have to move Susanna up in his estimation.

"Do you not want to meet Lord and Lady Lyndon?" Marlowe shrugged.

"Can you be certain they are not your parents? Can you be certain you are not Lady Elizabeth?"

Marlowe looked up, and her expression was softer than Dane had seen it. She almost looked...vulnerable. She looked terribly beautiful. Dane could not look away, and he held his breath, waiting for her answer.

"No," she whispered. "I'm not certain. I..." She shook her head, unwilling to share whatever it was she knew of who she might be.

"Then why not at least meet the Lyndons? Can you imagine how long they have waited for this day? Can you imagine how happy they will be to meet the little girl they lost all those years before? I do not know the Lyndons well, but I have heard that both the marchioness and the marquess were devastated when their daughter was abducted. They never stopped searching for her. The loss turned Lady Lyndon's hair white, and some thought she would die from grief. She did not seem to want to continue living."

Marlowe looked down, her fingers twined, saying nothing. She looked so small in the chair, so young. Dane wanted to go to her and hold her, which was ridiculous.

"Can you deny them this chance to meet their daughter, their only child?"

Marlowe looked up, her eyes bright and suspiciously

red. Had she been crying? "But don't you see, that's the reason I shouldn't meet them. Look at me." She gestured to her clothing, but Dane had the sense she was gesturing to her entire being. "They won't want the likes of me as their daughter."

"Of course they will. Do you think they care how you speak or dress? You are their child."

But Dane understood what Marlowe was saying. He did not know the Lyndons either, but unless they were truly amazing people, Marlowe would not be at all who they wanted to claim as a daughter. He wanted to tell Susanna not to give Marlowe false hope, but he wanted Susanna to be right more than anything else. Damn him if he didn't like a happy ending as much as the next person.

Not to mention, either way, she wasn't leaving until Brook returned. If warm feelings about a reunion with her long-lost parents kept her at Derring House, then so be it. He would play along.

"But look at me," Marlowe said. "I don't talk like you or dress like you or do that bending at the knee thing."

"Is that all?" Susanna asked. "I can fix that. Your speech is not so bad. One reason *I* am convinced you are Lady Elizabeth is because at times I hear the refined accent in your speech. We need only draw it out further. You can borrow any of my dresses. I have far too many, and I can teach you to curtsy. I can teach you all the rules. Oh, Miss Marlowe!" Susanna clasped the girl's hands in hers. "This will be fun."

Without waiting for an answer, Susanna rose and rushed to the door. She flung it open and said,

"Where is Maggie? Where is my lady's maid? Fetch her, will you, Nathaniel?"

"Yes, my lady."

Still in the dining room, Marlowe looked at Dane. He gave her a slow smile. "Now you've done it."

Oh, this ought to be thoroughly diverting.

Six

HE WAS RIGHT. MARLOWE HAD DONE IT. SHE STOOD IN Lady Susanna's frilly pink-and-white bedchamber as Dane's sister directed her servants to pull dress after dress *after dress* from her dressing room. Marlowe looked about curiously. The room was smaller than Dane's and much, much more feminine. Marlowe had never seen anything so feminine. The curtains were edged with lace, the walls were the palest pink, and the girl's dressing table was so dainty Marlowe was afraid if she leaned on it, it would topple over.

The bed had a white counterpane and fluffy pillows scattered about, now all but hidden under the growing pile of gowns. Who ever heard of white bedclothes? They would be soiled in a matter of moments in Seven Dials. On the little table beside the bed, three books had been stacked. Three. Marlowe had never seen so many books in one person's possession. She knew books were valuable to those who could read them. Sometimes the cubs came home with a few books filched during one of the better-rackets. Satin always sold them for a tidy sum.

Curious, Marlowe fingered one of the books, opening the cover and looking at the letters on the page. She could not make out all the words, but she recognized *the* and *of*. One of the servants made a tsking sound, and Marlowe closed the book, glancing at the mountain of dresses now teetering on the bed. She waved her hands. "Stop! I only need one dress."

Lady Susanna poked her head from the dressing room. "Nonsense. You need at least three a day. A morning dress, a dinner dress, a—"

"Three?" She began to back toward the door. "I'd spend half my day changing clothes."

Susanna nodded. "It is often a nuisance."

A nuisance? Marlowe had spent her entire life owning no more than one dress at a time, and that one was replaced either when she outgrew it or it fell apart and could no longer be remade. She could not imagine owning three gowns at once, much less wearing all three in one day. She did not belong here, in this world where everyone used pretty words and lived like kings. Even if she were this Lady Elizabeth, what would her parents think of her? They would be horrified that she knew nothing of their rules. Surely they would not want a daughter like her. Better for them if she was dead.

And why had she allowed this girl to persuade her to even try to be Lady Elizabeth? It had been a pleasant dream, when she needed to think of something other than the cold, miserable conditions in the flash ken. Didn't every girl secretly dream she was a princess who only need reclaim her rightful throne? Marlowe had so few dreams in her life. Did she really want to kill this one so completely and publicly?

Everyone would laugh at her. *Look at that little beggar girl, thinking she is better than she is.* Dane didn't even think of her as a person. Would her parents be any different?

Marlowe backed up farther. "I changed my mind. This is not a good idea."

"Of course it is."

Before Marlowe could reach for the latch, Lady Susanna scampered over to her and grabbed her hand. She was fast for a gentry mort. "We already discussed it."

"And I changed my mind."

Lady Susanna squeezed her hand, and Marlowe stared down at it with surprise. It was such a simple, friendly gesture. In her world, those were few and hard to come by. This girl offered them so freely and easily. "Why have you changed your mind? What are you afraid of?"

Marlowe's back straightened, and her chin shot up. "I'm not afraid of anything."

"Good. Then let's begin." She drew Marlowe back into the room, and she went without much protest. Where else would she go? Back to the flash ken? Satin would beat her senseless for allowing herself to be abducted. She could stave off the punishment by giving him something of value in return: information about how to crack this house. If she led the better-racket and returned with her arms full of cargo, all might be forgiven.

But one look at Lady Susanna, and Marlowe did not want to give Satin any of the girl's lovely things. Marlowe didn't care about Lord Dane. He could go to the bloody devil. His brother and his shrew of a mother as well. She might not like them, but did they deserve to have their home violated? They had only been trying to help her in their selfish, misguided way.

No, she did not want to give these people to Satin, did not want to hurt them. And as she rather valued her own life, she did not know how she could go back to the flash ken otherwise.

And so she was stuck for the present.

Lady Susanna held out several frilly underthings and said, "Perhaps a bath first?"

"No!" Marlowe screeched. "Not another."

"She looks clean enough, my lady," one of the maids said.

Marlowe nodded vigorously. "I had a bath last night. I'm not due for another for months now." Years, if she could help it.

Lady Susanna laughed as though Marlowe had made a jest. "We shall see about that. Very well, then, strip off those clothes, and let's dress you in one of these."

Marlowe looked at the two maids and the girl standing before her. "What? Strip off my clothes here? With all of you watching me?"

"Oh! You are modest. Very well." She pushed the underthings into Marlowe's hand and pointed toward a rectangular stand painted with flowers. "You may undress behind that screen. You won't be able to lace the stays yourself, so Maggie will help you."

Marlowe looked at the one Lady Susanna gestured to. She was a woman of perhaps thirty, with dark hair and plump cheeks. "There ain't nothing you have I haven't seen before, miss," Maggie said. "But

I imagine I can lace you with my eyes closed, if that's what you want."

Marlowe wanted to escape this prison where everyone wanted to throw one in water and stuff them in uncomfortable clothing. That was what she wanted. With a sigh, she went behind the screen and stripped out of her trousers and shirt.

"Put on the chemise first," Lady Susanna said.

"The what?" Marlowe examined the garments.

"The shift," someone, probably Maggie, said.

Marlowe pulled it over her head and then donned the petticoats. She'd never had such a full, lovely petticoat before. There were stockings and garters, but she had no idea how to dress in those. She'd leave them off. No one would see her legs anyway. Next came the stays, and she marveled at the fancy embroidery on the silk material. She had never seen anything so fancy. They were also longer than the stays she was used to. She'd always worn short stays, and these would reach all the way to her hips.

"Ready?" Maggie asked.

Marlowe sighed. "Yes."

A moment later, the slavey appeared behind the screen. She didn't spare Marlowe a glance, simply turned her and began to fuss with her clothing. Apparently, Marlowe hadn't put the chemise or the petticoats on right, because Maggie yanked them all about, untying and retying them. She even removed the petticoat, informing Marlowe the stays should have been put on first. Marlowe felt as though she were a rope in a tug-of-war. Maggie had clearly been telling the truth when she said she was not interested in what Marlowe had underneath the clothing. She turned Marlowe toward the screen and began to lace the stays. At the first sharp tug, Marlowe inhaled with surprise, and Maggie said, "Good. That helps."

The center busk immediately pressed into her flesh and made her stand taller. "I won't be able to bend," Marlowe complained.

"A lady doesn't need to bend."

Marlowe definitely did not want to be a lady, if that was the requirement. Maggie finished with the stays, turned Marlowe about, and took hold of her chest, which was now lifted and separated quite shockingly. "Let go of my bubbies!" Marlowe protested. Maggie ignored her, pushing and yanking until they were half out of the bloody stays. What was the point of the stays if she was only going to fall out of them?

Finally Marlowe slapped at the maid's hands and moved away. She wanted out from behind that screen. "Not so quick," Maggie said, tugging her back and helping her step into the petticoat. "And now stockings."

Marlowe shook her head. "I couldn't put them on if I wanted. I can't possibly bend."

She heard giggling from the other side of the screen, and Lady Susanna said, "In a quarter of an hour, you won't even notice the busk."

"I'll do it," Maggie said, reaching for Marlowe's ankle. Marlowe kicked at her.

"No! What is the point? No one will know I am not wearing them."

"I will know," Maggie said. "Now, there are two ways to go about this—I do it, or you do it. But one way or another, these stockings go on your feet. Which will it be?"

"Oh, Marlowe," Susanna said, "I recommend you allow Maggie to put them on."

Marlowe rolled her eyes. "Fine." She surrendered her foot, and Maggie yanked the stockings on, pulling them up her bare leg and tying the garters to hold them in place. Finally, the maid stood and pronounced her satisfactory. "I don't have my dress on yet," Marlowe said.

"Oh, do come and dress out here so we can see," Susanna said. "Certainly you are decent enough now."

"Fine." Marlowe stepped out from behind the screen and moved toward the dressing table. Susanna, quick as ever, grabbed her hand and yanked her away.

"Not yet. I want you to be surprised. Oh! You look lovely already."

Marlowe looked down at her half-exposed breasts. "I look like I might catch my death."

Susanna shook her head. "There are many women who would kill for a bosom like yours. Myself included."

Marlowe looked at Susanna's bubbies, which seemed perfectly fine to her, and shrugged. "To me, they're an annoyance. I usually bind them. If I stick them out like this, it gives the cubs ideas."

"And the cubs are your friends?"

"You might say that. Business associates, really."

"Thieves," Maggie hissed under her breath.

"Maggie!" Lady Susanna said, her tone chastising. She looked at Marlowe. "Well, I can certainly understand you hiding your charms from men such as that, but I assure you gentlemen are much different."

Marlowe snorted, and Lady Susanna blinked at her. Marlowe stared at the girl. Was she really so naive? "Gentlemen are the worst of the lot. I see 'em coming into Seven Dials all the time, slumming it and looking for a bit of muslin."

Lady Susanna's eyes were wide. "Really?"

Maggie cleared her throat. "That's not an appropriate topic for discussion."

"Doesn't make it any less true. What would you say to a small wager?"

Lady Susanna shifted, looking uneasy. "My mother does not like me to gamble."

"Then don't tell her. You can trust Maggie and—" She gestured to the other maid.

"Jane. Very well. What's the wager?"

"The first thing your brother looks at when he sees me is my bubbies."

Lady Susanna's mouth dropped open, and her cheeks went bright red. "Dane? He wouldn't."

"He's a man."

"But he"—she seemed to stumble for the right words—"he is an earl, you understand? An eligible earl, and ladies throw themselves at him all the time. He doesn't even blink an eye. I don't think he notices."

Marlowe could well believe ladies threw themselves at him, but she didn't believe for an instant he didn't notice. He had enough sense—oh, very well—enough honor not to appear to notice when in the company of his sister. "Then you accept the wager?" she asked.

Lady Susanna seemed to think for a moment. "I do. What are we wagering?"

Marlowe looked about the room for something she

might want. Her gaze settled on the pile of books. "That book on the top," she said, pointing to it.

"The sonnets of Shakespeare?"

Shakespeare, yes. She'd once seen a play of his. "Yes, that one."

"Can you read?"

Marlowe put her hands on her hips. "Does it matter? You don't think I'll win, at any rate. Do we have a wager?"

"What will you give my lady if she wins?" Maggie asked.

Marlowe looked at Lady Susanna, who seemed to think for a long moment. Then she whispered, "I want an adventure."

Her maid's brows shot up, but Marlowe smiled. "An adventure it is," she said. She and Lady Susanna would get along very well indeed.

Lady Susanna crossed to the bed and lifted a pink gown. "Let's start with this one."

"Let's not." Marlowe shook her head. Pink? She was not wearing pink.

Susanna frowned. "What is wrong with this one? You do not like it?"

"It's pink," Marlowe said. Susanna simply continued to stare at her. Marlowe spread her hands. "It's pink!"

"I think you'd look very well in pink. Try it on, and if we don't like it, we can try another."

"Another?" Marlowe gaped. How many would she have to try on? She had to take control of this, or she'd be wearing ribbons and bows next. "I'm not wearing the pink."

"What color would you like?"

"Black."

Susanna's eyebrows came together. "Are you in mourning?"

"I find black matches my mood."

Susanna laughed, and Marlowe stared at the girl. Was it possible she was not completely right in the head?

"Oh, Marlowe. You do amuse me."

Yes, the girl was definitely daft.

"How about this blue dress? And don't argue. Maggie, can you help her?"

Before Marlowe had even opened her mouth to protest—the dress was pale blue and had ribbons— Maggie had dropped it over her head, and Marlowe couldn't see a thing except muslin and lace. She was engulfed in the sweet smell of flowers, obviously the scent Susanna wore, before her head was free again. Then Maggie turned her and buttoned her up the back, pulling and yanking to make sure everything was in place.

Marlowe looked down. The gown was not so bad. The neckline was far more modest than any other dress she'd ever had. Still, she felt like one of those ladies on a ship, with her chest pushed out for all to see.

"Now we must do something about your hair," Susanna said, and before Marlowe knew it, she was pushed into a chair, and her hair was yanked and tugged and brushed within an inch of its life.

"Ow!" she complained. Maggie the Cruel, as Marlowe had begin to think of her, did not blink an eye. She and Jane pulled Marlowe's hair so tightly, Marlowe thought her face must have been contorted into a wide smile. Finally, the torture ended, and

Marlowe was released. She rose, held a hand out to keep her tormentors at bay, and hissed, "Stay back! If you touch me again, you'll be sorry. No one is worth this torture. I don't care if it's the bloody king."

"Now watch your language, miss," Maggie ordered.

Lady Susanna, eyes wide again, merely took her arm and led her to a long, oval mirror in the corner. Marlowe was about to shake the girl's hand off when she caught a glimpse of the woman in the mirror. The woman's mouth dropped open. "What did you do?" the woman asked. Marlowe touched her face, and the woman in the mirror followed suit. It was really her in the glass. It was really Marlowe.

But she was completely out of twig and didn't look anything like Marlowe now. She looked like she could be a princess. She looked like a bloody gentry mort. If Gideon could see her now, he wouldn't believe his eyes. He'd think she was a bubble, and probably try to steal her reticule. If she'd had a reticule.

"You don't like it?" Lady Susanna asked.

Did she like it? She didn't even recognize herself. Perhaps if she dressed like this all the time, Satin wouldn't recognize her either. Of course, as disguises went, this one was rather painful, what with all the skirts and the piece of wood between her bubbies and the pins stuck in her hair. "It will do," she said cautiously. But it was strange to look so…pretty and feminine. She was used to making every effort to look like an invisible boy. She would not be ignored dressed like this.

"You will certainly keep me modest," Susanna said. "Come, let's show Dane."

Marlowe had been turning away from the mirror, but now she halted. "Your brother?"

Susanna's brow arched. "I believe we had a wager."

Marlowe looked down at her chest. It was covered, but still quite pronounced. She had no doubt she would win the wager, but she was not so certain she wanted to be seen looking like this. After all, she had ribbons all over. There was even a blue ribbon in her hair. "We could show him later. Surely, he has other business to attend to."

"Afraid you won't win?"

"No!" Marlowe shot back. "Afraid he'll laugh at all of these silly fripperies I'm covered with," she muttered. Marlowe tugged at the ribbon on the dress, and Susanna smiled.

"He will be impressed. Come on." She grabbed Marlowe's arm and pulled her.

❧

Dane was in his library, attempting to read correspondence. Last week his land steward had written to him about a drainage issue at one of his properties in Shropshire, and Dane had not yet responded. He began to do so now, quill in hand, but he couldn't seem to concentrate on matters of drainage. Not when that little vixen was closeted with his sister. What was taking them so long? Had the little urchin slit Susanna's throat and escaped out the window?

Forgetting his letter, he rose and paced his library. It was too early for brandy, although if he'd been at his club—as he wanted to be—he would have already had at least two. But his mother would remark on it if he smelled like spirits before four. He didn't generally care much about her rules. After all, he was the earl, but he had taxed her nerves with Marlowe's appearance already, and he did not want to stretch them any thinner. He did not relish a lecture.

Dane lifted a paper concerning one of the bills in Parliament. He really should familiarize himself with it prior to the vote, but he'd read only a line before he thought he'd heard a sound. He went to the door, opened it, and peered out. Crawford blinked back at him from the entrance hall.

"Is my brother home yet?"

"No, my lord."

"Any word?"

"No, my lord."

Dane shut the door again and continued pacing. Perhaps just a sip of brandy… A knock sounded on the door, and he called, "Come in! Did a note from Brook come after all, Crawford?"

"It's not Crawford," Susanna said.

Dane turned. No, it was definitely not Crawford. His gaze swept over the dark-haired beauty who stood just behind Susanna. She was short and shapely with a wide mouth quirked in something of a smirk. His gaze returned to her eyes. There was something about her eyes that was familiar.

"I believe I won," Susanna said quietly. "He's looking at your eyes."

"Bloody hell," she cursed.

"Marlowe?" Dane said, his head snapping back. "How the devil did you do that?"

"She looks every inch the lady, doesn't she?"

Susanna said. Dane couldn't argue. She did look every inch the lady, except…

"She's not wearing any shoes."

Susanna inhaled sharply. "I cannot believe I forgot! I will return in a moment." And she was gone.

Marlowe shrugged. "She can't even see my feet." She pushed into the room. "What is this place called?"

"A library," Dane said, watching her turn in a circle and take in the dark paneling, the floor-to-ceiling bookshelves, and his massive oak desk. God, she was lovely. Perfectly, completely lovely. His mouth was dry just looking at her.

"It's yours?" she asked, flicking a gaze at him. With her hair away from her face, her eyes looked even larger and bluer. Now that they were alone together, he was even more aware of what an alluring woman she was. He couldn't help admire her neck, bared as it was by the upsweep of her hair. Dane noted it was quite a long, graceful column. Perfect for kissing. A surge of desire swept through him, and he fought to hold it at bay.

"It is for everyone's use, but I generally occupy it during the day. I work here."

She snorted. "You work?" She tossed him another glance. "That's a sham."

"It's not a sham. I have estates to manage, both mine and those of my wards, parliamentary affairs to see to."

She turned to him. "Parliament? Where they make the laws?"

"Yes." The gown Susanna had given her did not hug her curves like the trousers and shirt she'd been wearing, but it did distracting things to her bosom. A man might wonder what she'd look like in an evening gown, when a bit of décolletage was allowed.

"That explains it," she said, and then she scowled at him. "*Now* you look at my bubbies. Why couldn't you have done that when your sister was here?"

By sheer force of will, Dane bit back his reply. He'd been caught looking, like a naughty boy, and he jerked his gaze back to her face. "I'm sure I don't know what you mean." And when had he become such a complete prig? He deserved the eye roll she gave him. "That explains what?" he said, grasping at their earlier conversation, at anything to turn the topic from her "bubbies." He cleared his throat. "You do not approve of Parliament?"

"What's it ever done for me?"

"Quite a lot, actually—"

"Pish," she said, waving her hand. "You don't care about the likes of me. You care about them Frenchies or your fancy country houses. What about the orphans? What about the bawds selling their bodies to feed their brats? No one cares about them."

"That's not true. There are plenty of men acting on behalf of the lower classes and less fortunate." Not that he was one of them. "Look at William Wilberforce and the Slave Trade Act."

"Never heard of him."

Dane was not surprised. "You speak of orphans or fallen women. There are places of refuge—"

"Ha! Workhouses? You think anyone can survive in a place like that? Better to stay on the street, where at least you're free."

"Then the lower classes deserve their fate. The government cannot help those who don't want it." There was the prig again.

"True enough. I don't want the kind of help you're offering." She turned away from him, but Dane caught her elbow and turned her back. He forced himself to restrict his touch to her elbow.

"What kind of help *do* you want, Marlowe?"

She tugged on her arm, but he didn't release it. Susanna hadn't given Marlowe gloves either, and he could feel her silky skin under his fingertips. Amazing that a woman who had lived such a hard life managed to possess such silky skin.

"Let us assume, for the moment, you are not Lady Elizabeth. In which case we—or Brook, at least—owe you something for the inconvenience of abducting you and holding you here."

"About time you realized that." She yanked her elbow again, but Dane only yanked back, pulling her closer. That was a mistake. His gaze wanted to drop to her generous breasts again.

"What is it you want? Blunt? How much? Five pounds? Ten? That's a fortune for someone like you."

She stared at him. He was close enough to see the exact color of her eyes now, so impossibly blue. "Books," she said simply.

Dane dropped her elbow. He'd been so certain she would want the blunt. "Books? Why? You can't read."

She scowled and walked away from him. "You wouldn't understand."

But he did. He might be a bit slow today—dazzled as he was by the transformation in her—but he was not a complete and utter fool. "You want to learn to read?"

She shrugged. "Maybe."

"Perhaps Susanna might teach you." He sauntered over to one of the library's bookcases. "Which book to begin with?" he wondered aloud.

"I know the one I want," she said, surprising him.

"What is it?"

"Your sister has it in her room. It's Shakespeare."

Dane felt his brows rise higher. "That seems a bit…challenging."

"That's what I want to read."

The sound of footsteps outside the door made both of them turn. Susanna pushed it open farther, and said, "Here we are!" She held a pair of leather half boots in her hand. "Try these."

Marlowe's eyes widened. "Those are too fine."

"Put them on." Dane watched as Susanna handed them to her, and Marlowe sat on the chair before his desk, crossed one leg over the other, and pulled on a boot. She was displaying quite a bit of ankle and calf, but he tried not to look. Tried not to imagine tracing the slope of her calf with his tongue. He cleared his throat. "Susanna, Marlowe tells me you have a volume of Shakespeare in your room."

She blushed. "Oh." She looked down. "I know Mama doesn't like me to read Shakespeare, but—"

"I don't care what you read. Marlowe was hoping to learn to read it."

"Really?" Susanna's face brightened, though Dane was not certain if the change was because he approved of the Shakespeare or because he'd given her a task to complete.

"You don't have to teach me," Marlowe said, switching legs and sliding the other boot on. "I didn't win the bet."

"What bet?" Dane asked.

"Nothing," Susanna said quickly. "I would have given you the book anyway. Oh, do stand up, so we can see." She gestured to Marlowe, who rose and pushed a toe out. Dane had little interest in women's boots, but he would admit Marlowe looked very well in them. A pretty gold necklace, a smart hat, some gloves, and she would look like any other lady of his acquaintance. Astounding. He would never have imagined the dirt-covered urchin he'd hauled into the kitchens last night could look so lovely this morning. Almost like one of them.

The door opened, and Crawford entered.

"Oh, Crawford, I am glad you are here," Susanna said. "Would you ask one of the chambermaids to bring down the volume of'—she looked about, probably to ensure her mother was not near—"Shakespeare beside my bed?"

"Yes, my lady. My lord, your brother has returned." He did not add *prodigal*, but Dane did it for him.

"Thank God." Dane started for the door. "Where is he?"

"He retired directly to his room, my lord. He asked not to be disturbed."

Dane glowered. "Oh, he did, did he? We'll see about that." And he stomped out of the library.

"Dane!" Susanna called. "May we use the library?"

"It is at your disposal, dear sister." Dane took the steps two at a time and did not pause to knock on Brook's door. He pushed it open and walked in on Brook's valet, who was collecting Brook's soiled clothes from the royal-blue-and-gold Aubusson rug. "Where is he, Hunt?"

"In his dressing room, my lord. Shall I fet—"

Dane strode into the room, where Brook stood in a dressing robe. His blondish-brown hair was slicked back from his forehead and dripped onto the robe's collar. "I think the blue coat today, Hunt," he said, turning toward Dane. "But you're not Hunt."

Dane glowered further, if that was possible. "No, I am not. Where the bloody, goddamn hell have you been?"

Brook raised a brow. "Rough night?" He moved toward the door and gestured for Dane to follow him. Dane trudged after him.

"Yes, as a matter of fact. You left that little hellion here under my care."

"Hellion?" For a moment his brother appeared confused. Dane was going to strangle him. "Ah, Lady Elizabeth." Brook glanced at his valet, who appeared quite absorbed in his task of folding clothes over and over. "Hunt, I think the blue coat today."

"There's very little of the *lady* about her."

Brook nodded. "She is a bit rough."

"*A bit rough?* The chit almost killed me last night. She had a dagger in her boot, and I woke with it pressed to my throat." Very well, that was a bit of an exaggeration, but there had been a dagger, and she might have pressed it to his throat, given a few more minutes.

Brook frowned. "Was she sleeping in your room?"

"Where was I supposed to put her? In Susanna's room?"

"What about one of the guest rooms?"

"Then we would have awakened to find her gone, and the house robbed of everything not nailed down."

"Ah." Brook had the gall to look thoughtful. Thoughtful! After the night Dane had spent! "She is resistant to the idea that she's Lady Elizabeth."

"What gave you that idea? When we had to abduct her? When we brought her kicking and screaming into the house?"

"Where is she now?" Brook asked as his valet returned, arms laden with clothing. Brook handed his man the dressing gown and pulled on breeches. It occurred to Dane that Brook was very possibly dressing to go out.

"Where the devil are you going?"

"Bow Street. I have an important piece of information regarding one of my investigations."

"You aren't going anywhere," Dane said. "I forbid it. You will deal with that woman first."

"I *have* dealt with her," Brook said, accepting his valet's help with his shirt. "I sent word to Lord and Lady Lyndon's town house."

"And? When will they be here to collect her?"

Brook raised his chin as Hunt tied his cravat. "I cannot say. Their knocker had been removed, and when the man I sent inquired of the servants, the butler informed him that the marquess and his wife were in Scotland, hunting."

"Scotland?" Dane felt the floor drop away beneath him. He swayed.

"Yes, annual trip, it seems. I will send word to their hunting lodge in Scotland, of course, but—"

"That will take days to reach them," Dane finished. Not to mention the days it would take for them to journey back, and that was if they left immediately.

"It's the height of the Season. Who the hell goes hunting in Scotland?"

Brook shrugged. "Apparently, this is the time one stalks roe deer bucks." He stuck an arm into his coat, followed by the other. Hunt struggled to pull the tight garment into place.

"If you think you're going somewhere without Marlowe—Lady Elizabeth—think again. I am not her guardian."

"Fine. I will take her with me. How much trouble can she be?" he said with an eye roll. "You act as though she is a dangerous criminal, rather than a defenseless girl who is the victim of such criminals."

Dane stared at Brook. "Whatever that girl is, she's no victim."

"Where is she now?" Brook asked, starting for the door of his bedchamber. "I'll fetch her and be on my way."

"In the library," Dane said, following. Why the hell was he always following his brother? It should have been the other way around. "Susanna is teaching her to read Shakespeare."

"Ah, dangerous criminal activity. Shakespeare. I shudder to think what might come next. Byron? Say it isn't so."

"Stubble it," Dane said, a warning in his voice. The two brothers were halfway down the stairs when they heard the commotion. Dane merely frowned at the sound of a man speaking rapidly to Crawford. Brook hurried forward. But as Dane approached the scene, he saw why his brother had been concerned. The man standing in their vestibule—well, leaning against a side table, if one was to be precise—clutched his ribs and dripped blood on the floor.

"Farquhar? What happened, man?" Brook asked

"Just a scratch," Mr. Farquhar said in a scratchy Scottish accent. "But you are needed immediately, Sir Brook."

"Of course. I'll come directly."

"Oh, no, you won't!" Dane yelled even as Brook assisted Farquhar through the door Crawford held open. "You'll bring that little thief with you!"

Brook threw a scowl over his shoulder. "No time for that now, Dane," he said in a tone that implied this should be patently obvious. "I'll come back for her in an hour." And with that, he crawled into a carriage behind the wounded man and was gone.

Dane stood staring at the street, and then he looked at Crawford. "He won't be back within the hour, will he?"

"No, my lord."

"We are stuck with her, aren't we, Crawford?"

"Yes, my lord."

And that was when they heard the scream.

Seven

"WHAT IS THE MEANING OF THIS?" THE COUNTESS OF Dane demanded from the entrance to the library. Marlowe did not jump, only because she was accustomed to such unexpected outbursts from Satin. Poor Susanna leapt almost a foot in her chair. They'd been seated behind Dane's desk, the book of poems laid out before them.

"Mother!" Susanna jumped to her feet. Marlowe did the same, figuring that imitating Susanna was probably wise at this point.

"What is that—that *person* still doing here?"

"She—" Susanna began.

"And why is she wearing one of your gowns, Susanna?"

"I should hardly think it proper for her to wear trousers, Mama," Susanna stuttered. Marlowe noted Susanna was shaking all over, her hands trembling, and a subtle quake vibrating through her thin body.

"And what is this?" the woman asked as she strode forward and snatched the book from the desk.

"Hey, that's mine!" Marlowe said, snatching it back. But the countess had seen.

"Shakespeare? You are reading Shakespeare? That is highly inappropriate for a young lady such as yourself. And you"—she gestured to Marlowe—"how dare you pull that book out of my hands? Who do you think you are?"

"Who do *you* think you are?" Marlowe shot back. "This is *my* book. She gave it to me."

"This is it. The end!" Lady Dane said with a whirl. Just then Dane and his butler barreled into the room.

"Mother, what happened?"

"Do not *Mother* me," Lady Dane replied, pointing a finger at him. Apparently, no one was free from her censure. The butler quickly slipped away, and Marlowe wished she could do the same. "I have had enough of this person and her antics. Where is your brother? He must take her away *immediately*."

Dane glanced at her, and Marlowe felt a shiver of unease crawl up her spine. Now where were they going to keep her?

"About Brook," Dane began.

"Oh, never mind!" Lady Dane said with a wave of her imperious hand. "If she will not leave, we will. Susanna, have Maggie pack your things. We will go to Northbridge Abbey."

"The country?" Susanna asked, her brows high. "But it is the height of the Season."

"I do not care if the king invited you to dine, we will not spend another minute in this house with that *person*." She pointed at Marlowe again, and Marlowe stuck her tongue out.

"Marlowe!" Dane warned her.

"Yes, Mother," Susanna said, sending Marlowe a regretful look. Marlowe sighed. So much for her chance to have a female friend.

The door opened again, and the butler cleared his throat. "The Duchess of Abingdon is here. Shall I show her to the drawing room?"

"Her Grace?"

Marlowe marveled at how quickly the countess's red cheeks lost all of their coloring and her skin turned deathly pale.

"It *is* our at-home day," Susanna said. Marlowe did not know what that meant, but apparently it hampered the plan to run away before Marlowe could infect them with her undesirability.

"How could I have forgotten? *You*"—she pointed to Marlowe—"stay here. If the duchess sees you—"

"Must I be kept waiting all day?" an imperious voice intoned from the vestibule. "Or do you possess a drawing room where I might at least sit down?" A woman dressed in dark purple appeared behind the butler. She was short and round, but the most regal woman Marlowe had ever seen. She tapped the butler with her walking stick and stepped into the library. Her gaze swept over the company. "This is quite the gathering."

"Duchess!" the countess said, hastily moving to block the woman's view of Marlowe. She bent her knees—what was that thing called again?—and made a show of fawning over the older woman. "We are so delighted by your call. Please, do allow me to show you to the drawing room. Crawford, ring for tea. Susanna!"

Susanna raced to her mother's side, eager to follow the countess's orders. But the duchess did not move.

Her gaze rose until she was looking at Dane in the face. He came forward, bowed, and kissed her gloved hand. "Duchess."

"Lord Dane, how lovely to see you. Come, you must sit with us for a quarter hour. It will not be too much of an imposition, I hope."

"Not at all, Duchess." Dane gave the woman a smile Marlowe did not think she had seen him use before. She did not know how to term it, except extremely charming.

"And who is this young lady?" the duchess asked, gesturing to Marlowe.

"No one!" the countess said at the same time Dane said, "A distant cousin."

The duchess's brows rose. The countess pressed her lips together and said stiffly, "She is a distant cousin come to visit for a very short while. You will be quite well in the library, will you not, Miss…"

"Marlowe," Susanna supplied.

"Rubbish." The duchess waved an arm. "She must join us for tea." The woman led the countess and Lady Susanna out of the room, while Dane stayed behind, presumably to collect Marlowe.

Marlowe shook her head when the duchess was through the door. "I don't want to go," she whispered.

"None of us do," Dane said, "but when the duchess summons you, you obey."

"Why? Is this her house?"

His look darkened. "It is my house, and she is a guest. As are you. Please join us."

Marlowe thought about arguing, but she was curious as to why everyone felt the need to scramble over themselves to please this duchess, like the cubs tried to please Satin. This duchess might be a useful person to know.

And there had been the mention of tea. Surely that meant there would be food to eat. "Since you said *please*," Marlowe replied, coming around the desk. He held out his arm to her, but she breezed past him. She did not want to touch him if it was not necessary. But before she could escape, he caught her arm and pulled her back. She gasped in a breath when he hauled her against him. For a moment, she was dizzy at the feel of his body against hers. Her gaze met his, and the world seemed to spin.

"Do not embarrass me or my mother, Marlowe," he said, a warning in his voice.

She blinked. She could not think of a single thing to say, and her gaze dropped to his mouth without her permission. What would those lips feel like pressed against hers? What would his hands feel like on her body?

"Marlowe?"

She jerked her gaze up again. He leaned close, his lips brushing her cheek and then grazing against her ear. She shivered, and her legs wobbled. "You may look beautiful," he whispered, his breath tickling her ear, "but I haven't forgotten what you are and where you come from."

With a jerk, she stumbled back, putting as much distance between them as possible. "Don't worry, *Maxwell*. I know exactly who I am." She whirled and walked away.

Once in the drawing room, Marlowe stopped cold.

She'd had a moment to recover from Dane's closeness. She didn't know why she should be affected by him so. She must be weak from hunger. But all thoughts of food vanished—well, almost—when she took in the room. It seemed every room in the house was more beautiful than the last. This one was rectangular and quite spacious. The large windows allowed in so much light, Marlowe felt almost as though she were outside. There were more chairs and couches than she could count, and just now a footman wheeled in a cart with several very promising-looking trays.

Dane entered behind her. "Sit down," Dane whispered in her ear, "and keep quiet."

Marlowe took a step forward then halted again. Where should she sit? There were far too many choices for someone used to sitting on the cold, hard ground. She was actually rather grateful when Dane steered her to a couch and then took a seat beside her. Of course, she immediately realized she was too far from the tea cart. She was already salivating at the cakes and sandwiches displayed on those trays.

The countess poured the tea and made some comment or other to the duchess, who then remarked, "Of course, with my annual ball commencing tomorrow night, I am on the verge of collapse. It is so exhausting to plan a ball, do you not think?"

Marlowe did not think the duchess looked ready to collapse at all. In fact, she had already bitten into a tea cake, and Marlowe was worried that the countess was taking so long pouring the tea, all of the sweets would be gone before she had a chance to try one. She leaned forward, ready to filch a cake, but Dane grabbed her elbow and hauled her back. "Sit still," he grumbled in her ear.

"Oh, but your balls are always the most wonderful affairs," the countess said, handing Susanna a teacup.

"Thank you." The duchess fixed her gaze on Dane, and Marlowe aborted her next attempt to snatch a cake when the duchess's gaze flitted briefly to her. "Lord Dane, I must admit I was surprised and dismayed to learn you had not accepted the invitation to my ball."

"I…" Dane began, then he looked at her. Marlowe frowned at him. Why the devil was he looking at her? "I am afraid I have a prior commitment. I promised Miss Marlowe I would take her to the theater."

"Oh?" The duchess looked at Marlowe. "Your cousin."

"*Distant* cousin," the countess said. "Very distant."

"I see." The duchess sipped her tea and reached for another cake. Marlowe tried to scoot forward to grasp one herself, but Dane wrapped an arm around her, hidden from the view of the duchess, and held her firmly in place. The countess handed her a teacup, but he accepted that as well and set it where she could not reach.

"Clearly, I must extend the invitation to Miss Marlowe. Then all of you may come together."

"No!" the countess cried.

"Duchess," Dane said, drowning his mother out. "That is very kind of you, but not necessary."

"Rubbish. The ladies will be so disappointed if you are not in attendance, my lord. Unless…" She studied him and then looked at Marlowe again. Marlowe felt Dane remove his hand. Now was her chance to steal a cake, but the duchess was staring at her. "Unless you have an announcement, my lord?"

"Absolutely not!" the countess cried again. "No!"

"Ah." The duchess smiled. "I see we must wait to wish you happy. In any case"—she rose, and everyone else followed suit. Dane dragged Marlowe to her feet—"I must return to oversee the preparations. I look forward to seeing you tomorrow night."

"Oh, but we will be at Northbridge then," Susanna said.

The countess whirled. "Do not be silly, Susanna. We will be at the duchess's ball, of course."

The duchess nodded and waved the countess away. "I shall see myself out."

Everyone looked after her, and Marlowe took the opportunity to shove two cakes in her mouth and stuff three more into her hands, which she then hid behind her back.

"So we are not going to Northbridge Abbey?" Susanna said when the door had closed behind the duchess.

"We are going to Northbridge," the countess said, "but not until after the duchess's ball. If I had not been so distraught earlier"—she glared at Marlowe, who had just popped another cake into her mouth—"I would have remembered the ball is tomorrow night."

Dane clasped his hands behind his back. "I will cry off. I've had my fill of balls."

"No, you will not," his mother said. "You will anger the duchess."

"Surely you do not intend to bring Marlowe?" he said, gesturing to her and frowning when he saw she was reaching for another cake.

"I do not see what choice we have," his mother said, putting a hand to her forehead. "I feel a megrim coming on."

"But, Dane," Susanna argued, "if she is the daughter of Lord and Lady Lyndon, they may wish to spend time with her before she is introduced publicly."

"The daughter of the Marquess of Lyndon!" the countess exclaimed. "Is that the story she is telling you?"

Marlowe put her hands on her hips, accidentally squashing one of the tea cakes. "And why is that so hard to believe?" she said, mouth still full of cream. "I could be Lady Elizabeth."

"If you are Lady Elizabeth," the countess said, "I will get on my knees and kiss your feet! You are a common beggar, that's what you are."

"I've never begged a day in my life," Marlowe said. "Never needed to."

"Because you steal what you want," the countess said.

Dane stepped forward. "Unfortunately, the question of Marlowe's true parentage will have to wait. Brook says the Lyndons are hunting in Scotland at present. It will be several days before they can be reached."

The countess sank onto a couch. "I need a tonic. Fetch Edwards. She knows what to make."

"Mama, let me take you to your room," Susanna said, assisting the countess. When they were gone, Marlowe sat down and pulled the tea tray to her chair, lifting a sandwich and trying it.

"You are going to weigh ten stone if you keep eating like that," Dane said.

Marlowe shrugged. "I can't let it go to waste."

He sat down opposite her, rested his elbows on his

knees, and dropped his head in his hands. Marlowe ate another sandwich, trying to ignore how dejected the earl looked. She didn't really care if he was dejected, did she? Of course, watching him pout made enjoying her meal a bit tricky. Finally, she sighed and said, "What is it?"

He looked up at her, his eyes weary. "Nothing. You go on eating cakes."

"I can hardly do so in peace with you looking like someone just choused you out of your last shilling."

"It's time to make a decision, Marlowe," he said, and she didn't much care for the look in his eyes. They were full of determination.

"What kind of decision?" She suddenly felt quite full, and set the tea cake she'd been holding back on the tray.

"You must decide whether you will stay or go. Brook is occupied with another investigation, and the Lyndons may not be back in Town for weeks. I can't keep you here against your will any longer."

"Then let me go," she said immediately, but for the first time she was not certain she meant it.

"Is that what you want?"

"Yes." Was it?

"Then you are free to go." He sat back and spread his arms over the back of the couch. She narrowed her eyes at him.

"Just like that? I can go?"

"You may go. I won't stop you."

"Ha!" She jumped up, snatched several tea cakes, and started for the drawing-room doors. When she reached them, she pushed them open, then peered back at him. He was still sitting on the couch. He wasn't even looking at her. She really could simply walk through the door. She scampered down the steps, into the vestibule, and saw the butler. "He"— she notched her head up to indicate the drawing room—"says I can go."

"Very well. Good day to you." The butler opened the door, and Marlowe looked over her shoulder.

Dane wasn't coming for her. He was really setting her free. She stepped outside, into the sunshine and the brisk spring air, and stood on the stoop, staring down at the boot scraper. She knew which way the flash ken lay. She'd never had any trouble finding her bearings in the city. If she walked quickly, she could reach it in less than an hour. Wouldn't Gideon be surprised when he saw her dressed so finely? Satin's eyes would nigh pop out of his head.

Of course, she would have to give some sort of explanation, and she'd have to think of a way to talk Satin out of robbing Dane's house. He would want her to go back, to make a pretense of visiting, so she could pocket a few valuable items. Satin would be full of plans, and Marlowe would have to go along with them. She might protest, but after a few beatings and days of starvation, she'd agree. She knew she would. And why not? She'd never cared about the swells before. They had far more than they deserved. They wouldn't miss a few glim-sticks or feeders.

But the fact was, Marlowe did not want to steal from Dane—or from anyone. For the first time, she wondered what it would be like to have her own house, her own candlesticks, her own forks. What if she had a home instead of a space on the floor of a dirty flash ken? What if she had a family who loved her instead of a bunch of cubs always looking to double-cross her for their own gain?

She had Gideon. That much was true. He was like family, but though Gideon protected her from the worst of Satin's tirades, he couldn't save her completely. Not without getting himself killed.

Marlowe sat down on the step and nibbled one of the tea cakes. It tasted almost stale to her now. Dane had said she needed to make a decision. If she returned, she was back under Satin's control. She was back to being a thief, back to starving, back to running from the Charleys and the Watch and dodging Satin's fists.

If she stayed…

What was wrong with her? How could she even *think* of staying?

Because if she stayed, she had a soft bed, clean clothes, a full belly, and a chance. What if she was Lady Elizabeth? What if Lord and Lady Lyndon were her parents? What if Satin had stolen her away from the life she should have had, the parents who loved her?

Loved her.

No one had ever loved her, but these Lyndons loved their daughter. They'd gone on searching for her all these years. They must have loved her very much.

Marlowe clenched her hands together and closed her eyes. She had spent years pushing the memories down, years fearing the vulnerability they brought with them, but now she opened herself to them. The sounds of the carriage wheels on the streets, the hawkers' distant cries, the church bells tolling the hour faded away. She remembered…warmth. The memory must have come from some time before Satin, because she had never felt warm when she'd lived with him.

She remembered…softness. Again, where had a memory of softness come from, if not a time before Satin? She shut her eyes more tightly and remembered rocking, a soft bosom, the scent of…some sort of flower. She didn't know the name. An image of a man in a coat and the sort of neckcloth Dane called a cravat came to her mind. He was going out, and he gathered her in his strong embrace and kissed her, the hair on his chin scratching her.

She turned, and there was a woman—

Marlowe opened her eyes. No, she could not remember her, could not see her now. Tears were already threatening to spill over. *Mama*. Marlowe clenched her hands until her blunt fingernails dug painfully into her flesh. There was no crying. No sniveling. She must be strong—except, what if she did not have to be strong anymore? What if, for once in her life, she did not have to take care of herself?

She turned and looked at the town house behind her. This was not her world, but perhaps it could be. The other cubs would have killed for a chance to live in a place like this. Should she abandon her one chance before she even had all the facts? If she was Lady Elizabeth, her whole life would change. If she wasn't, well, then, no harm done. She'd go back to Satin, and everything would be like it had been before.

Except, as she rose, she knew if she walked back into that house, nothing would ever be like it had been before.

❧

Dane closed his eyes and laid his head on the back of the settee. She was gone. She'd actually walked away. It had surprised him. He'd thought a thief like her would see the value in staying, would see the opportunity it provided. Either she was not a very good thief, or she actually had morals. Scruples. Terrifying thought, that. He'd have to start thinking of her—of all her ilk—differently.

The house was suddenly eerily quiet. It must have been quiet before she'd come, but he'd never noticed how silent it was before. He should take advantage of the quiet and return to his library to work. But he knew he'd find the volume of Shakespeare on his desk, and he'd think of her.

Perhaps she'd taken it with her, although since she couldn't eat it, she'd probably left it. And what did he care if she'd left a book on his desk? What did he care if he'd think of her when he looked at the chair in his room or climbed into bed? She was gone. He was done with her, and good riddance.

The drawing-room doors opened, and Crawford stepped inside. "Is she gone?" Dane asked, letting his head fall back again.

"Yes, my lord."

He sighed. "Well, it was a diverting few hours, wasn't it, Crawford? I suppose it's back to the ledgers and the balls and the bickering in Parliament." And it was back to the simpering misses, the daughters of barons and viscounts, hoping to improve their stations by marrying an earl like him. Back to conversations about hats and horses and the weather. "Do you know, Crawford," Dane said, "she and I never once discussed the weather."

"That is too bad, my lord."

"Is it? I detest discussions about the weather. Marlowe was…interesting."

"To say the very least, my lord."

"And she was"—he'd thought about saying *beautiful*, but that might shock Crawford—"really quite pretty in Lady Susanna's gown. I could almost imagine she really was Lady Elizabeth."

"Yes, my lord."

"But she's gone now," Dane said.

"For the most part, my lord."

Dane sat forward. "What do you mean?"

"She is sitting on the front step, my lord."

"Doing what?"

"Nothing that I can ascertain, my lord. Just sitting."

"Why?"

"I do not know, my lord. I came to inquire as to whether you want me to ask her why she is still sitting there? Or should we send a footman to shoo her away?"

"Like a stray dog?"

"Exactly, my lord."

Could he fault Crawford for seeing her as such when he was no different? "I'll speak to her."

"You, my lord?"

Dane rose now, feeling unaccountably invigorated. "Perhaps she forgot something."

"Forgot, my lord?" Crawford followed Dane out of the drawing room. "We burned her clothing, your lordship."

"There was a book of Shakespeare," he said, jogging down the stairs and arrowing toward his library, moving quickly now, worried he might miss his chance.

"My lord, I assure you that girl cannot read."

"A gift is a gift, Crawford," Dane said entering the library and sweeping the book from his desk and into his arms.

"As you say, your lordship." Crawford had resumed his position at the front door, and he opened it now. Marlowe turned, looking rather surprised to see him. It was just as Crawford had said. She was seated on the stoop, the midmorning sun glinting on her light brown hair and making some of the strands shine like gold. She pushed up, and Dane waved the book in his hand.

"You forgot something."

Her brow furrowed, and then she gave a short laugh. "That book is your sister's."

"I believe she made a gift of it to you." He took her hand and pressed the volume into it.

Marlowe looked down. "I can't read it, and Satin will just sell it." She held it out to him. "You keep it."

Dane didn't reach for the book. "Why are you still here, Marlowe?"

She shook her head, looked over her shoulder at the street. Dane imagined they were making quite a scene for the neighbors passing by. The Earl of Dane standing on his stoop, talking with a beautiful young woman. Oh, the rumors would fly. The gossips would have him married by the end of the day.

But he didn't care. He held out his arm. "Fancy a walk?"

Her brows rose. "A walk? To where?"

"Just a walk."

"Why?"

He laughed. "Because the sun is out and the day is mild and we might as well enjoy it."

"So you walk as a diversion?"

"I am no great walker, but many do, yes. Come along. You might enjoy it." He offered his arm, and she merely blinked at it. With a sigh, Dane took her hand and placed it on the crook of his elbow. Keeping his hand on hers, he led her from the stoop. Neither of them were wearing gloves. She didn't own a pair, and he hadn't anticipated walking, and had left his inside. He might have paused to retrieve them, but by then, Marlowe could have been halfway back to St. Giles. So it was that his flesh grazed hers rather intimately.

Her hand was small, which he supposed was an advantage for a pickpocket, and rough. He had not held many ladies' hands, but the few he'd held were usually plump and soft. Marlowe's hand was long, thin, and scarred with scratches, calluses, and even a burn mark. Her nails were blunt but clean—thanks to her bath—and despite the abuse her hands had obviously endured, they were rather elegant. It was her long fingers, which would have been perfect for playing the pianoforte or drawing—two lady's accomplishments she had probably never even considered, much less attempted.

Dane had the ungentlemanly urge to glide his hand from hers up to her dainty wrist and then to her pale forearm. He wondered if the skin was softer there. He remembered soft skin from last night when she'd been in his bed. Better not to think of that at the moment. It wouldn't be repeated, and if she was Lady Elizabeth, it had better never be mentioned.

He'd turned her unconsciously toward the park at Berkeley Square, and as they neared the green area, he realized this path had probably been a mistake. He would undoubtedly meet with acquaintances, and how was he to introduce Marlowe? But he had chosen his path now, and perhaps it was too early for many of the *ton* to be out and about except on social calls.

"What do you"—she began and then paused— "what does one do on a walk?"

He smiled. She was trying to mimic her betters, and he found that strangely endearing. She already had a good grasp on the accent, almost as though she'd been born speaking well and had merely laid the ability aside. Or perhaps she had cultivated the accent in order to further some scheme or other. How could he know?

"One enjoys the fresh air."

She looked up at him, her expression incredulous. "The smell of horse s—manure and coal fires?"

He grinned. "Very well, fresh air might be enjoyed only in the country. One day I will take you to walk or ride in Hyde Park. There are paths on which one forgets he is even in a city." Why was he saying this? Acting as though their acquaintance would continue?

"I've been to Hyde Park."

"Yes, but this time you would leave without having filled your pockets with others' valuables."

She shrugged, not appearing reprimanded in the least. "What else does one do on a walk?"

He thought for a moment, surprised he was still having to resist the urge to slide his hand up her arm. "Oh, one usually discusses the weather."

She looked at the sky. "Why? You can see it as well as I can."

"That's not the point. Here, I'll begin. What do you think of this sunny weather we're having?"

She cut her gaze to him. Her expression was one of extreme patience. She quite obviously thought he was daft. "It's…sunny."

"Yes, a welcome change, as it's been so dreary the last few days." Even he was impressed by that statement. He had never waxed so eloquent on the weather.

"What do you care if it's dreary? You don't have to be out in it." Her statement was so unexpected, Dane burst out laughing. It was probably quite true from her view. He had never considered that the lower classes might think of the weather quite differently than he and his ilk. To him, it was a banal topic. To them, extensive rain or cold might be more than just an inconvenience. What did people who could not afford coal do in winter?

They'd paused on the edge of the grass at Berkeley Square, where several governesses and nannies were out and about with their young charges. Dane released Marlowe's arm and turned to her. "I like you, Marlowe." And he did. Anyone who disdained talk of the weather could not be all bad.

Her eyes, blue like the clear sky today, narrowed at his comment. "What do you want?"

He grinned. "Always suspicious. Very well. I want to know why you were still sitting in front of my town house."

She didn't answer, merely crossed her arms over her bosom and stared at the park.

"You were free to go," he said. "I thought that was what you wanted."

She nodded. "It was. I mean, it is."

"Then why are you still here? Do you want Mrs. Worthing to make you a lunch to take along?"

She turned toward him, eyes wide. "Would she?"

He laughed. "If that's what you're waiting for."

"Humph." She blew out a breath. "You're certainly in a hurry to be rid of me."

"Not at all. In fact, I want you to stay." Had he really just said that? He had, and he'd even meant it. Life had been far more interesting with Marlowe in it. If he'd been thinking as an earl ought, he would have had Crawford shove her off the stoop. She didn't belong in Mayfair. She didn't belong in his home. Despite all appearances, she was still a thief, a criminal. She might turn out to be Lady Elizabeth, but she might not. That was not really his concern.

But he wasn't thinking as a proper earl. He was thinking as a man, a man who was suffering acute ennui from all of his proper engagements. A man who still enjoyed the company of a beautiful and... vivacious—that was a good way to put it—woman.

She was staring at him, her expression bewildered. "Why?"

"I have my reasons."

"Nefarious ones, I'm sure."

He raised his brows. "That's an impressive word. I cannot say it has been used to describe me very often, if ever." He turned to her. "Answer the question, Marlowe, why were you still on my stoop?"

She sighed, and her shoulders slumped, making her look so small and fragile. Dane clasped his hands together to keep from touching her, from pulling her to him for a comforting embrace.

"I'd be a fool to leave," she said finally, though he doubted that was what she'd been thinking. "Why go back to the flash ken when I can live it up with the swells?"

"Why, indeed? You said something about Satin coming for you."

A shadow crossed her face, but she blinked it away. "I can handle Satin. Besides, how would he ever recognize me, looking like this?"

"True."

A long silence descended. He didn't break it, merely watched the children playing a game of tag. Finally, she said quietly, "I just thought that maybe there was a chance. And if there was a chance I was—I am this Lady Elizabeth—I should stick around and see it through."

"So you're staying?"

"I…" She looked up at him and frowned. Now what was bothering her? She had the most expressive face. "If I can, that is."

Ah, she did not like asking him. He imagined she rarely asked anyone for anything. He might have made it difficult for her. Instead, he said, "Shall we continue to introduce you as a distant cousin?"

"I don't even know what that means."

"And you're willing to attend the Duchess of Abingdon's ball?"

"Is your head cracked? I can't go to a ball!"

"If you stay, you'll have to. My mother will not allow it to be known that she's been sheltering one of the…lower order in our house." He also could not allow that, even if he was starting to like her.

"Then I should stay back, where there's no chance I embarrass everyone with my *lower order* behavior."

"But what you do not understand, Marlowe, is that my mother's sole objective in life is to marry my sister to a wealthy, honorable family. That won't be accomplished by annoying the Duchess of Abingdon. If you stay, I fear you'll have to go to the ball. Susanna and I will keep you out of trouble, and you can complain of a megrim so we must depart early."

Marlowe was watching the children playing now too, and he wondered if she'd even heard him. The children had a ball, and one boy was kicking it while a little girl chased him. "Come on!" the boy yelled, and Marlowe flinched, almost as though she had been struck.

"What is it?" he asked, but she didn't acknowledge him. She stared at the boy and the ball. "Marlowe?" He reached out and touched her arm. It was ice cold. She drew her arm back and stared at him, her eyes not seeing him. "What the devil? Marlowe, what is it?"

"I'm fine. I–it's nothing."

But it was not nothing. She was shaking like a leaf. "I have to go."

He took her arm before she could bolt, and directed

her toward Gunther's Ice House, which was just across the way. "Let's sit down."

For a few moments, she allowed him to lead her, and then she withdrew her arm and looked about. "Where are you taking me?"

"Gunther's." He gestured to the small shop nearby.

"It doesn't look open."

"They will open it for me."

"Fine." She looked back over her shoulder, studying the children a last time before she allowed him to lead her away. Dane didn't know what concerned him more—the haunted look on her face or the fact that she didn't protest when he took her arm. Something told him life with Marlowe was about to become even more interesting.

Eight

SEVERAL MINUTES HAD PASSED BEFORE MARLOWE realized where she was. When she did, she looked around and blinked at the small, clean shop, the concerned clerk wringing his hands nearby, and the little table where she'd been seated.

"—I asked if you wanted an ice," Dane was saying. She blinked up at him. The look on his face indicated he had probably asked her this question once, if not twice already. Why would she want ice? "It's food," Dane said.

"Oh, in that case, yes, please."

He spoke to the clerk, and she looked around again, seeing the green grass of the park through the windows. Something about that boy and the ball had been so familiar—and oddly terrifying. She was still shaking, and she did not understand it.

Dane sat across from her, looking elegant and at ease. This was his world, and he moved in it with enviable confidence. He would have moved in her world with that same confidence. Like Satin, he was a born leader. It seemed strange that she should see him thus, since she had always associated leadership with brute strength and intimidation. Satin was obeyed because the rogues were too scared to disobey. Dane was not violent—not from what she'd witnessed—and he still commanded respect. Was it the blunt in his pocket? The power in the title he'd been born with? Or something else? How much of his confidence was given to him by God and how much from growing up as the heir to a title?

The clerk returned with two small bowls of colored ice. She looked at hers then watched as Dane lifted his spoon and brought a portion to his mouth. "Have you never had an ice before?"

She shook her head.

He motioned to her cup with his spoon. "Try it. It's most refreshing, especially on a warm day."

Eat ice? What else would these swells think of? She'd eaten plenty of ice—melted it over meager fires for drinking water, had it stuffed in her mouth during scuffles with another cub, woke up with a thin layer of it on her threadbare blanket. She was no lover of ice. But she had never eaten colored ice, and so she dipped her spoon in and tasted it. Her eyes widened. "It's sweet," she said.

Dane nodded. "Strawberry."

She'd stolen a handful of strawberries once and gobbled them down eagerly. They had not tasted like this.

"Slow down, or your head will ache," Dane said. "If you want another when you've finished, I'll buy you one, though I can't think where you would put it."

Marlowe continued shoveling ice into her mouth,

but Dane had a point. She was uncomfortably full. It was a strange and slightly unpleasant feeling. She never thought she would dislike being full.

"What was troubling you in the park?" he asked, setting his spoon aside and watching her eat. She wondered if he was simply going to allow his food to go to waste.

Marlowe shrugged. "Just someone walking over my grave, I guess."

"Is that all?" Dane frowned. "You were trembling and ice cold."

She finished her ice and stared at his bowl, which had been abandoned. Dane shook his head and pushed it toward her. "You are going to make yourself sick."

Marlowe spooned more ice into her mouth. She was definitely cold now, but the ice was so sweet, she could not seem to stop eating it. And there were worse things to be sick from than eating too much. She heard the children calling one another outside again, the boy yelling, "Come on!" and she glanced at Dane.

"There was something familiar about that boy."

"You can't know him."

"I've never seen him before. I can't explain it, but as I watched him play with that little girl, I felt as though I had seen it all before."

"Perhaps it reminded you of when you played as a child."

She stared at him. "I never played. We worked for our keep."

Dane sat back. "That sounds like a dreary childhood."

"It was better than some. Have you ever walked through St. Giles? Walked through Seven Dials?"

"Of course. I went there a time or two in my youth."

She let out a bitter laugh. "Ah, yes. A visit to the rookeries for the bored young gentleman. It's not quite so entertaining when you live there and you watch the children starve on the streets. You watch a woman sit in her dirty doorway, two filthy brats hanging on her, and another in her belly. Her eyes are empty because she can't feed the two she's got. How's she going to feed another? There's never enough food, and always too much to drink, and everywhere you look, there's dirt and cold and someone's brat sniveling."

He blinked at her. "I never thought of it like that."

"No, you wouldn't. Your world is clean and warm and filled with"—she gestured to the empty bowls—"ices. That's not my world."

"Don't you think it could be? Perhaps watching that boy and girl play affected you because you once played like that. Before you were taken."

She shivered. "If that's true—and I'm not saying it is—but if it is, then where do I belong?"

"I don't follow."

"Is your position something you were born into, or were you raised to be who you are? Even if I was born Lady Elizabeth, I was raised—if you can call it that—to be Marlowe."

He stared at her for a long moment. "That's an interesting question."

"Interesting how?"

"Because I didn't expect you to say it."

She scowled at him, brows coming together. "You may not believe it, but I have a mind. I'm a person just like you."

He waved a hand as though to brush the comment aside. "Very well, let's discuss philosophy. I believe it was Rousseau who said, 'We do not know what our nature permits us to be.'"

"Which means what?"

He smiled. "Since we're speaking of philosophy, I'll play tutor and make you answer that question yourself. What does it mean?"

She thought for a long moment. "That I can be anything."

He nodded. "Very good."

She went on. "It also means rich young nobs shouldn't go into the rookeries thinking they're better than those who live there, because the nobs somehow deserve their place, while we deserve ours."

"Touché."

"No one deserves to live like that," she said. "Not even a dog."

He rose and held out his hand. She looked at it. "I don't need help."

"Allow me this small courtesy." If he was offering a courtesy, maybe she'd said something that got through to him.

She put her hand in his and allowed him to help her rise. His hand was so large it completely covered hers. She had the oddest sensation that she was safe with him. Her instincts must have been off, because she wasn't safe at all. She couldn't trust him, any more than she could trust any of these swells. She could trust Gideon and the Covent Garden Cubs. That was all. She had to remember that.

He led her back into the sunlight, and they strolled

along the park again, toward his town house. It felt odd to watch people walk by her and not to mark them. Not that she didn't evaluate them. That man walking briskly was in such a hurry that she could bump into him, do a dive, and he'd probably keep right on walking. That woman walking two yapping dogs was another easy bubble. Marlowe could have riled the dogs and stalled her up, then done the trick. The woman might not have much blunt in her reticule, but she probably had a wipe in there. There was a market for silk handkerchiefs, and dolly shops who'd buy them, no questions asked.

For once Dane wasn't going on about the weather, and she could study the people she passed, and the buildings. She had the knack of never being lost. She always knew which direction pointed to Seven Dials, but she rarely took the time to look about her and simply enjoy the surroundings. They walked on, along a busy street, and she saw the turn to the block where Derring House was located just up ahead. That street was quieter, the homes larger and more stately. But as they neared the turn, her back prickled and her scalp crawled. She must have stiffened, because Dane said, "What's wrong?"

"Nothing." But that wasn't true. Something was wrong. Something was very wrong. And then she saw it. She saw *him*. The cub was watching her, marking her. He lounged against a door, looking as though he was waiting for his employer to come out of a shop, but she knew the look of him. He only gave the appearance of being idle. His eyes were as keen as a hawk's. And she recognized him too. He wasn't one of Satin's, but she'd seen him a time or two. He was one of the Fleet Street Cubs.

The Fleet Street Cubs loved nothing better than a public execution. Then half the city would come out to watch the convicts from Newgate or Fleet Prison hanged. While the crowds were watching the spectacle, they weren't watching their pockets. Easy pickings.

Satin looked down on the Fleet Street Cubs, saying they got rich off the misery of their own kind. After all, who was being hanged up there if not thieves? But Marlowe had never known Satin to turn down a coin, no matter where it came from.

For an instant, her gaze met the cub's. He looked away quickly, with seeming respect. After all, she was dressed as a lady. Marlowe held her breath, and then his gaze snapped back. He stared at her openly, and she could almost see his mind working, struggling to place her. And then she and Dane passed him, and he was behind her. But she knew she was in trouble. The cub might not know her yet, but his mind would keep working on the riddle of who she was. When he solved it, he'd go to Satin.

When they reached the town house, Dane paused. Marlowe's thoughts were still back on the cub they'd passed, and she looked over her shoulder to make sure he hadn't followed them. She didn't see him, but he wouldn't have been a very good rogue if she did.

"You realize, when we go inside, preparations for the ball will be in full force."

"The lady said it's tomorrow."

"Yes, but my mother will worry about what

Susanna is to wear, and Susanna—and my mother—will worry over what you are to wear and how your hair should be styled and whether to bring a wrap or not, a fan or not…" He circled his hand as if to indicate all of this would go on and on.

"It sounds like a nightmare."

Dane laughed. He seemed to laugh quite often. She'd never met a man who laughed so much—at least not one who wasn't daft in the head. "The ladies are supposed to like all the fuss."

"Why?"

"How the devil do I know? In any case, one question may be neglected amid all the primping, and that is perhaps the most important question. Do you dance?"

"Dance? Like a jig?"

"No. I'm not speaking of romping around after you've had a few sips of Blue Ruin. I'm speaking of waltzing, the quadrille, a country dance."

Marlowe had no idea what he was talking about, but she could count on one hand the number of times she'd danced. There simply was little cause for dancing or celebration in her life, and if she had a few coins, she wouldn't have spent them on gin. She would have bought something to fill her belly. She had danced with Gideon once. He'd twirled her about and showed her some complicated step he said he learned watching the nobs when looking at a place before the crack. She'd fallen all over her feet and tumbled onto her bottom, laughing all the way. Somehow she thought Dane and the duchess would be less than amused.

"I don't dance."

"And we won't attempt to teach you in a day.

We'll say you twisted your ankle, and I will stay by your side to ward off admirers."

"Admirers? Ha!" She rolled her eyes and waited for Dane to give one of his characteristic laughs. But he wasn't laughing.

"I am completely serious," he said. "Men will take notice of you."

"Because they'll see I don't belong."

"Because they will see that you're beautiful."

Marlowe stumbled back, her eyes bulging with shock. Why did he keep calling her beautiful? No one ever said anything more complimentary to her than "You'll do." Dane was a handsome man. She tried not to look too directly at him for fear of staring overly long. He was rich and titled. He probably knew hundreds of beautiful women, and he thought *her* beautiful? "I'm not beautiful," she said. "I'm…" She gestured to herself to indicate she was—whatever she was.

Dane raised a brow. "You are?"

"Quick, canny, nimble."

"I am certain you are all of those things, but you are also beautiful. Have you looked in a mirror?"

She had, and she hadn't even recognized herself. The Marlowe she knew was flat-chested and wore trousers and a perpetual layer of dirt. The Marlowe she knew scowled and swore and spit. She didn't flutter her lashes or sashay her hips or do any of the things gentlemen seemed to think made a woman a rum blowen. "This"—she gestured to her gown—"this isn't who I am."

"Don't you think it could be?" he asked. She

thought he might say more, but at that moment, the butler opened the door and peered out with an expectant look.

"Your mother is asking for you, my lord. Shall I tell her you have taken up residence on the front walk?"

Dane let out a sigh. "No, Crawford. We are returning now." He gestured to Marlowe, indicating she should lead. Marlowe took one last look behind her. She didn't spot the cub. Perhaps he hadn't followed her, after all. She could still walk away. She could turn and head for Seven Dials and the flash ken. And then she thought again of the little boy and his ball, and she looked back at the town house.

Marlowe didn't know where she belonged, but she would find out.

❦

Gideon wasn't sleeping. Around him the cubs snuffled and snored, sleeping the sleep of the dead. He should be asleep too. He'd been out diving until the wee hours of the morning—at least that's what he'd told Satin. In reality, he'd been searching for Marlowe. Gideon didn't understand what had happened to her. One minute she'd been there, and the next she was gone. Joe said he'd seen a jack stop, a man had carried her to the coach, shoved her inside, and driven away.

He'd run after the jack, in the direction Joe had indicated, but there had been too many coaches. He didn't know which one or the direction it had gone. He'd returned empty-handed to the house they'd marked. The noise had alerted the residents, and Gideon had called off the racket. Satin had been furious, not only to lose the cargo from the racket, but also one of his rogues. And not just any cub—his best filching mort.

Why the hell would someone in a jack take Marlowe? Had she dived in the wrong bubble's pocket? Had a Brother of the Gussit seen her and decided she'd make a good addition to his bawdy house? Gideon hoped not. Marlowe didn't have the first idea how to play pretty and coy. She'd never survive a brothel.

It didn't make sense, and the more Gideon searched for Marlowe, the less sense it made. He'd even considered that Satin might be behind the abduction. Gideon knew the upright man had plans for Marlowe. Was this one of them?

Gideon had been one of the first cubs in Satin's gang. He'd been about ten when he'd joined, and he'd joined willingly—unlike Marlowe, who Satin had brought in a year or so later. Gideon was old enough to remember his parents. He could remember the shabby room where he'd lived with them and his grandmother. His mother and his father worked, and his grandmother kept watch over him. There wasn't money for school, but she'd taught him how to read and write. She used to tell Gideon stories of when she'd been a girl, and how she once saw a parade where the king waved to her from his coach.

Gideon had been hungry sometimes, but he was well cared for. He didn't see his mother or father often. They worked too much, but he knew they loved him, though his father cuffed him a bit more than Gideon liked. And then there'd been a fever, and it had taken his mother and grandmother. Gideon's father had not dealt with the loss well, and he started drinking heavily. The cuffing grew more frequent, turning into beatings.

And then one night his father hadn't come home. One of the men his father drank with knocked on the door and told him his father had been killed in a fight in a public house. Gideon was an orphan at seven. He'd gone to an orphanage, but life there had been unbearable. The food was disgusting, and he'd been hungry all the time. He'd been tall for his age, and he'd learned to fight by defending himself from his father, so Gideon held his own against the bullies who ran the place.

But when he'd run away, for the sixth or seventh time, and he met Satin, he didn't hesitate to join the gang, even though his mother had always taught him filching was wrong. It had to be better than life in the orphanage. And in some ways it had been. Satin was a cruel man, but he was generally predictable. He didn't attack without cause or warning. Gideon could live with that.

He'd been thinking of how to accuse Satin of taking Marlowe without *sounding* like he was accusing Satin, when he remembered what Marlowe had told him about the bubble she'd seen on Piccadilly, the one who'd called her Elizabeth. The one who worked for Bow Street. Now Gideon knew Bow Street Runners. Most were corrupt, or at the very least, worked exclusively for the swells, who could pay for their services. He'd worked with a few Runners. He'd steal a few valuables and then negotiate with the Runners to set a high ransom. When the nob paid the ransom, he'd give a portion of it to the Runners. They were getting the better end of the deal, because they'd collect not only a portion of the ransom but also the fee from the nobs for "finding" the stolen items.

Gideon had also seen other gangs decimated when Runners convinced a few fool cubs to attempt a better-racket, then caught the cubs in the act, thereby collecting the reward. The cubs went to the stone pitcher and hanged.

Gideon didn't trust Runners, and for good reason. He'd taught Marlowe not to trust them either. She wouldn't have willingly gone with a thief-taker, and Joe had said she'd been kicking and screaming...

Someone tapped on the door to the flash ken, and Gideon's eyes snapped open. He didn't move or give any other indication he was awake, though. Satin and Beezle had been murmuring for the last half hour, planning something Gideon would have to carry out, no doubt. He'd tried to listen, but their voices were pitched too low. Now both men ceased speaking, and Beezle went to the door. So it wasn't anyone Satin was expecting. If it had been one of the cubs, he would have given the code word, then knocked and come in.

Beezle reached the door, then peered back at the sleeping cubs. Gideon closed his eyes again, pretending to sleep, though he doubted Beezle could see much in the dark of the flash ken. Slowly, he opened his eyes again and watched as Beezle opened the door, his knife at the ready. Whoever was outside said something Beezle thought Satin needed to hear, and the cub returned and motioned for Satin to step outside.

Gideon waited until the door closed behind Beezle

and Satin, then rose and made his way silently and deftly around the sleeping figures. He crouched beside it and put his ear to the wall. The walls of the flash ken were so thin, the building so poorly constructed, he could easily hear the conversation taking place outside.

"You saw her *where*?" Satin asked.

"Mayfair," the cub said. "I was out for a walk—"

"Sure you were," Beezle said with a laugh.

"Hey, if Dagget finds out I came to see you, he'll slit my throat. Do ye want to know or not?"

"Shut it, Beezle," Satin growled.

Gideon swallowed. Dagget was the arch rogue of a crew of rogues in Fleet Street. Gideon had seen the man a time or two. As far as he could tell, the cubs in Fleet Street didn't have it any better than the Covent Garden Cubs. Their boys had to have spines of steel to bilk right in the shadow of the gallows. It was like seeing yourself hanging there if you made one wrong move.

"Go on," Satin said.

"She were dressed all fancy-like, and her hair were all…" He must have made some gesture, because Satin grunted in response. The cub had to be speaking of Marlowe. But why would she be dressed like a rum mort and walking in Mayfair? And if she was, why wouldn't Satin know about it? She didn't have something on the side. Gideon would have been in on it.

"She looked like a right proper lady, and she were walking with a swell."

"Tell me about him," Satin said.

"Looked like any other swell. Fancy dress, nose in the air."

"Did you find out his name?"

"No."

"Useless," Satin said. "How am I supposed to find her?"

"I know where he lives."

Silence descended. Gideon held his breath.

"Where?"

Silence again. Finally, "That information will cost ye."

Gideon shook his head. The cub's information better prove useful, or Satin would go after him personally.

"Beezle, give the man a shilling."

"Two," the cub said. "This is good information."

"If it's not…" Satin said. He didn't need to finish. The threat was clear.

Gideon heard the clink of the shillings, and held his breath.

"Tell me," Satin said.

The cub rattled off the number and name of a street in Mayfair. Gideon wasn't as familiar with the area as he was with St. Giles, but Berkeley Street had to be near Berkeley Square. What the devil would Marlowe be doing in Berkeley Square?

"And you're certain I'll find her at this house?"

"I saw her go inside meself."

Gideon didn't wait to hear the rest. He crept back to his spot on the floor and lay down again, closing his eyes just as the door opened, admitting Beezle and Satin. They went back to murmuring, and now Gideon knew what they planned. He had to find a way to reach Marlowe first.

Nine

MARLOWE DREW BACK HER FIST, READY TO STRIKE. If Lady Dane made one more insulting remark, she would bash her so hard she landed on her arse and slid out the door. Something of her intent must have shown on her face, because Lady Susanna threw her a worried look. Marlowe lowered her fist and took a deep breath. She gave Susanna a tight smile and returned to listening half-heartedly as Lady Dane enumerated all of the myriad rules she must follow at the ball.

Marlowe had already heard it three times. Did the countess think she was an idiot? Satin told her something once, and she was expected to remember it. She did not need to be told three times how to address a duchess, or that she should ask for the *ladies' retiring room* instead of saying "Where can I take a—"

"Are you attending me, Miss Marlowe?"

Marlowe ground her teeth. "Yes."

The countess raised her brows.

"Yes, *my lady*."

"Good." The countess clasped her hands behind her

back and began another circuit of the room. *Marlowe's room.* It wasn't her room, in truth. It was the room Mrs. Barstowe had given her when she and Dane returned from their walk the day before. Marlowe had never had a room to herself. She had never had a space to call her own. A family of six could have lived in the room where she alone had slept last night. At least she'd tried to sleep.

All of her life she had dreamed of having a full belly and a warm bed. She'd had both last night, and yet sleep eluded her. She'd lain on the soft bed, the soft covers pulled to her chin, dressed in a soft night rail, and stared at the ceiling. She was used to the sounds of the flash ken, and this room—this house—was too quiet. The fire crackled, and she had propped herself on her elbows to catch a glimpse of it. She was not used to the sound of a fire crackling in a hearth. After what had seemed like days, she rose, pushed her feet into the slippers Lady Susanna had given her—what an extravagance—and strolled about the room.

She'd had a look at it earlier, tallying the worth of every little bauble and trinket. She could count pretty high, but she didn't think she could count as high as the blunt she'd make if she fenced all of these goods. She stopped at the door and tested the handle. The door opened easily, and Marlowe peered into the dark corridor. The house was chilly away from the fire, and she hastily closed the door again. But it was still unlocked. She could leave at any time. She could walk right out the door, down the stairs, and into the street. No one would stop her.

One of the slaveys kept guard at night, but Marlowe

did not think he would or could stop her. She could handle one man.

But she hadn't left. She'd stayed all night, and she'd even fallen asleep at some point on the soft bed.

Something inside her had to know who she really was. Marlowe or Lady Elizabeth? She wanted the truth. She wanted to know her parents. She wanted to have a choice about the life she would live. A choice—that was the true gift. She'd never had a choice about anything in her life. She did the jobs Satin gave her. She ate what was put in front of her. She slept where she was kicked. She wore whatever clothes she could find.

Now Marlowe glanced at the bed and the lovely ball gown that had been placed there. It was the most amazing shade of violet. Marlowe had never seen anyone wear such a color. The fabric was the finest satin. When she'd tried it on earlier, it had glided across her body. The underskirt was lavender, which was also quite lovely. Marlowe did not know how she dared wear the dress. It had been made for Susanna, but the girl assured her she'd never worn it.

"It didn't suit my coloring," she'd said earlier. Marlowe had gaped. Did people actually choose clothing based on color? And they didn't wear clothing simply because the color didn't flatter them? At times she really wanted to knock these swells down for their selfishness.

"Miss Marlowe!"

Marlowe snapped her gaze from the gown and scowled at Lady Dane.

"Are you attending? And do *not* look at me with

that frown on your face. You must compose your expression into a pleasing and serene half smile."

Marlowe cocked a brow, and Lady Dane sighed dramatically. Marlowe clenched her fist again.

"Susanna, show her, please."

Susanna immediately pushed her mouth into the most ridiculous grin Marlowe had ever seen. She burst out laughing, and Susanna could not help but follow. The two girls laughed for several minutes before Lady Dane threw her hands in the air. "I surrender! Make a fool of yourself, if you must. Do not say I did not try to help you." And she swept out of the room, her skirts swishing.

Susanna stopped laughing, and her eyes grew wide. "Oh, dear. I had better go after her."

"Go ahead," Marlowe said, "and tell her not to worry about me." Though Marlowe didn't care if the countess worried or not. The words were for Susanna. "I have been imitating my betters for most of my life. No one at the ball will think me out of place."

"Of course not," Susanna said, squeezing her arm. Marlowe looked down at it. The girl was always hugging her or putting a hand on her shoulder. It was jarring. "And try not to be so hard on my mother. The more frightened she is, the more dictatorial she becomes." Susanna ran to the door, opened it, and chased after her mother. But a moment later, she stuck her head back in again. "I'll send Jane to you in a little while. She can help you dress." And then the girl was gone again.

Marlowe slumped into a chair and stared at the fire. Lady Dane was frightened? Ha! Perhaps that was why Satin was such a bully. He was probably frightened too. She wanted to laugh. Some people were just born to be cruel, and though Lady Dane's cruelty wasn't punctuated with kicks and slaps, her words cut more than Marlowe wanted them to.

She felt like the ugliest, clumsiest, most ignorant person ever to have walked the earth. Lady Dane found something wrong in every single thing she did, which only made Marlowe more determined than ever to succeed. She would go to the bloody ball, and she would—how did the countess put it?—conduct herself with aplomb. And, God willing, she would meet Lord and Lady Lyndon soon and put an end to this whole farce. She would know, once and for all, who she was and where she belonged.

Marlowe stood, too restless to sit for long, and paced her room again. *Her room*. She could hardly believe it. Part of her did not believe it. Part of her waited for the whole charade to come crashing down. She had thought it might topple last night. She'd been pacing like this and stopped to open the curtains and peer out. She'd never lived anywhere with curtains or a window, and she found she liked looking out. The view of the small garden was endlessly fascinating to her. Marlowe went to the windows now, and looked out. She would have preferred a view of the street, so she might see who was coming and going.

Her gaze was drawn to a small clump of rose bushes at the back of the garden. In the daylight, it looked smaller than it had last night. She'd imagined shadows in that clump of bushes, imagined she saw something move. But Satin couldn't have found her. Not yet. Unless the cub…

She bit the pad of her thumb and pushed the thought away. Even if the arch rogue found her, how would he reach her? The house was guarded. She was safe inside. Except she knew Satin, and she knew when he wanted something, or someone, he got it.

Marlowe wondered if she should tell Lord Dane about her suspicions. He would probably say she had been imagining things. Although, in truth, she did not know what he might say. She did not know him very well at all, and he'd seemed to have forgotten about her completely. She hadn't seen him at all after their walk the day before. The slaveys had informed her he was dining at his club, and the ladies were taking dinner in their rooms. A mopsqueezer had brought Marlowe a dinner tray, and Marlowe had eaten by herself. When she'd gone down for breakfast the next morning, Dane hadn't been there either. Strange that she should have been disappointed. She must have eaten too much of the rich food to imagine that she wanted to see him. He annoyed her more than anything else.

He was a bang-up cove. That much was true, but she'd known other handsome men. She could not think of any at the moment…oh! Of course, Gideon was a rum duke, though he was more of a brother to her than anything else. She thought she might understand now what Gideon meant about sparks when kissing. Marlowe imagined she would feel all sorts of sparks if Dane ever kissed her.

Of course, that was a foolish girl's fantasy, and Marlowe was no fool girl. Dane was never going to kiss her. She'd probably give him a black eye if he did.

But perhaps she might let him kiss her first, just to see what it felt like…

Marlowe pressed a fist to her belly. It felt fluttery and tingly. She must have eaten too many tea cakes.

There was a knock on the door, and the mop-squeezer Jane entered, bobbing a slight curtsy, which though not nearly as deep as those she gave Lady Susanna or the countess, still surprised Marlowe. "You don't have to do all that bowing and bobbing with me," she said. "I'm the last person to deserve it. Or want it."

"His lordship asked us to treat you as we would one of the family," the girl said.

Marlowe blinked in surprise. Why would he have said that? Because there was a small chance she might be Lady Elizabeth? "I don't want to cause you any trouble, but please, no more bows."

"Of course, miss."

"Marlowe. I'm no *miss*." Marlowe sighed. "Come on, then. Let's get this over with."

Several hours later, Marlowe was half-asleep in her chair as Jane shoved yet another pin in her hair. Marlowe was beyond impatience and had drifted into pure boredom. She had new respect for these rum morts of society. They must have nerves of steel to sit through this sort of thing day in and day out. A knock at the door made her blink, and Jane said, "Do you want me to answer it?"

"No. I must have fallen asleep. Come in!"

Susanna peered around the door, and her face broke into a huge grin. Marlowe couldn't help but smile back.

"Look at you!" Susanna said. "You look like a princess!"

Marlowe glanced in the mirror and blinked at the girl staring back at her. It was her, only her face looked…different.

"Stand up. Let me see!" Susanna said. Marlowe rose obediently, feeling the satin dress pool around her. The material was so light, she felt as though she wasn't wearing a thing. It whispered across her flesh in a way that made her shiver. The neckline was low, and her arms bare, so she felt almost naked as it was. The foolish part was that Jane had insisted she wear gloves past her elbows. Her hands were covered, but her bubbies were hanging out!

Susanna let out a satisfied sigh and clasped her hands together. "You look beautiful. That gown suits you so much better than it ever did me. It's almost as if it was made for you!"

Marlowe looked down at the gown. "Jane had to shorten it."

"Just a bit," Jane admitted, "but it was nothing."

"And your hair!" Susanna exclaimed. "It's so lovely. Jane, I had no idea you were so talented. You must dress my hair sometime."

"Not likely," Jane said. "Maggie would have my head."

The two women laughed as Marlowe turned to look in the nearby mirror to catch a glimpse of herself. For a long moment, she simply stared. She was used to seeing herself in a fancy gown now. She'd seen herself all day in Susanna's, but this gown was far more— what was the word Susanna had used?—elegant than the one she'd worn earlier. This gown seemed to shimmer. And the rich violet color was far lusher than

she was used to. She'd spent her life in grays and blacks
and browns. Never had she imagined wearing purple.
It made her eyes look so much more blue, a deep
blue. They were almost too large for her face, and her
face looked quite large with all of her hair pulled back
and up. She didn't realize she had quite so much hair.
Jane had coiled it in a thick rope and wound it around
the back of her head in a style Marlowe thought was
almost artistic.

"Do you like it?" Susanna asked, and Marlowe realized they had ceased speaking and were watching her.

"Your hair is all the same length, but I could cut it
if you'd like fringe," Jane said.

"No!" Susanna said quickly. "She looks perfect
as she is. Well, almost perfect. I brought you this to
wear." She held out her hand.

Marlowe turned away from the mirror and watched
as Susanna opened her fist to reveal a small gold
necklace. Marlowe could feel her jaw drop. She could
not stop herself from stepping forward. The necklace
was so small and delicate—so beautiful. She shook her
head. "I can't wear that."

"Why not?" Susanna asked. "With the neckline,
you need something, although you look lovely with
no adornment. Still, I would be honored if you'd
wear it."

"But what if I lose it?"

Susanna shook her head. "You won't."

Marlowe didn't know what else to say. She turned
and allowed Susanna to fasten the chain around her
neck. When she looked in the mirror again, the gold
shimmered and sparkled. She touched it reverently.

She had never worn anything so beautiful. She had never worn anything worth such a fortune. No one had ever thought her worthy of it before.

"Thank you," she said simply, feeling as though the simple sentiment couldn't possibly be enough to express how moved she was.

"You're welcome. We'd better go down. I don't want to keep Mama waiting. Crawford has a wrap for you."

Of course he did. Susanna had thought of everything. Marlowe followed Susanna out of the room, her insides beginning to tremble. She hadn't been apprehensive about the ball before, but now that she was on her way, she could not help but worry. What if she said the wrong thing? Did the wrong thing? What if she forgot her accent and sounded like she ought to be out on the streets?

She'd never cared about such matters before, and now that she was dressed up and adorned, she felt more like a doll than a person. Susanna had been so kind, and her brother too, in his way. She did not want to embarrass them.

"Lady Susanna," she said, trying to ignore the flutters of nerves, "I haven't forgotten I owe you an adventure."

The girl looked back at her with an expression of pure mischief on her face. "I was wondering when we'd come to that. Honestly, readying you for this ball was adventure enough for me."

Marlowe shook her head. "No. I'll find a real adventure for you."

"That will be difficult, since we're leaving directly for the country, but thank you, Marlowe." Her expression had turned sad, and Marlowe cursed Lady Dane under her breath. The woman was such a tyrant.

As they started down the stairs, Marlowe realized not only the tyrant countess but her son would be waiting at the bottom. Her belly began to flutter again, making her feel as though she might cast up her dinner. Would he approve of the dress? Would she even make it through the ball without becoming sick on some important person or other? She must truly dislike Dane to feel ill every time she thought about him.

But when they reached the vestibule, only the butler was waiting for them. He helped Lady Susanna and then Marlowe don wraps, and informed them the countess and the earl were on their way.

A few moments later, both appeared. Marlowe almost forgot to breathe when she saw Dane. His wavy hair had been carefully arranged to fall over his forehead, and one lock of it curled against his cheek. His dark eyebrows rose when he saw her, and his lips curved in a sort of half smile. She did not know the name for the expression, but again, her belly lurched.

He was dressed in a black coat and a white shirt with a neckcloth that seemed to flow down his chest in ripples. Everything, including his waistcoat, was starched and white and perfect. His breeches were also black and quite snug, and his calves were shown off to advantage without his riding boots. She'd always preferred trousers on men, but now she could see the advantage of breeches.

"You look lovely," he said. He took Susanna's

hand and bowed over it, kissing her gloved knuckles, and then repeated the gesture with Marlowe. She almost laughed. It was the sort of thing she and Gideon would have done in jest, but when Dane did it, it was quite charming. She wondered if he had been speaking to Susanna or both of them when he'd given the compliment. Did he think she looked lovely? And why the bloody hell did she even care what he thought? She was turning into some sort of silly ninny.

"Yes, you will do," the countess said with a quick nod. Marlowe refrained from rolling her eyes. She imagined it was the first of many times she would have to exercise such willpower this night.

The four of them departed and clambered into the earl's coach. Marlowe climbed in after the countess and her daughter, and Susanna indicated a spot beside her. "Sit here, Marlowe. You will feel more comfortable facing forward."

"I…no, thank you." Anything to avoid the countess. She sat across from Susanna and her mother and was surprised when Dane sat beside her.

"You do not want to sit facing forward?" he asked.

"Is that what I am supposed to do?"

"Good heavens!" the countess said. "Dane, do tell Johnny Coachman to drive on."

And so she sat facing backward, staring out of the curtained windows and ignoring the little conversation occurring around her. Finally, Dane interrupted her thoughts. "What do you think?"

"The world seems to stream by very quickly," she said.

"Does it?" He peered out as if to verify this fact. "Have you never been in a coach before?"

"Not when I could see anything," she said, referring to the night he'd abducted her and covered her head with a sack.

"Really?" Susanna asked. "Not even a hackney cab?"

Marlowe shook her head. "If I had somewhere to go, I walked. There's nothing wrong with my legs."

"True, but what if you had to travel a great distance?"

Marlowe shrugged. "No—"

"Do not move your shoulders in that fashion," the countess scolded. "It is not ladylike."

Marlowe wondered if anyone could see her roll her eyes in the darkness of the carriage.

"Haven't you ever been out of the city?" Dane asked.

"Course I have. I've been to Field Lane."

The countess inhaled sharply, and Marlowe nodded. The lady should inhale sharply. Field Lane was no place for the likes of her. She would have been eaten alive.

"It's true that Field Lane is slightly beyond the city's parameters," Dane said, "but I meant haven't you ever been to the country?"

"No. Why would I go there?"

"Why indeed?" his mother murmured.

"I've never been out of London, never ridden in a coach, never worn a fancy dress like this one," Marlowe said. "I've never been to a ball. Maybe you'd better leave me in the carriage." Her hopes almost began to rise at the suggestion. Perhaps she could find a way out of this predicament.

"Certainly not," the countess said. Marlowe sighed.

She'd hoped Xanthippe at least would be on her side. "The duchess invited you, and you will attend. But you will not speak unless it is absolutely necessary. No talk of Field Lane!"

Marlowe sincerely hoped the woman did not begin her long lecture of rules again. As though she didn't know enough not to bring up the dolly shops of Shoe Lane and Saffron Hill.

"I am certain Miss Marlowe has had many experiences we have not," Susanna remarked. Marlowe narrowed her eyes at the girl. She'd sounded far too interested in the sorts of experiences Marlowe had had.

"That's true," Marlowe said, "but they're not the sort of things you want to try. Although there's something to be said for walking the city at night. Parts of it are so quiet, so dark, that I can almost imagine I'm the only one who lives here. And on a clear night, when you can see the stars, I like to go to the Thames and watch their reflection in the water. They glitter like I imagine diamonds might."

"That sounds exquisite," Susanna said.

"Humph," said the countess. "The river stinks."

"That's true," Marlowe admitted. "But I didn't mind so much. The only thing I ever minded was the hunger. I don't like being hungry."

"We've noticed," Dane said.

"But even that can be forgotten. Many a cold night I've stood with a group of people around a fire and listened to story after story. I could lose myself in those stories. That's why I wanted to read Shakespeare," she said, looking at Susanna. "I've heard some of his stories."

"Well, then, you shall learn," Susanna said.

Dane did not speak, but she could feel his eyes on her for a long moment. And then he turned away and looked out the window on the other side. Marlowe went back to her window as well, watching the faces of the people they passed, people who stared in awe at such a fine conveyance and wondered what gods might be inside. She remembered watching a time or two as a fancy carriage passed her on the streets. She might catch a glimpse of a lady's face in the window, but usually the curtains were closed, and the occupants were a mystery. They passed a family walking on the street, and Marlowe waved to a little girl looking up at them. The little girl's eyes went wide.

Marlowe almost chuckled. Now the child would have a story to tell. Of course, no one would be very impressed had they known who she was. No one special, just someone pretending.

Finally, they arrived at the ball. At some point they had encountered other carriages also en route, and the line of vehicles made very slow progress. Marlowe thought she could have walked more quickly, but the countess forbade her from climbing out.

The progression of carriages finally moved forward, and Dane's carriage crawled to the front of the duchess's house. A slavey opened a door, and Marlowe waited for the family to exit. When Dane handed her down, she stood completely still and stared. The house was so bright it must have looked like daylight inside. She could not imagine how many candles must be burning. The cost of the candles alone was a fortune she could not imagine. Music floated out from the house's open doors. It was a beautiful noise, what she imagined an angel's song might sound like. Of course, she'd heard music before, but a fiddler in a public house could not compare to the vibrant sounds she heard coming from within.

"Do stop gaping and come along," Lady Dane said, but Marlowe hardly heard. Dane took her arm and ushered her forward. There was so much to see. Everywhere she looked, men and women milled about, wearing clothing more beautiful than any she'd ever imagined.

And the jewels. If she got her hands on one measly earbob a lady dropped, Marlowe would be rich. She touched the gold chain Susanna had allowed her to wear and swore tonight she'd steal nothing. She'd already been the recipient of so many gifts. She wanted to deserve them.

Footmen in blue-and-gold livery lined the steps leading to the house before them. There must have been ten in all. Ten male servants, plus those opening carriage doors and serving inside. How many servants did the duchess employ?

Dane leaned close to her ear. "Lift your skirts."

She drew back. "Fat chance!"

Lady Dane threw her an angry look. Marlowe took a breath. It was time to play her part. "I meant, I beg your pardon, sir!"

"It's *lord,* not *sir*, and I only meant you might want to lift the hem of the gown so you do not trip on it as we climb the steps."

"Oh."

"What did you think I meant?" He had a smile

on his face, as though he thought all of this quite entertaining. She supposed, in his position, she might find it entertaining too. As it was, she was not entertained in the least. The more she considered this a job to be done, the easier it would be to survive. And Dane did say he would take her home early. Hopefully, he would tell her when to start feigning a megrim.

They ascended the steps and were greeted by another slavey who took their wraps. Susanna and the countess simply handed them over, but Marlowe was not so trusting. "What are you going to do with it?" she asked before she handed him the lovely India shawl Susanna had lent her.

"Take it to the coatroom, miss," the footman said, looking a bit surprised.

"Will I get—will it be returned to me?"

"Of course." Now he looked a bit offended. Ha! Well, if he only knew the blunt he could make fencing pelisses and wraps.

Another footman—they were positively legion—stepped forward to lead them to the ballroom. The countess was shaking her head, and Dane was smiling again. Marlowe knew she had made another misstep, but she could not seem to help it. If things did not improve, this night would be interminable.

Once they reached the ballroom, Dane handed the butler his invitation and then gestured to Marlowe. "Miss Marlowe is an addition to our party. It was Her Grace's suggestion."

"Very good, my lord," the butler said without even looking at Marlowe. He cleared his throat. "The Earl of Dane, the Countess of Dane, the Lady Susanna Derring, and Miss Marlowe."

Marlowe thought it might have been her imagination, but several heads turned when her name was mentioned. And then they were moving forward again, toward a short line of men and women. "The receiving line," Dane murmured in her ear. She wished he would stop whispering in her ear. His breath tickled and made her skin tingle. She felt far too warm, and it was most annoying. "Do not ask any questions. Just smile and nod. Watch my sister."

Marlowe did as she was told. She curtsied until her legs wanted to buckle, she smiled until her face wanted to crack, and she did not open her mouth except to murmur, "It is a pleasure." She greeted the Duke and Duchess of Abingdon's six children, their husbands and wives, as well as the duke and duchess themselves. Marlowe remembered the duchess from the previous day, and she was glad to see at least one familiar face.

Dane was about to lead her away, and Marlowe had even let out the slow breath she'd been holding, when the duchess spoke again. "Miss Marlowe, when we met yesterday afternoon, I did not learn your Christian name."

"Ahhh…it was a pleasure, Duchess," Marlowe said, looking at Dane.

"I am certain it was a pleasure, but what is your given name, gel, and where are you from? I cannot quite place your accent."

Dane cleared his throat. "She is our cousin from the north, Duchess."

"I see," the duchess said, leaning her short, round

body forward. Even Marlowe, who was rather short, could see the feather bobbing on the top of her head. "Where in the north?"

"Ah…Bath," Marlowe said, naming the first place that came to mind. Satin had business in Bath at times.

"Bath?" the duchess asked, her brows rising.

"Yorkshire," Dane said smoothly. He glanced at Marlowe. "You know very well Bath is not in the north."

She smiled. "How silly of me. Yes, I'm from Yorkshire."

"My brother has connections in Yorkshire. Do you know Viscount Grennoch? I believe his family name is Marlowe."

"I can't say that I do."

"Miss Marlowe is rather reclusive, Duchess," Dane said. "That is why we invited her to Town. We wanted to broaden her horizons a bit."

Marlowe bit back a laugh. As though she needed her horizons broadened.

"And what did you say your name was?" the duchess asked.

"Marlowe."

"Yes, but your given name, gel."

Marlowe glanced at Dane.

"You do not need to look at him to tell you your name, do you?"

"No. It's…" She could not think. She had always been good at thinking on her feet, but she was shaken. The music, the lights, remembering to use the correct accent, all this talk of York-whatever-it-was.

"Do you mean to tell me your name is Marlowe Marlowe?"

"No," Dane said at the same time Marlowe said, "Yes."

The duchess blinked. "Well, which is it?"

"My parents liked the name so much, it is also my given name."

"How odd," the duchess said.

"But her middle name is Elizabeth," Dane said. "We often call her that, don't we, Elizabeth?"

Marlowe did not answer. A reply did not seem to be required. "Enjoy the ball, Miss Marlowe," the duchess said. "I do hope to see you dancing in the first set."

Dane pulled her away, just as Marlowe murmured, "Not bloody likely." She wouldn't have to feign a megrim, after all. She could already feel one beginning.

Ten

DANE TUGGED MARLOWE TO WHERE HIS MOTHER AND sister were standing and watching them anxiously. "Now what?" his mother hissed.

"Everything is fine," Dane assured her. "Miss Marlowe Marlowe was having a discussion with Her Grace about mutual friends in Yorkshire." He did not know why he found this amusing. If the duchess ever learned who Marlowe really was, the Dane name would be tarnished for decades to come. His family honor was not something he took lightly. But when he was with Marlowe, his upper-class sensibilities seemed so foolish and inconsequential, which was amazing in itself. He'd spent the last few years of his life proposing bills to keep the classes separated. Why now was this girl from the lowest class charming him?

And why did he find it so amusing when Marlowe glared at him and his mother closed her eyes. "I do not think my nerves can withstand this."

"She is doing quite well, Mother. You have nothing to worry about."

A gentleman approached, and the company spoke

to him briefly. When he inquired about reserving a set with Susanna, Dane lost interest and glanced about the room. It was filled with the usual company—poor younger sons looking for rich heiresses, desperate girls in their third seasons, debutantes who were already weary of the Season's mad rush, and his least favorite, the meddling mamas. God save him from those grasping fingers.

"Did you mean what you said?" Marlowe asked. He looked down at her and almost forgot who she was. For an instant, she'd looked like she belonged. She was as beautiful as any other lady here, and as well dressed. When the footman had removed her wrap, Dane might have intervened before she practically accused the poor chap of planning to steal it, if he hadn't been struck speechless by the look of her in the violet gown. He'd seen Susanna wear it, and he'd barely noted the gown. On Marlowe, the material seemed to hug her curves and slide over her lush body. The bodice was low cut, as were most evening gowns, and now he could not quite keep his gaze from lowering to that delicious span of pale flesh on display.

Dane prided himself on behaving like a gentleman. He did not leer at ladies, but he was certainly leering now. He raised his gaze, and there was that hard twist of her mouth. That was what set her apart from the rest in attendance. There was no softness in her, no frivolity. "I beg your pardon," he said.

"You should."

Ah, so she'd seen his gaze dip.

"I asked if you meant what you said."

He raised a brow quizzically.

"Do you truly think I am doing well?" There was a hesitation before she spoke, as though she were weighing the correct words to use, and her accent was not quite right. He'd managed to convince the duchess Marlowe sounded as though she was from the north. He had no idea if she sounded thus or not. To him, her accent sounded rusty from lack of use. Was it because she did not practice aping her betters very often, or because she'd had the accent as a child and lost it?

"I do," he said, finally. "Far better than I imagined you would. Shall I fetch you a refreshment?"

Her eyes widened. "And leave me alone with your mother?"

He laughed. "Somehow I think you are up to the challenge." He gave her and his mother and sister stiff, formal bows. "I will return momentarily with refreshments for all."

His mother frowned at him. Footmen were circling with glasses on silver trays. Dane did not need to seek one out, but he needed some distance between himself and Marlowe. No sooner had he stepped away, than he was waylaid by Mr. Heyward, the younger son of Baron Wye. He was an amiable fellow, although he played with a rather fast set. Dane himself had never been one for too much drink and debauchery. There was his family name to think of. Not to mention, his mother would have had his head on a platter if Dane's name was associated with the sorts of entertainments Heyward frequented.

"Dane," Heyward said with a nod. He lifted a glass of champagne from a passing footman and handed it to

Dane, then took another for himself. "I didn't expect to see you here."

"I didn't expect to attend, but my services were required."

The men stood, watching the train of guests entering the ballroom. From his vantage point across the room, Dane could see Marlowe and his family. His mother and sister had their heads together, while Marlowe stood straight and stiff, her eyes assessing everything and everyone. She was probably calculating each item's worth.

"You have put yourself in the midst of the Marriage Mart, my friend," Heyward said. "Have you chosen a new countess, or will you let one of the brigade of desperate mamas do that for you?"

"I am simply escorting my cousin to the ball. She is new in Town and unaccustomed to such entertainments."

Heyward squinted across the room. "Lovely cousin. Miss Marlowe, is that correct?"

"Yes."

"And where have you been hiding her?"

Dane scowled. The last thing he needed was half the men of the *ton* frothing about the mouth and yipping for Marlowe's attention. "Northumberland," he said, thinking a bit of mystery about her true origins might perpetuate their ruse until the Lyndons returned. As Dane watched, another gentleman approached Susanna. Dane almost smiled as the man gave Marlowe a nervous smile. She ignored him completely. Her gaze was locked on Dane, her blue eyes deep and vivid, even from this distance. No wonder the puppy dared not approach her. She had little elegance in her, but everything about her spoke of confidence. She held her head high and looked others directly in the eye. If his mother would have allowed it, she probably would have crossed her arms over her chest and leaned one shoulder negligently against a wall.

And yet, for all her self-assurance, she was distinctly feminine. It was not a studied femininity of fluttering lashes and tremulous smiles. It was something more earthly, something lush and voluptuous. She had not quite harnessed it yet, but when she did, few men would be able to resist her, and every woman would hate her. No wonder Heyward, with his preference for courtesans, took an interest in Marlowe. She had the potential for that sort of brazen seductiveness.

Belatedly, Dane realized he was being addressed, and he turned to see Heyward exchanging pleasantries with the Duchess of Aycliffe and her daughter, Lady Edith. Heyward bowed and kissed Lady Edith's hand, but the woman's gaze was on Dane.

He could not say he minded attracting her attention. She was the perfect duke's daughter. She had a stately demeanor and was tall enough to be considered regal. She had the perfect English complexion—roses and cream—and a head full of blond curls. Her green eyes were a bit large for her face, her mouth a bit small, and her expression a bit icy, but there was not a man alive who could deny her beauty. Or that she would make the perfect countess—or marchioness or baroness. If Dane were to court Lady Edith, his mother would probably expire from happiness.

"My lady," Dane said, stepping forward and playing his part. After much bowing and curtsying and talk of the weather—Dane's favorite topic—the Duchess of Aycliffe drew Mr. Heyward aside and left Lady Edith and Dane to converse alone momentarily. Dane was not surprised. After all, the Duchess of Aycliffe had no interest in seeing her daughter married to the prodigal second son of a baron. She would set her sights much higher—on an earl, like himself.

"It is a pleasure to see you again, Lady Edith," Dane said easily. "It has been an age since we last met."

She blinked at him. "Actually, we spoke the other night at Lady Yorke's soiree."

"Yes, but even a day without seeing you feels like an age to me," Dane said, covering his surprise at having forgotten seeing her so recently. The truth was, since Marlowe had entered his life, everything else had seemed to fade into a colorless, dull tapestry—his life Before Marlowe. He hadn't realized he'd seen life as such, but now that he did, he felt his spine prickle uncomfortably.

"Why, thank you, my lord. I was surprised to see Sir Brook the other night. I read frequently of his heroics."

"Yes, Brook is quite the hero." Dane sighed. Had he known he would have to spend half the evening extolling his brother's virtues to the fairer sex, he would have gone directly to the card room. There were no ladies there to sigh over his brother's good deeds.

"How did he ever manage to locate Lord Chesham's younger brother? We all thought the poor boy was lost forever."

"Brook is like a dog with a bone," Dane said. He could not think of a less romantic image, but Lady Edith did not seem dissuaded.

"And now I heard a rumor that Lord and Lady Lyndon have hired Sir Brook to find their kidnapped daughter. Is it true?"

Dane stiffened. As far as he was aware, both the Lyndons and Sir Brook had kept their association a secret. And Dane certainly did not want rampant speculation swirling about that Marlowe was Lady Elizabeth. If she was not, it would only be harder for the Lyndons if everyone knew of their disappointment and Brook's mistake. Though, for his part, Dane wouldn't have minded seeing Brook make a mistake.

Dane took a breath. "I have no idea, my lady. The last I heard, Lord and Lady Lyndon were in Scotland, and I have not seen my brother. I believe Bow Street keeps him busy recovering stolen goods." There. That sounded rather menial.

"Anything of interest?" Lady Edith asked. "A priceless painting or jewels?"

Dane let out a slow breath and was saved from replying when the Duke and Duchess of Abingdon announced the commencement of the dancing. The orchestra began to play a minuet, and Dane watched as his sister took her place on the dance floor. Lady Edith's partner claimed her, and with a curtsy, she also moved away. Heyward leaned close to Dane. "Did she convince you to dance a waltz with her?"

Dane shook his head. "She wanted only to talk of my brother."

Heyward chuckled. "Sir Brook is the bane of many men less heroic."

Dane grunted. He watched the dancing halfheartedly, having observed the scene countless times before.

He was certain his mother would chastise him for not asking a young lady to partner him. But he was here to keep watch over Marlowe, not dance.

Marlowe! Dane's head whipped across the room, and to his horror, he saw she was standing alone. No, not alone. His mother was not with her, but a gentleman was, if Lord Siddon might be called a gentleman. He was a known rake, and Dane was surprised the Duchess of Abingdon had invited the man.

"I wondered when you would notice Siddon and your cousin," Heyward said.

"Deuce take it," Dane mumbled. Now that the dancing had begun, he would have to walk the perimeter of the room to reach Marlowe, and who knew what traps laid by the scheming mamas lay in wait?

"Hurry and save her," Heyward said with a chuckle.

"Go to hell," Dane said, starting away.

"Better there than the altar!" Heyward called.

Dane pushed his way through the groups of people watching the dance. He knew almost every single one, but he did not stop to exchange pleasantries, which earned him more than a few frowns and raised eyebrows. He plowed forward with a single-minded purpose, ignoring the fans and handkerchiefs that fell in his path, dropped by young ladies hoping he would stoop and retrieve them, thereby giving them a chance to impress him with their beauty or wit.

But Dane did not want to play the gentleman. He found that role more difficult to swallow of late. He stepped over the offerings and finally arrived, out of breath, at Marlowe's side.

"Lord Dane," Siddon said. "Miss Marlowe and

I were just discussing you. She said you had left to bring her refreshment." The man's eyes lowered to the half-empty glass of champagne in Dane's hand. For her part, Marlowe looked calm and composed and slightly amused.

And beautiful. God, she was so incredibly beautiful. No wonder she'd attracted Siddon. Dane could only be relieved she didn't have more admirers swarming about her. "And now I have returned," Dane said. He leveled a gaze at Siddon. "Thank you for keeping her company."

"Oh, I neither deserve nor desire any thanks," Siddon said. "It was my pleasure. In fact, Miss Marlowe just reserved the waltz for me."

Dane glanced at her, but she shrugged as though she had no idea what Siddon was speaking of. She probably didn't. "I'm afraid that's impossible," Dane said. "She's already promised the waltz to me."

"Then another dance." Siddon smiled at Marlowe, who gave him a cool, assessing look.

"All of her dances are claimed," Dane said. "Excuse us." He took Marlowe's elbow and led her away.

"I could have done that myself," Marlowe said. "I thought I was supposed to be polite."

"Not to the likes of him," Dane said. "Where is my mother? She should not have left you alone."

Marlowe shrugged. "I am sorry to have dragged you away from your flirtation. If you want, I can pretend I have a megrim now and leave on my own." She looked up at him. "Or must I wait until after our dance?"

"We are *not* dancing," Dane said. Waltzing with

Marlowe would be his undoing. "We determined that already."

They stood in silence for a moment, Marlowe's gaze on the dancers in the center of the ballroom. "How does everyone know which way to turn? Which way to step?"

Dane opened his mouth to reply, and then hesitated. She was going to think his answer absolutely ridiculous. And, of course, from her viewpoint it was. She had spent her life attempting to survive. How completely frivolous it would seem to her that his mother had spent funds to pay a dancing instructor to teach him. "Some of the dances one learns by watching," he said.

Her gaze snapped to his face. She seemed to always be able to tell when he was attempting to hide something. "And others?" she asked.

"Others are taught. Susanna, Brook, and I had a dancing instructor."

He expected her to snort and make a scathing comment, but she only nodded and looked back at the dancers. "That must have been lovely." Her voice sounded so wistful, so filled with yearning, that he actually felt his heart tighten.

"I think Susanna enjoyed it, but Brook and I suffered through. The last thing a young boy wants is to be stuck inside and forced to learn the steps of the quadrille. And then to have to partner his sister."

A ghost of a smile played on her lips as she watched the dancers. "I can imagine. But look at your sister now. She is the most graceful dancer by far. I'm sure she feels like a princess."

Dane glanced at his sister, but he could not stop his gaze from returning to Marlowe. He did not know if Susanna felt like a princess, but he knew one lady who certainly deserved to feel like a princess. And shouldn't every girl feel beautiful and royal at least once in her life?

He'd strictly forbidden her from dancing—and with good reason. She did not know the dances. But he had not considered that she would want to dance. He had not considered that this might be her one and only ball. This might be Marlowe's only chance to feel like a princess before she had to return to the squalor of St. Giles. The waltz was not a difficult dance. He could lead her through it. She deserved one dance, one chance to be swept across the ballroom.

Dane lifted two glasses of champagne from the tray of a passing footman, handed one to Marlowe, and downed the other. She watched him, brows raised. "Thirsty?"

"I need fortification."

Her brow furrowed. "Forti—like a castle?"

He chuckled. "Courage. My mother is going to murder me." The set was coming to a close, and Dane could only pray his mother had left the ballroom and would stay away for the next half hour. And that was about as likely as George IV and Caroline of Brunswick reconciling. He took her glass and his own and motioned to a footman. When the servant approached, he set the glasses on a tray.

"Why is that?" she asked.

Dane took her arm. "Because, Miss Marlowe, you and I are going to dance a waltz."

She shook her head. "But you said no dancing."

"I changed my mind." He nodded to the dance floor. "Come."

"No. I don't know how to dance a waltz." Her accent had lost a bit of its polish, confirming her nervousness at his suggestion. But she did not need to talk to dance—at least not to anyone but him.

"I'll show you. Just follow my lead." He tried to steer her toward the floor, but she resisted.

"No!" she hissed. "I don't want to dance."

Dane gave her a long look. Her blue eyes met his, and he raised a brow. "Yes, you do."

Her gaze held steady, and he thought, for an instant, he might have misjudged. And then, slowly, her gaze lowered and dropped to the floor. Dane released her elbow. If he would do this, he would do it properly. He would make her feel like a princess. He executed a deep bow, sweeping his hand with a flourish. "Miss Marlowe, may I have the pleasure of this dance?"

She didn't answer, and he glanced up at her. Her mouth had dropped open, and there was laughter in her eyes. "What are you doing?"

"The correct response is *yes, my lord.*" He straightened and held out a hand. The invitation could not be clearer. All she had to do was accept it.

She stared at his hand for what seemed an eternity. Dane had time to consider what he would do if she refused. At least a dozen people in the ballroom had seen his bow. There was no question as to his purpose. Before the night was over, the story would be all over the *ton* as to how his gallant request for a dance had been denied. He wouldn't have the pleasure of holding her in his arms before his mother murdered him.

But just as Dane had resigned himself to a cold, lonely death, Marlowe's warm hand joined his. "Yes, my lord," she said, her accent in place once again.

Dane almost wished she hadn't used it. He liked her real voice so much more than this affected one. With a smile, he led her to the dance floor amidst the other couples. Susanna, who was still a debutante, was not dancing the waltz. It was not an appropriate dance for innocents, and Dane had a moment to wonder if he'd done Marlowe more harm than good by leading her out there. But then the music began, and he had no more time to think. He swept her into his arms and, with minimal instruction, began to lead her across the floor.

She was a quick learner. He had but to count the rhythm for her once and show her how to position her arm and hold her skirts, and she was following him as though she'd danced the waltz a thousand times. He'd anticipated having to talk her through the first few minutes, having to suggest she relax her rigid body, having to count the beats for her. None of it was necessary. She danced so easily, she was almost an extension of him. Did she realize the entire room was probably watching them? He glanced at her face and saw nothing but pure joy. The smile on her lips took his breath away, and he forgot about his mother, the duchess, the entire ballroom. If dancing could make Marlowe smile, he would waltz with her every hour of every day.

"Do you like it?" he asked, though he could see quite plainly she did.

"It's like flying!" she said, her voice breathless.

Dane laughed. "I'll show you flying." And he turned her, spinning her until he was certain she was dizzy. She laughed, and when she looked at him, her face was pleasantly flushed. In that moment, he thought her the most ravishing creature he had ever encountered.

"More," she breathed. And Dane could not resist. He twirled her again, catching her back to him and pulling her in close. He danced faster, passing other couples, and sweeping her across the room. He held her tightly, ensuring she would not lose her footing—at least that was what he told himself. But he could not deny the closeness of her body affected him. She was warm where his gloved hand touched her bare back. He knew her skin was as soft as the satin of her dress. He remembered marveling at the feel of it when she'd been in his bed. Now he had the urge to stroke that bare flesh, to remove his glove and touch her, skin to skin. Even greater was the urge to slide the hand at her waist down and over the curve of her hip. He could feel it there, where her waist indented, and he longed to fit his hand to that gentle swell.

This was why the waltz was not for innocents. How could a man look down at her and not want to kiss her, not imagine himself taking her to bed, undressing her, kissing those ample breasts? If there was such a man, Dane was not he. He wanted her, and when he met her gaze, the dark blue of her eyes told him she wanted him too. As their gazes held, her lips parted slightly into an O, and Dane's hand on her back closed into a fist to keep from sliding to her neck, cupping it, and bringing his lips down to hers. He could imagine kissing those perfectly pink lips. He could imagine sliding his tongue between her lips and tasting her. Would she taste of champagne or something darker, more alluring?

She took a deep breath, and her breasts brushed his chest. He wore a shirt and a coat, and he could not feel the softness or the heat of them, but he was as aware of the movement as he was of his own heart racing.

"I feel a bit warm," she said, her voice husky and breathless. Dane wanted to groan aloud. He'd known dancing with her would be a mistake.

"Perhaps we should step outside."

"Yes," she said with a nod. He turned her until they were near the doors to the garden, and then he took her hand and led her through one of them. A footman nodded at them and offered a tray of champagne, but Dane waved it away. They stepped into the cool night air, and it felt refreshing against his heated skin.

She wore gloves, and he could not feel her flesh, but he could feel the way her hand trembled in his. She was as affected as he was by the dance. He should lead her back inside, perhaps give her another moment to catch her breath, but that was all. The lights from the ballroom lit the garden, with aid from several lanterns, and he could see she was struggling to catch her breath.

One minute more, and he would bring her back inside.

"Shall we walk?" he asked. No, that was not what he'd meant to say. He should take it back.

"More walking?" she asked.

"Yes, but this time we won't speak of the weather." They wouldn't speak at all, and that was why he should take her back inside. He should play the gentleman. He knew the rules. A gentleman did not lead a lady into the darkness, where the couple could not be observed. A gentleman did not draw a lady against him. A gentleman did not steal kisses from someone to whom he was not betrothed.

But Dane could not stop himself. He didn't understand it. He'd never had trouble resisting such temptations before. But with Marlowe, Dane suddenly felt so bloody sick of playing the gentleman. He paused in the darkness behind a hedge and turned to face her. In the shadows, he could see little of her, save the white of her gloves. He took a step toward her, pulling her into his arms. She didn't resist. He wished she would. He wished someone would stop him, because he feared once he took this step, he would never be able to go back. Once he kissed her, he would never be able to resist doing so again.

But she went willingly into his arms, her body soft and supple against his. She was so delightfully warm, so petite, so lush. He wanted to ravish her and protect her all at the same time. The rush of sensations was enough to make him curse. Instead, he bent his head and did the one thing he knew would shut out everything else.

He kissed her.

The moment his lips brushed hers, everything inside him came alive. It was as though he'd been wearing a heavy cloak, one that weighed him down and muted all sensation. Now he'd shrugged it off, and he could feel again. He was so damn light that he could have run for miles and not tired. He brushed his lips against hers again, feeling the frisson course through his entire body. He was suddenly too warm and yet not warm enough. Had he ever been warm before? Nothing could compare to the heat he felt with her body pressed against his. His hand flexed on her back, and he wished he'd taken off his gloves so he could trace her skin with his bare fingers.

Marlowe's hands, which had been at her side, moved now. She brought them to his chest and rested them there. He half-expected her to push him back, but she didn't. She didn't kiss him back, either. She simply stood, seemingly undecided. Dane wanted to crush his mouth to hers, to sate the need building every time his flesh brushed against hers. But he couldn't forget he was a gentleman, and she—whether she was Lady Elizabeth or not—deserved his respect.

"I apologize," he said, releasing her. "I overstepped." She didn't remove her hands from his coat, and he tried to discern her expression in the darkness, but her head was lowered, and he couldn't see. "Allow me to escort you back inside. I assure you this won't happen again."

Now she looked up at him, and he saw the flush of her cheeks and the way her breathing was uneven and fast. "Why?"

"I beg your pardon?"

She shook her head, probably annoyed at his politeness. "Why won't it happen again?"

"I…because I overstepped."

She shook her head. "I don't understand. You don't want to kiss me?"

He stared at her. Hell, but he wanted much more than that. "I do want to kiss you."

"Then why apologize?"

"Because this"—he indicated the dark, deserted section of the garden—"is not appropriate. I'm a gentleman and should respect—"

She slid her hand up his chest, resting her finger on his lips, effectively silencing him. "I've never had much use for gentlemen." She stepped closer, so her body was flush with his again. "All of this talk— *overstepped* and *pardon* and *appropriate*—means nothing to me. Kiss me again."

Now it was Dane's turn to question. "Why?"

"Because I finally understand what Gideon meant about sparks. Kiss me."

Who was he to deny a direct request? Her arms wrapped around his neck, and he lowered his lips, pressing them against hers. She let out a soft sigh, and he closed his arms around her body, feeling it tremble against his. He needed to take this slowly, so as not to frighten her. He had no idea what sort of experience she had—if any. His own was not extensive, but the women he'd known had never trembled in his arms. Could she be an innocent? He supposed chastity was not reserved for the upper classes. He moved his lips against hers gently, carefully, resisting the urge to delve inside and taste her.

Her fingers threaded into his hair, and she pulled him down. Dane lifted his head. "Marlowe—"

"Kiss me," she said, her voice low and ragged.

"I don't want to frighten you."

"With that? I wouldn't even call that a kiss, much less a frightening one."

Dane raised his brows. "Is that a challenge?"

"Too much of a gentleman to take it?"

Dane pulled off his gloves. "You tell me." Throwing restraint and his gloves to the ground, Dane yanked her against him and claimed her lips with his. This time he didn't wait for her to accustom herself to his touch; he teased her lips open with his tongue and entered her. She let out a small gasp, but he didn't retreat. His hand slid up her back, and there was that silky skin he'd been longing to touch. He spread his hand over the cool skin of her back, tracing it until he reached the nape of her neck. He closed his fingers protectively around her, angling her head for better access. His tongue tangled with hers as his mouth slanted over hers. She tasted of champagne, and when she tentatively stroked her tongue along his, he almost lost all control. His hand fisted in her hair, and he deepened the kiss until he was drowning in her.

Every fiber of his body was alive. He could feel the soft thickness of her hair on his fingers, the smooth satin of her gown, the whisper of the night breeze, and hear the low strains of the orchestra inside the ball. And he could feel her breaths coming short and ragged, and his own matched hers. If he allowed this to continue, he'd lose his last ounce of control, lay her down, and take her right there. Instead, he drew back, keeping one hand about her waist to steady her. He drew in a labored breath.

"That was a kiss," she said, her voice breathy. "Do it again."

"*No.*" He held out a hand, as though to convince his body his mind meant what it had ordered his lips to convey. "We've already been away too long. We should make our excuses and return home."

"Your home."

"Yes. My town house." He saw now he'd mussed her hair. The careful coiffure was ruined, pieces of hair beginning to spill down her dress. He doubted she knew how to fix it. Perhaps it would be better for him to make both of their excuses, fetch her wrap, and escort her out without going through the ballroom. There would be talk enough without adding to it by presenting her with a disheveled appearance. He bent to lift his gloves.

"And what happens when we return to your home?"

"We go to bed," he said, pulling the gloves on. "Alone," he added quickly. "Marlowe, this was a mistake. It cannot go any further."

"Do you think I want it to? I'm not your ladybird."

"No, you are not." He tugged the last glove into place. "I will fetch your wrap and make our excuses. Do you mind waiting here? I'm afraid I've damaged your coiffure."

"My what?"

"Your hair."

She touched it. "Oh. You don't want them to know you were kissing me."

"I don't care who knows, but it would be better for your reputation if we kept this between us."

"Liar. You're terrified I'm not really Lady Elizabeth

and everyone will know you were dancing with nothing but a thief from Seven Dials."

The accusation stung, not least of all because there was truth in it. Dane straightened his coat. "I will return in a few moments. Stay here." He turned and walked away from her, cursing because he had no one to blame but himself. He'd known he should not kiss her. Hell, he'd known he shouldn't allow Brook to bring her into Derring House. This was the inevitable result—an attack on his character from—

Damn it! She *was* a thief from Seven Dials. Even if she was Lady Elizabeth, she was a criminal as well. Was he supposed to ignore that fact? Was he supposed to forget he was an earl with the responsibility to uphold his family name? Was he supposed to pretend he'd never been held up by highwaymen or had his home ransacked? But he couldn't blame her for his lapse tonight. She was not the one with responsibilities to consider. He was treading a fine line with her, and he'd best remember which side to stay on.

Eleven

MARLOWE STOOD IN THE GARDEN, FEELING CHILLED now that Dane was walking away. She was a numbskull, forgetting for a moment who and what he was. It was the spark that had done it. She didn't know that kissing could feel like that. She felt sick to her stomach and shaky and terrified all at the same time. It was like suffering from a particularly awful ague, except she didn't want it to go away.

Something was definitely wrong with her. She wasn't thinking clearly. Why had she let him kiss her? Why had she asked him to kiss her again? She knew he didn't want her. She knew better than to let some swell paw at her, though he hadn't exactly pawed. He'd been tender and gentle, and that had been its own form of persuasion. If he'd grabbed her or been rough, she might have fought him. How did one fight against tenderness?

How did one remember he was a nob and she would never be anything but a villain? If she let him, he would use her, and then she'd end up with a swollen belly and a brat she couldn't care for. She'd be selling her body on the streets like every other bawd who'd been weak enough to listen to a man's charming words.

Marlowe wasn't a pigeon, easily duped and cheated. "Well, well, well…"

Marlowe's back prickled, and she inhaled sharply before turning. She knew that voice, but he couldn't be here. She had to be imagining this. Satin stepped out of the shadows and gave her a low bow. "Don't you look like a frigot well rigged."

She looked down at Susanna's gown and swallowed. A thousand questions filled her mind. How had he found her? How had he managed to sneak inside the garden? What did he intend to do to her now?

"Satin," she said, her voice shaking.

"Let me see you, Marlowe." He made a motion with his finger, encouraging her to turn for him. She stood rooted in place. "Turns out you're a rum blowen. Didn't think you had it in you, but you were hiding these looks under all that dirt."

"How did you find me?" But she knew. The cub who had spotted her on the walk back from Hyde Park had snitched on her, sold her for a song, she was certain. And why not? In his place, she would have done the same. Satin was a powerful ally.

"The real question, Marlowe," Satin said, leaning close and giving her a whiff of his fetid breath, "is why didn't you find me? Thought you were well rid of me, didn't ye?"

"No." She shook her head. She'd never thought that, not really. She'd known he would find her, but she'd allowed herself to pretend she was safe.

"And don't tell me you were planning to bring me into this racket. I weren't born yesterday."

"It's not a—" But she stopped herself. Satin would never believe her if she told him the truth, and it didn't matter anyway. He'd found her. The game was spoiled. "I didn't want to bring you in." She had to leave here before Dane came back. She didn't want Satin to see him. Or maybe she didn't want Dane to see Satin. She was amazed at what only a day or so could do. Suddenly, Satin looked impossibly filthy. She'd always thought him a bit cleaner than the rest, but now it seemed he stank to heaven. "I've done the trick, and the game is over now."

"Is it?" he said, crossing his arms over his chest.

She gestured to her gown. "We can sell this for a small fortune. The cubs will have full bellies tonight, and you'll have a bit left for yourself." She'd have to find a way to make sure the gold necklace was returned to Susanna. Satin had seen it. He never missed a trick, but she couldn't let it be sold with the rest.

"And why would we sell it? You look like a pure to me. Looking like that, we could bilk some swell out of ten times the cost of that gown."

Marlowe clamped her mouth shut and clenched her fists. She'd die before she became Satin's buttock and file. "I never took you for a cock-bawd. Have you turned pimp?"

"Not yet, but you're like to make me consider it. I've been considering something else too."

"What's that?" Oh, she did not want to know. Truly, she did not.

"Why you're so eager to claim the game is over.

Ye're livin' in one of them fancy houses in Mayfair, and all you got is this frock? There's more where that came from."

Oh, yes, there was much more. So much more that Satin's eyes would probably pop right from his head if he saw it.

"There's more, but the cove is down," she lied. "I have to get out now."

"He suspects?" he asked, picking his teeth with a long fingernail.

"Yes."

Suddenly, his hand was around her neck. She staggered until he pushed her down on a stone bench, where he leaned over her. Her vision dimmed, and when she forced her eyes open again, his face was an inch from hers. And still she prayed Dane stayed away. She didn't want him to find her like this. Worse yet, she worried what Satin would do to the man if he interrupted. "Then make them unsuspicious," Satin said. "Ye're a good liar, Marlowe, but you can't fool me. You and me, we row in the same boat. You understand?"

She tried to nod.

"I can't hear you." He lifted her head and slammed it back on the bench. Now she saw stars that had nothing to do with the foggy sky above them.

"Y-yes."

"You and me, we're going to devise a racket. You're the plant. You look at the place, and then we're going to crack it together. You got that?"

"Yes, but, Satin, this isn't just any swell. He's an earl. If we're caught—"

"We hang. At least we're going after something worth hanging for. Tomorrow night, you meet me in the back of the garden by the shrubs. You know the ones I mean?"

She did. And she hadn't imagined seeing movement there. Satin had been watching her. He shook her by the neck. "I can't hear you, girl."

"Yes."

"When the clock chimes two, you'd better be there, or I'm coming in to get you."

"I'll be there."

"And don't bring me any cock-and-bull story. You have a game, and you come alone. You cry beef, Marlowe, and I'll see you nibb'd with me."

Just as quickly as he'd grabbed her, he released her. She lay on the bench, blinking the pain and tears away. Damn tears. She would not cry. She sat, watching as Satin brushed his ragged coat clean of the imagined dirt from his attack. "A pleasure doing business with you, Marlowe." He tipped his hat. "Until we meet again."

Before she could protest, he wrapped his fingers under the gold chain and yanked it off her neck. "No!" she cried, rising.

He held up a hand, and she flinched back. "There'd better be more where this came from." Whistling to himself, Satin dropped the necklace in the pocket of his coat and strolled away, hands tucked in his trouser pockets. Marlowe closed her eyes and sank to the bench. She had precious few options. She could run away, but Satin would still go after Dane. He had the idea now, and he wouldn't let it go easily. She could warn Dane, but would he even believe her? And if he did, he was more likely to have her thrown in gaol than to let her escape.

And if she did escape, what would happen to Gideon and the rest of the cubs? Satin knew she and Gid were close. He'd punish her friends if he couldn't hurt her. And even if she figured Gideon could take care of himself, even if she managed to get away, what then? She didn't have any skills or any references. She'd be back to the game to stay alive, and once she started the buz again, Satin would find her. Pickpockets knew one another, and Satin had a wide range of friends and accomplices.

"Marlowe?"

Her head jerked up at the sound of Dane's voice, and she hastily tried to straighten her hair and gown. He stepped into the little garden nook. "There you are—what the hell happened to you?"

Damn it. She must look worse than she thought. "I f-fell. I couldn't see in the darkness, and I tripped. I must look awful."

He wrapped the shawl around her shoulders. "Let's see you home."

She almost laughed. *Home.* It was not her home, nor would it ever be. He led her back toward the house and inside through a different door. "If we take this route, we avoid the ballroom." He turned to look at her, and his eyes gave away nothing. Perhaps she did not look as bad as she thought. With his hand firmly on her elbow, he led her to the vestibule. Guests were still arriving, and Dane shielded her with his body, leading her outside and setting her in the shadows.

They had to wait for what seemed an eternity for the coach, and when they climbed inside, the vehicle moved at a snail's pace. The lanterns inside the coach had been lit, and Marlowe kept her face averted. Dane sat across from her, arms crossed, not seeming interested in chatting. Finally, she darted a glance up at him and noted he was staring out the window.

Except that the drapes had been closed. He was on to her. She could sham Abram and pretend to be sick. That was probably her last chance. "I don't feel very well," she said. "I think I may be ill." She clutched her belly and doubled over, tilting her head so she could see his face.

Slowly, he glanced at her. There was no trace of sympathy on his features. "I imagine those bruises on your neck are rather painful."

She forgot her supposed stomach ailment and brought a hand to her throat. It did feel tender. Satin, that bloody cockchafer! He shouldn't have marked her. But she knew exactly what had happened. Dane had believed her story about falling until he'd seen her in the light from the house. She hadn't thought to cover her neck, and the marks must have been clear.

"Will you tell me what happened, or continue to lie to me?"

"I can't tell you," she said.

"Did one of the guests assault you? Give me his name or a description. I'll issue a challenge within the hour."

She blinked at him. "One of the guests? No. I...do you mean you'd fight a duel?"

He merely looked at her.

She gaped. She knew it was unladylike. She knew

if the countess had been here she would have ordered her to shut her mouth, but Marlowe could not seem to help it. "You would duel over *me*?"

"Is that so hard to believe?"

"Yes!"

He merely cocked his head. "Because?"

"Because I'm no one. Nothing. Not worth dying for."

"They don't know that. We introduced you as my cousin."

Marlowe felt a sharp blast of cold pierce her heart. "So this is about your honor, not mine. You can't have one of your own treated like a common thief from the rookeries. Well, you needn't issue your challenge, Dane, it wasn't a guest from the party."

"Then who was it?"

She shook her head. "It doesn't matter."

He was beside her on the seat in a matter of seconds. The coach had seemed spacious mere moments before, but now everything was far too small and cramped. "A man does this to you"—lightly, he angled her chin up, and she yanked it down, not wanting him to see the injury—"and you tell me it doesn't matter."

"You can't help me." The coach finally picked up speed, and she bounced, hitting the back of her head on the seat. The squabs were soft, but she still winced. Immediately, Dane's hand went to the back of her head. She hissed in a cry of pain as his fingers probed the knot forming there. Dane pulled his hand away and stared at the tinge of blood on his fingers.

"You have no idea what I'm capable of."

She shook her head. "You're a spoiled, pampered

lord. You have everything you could ever want. I doubt you could even imagine what my life has been like, much less solve any of my problems. Stick to your books and your balls and your"—she gestured to his neckcloth—"cretins."

He cleared his throat. "It's a *cravat*." He moved back across the carriage.

"Oh, do forgive me, my lord, for mixing up yer fancy words."

Dane pinched the bridge of his nose, then lowered his hands and looked up at her with those deep brown eyes. "I want to help you, Marlowe. I *can* help you, but you have to let me in. When you're ready to trust me, let me know."

The rest of the ride home was made in silence. When they arrived at the town house, Dane went straight to his room, but he must have issued some orders before he retired, because just as Marlowe donned a robe and dismissed Jane, the servant returned and apologized as two footmen carried a hip bath and buckets of water into the room.

"What is this?"

"I'm sorry, miss, but his lordship asked us to bring it." The poor girl looked terrified, and Marlowe decided to hold her anger. There was no point in taking it out on the slaveys, who had worked so hard to haul all of that water to her room.

"Thank you," Marlowe managed to grit out.

Jane let out a breath she must have been holding. "His lordship said you'd want to wash your hair. Shall I help with that?"

"No!"

Jane jumped back.

"I mean, no, thank you. I can do it myself." The last thing she wanted was an audience while she bathed. Or rather, didn't bathe. It had been only a few days since she'd taken her *last* bath!

Finally, the bath was ready, and Marlowe was left alone. She'd very rarely been alone in her life, and the sensation was strange and not entirely welcome. But at least she could worry about Satin in peace. She sank down on the floor and buried her head in her hands. No solution jumped out at her, and she found herself shivering on the cold floor. How quickly she'd gone soft. She moved closer to the fire, which meant closer to the bath. She could feel the heat from the water, and she trailed her fingers in the warm liquid. They came away smelling sweet but pleasant. Perhaps if she dipped her feet in the water, it would warm her.

Hiking her night rail to her knees, she balanced on the edge of the tub and dipped her feet into the soapy water. She was instantly warmed, and she might have relaxed if her head and neck didn't pain her so much. She touched the back of her head gingerly and felt the matted hair where the blood had dried. She could wait for it to harden and fall out on its own, or she could wash it out.

The thought of wet hair made her shudder. It couldn't be healthy, but she could hardly lie down on those clean white sheets with blood and grime in her hair. With a curse, she threw off the night rail and submerged herself in the bath, knees to her chin. She scrubbed as best she could, and then dried off with the soft towels Jane had left. Last, she dipped her head in the water and rinsed her hair several times. Wrapping her hair in a towel, she sat by the fire and allowed it to dry.

For a long while, she marveled that she was in this place. Who would have ever thought Marlowe would be sitting by the fire in a room like this with the idle time to allow her hair to dry? Her belly was full, she was reasonably warm, and she was clean and dressed in soft clothing. The memory of this must be enough to last her through the dark times to come.

One realization was becoming clear. If Lord and Lady Lyndon were her parents, she didn't want to meet them. She'd only put them in danger. She couldn't live with herself if that happened.

A soft knock on the door sounded, and Marlowe jumped. A moment later, Susanna opened the door and peeked in. "Oh, good. You're not sleeping."

Marlowe's hand immediately went to her neck. How was she going to explain the lost necklace? The girl would think she'd stolen it. Susanna stepped inside and closed the door behind her. "I have only a moment. Mama insists we pack tonight."

"You're leaving," Marlowe said.

"Yes." Susanna rolled her eyes. "Mama is convinced you're the very devil, and just being in your presence will corrupt me."

Marlowe didn't think that assessment was far from the truth, after what had happened tonight.

"But I didn't want to leave without saying goodbye. I hope you meet your parents and everything goes well with them."

Marlowe wasn't certain what to say. That there was

no chance of that? Still, it was kind of the girl to offer the words. "Thank you," she said simply. Susanna looked back at the door and moved closer.

"You and Dane caused quite a stir at the ball," she said in hushed tones. "After you waltzed, everyone was talking about you. They wanted to know who the mystery beauty was."

Marlowe made a face, but Susanna held her hands up. "I'm telling the truth! Everyone was talking about you."

"About how awfully I danced."

"About how lovely you looked. Really, Marlowe, you looked like you had danced the waltz a thousand times. I know Dane is a good dancer, but even I was struck a little dumb. What happened to you after the dance? You disappeared."

Marlowe wished she could confide in the girl, could confide in someone, but Susanna couldn't help her. "Dane thought it was time I left. Before I did something to embarrass him or myself."

Susanna gave a bark of laughter. "More likely he didn't like the other men looking at you. You would have been crushed with the gentlemen vying for your hand."

The girl exaggerated, of course, but Marlowe couldn't help but like her. She was so naive. So sweet. "About your necklace," Marlowe began.

Susanna waved her hand. "You can give it to me later. I have to pack, and I'd better begin, or I'll not have a wink of sleep." She started for the door. "I just wanted to say good night and good-bye." She paused and rushed back to Marlowe, throwing her arms around her. Marlowe almost toppled over. "I'm sorry," Susanna gushed. "I know you probably hate this, but you just look so small sitting here by yourself." She pulled back. "I hope I see you again very soon." With a quick kiss on Marlowe's cheek, the girl was gone.

Marlowe watched the door close and then touched her cheek. What a strange gesture. She had to protect these people, and there was only one way to do that.

Rid the world of Satin.

Marlowe paced her room, her thoughts all in a rush. And when she decided on her plan of action, she sat down hard on the bed and closed her eyes. It could work. It could very well work. But she'd need Dane's help. There was no other way.

Taking a deep breath, she pulled her wrapper close around her neck to cover the bruises and carefully opened the bedroom door. The hallway was dark and quiet, but she didn't take a candle. The dark was her ally in this. She wished she weren't wearing white, but if she was discovered, she'd simply say she'd become lost while searching for the kitchen. They'd believe she was looking for more to eat.

Silently closing the door, she stood in the hallway and pictured the house in her mind. Dane's room was on the other side of it. She'd have to pass the countess's room and Susanna's to reach it. Moving stealthily, she crept past both doors. Light still burned under each, and she could hear the sound of voices. At one point, the countess's door opened, and her abigail, Edwards, emerged, carrying a glim-stick and a pile of clothing. Marlowe hunched down beside a chair and did not move until the light disappeared.

She rose again and continued her trek along the corridor. She passed a set of stairs and entered the male section of the house. It was quiet and dark here, and she stopped in front of Dane's door. No light shone under it. He was probably sleeping. Well, she'd just have to wake him up. She tried the handle and was pleasantly surprised to find it unlocked. These people really stood no chance against Satin. They didn't even lock their bedchambers.

She stepped into the room and closed the door behind her. A low fire burned in the hearth, but other than the crackle of the blaze, she heard nothing. She crept forward, toward the bed. She remembered where the furnishings were and sidestepped the chair where she'd spent part of her first night in the house. Finally, she stood next to the bed.

He was there. The covers had been pulled to his chest, which was bare, and he had one hand thrown up beside his head on the pillow. His face was peaceful in sleep, his dark hair tousled on the pillow. She could see the muscles in his arm, and with her gaze, she traced the limb down to his chest, which also appeared to be rather muscled. Maybe these swells did more than she gave them credit for.

The signs of his strength reassured her, and she reached out and poked his chest. "Dane, wake up."

He didn't move. She poked him again. "Dane? It's Marlowe. I have to speak to you."

When he still didn't move, she patted his cheek several times. With lightning speed, he grasped her hand in his and hauled her half onto the bed. He opened his eyes and stared at her. "What are you doing?"

"Let me go!" She struggled, but he wouldn't release her hand. Her feet were all but off the floor. "I need to speak with you. I was just trying to wake you."

He released her hand, and she slid back to the floor as he sat. The bedclothes dipped down, pooling about his waist. She could see his naked back, could see where the bare skin dipped down to his buttocks. He was not wearing any clothing.

Maybe this hadn't been such a prime idea.

He pushed his hair back and out of his eyes, which was hopeless, because it fell right back over his forehead again. But then he turned those deep brown eyes on her. "You shouldn't be in here. It's improper."

Marlowe rolled her eyes. "I don't care about that. Earlier tonight you said I could trust you. Can I still trust you?"

His eyes narrowed. "Is this about what happened in the garden?" He gestured to her throat. She'd forgotten to cover it, and pulled the wrapper about it again.

"Yes. I need you to send for your brother. I need a Bow Street Runner."

"Why?"

"Because I do, that's why. Are you going to help me or not?"

He didn't answer her, merely stared at her for so long she thought he could see right through her. The way his gaze touched her made heat creep from the middle of her chest to her arms and legs and down to her feet. Her heart sped up, pounding so hard she feared it might burst. And her body tingled. She shifted uncomfortably, trying to rid herself of the sensation. What was wrong with her? How was it he could make her feel ill with just a look?

"Turn around," he said finally.

"What?"

"I won't have this conversation while I'm naked in bed. I will have to dress. Turn around. Unless you want to watch?"

"You don't have anything I haven't seen already." But she turned around, because seeing it on other men had never made her heart pound or her cheeks flame. Maybe all the baths had finally ensured she caught a chill that would kill her. That was probably why she felt so warm. She heard him moving about behind her, and finally he said, "You can turn back."

He stood beside the bed, dressed in trousers and nothing else. The firelight played on the hard planes of his chest, and she could not seem to look away for a moment. "You forgot your shirt," she said finally.

"And you forgot to wait until morning to speak with me. Tell me why you think you need my brother."

"No. The less you know, the better."

He crossed his arms over his chest. "You don't really trust me."

"If I didn't trust you, would I be in here right now?" It was really quite difficult to tear her gaze from that bare chest.

He arched a brow. "Do you think I'll ravish you?"

She frowned. "Ravish?"

He made a circular gesture with his hands, as though searching for another word. "Bed you?"

"No. You're far too much of a gentleman for that."

He was before her in an instant, his body almost flush with hers. "I don't feel very much like a gentleman at the moment."

She blinked at him. "You *want* to bed me?"

He gave a sharp laugh and raked a hand through his hair. "How can you be so naive? You must be to come in here and tempt me like this."

Her brows winged upward. "I *tempt* you?"

"Yes. If I weren't holding on to the last vestiges of my honor, I'd—"

She stared at him. His fists were clenched, and his jaw tight. He was really fighting to control himself. And *she* had made him feel this way? Her belly did another roll. She was not at all well, but she couldn't stop herself from asking, "What would you do?"

"This." His arm came around her, strong and steady, and he pulled her against his hard chest. His flesh was hot through the thin material of her night rail. She'd forgotten she was wearing her wrapper, and it had fallen open so she pressed directly against him. She waited for him to crush his mouth against hers. Sometimes men who didn't know she had a quick right knee would try that. But she stared at his chest for a long moment, stared at the way it rose and fell, as though he was out of breath. And when he still didn't take her, she looked up. His hand touched her cheek, the fingers grazing her skin so lightly she shivered. He cupped her chin and looked down at her with an expression she didn't understand.

"What are you doing?"

"Ravishing you," he whispered. His lips brushed

over hers as they had in the garden earlier tonight, and she shivered again. She had most definitely caught a chill. Still, she didn't find his lips unpleasant. Just as she had in the garden, she felt a spark, and she angled her face up so he might kiss her more thoroughly. But he moved with maddening slowness, his lips teasing hers until her whole body ached and strained for something more. She didn't know what was wrong with her. She only knew that she did not want him to stop.

She brought her hands up, and they landed on the bare skin of his waist. She felt him tense, but she didn't draw her hands away. She slid them up his back, feeling his muscles bunch and strain under her fingers. With a low growl, he slanted his mouth over hers, and she dug her fingers into his back to keep herself from spinning out of control. She couldn't breathe, couldn't think, couldn't feel her legs. Every part of her was numb except for where his touch branded her. His lips moved over hers, and she tried to match his movements with her own. When it proved hopeless, she simply surrendered to his kisses, letting him show her what he wanted.

He teased her mouth open, and his tongue dipped inside. She had seen men kiss like this before, and had always thought it the strangest, most disgusting sort of thing. Now she felt a tremor race through her body. Tentatively, she touched her tongue to his, and he hissed in a breath, and the hand on her waist tightened. He withdrew, angling his head and kissing her deeply, but she wanted his tongue again. She touched hers to his lips, and he went rigid. And then his hand moved into her hair, cupping her head and bringing them closer together. His lips had not closed, so she delved farther until his tongue met hers. Again, she felt a small jolt of surprise, as though the house moved beneath her feet.

And then he stroked her tongue with his, and she could not contain a gasp. She was falling, too ill to stand upright any longer. He caught her, lifting her and sweeping her into his arms. And still he didn't stop kissing her. She didn't know where his lips ended and hers began, whether she was kissing him or he was kissing her. She only knew he was holding her, and she was safe. What a strange feeling. Why should she feel safe with this man? She'd so very rarely ever felt safe in her entire life.

She felt the soft mattress beneath her back, and he was bending over her. His mouth left her, and the stubble of his cheek brushed against the skin of her face. His lips traced a hot path from her jaw down to her neck, and that was a completely new experience. His mouth tickled and tantalized until she felt herself arching to give him better access. But instead of continuing his kisses, he rested his forehead against her shoulder.

"Marlowe."

She blinked, shaken out of her trance by his use of her name. Suddenly she realized she was lying on his bed, and the weight on top of her was Dane himself. His large body covered hers. He rested the bulk of his weight on his arms, which were on either side of her, but his legs were between hers, having nudged hers open at some point.

"What are you doing?" she asked, pushing him

back and trying to sit. He didn't fight her, merely rolled off her and lay back on the bed beside her, one hand across his face. She didn't understand it. No man had ever released her without her having to make him aware she knew how to use her fists and her knee. But Dane made no protest, and she glanced at him curiously. He looked so beautiful, lying there in only his trousers. She longed to run her hand over his chest, but she had come to his room for a reason...Satin. Yes. She was wasting time.

"I apologize," he said, his voice muffled by the hand over his face. "As you can see, I'm no gentleman."

She laughed, and he drew his arm away to peer at her. "You find that amusing?"

"Yes. You are the most...gentlemanly gentleman I have ever met. I push you away, and you stop. I didn't even have to use my knee."

He raised a brow. "You've had to do that often?"

"Of course. Sometimes a man drinks too much and forgets I'm not the gang's dell, or one of the cubs thinks he needs to show off to the others. I make sure they remember what's what."

"I see."

"But you! You haven't even tried to touch my bubbies."

"Bu—your bosom?" His gaze slid to it now, and she felt that prickly heat again.

"Most men grab for my bubbies right away."

He raised his brows. "It's not because I don't want to grab them, I assure you. I am exercising enormous restraint." His brow darkened. "Despite repeated temptation."

"And that's why you're a gentleman."

He made no response, simply lay still on the bed beside her, staring at her for a long, long moment. She began to feel as though she must have a wart on her face, because he looked at her so long. "Why are you looking at me like that?"

"Because you confuse me, Marlowe. You're naive one moment and seemingly full of experience the next. I could swear you've never been kissed, but you tell me men paw you routinely."

She flipped onto her knees and glared down at him. "I'm not a bawd. If a man touches me, he gets the benefit of my fist."

"But you didn't hit me."

She opened her mouth and closed it again. She had not seen that argument coming. Why hadn't she hit him? "I liked the way you kissed me," she said slowly, the revelation coming to her as she spoke.

He groaned and closed his eyes.

"Are you ill?" she asked.

He shook his head. "Not in the way you mean."

He didn't speak again, and the silence lengthened. She sat back on her heels, thinking about the difference between Dane and the other men who'd—as he put it—pawed her. He was a gentleman, it was true, but it was more than that. "When you kiss me, I feel a spark," she said.

He opened his eyes. "You said something about sparks in the garden. And a man named Gideon. Is that your lover?"

"*No*. He's a friend."

"A thief?"

"A crony. Me and him, we watch out for each other."

"And he spoke to you of sparks?"

Marlowe ducked her head. She didn't want to talk about this. Why had she even mentioned sparks? She must have something wrong with her head to talk to him like this. "We kissed a few times," she admitted. "When we were younger."

Dane sat. "I see. And?"

She shrugged. "Gid said there was no spark. We made better friends. Besides, Satin would have killed us if he found us prigging."

"And have you ever, ah, prigged?" Dane asked.

She gave him a sidelong glance. "That's a rather personal question."

"You don't have to answer it."

"I told you I'm no bawd," she said, notching her chin up.

"Then you're a virgin." He passed a hand over his face. "What am I doing?" he muttered.

But Marlowe felt suddenly exposed and vulnerable. "What about you? Are you a...a virgin?"

He looked up at her. "We're not talking about me."

She gave him a push then set her hands on her hips. "I told you."

His mouth crooked in a sort of smile. "I suppose fair is fair."

"Exactly."

"No, I'm not. But I'm no rake. I don't debauch virgins."

"I suppose you have a rum-blowen set up somewhere for your convenience."

"A mistress? No. If I did, I wouldn't be half as

frustrated," he muttered.

"I didn't come in here to kiss you."

"No. You want my brother, as does every other woman in the city."

She didn't try to understand him. "I need a Bow Street Runner."

"Why?"

She held up a hand. "I told you—"

He grabbed her wrist. "And now I'm telling *you*. If you want my help, you'd better tell me something. You can start with who did this to you in the garden." He gestured to her throat.

"You want to know who did it?" She was angry now. Why did the idiot man have to be so difficult? "It was Satin. He found me, and he knows where you live, and he wants to crack this house with my help."

Dane stared at her, his expression one of shock.

"I don't want to help him, but I'm dead if I don't. So I figure I have one chance."

"Which is?"

"I get him before he can get me."

Twelve

DANE STARED AT THE GIRL SITTING ON HIS BED IN HER white night rail and flimsy robe. She'd forgotten to cover her neck again, and he could see the red marks Satin had left on her pale skin. It was clear, even in the dim light, the marks were in the shape of fingers. He hadn't seen that earlier. That might be for the best, because if he had, he might have gone after the bastard and killed him.

If the bastard hadn't killed him first. This Satin was obviously fearless. He'd had the gall to accost a woman attending the Duchess of Abingdon's ball, despite the threat of both discovery and harsh reprisal. And why should he fear? What reprisal would there be? If he'd been discovered, all he had to do was reveal Marlowe was not who she seemed. The gentlemen might have made some attempt to protect her in the moment, but no one would protect her tomorrow or next week or next month.

Dane looked at her again, noted she'd washed her hair, washed the blood out. The dark tresses tumbled down her back, and he'd felt the dampness weighing it down. He hadn't actually thought she'd use the bath he'd ordered for her, but now that she had, he could smell the scent of the apricot soap she'd used. It teased him enough that he wanted to lean closer and sniff it, bury his lips in her neck and allow the sweetness to surround him.

He shook his head, uncertain how he'd come to this place. He'd been going about his life, living it the way any titled man would, and then she'd been dropped in without his invitation. He should have had nothing to do with her. She was Brook's concern, not his. But Dane found himself thinking of her far too often. He found himself desiring her more than was wise. He found her kneeling in his bed in the middle of the night, wearing little more than a thin linen wrapper. And what were they speaking of? Destroying a crime lord.

How he missed his old life. He didn't waste time thinking about the plight of the poor or the plans of crime lords. Dane's life had been staid and respectable. It had also been tedious and predictable. He'd done the same things, day in and day out. Saw the same people. Attended the same events. He could have played his part in his sleep.

Now he was awake, and he wasn't certain he liked it. But how did one go back? How did he forget about the poor and the orphans and the thieves? How did he resign himself to that familiar, banal existence? He'd wanted adventure. That was why he'd gone with Brook on that fateful night when they'd taken Marlowe. And now he had an adventure.

He swallowed and cleared his throat. "Might you repeat that last bit?"

She rolled her eyes. He didn't blame her. He would have rolled his eyes if he'd been her. He sounded like such a prig. "I said, I'll get Satin before he can get me."

He did not want to ask the next question, but he couldn't find a way around it. "Are we speaking of murder?"

She gaped at him. "I'm no killer. Besides, how would I mill Satin? I don't have a weapon besides my knife, and he'd just knock it out of my hand."

"Then you want me to…mill him?"

"What? *You?*" She started laughing, and Dane frowned. His frown turned to a scowl when her laugh continued. And continued.

"Why is the idea of me killing Satin so amusing?"

She pressed her lips together and attempted to look serious. "Right. It's just…*you?* Mill Satin?" She dissolved into giggles again, falling over on his bed, weak from laughter.

"I have pistols," he said defensively. "Hunting rifles too. I can shoot."

"And the moment you stepped into Seven Dials, Satin would know you were there. You don't exactly blend in. You'd never get close enough to mill him. But my plan isn't to kill him, at least not that way. I told you, I need your brother or a thief-taker like him. Maybe one whose hands have a little dirt under the fingernails."

"Why?"

"Because I want him to tow Satin out, convince him to go in on a racket, convince Satin it's too prime to pass up. And then he can catch Satin in the act and sell him like a bullock in Smithfield. Lock him in the stone doublet."

He supposed the *stone doublet* referred to Newgate. "The Bow Street Runners would never do something like that. We stamped out that sort of corruption three or four years ago."

Marlowe laughed again, but this time it was a brittle, harsh laugh. "Oh, they do the trick all the time, and they get away with it too."

"But the Home Office conducted an inquiry. The offenders were caught and transported."

Marlowe shook her head, probably amused by his naiveté. And he'd called her naive.

"Why work for your bread when you can trick some young cub into stealing for you? Then you're a hero for catching the thief, and you collect the money from the nobs. Everyone wins. Except the cub."

"My brother would not participate in such a scheme."

"Never said he did, but plenty do. My question is will your brother help me? It would mean catching the arch rogue of the Covent Street Cubs. I need someone good, because Satin will know if he's being gulled."

Dane nodded and was silent. She was clever. He'd known that, but he hadn't known quite how clever until this moment. Her plan could actually work, but not if they employed Brook in the manner she suggested.

"So will you contact your brother, or not?" she asked.

"No," he said.

"Bastard!" She jumped off his bed and stormed toward the door. At the last moment, she turned. "I knew I shouldn't have trusted you. I was a fool to think you'd ever help someone like me."

"Marlowe."

"I'm leaving. Don't try and stop me." She grasped the door latch.

"Marlowe, stop yelling, or you'll wake the house."

"I don't care."

"I do, and if you want my help, you should keep our meeting tonight between the two of us."

Slowly, she turned to face him, her hand still on the latch. "I already told you how you can help. You refused."

"Because your plan won't work."

"And what do you know about it, *Lord* Dane? You've done a lot of scheming, have you?"

"No, but you said yourself that Satin will be suspicious if you send a Runner."

"I said if the Runner isn't convincing."

She was listening now, and Dane slid off the bed and crossed to her. "If you know about these ploys the Runners use, then Satin knows too. Would you ever trust a Runner, no matter how convincing?"

She stared at him, her mouth set in a hard, thin line. "No."

"And you think Satin will?"

She slumped. He could see her shoulders collapse. "No." She shook her head. "Bloody hell. That was my last hope. I'm done for." She looked up at him, her blue eyes round and suspiciously shiny. He wondered how much strength it took for her to hold back the tears. "*You're* done for."

"No, I'm not. I said I wouldn't fetch my brother. I never said I wouldn't help you."

"I'm listening." Her hands fisted on her hips in a show of skepticism he didn't appreciate.

"I'll convince Satin to go in on a—what do you call it? A racket?"

She closed her eyes. "It will never work."

"Why?"

"Because he'll know who you are."

"How? He might know this is the house of the Earl of Dane, but he's never met me. I could be anyone. I could be the younger son of a duke who wants a share of the old man's blunt. And perhaps I need Satin's help for that."

She didn't speak, which he took as a good sign.

"You said yourself I'd never fit in if I showed my face in Seven Dials. So I don't try to fit in. I go as a gentleman and make it known I'm looking for a thief to do a job for me. When Satin takes the bait…" He paused. That was the extent of his plan.

Marlowe's lips relaxed slightly. "We can figure that part out."

Dane smiled, but it was short-lived. "*We?*"

She stepped away from the door. "If you want to make sure Satin bites, then we go to him directly. Otherwise, chances are he just sends Gideon or Beezle to strip the ken. I wouldn't mind seeing Beezle dangle, but the other cubs don't deserve that. I'll take you to Satin. I'll tell him I have an even easier game than pilfering this place."

"How do we make certain he doesn't send one of the, ah, cubs to do the dirty work?"

"I make the racket sound so prime that he'll want it all for himself."

"You think it will work?"

"It has to. We don't have much time, though. We figure out the details and see him tomorrow night."

"Fine. In the meantime, we sleep." He yawned to punctuate his suggestion.

"How can I sleep? I have plans to make. You had better hire additional footmen, in case Satin decides to heave a cough without warning."

Dane waved. "I'll take care of it in the morning. Now, we sleep." He headed back to his bed and reached for his trousers before he realized she was still standing by his door. "Are you staying?" he asked. He almost wanted her to say yes. He *did* want her to say yes. He might have tried to convince her if he didn't know taking her to bed was the absolute worst decision he would ever make.

Well, the second worst decision. He was probably going to get himself killed going after this Satin. Dane sighed. He'd wanted adventure.

"I'm not staying. I just wanted to…"

When she didn't continue, Dane raised a brow. "Catch one more glimpse of my magnificent body?"

She rolled her eyes. "No."

"You wanted a kiss good night? I'd be more than happy to oblige."

"No. Never mind! I would have said thank you, but I forgot how much I hate you." With that, she pulled the door open and stormed out. Dane shook his head. She'd probably woken half the servants. He glanced at the clock—well, she'd woken those not already up and starting their day.

"You're welcome," he muttered, stripping down

and climbing back into bed. But it was a long time before he slept. A long time before he could no longer detect the lingering scent of that apricot soap or hear the echo of her voice.

The next morning—very well, afternoon—he rose, dressed, and considered asking Crawford to send her to his library. But then Dane didn't need the butler to tell him where she was. He knew already. Dane made his way to the dining room, well aware it was too late for breakfast, especially if his mother and sister had eaten then departed at dawn. But when he opened the door, there she was. No surprise, the cook had made certain she was fed. A plate was piled high before her, and from the littering of crumbs around her, he deduced that was not her first serving. Crawford himself stood in the corner, playing his favorite role of silent sentinel.

"Good morning," Dane said to Marlowe.

She scowled at him and stuffed anther sausage in her mouth. So much for his attempt at politeness. Dane took a seat at the head of the table, and Crawford approached. "Tea, my lord?"

"Coffee this morning, Crawford," he said.

"Very good, my lord."

"Did the countess and my sister leave any parting words for me?" he asked. He didn't really want to know, but if his mother had left a message, he was going to have to hear it at some point.

"Yes, my lord. Her ladyship said"—Crawford straightened as though about to give news of the utmost import—"she will not return until that vulgar woman has been removed. I am to send word when Lord and Lady Lyndon have rejected her."

Dane glanced at Marlowe. She'd stopped chewing for a moment, but now she swallowed and took a bite of toast. Her table manners were still quite appalling, though not quite as bad as when she'd first arrived. He supposed she was no longer starving.

"And if Lord and Lady Lyndon do not reject her?" Dane asked.

Crawford sniffed. "The countess left no instructions in that case." He poured Dane coffee and retreated to his corner.

Dane sipped the coffee. He wasn't fond of the taste, but he was still weary from the long night without much rest. He did not expect to rest any more until this ordeal with Satin was quite over. He did not know if Marlowe had slept at all last night either. She was wearing the same dress she had on the day before, and her hair had been brushed and pulled into a simple tail. Either she hadn't allowed the maid to dress it, or she hadn't wanted it pinned up. He liked her with her hair down. She looked more feminine and less like she might knee him in the groin at any moment.

"Miss Marlowe," he said for the benefit of Crawford, "I suppose you and I should have a discussion about the arrangements going forward."

"The…what?" she asked.

Dane rose. "If you would, meet me in the library when you have finished breaking your fast. Crawford, might I see you for a moment?"

Crawford gave Marlowe a suspicious glance, then said, "Yes, my lord."

Dane led the way to the library and closed the door. "I want you to hire several additional footmen. Only men you trust. Perhaps those we have used when we needed more staff for a ball or some such thing. You can find a few men?"

"Of course, my lord." He puffed up his chest. "May I ask why? Nathaniel and Jimmy are quite capable of seeing to anything you need."

Dane took a seat at his desk. "I'm not questioning their skills, but I want men to patrol the perimeter of the house for the next few days."

"Do you fear a theft, my lord?" He glanced back toward the dining room and Marlowe.

Dane did not want to tell Crawford the truth. The fewer people who knew of his plans with Marlowe, the better. "At the ball last night, several of our neighbors mentioned having their homes pilfered. I believe there may be a gang of thieves targeting the area. Until they are apprehended, I want more security."

Crawford's eyes widened, an indication he was shocked. "A gang of thieves, my lord? In Mayfair? I have heard nothing about it."

Of course he hadn't. Dane had made the whole thing up. "The Bow Street Runners do not want the thieves to know they are on to them. I rely on your discretion, Crawford."

"Certainly, my lord."

Dane ran a hand over the top of his kidney-shaped oak desk. He'd sat here so many hours that every grain of the wood was as familiar to him as his own hands. He knew every ink stain, every scratch, every nick. "There's one more thing, Crawford." Dane looked up.

"Miss Marlowe, my lord."

"Yes. Now that my mother and sister have

removed, it's quite improper for the two of us to be living here alone together." No matter that the house had a full complement of servants. Society would see Marlowe—or Lady Elizabeth, if that's who she was—and Dane as being quite alone together. "Even if Brook were here, and God knows where he is of late, it would still be improper. I rely on you to keep this situation from becoming public fodder."

"I will do my best, my lord. Is there no where else the girl might go?"

"Crawford, if she is Lord Lyndon's daughter, we owe her our hospitality. I won't turn her out."

"Of course not, my lord."

A tap on the door drew Dane's attention. "Thank you, Crawford. That will be all."

Crawford nodded and opened the door to Marlowe. With a sigh, Dane beckoned her inside.

❦

Marlowe couldn't have said why, but Dane looked different sitting behind the desk. More earl-like. Perhaps she had become used to seeing him lying in his bed, half-dressed. She actually preferred him that way, which was a thought she did not want to consider too closely.

The butler, his face pinched as usual, passed her and closed the door behind him, leaving her and Dane alone. "He doesn't like me much," she said, stating the obvious.

"He doesn't need to like you," Dane said, rising as she came forward. "But if he did, he would be your most valuable ally. As it is, I have instructed him to hire more footmen." He gestured to a chair on the other side of the desk. Marlowe blinked at it.

"Good. But if Satin wants to dub the gigger, he'll find a way. You can't be on guard forever."

"True, but if all goes according to plan, we won't have to be." He frowned at her. "You do realize that as long as you stand, I am obliged to stand?"

She hadn't realized that. No one had ever stood when she entered a room before she'd come here. "Sorry." She took the seat across from him, and he lowered himself into the chair behind the desk. "This feels stiff," she said.

"Perhaps that is a better arrangement for us. We tend to become...distracted when conversing in less formal situations."

Kissing. That was what he meant by *distracted*. She would never understand why he didn't just say what he meant. He talked around everything so much it made her head spin. "I've been thinking about our plan," she said, rising and pacing. Moving about always helped her to think more clearly. "There's a tavern right across from Satin's flash ken. You and I can get a room there. We'll be close enough to the gang to know what they're up to." She looked over at Dane and realized he was standing again. "Oh, sorry," she said and took her seat again. With a tight smile, he took his place behind the desk.

"And the name of this establishment?"

"I wouldn't exactly call it an *establishment*. But it's called Rouge Unicorn Cellar."

"Interesting."

"I know the husband and wife who own it. They

have no love for Satin, but they won't double-cross him either. We'll have to be careful."

"Always. And what happens after we have our room?"

"That's where we plant the seed." She rose and walked to the bookshelves, wondering how anyone could have possibly read all of the volumes it contained. How did anyone have time? She barely knew a few words, and it took her a painfully long time to piece those together. "Satin will come when he hears I'm back. Then you tell him the story about the duke. You have to make it sound bang-up prime."

"I'll do my best."

She turned. He was standing again, but she couldn't be bothered to sit. "And you can't show any interest in me."

"What do you mean?" He came around from the desk now, and she almost wished he'd stayed behind it. He looked so handsome in his buff breeches and dark blue coat. His boots were polished, and that cravat of his tied perfectly under his chin. As a thief, she had an eye for quality. As a woman, she had an eye for a rum duke. And the Earl of Dane, with his hair falling over his forehead and his deep brown eyes, was most definitely handsome.

"I mean, you can't act like you care about me. Not that you do. Care about me, that is."

His brows rose. "You think I don't care about you?"

She shrugged. "I just mean that if Satin sees any sort of weakness, he'll exploit it. So no kissing." She turned back to the bookshelf, feeling her face heat. She did not know why the discussion should make her insides flutter. Perhaps the sausage had been bad.

"No kissing. I understand." He was behind her now, rather close behind her if his voice was any indication. "What else should I not do?"

"Don't stand up for me. If he calls me names or kicks me, you can't intervene."

Dane blew out a breath, and she felt the warm air on the back of her neck. "I cannot guarantee that."

She turned and almost stumbled back against the bookshelf. Dane was quite close. "You have to. He's not going to hurt me. Not yet, anyway. He still needs me. I'm safe while he needs me."

Dane raised his hand and cupped her cheek. "What you must have been through, Marlowe." He ran a thumb over her cheek. "I wish I could take it all away."

What a strange thing to say. The touch of his thumb made her skin heat further. Her heart was pounding now, and she feared she really was not well. "You can't do that," she said, her voice far more breathless than she had intended.

"Do what?"

"Touch me like this."

"I see. It's more indication that I care about you."

"I didn't say that. I just said you can't appear like you care. Not that you do care."

"And what if I told you I *do* care? What if I told you I care *a great deal* about you?"

She shook her head. She didn't know the game he was playing, and she didn't want to understand it. She wanted to get away. Of course, if she'd wanted to move away, there was no reason she couldn't. He wasn't in her path. Her legs simply refused to move.

"You wouldn't believe me, would you? No one has ever cared about you."

No one had, not like this, at any rate. Gideon was her friend, and he'd done what he could to protect her, but he protected a lot of the cubs.

"Why would they?" she said. "I'm no one. I'm worse than no one. I'm a thief."

"I can't answer for the foolishness of everyone else who has ever met you, but I can tell you why I care about you."

He was standing far too close, and his thumb was making delicious circles on her cheek, dipping down to her jaw. She wished he would move away. If she cast up her accounts on his shoes, he would not feel nearly as tenderly about her. For some reason, she wanted to keep his good opinion. "Why?" she asked, knowing she should not ask, and unable to stop herself.

"Why do I like you? Oh, I've a weakness for intelligent women. I don't meet many." His thumb dipped down to her neck, brushing over the flesh until she shivered.

"Y-you think I'm intelligent?"

"Perhaps cunning is a better word."

She frowned. "I can't even read."

"You'll learn to in no time. Do you know what else I like about you?" His fingers stroked her neck, feathering down to her shoulder. "I like that you're unpretentious."

"Is that good?"

"Very good in my world. And, unlike most women I meet, you have an appetite."

"You mean I'm hungry?"

"Exactly." His hand slid down her arm and encased her hand in his warm one.

"But Crawford said I have the manners of a swine."

Dane laughed. "And you didn't strike him?"

"He moved too quickly." She smiled back.

Dane inhaled slowly. "And, of course, there's that."

"That?"

"Your smile. You're beautiful when you smile." He squeezed her hand, and she looked down at their linked fingers.

"If you're to convince Satin you don't care about me, you shouldn't do that."

"Hold your hand? What about this?" He released her hand and wrapped an arm about her waist, drawing her closer to his broad chest and the warmth of his body. He smelled faintly of soap and a musky spice.

"Not a good idea."

"No?" He leaned forward and kissed her forehead, her eyelid, her nose, her cheek. "I shouldn't do that either."

"Definitely not."

"And this"——he brushed his lips over hers——"is a very bad idea."

She murmured something incomprehensible, because she could no longer think. His lips, like his body, were warm and tasted slightly of coffee, sugar, and cream. His hand on her back flattened, and she felt thrilling little zings where his fingers pressed into her flesh. His mouth claimed hers, his tongue dipping inside to tease her and make her want more. When he broke the kiss, they were both breathless. "It's helpful to do this now," he said. "Just so we're clear on the rules."

"That was definitely against them."

"No kissing on the lips. Understood. What about here?" He touched her neck then brushed it with his lips. She almost jumped from the sensation.

"Def—"

But she didn't finish before his lips skated up her nape to tease her earlobe. And then he slid back down again, kissing her tenderly in the hollow at the base of her throat. "Is that allowed?" he asked, his breath feathering lightly against her skin.

"No."

"Shall I stop?"

"No." That was the wrong answer. She should have said yes, but she couldn't think. Her head was muddled with the mystery ailment, and she couldn't seem to make wise decisions. His lips felt so pleasant against her skin, so warm and delicious. She really didn't want him to stop.

He bent lower, his lips teasing the modest neckline of her blue day dress. His fingers caressed the small pins holding the bodice in place, and he looked up at her. His brown eyes were large with desire, but there was a sense of the playful too. He reminded her of a mischievous cub.

And then he withdrew the first pin.

She felt her own eyes widen.

"Do you want me to stop?" he asked as he withdrew another pin. His gaze was on her, not on the work of his fingers, but she could see the line of flesh he exposed, could feel the material dip where it had been secured over her breasts.

"I..."

Another pin fell victim.

"Yes?"

"W-what are you going to do?"

"Kiss you." Another pin opened, and the bodice folded over. "Nothing more." He reached up and pushed the material down from her bosom. She was still dressed. She wore stays and the chemise under the gown, but she was quite aware that the stays pushed her bubbies up so they swelled over the top of the chemise. And now they were aching uncomfortably. They felt heavy, and the points were hard and sensitive.

His warm hands slid down, curving so they rested on either side of her chest, just on her ribs and directly under her breasts. "May I?" he asked, ever the gentleman.

Yes, she thought. Whatever he was asking, the answer was yes. "May…" She could not seem to utter a word. Her tongue felt clumsy in her mouth.

"May I kiss you?" One of his thumbs extended, brushing over her hard point. "Here?"

"Yes," she whispered.

"Good," he said. "I think I might have died if you'd said no." He lowered his lips and brushed them against the swells of her flesh. Her skin tingled, and she felt a shot of heat in her lower belly. With his tongue, he traced a path to the other side and gave her tiny, torturous kisses. At some point she'd grabbed his arms, and she dug her fingers in now, using his strength to keep herself upright. Her legs felt wobbly. Judging by her list of symptoms, she probably had the plague.

He dipped his tongue in the crease between her

cleavage, and she let out a low moan. Inexplicably, she arched her back, pushing herself toward him.

"More?" he asked.

She should say no, but she wanted to see what else he would do. "If Satin suspects—"

"He's not here," Dane said, his breath warm on her flesh. "And I want to see you. May I see you?" His gaze was on her again, and he waited ever so patiently for her response. Marlowe knew if she told him no, he would stop. He would never have forced himself on her, though he was strong enough to overpower her. Not that he would have needed much strength, considering her current condition.

"Yes," she heard herself say.

"Thank you," he said simply. She almost wanted to smack him for his politeness, and then he reached up and tugged her chemise down, revealing her. She thought he might push his face into her chest, as she'd seen men do to the bawds at the Rouge Unicorn Cellar, but Dane didn't move at all. He merely looked at her, and he looked for so long she began to think there might be something wrong.

"I know they're big. Too big," she said. She moved to tug her chemise back, but he caught her hand.

"They're perfect," he said. His gaze met hers again. "You are perfect."

"No, I'm not. And they're not perfect. They're a nuisance, especially when I need to look like a boy."

"But I don't want you to look like a boy," he said. "You have the body of a woman with all of its curves." One hand caressed the slope of her heavy flesh, warming her. "And softness." He cupped her and squeezed gently. "And the hardness too." One of his thumbs brushed over her distended peak, making her gasp. "I like your nipples most of all," he said. "They're hard and pink and waiting for me to kiss them. May I kiss you here?" His thumbs caressed her nipples, and she thought she might die from the pleasure of his touch.

"Oh, yes."

He smiled and looked down at her chest again, at her nipples. "First I will kiss you here." He traced his lips over the swell of her bubbies and then around and down underneath. She trembled as he repeated the gesture on the other side. And then his thumb brushed against a nipple again, rolling it in a circle, while his wet, warm mouth closed on the other. At first his tongue teased her flesh, swirling around and flicking her until she was breathless. And then, even as his finger plucked at her exposed nipple, his lips closed on the other, and he sucked gently.

A shot of pure pleasure ripped through her, and she moaned despite herself. He'd pushed her up against the bookshelf now, and she could feel the spines of the volumes cool and hard against her warm back. He licked her again, and then his thumb replaced his tongue, and he took her other nipple into his mouth. It felt even better than the first, and she couldn't stop her head from lolling back until it pressed the books deeper into the shelf.

"You are so lovely," Dane said, lifting his lips. She opened her eyes and saw he was looking up at her. "You cannot know how much I want you right now."

"Show me," she said, her voice husky as his hands cupped her again.

"I would like to, but I'm not going to take you here, against a library shelf."

She closed her eyes then opened them again, trying to clear her head. What was she doing? She was no bawd. She didn't want a swollen belly or a brat to care for. "We can't do this."

He didn't argue. He merely nodded and released her. With care, he pulled her chemise back into place and tried to adjust her stays. She pushed his hands away. "I'll do it." She hadn't noticed when he'd set the pins on the shelf, but now he gathered them and wordlessly handed them to her. Then he showed her his back, she assumed to give her privacy while she righted her dress. Her fingers shook when she tried to pin the material in place, but she finally managed it. By then her cheeks had cooled and she wasn't quite so breathless.

"We should probably discuss our plan further," he said, still giving her his back. "I assume the sooner we start, the sooner this will be over."

She wanted to ask him what he meant by *this*. His dealings with her or the ordeal with Satin? But she didn't. Instead, she said, "You may turn around now. If you're ready, we can leave as soon as I tell you the game."

Thirteen

TWO HOURS LATER, DANE STOOD OUTSIDE THE ROUGE
Unicorn Cellar and decided he was daft. He supposed
he had been to Seven Dials once or twice on some
business, but he'd never been the sort of gentleman
who liked to visit the rookeries. He knew young
bucks who enjoyed that sort of thing. They liked the
danger or the change of scenery or the knowledge
they were defying their parents' wishes. Dane liked
comfort, a good brandy, and to keep the peace.

It was too late to keep the peace. His mother had
left Derring House in a huff, and Marlowe had been
disrupting his life since the first moment he'd laid
eyes on her. One look at the Rouge Unicorn Cellar,
and he rather doubted he would have either comfort
or good brandy inside. But he'd never been one to
shirk his duty. He couldn't leave Marlowe to deal
with this Satin by herself, and Dane couldn't risk his
house being pilfered again, especially when his mother
and sister might be home. Satin had to be stopped,
and Marlowe thought she knew how to do it. Dane
wasn't entirely clear about her plan, either, but he

knew his role. He was the youngest son of the Duke of Yorkshire. As far as he knew, there was no Duke of Yorkshire, but Marlowe hadn't seemed concerned about that. She said the title sounded important and wealthy, and Dane doubted this Satin was the sort to read Debrett's.

So here they stood, outside the public house in Seven Dials. She had paused to take stock of things, she said, and he gazed about him and resisted the urge to press a handkerchief to his nose. The stench was foul. Raw sewage lay in the streets wherever residents tossed it out windows. Piles of dirt and trash provided obstacles or convenient seats for the residents of the rookery. And Dane had the feeling every resident of the place was out of doors. Children were everywhere, swarming the streets, sitting in doorways, crawling in dirty alleys. Men and women alike sat idle on stoops or on the side of the street, appearing, for all intents and purposes, to simply be resting wherever they had fallen. He'd been propositioned by prostitutes at least half a dozen times since they'd walked past the large pillar that marked the entrance to Seven Dials. Marlowe, who was now dressed as a boy in trousers and a loose shirt, shooed the women away, sometimes calling them by name. The most recent altercation, with a woman Marlowe had called Cal, had almost come to blows. Marlowe had showed her dagger, and the woman backed down, grumbling all the way.

Dane wondered what he would have done if Marlowe had not won the day. Would he have been obliged to couple with the fearsome Cal? He shuddered. She'd had about three teeth in her mouth, something moving in her stringy hair, and open sores on her face. He did not think he could have completed the act if she'd been the one paying him.

He'd had his pocket picked several times too, and he wasn't certain if he still possessed his handkerchief. After the first pickpocket lifted his purse, Marlowe had gone after the lad and retrieved it. She hadn't given it back, either. The next few times, she'd just shooed the children away before he even knew he'd been targeted. So many children were begging and thieving. He should have looked around and felt vindicated. Wasn't this what he argued in Parliament? The rookeries were breeding grounds for crime, full of lazy men and women who'd rather steal than do an honest day's work. But he only felt sick as he looked around him at the sheer numbers of those suffering. It was overwhelming. England was supposed to be the greatest nation in the world. Why were these people allowed to live like this in the nation's capital? And why hadn't he ever cared before?

"Come on," Marlowe said finally, gesturing toward the door of the public house. "Everyone's asleep right now, but Satin usually posts a lookout. If we've been spotted, we'll not be alone for long."

Dane followed her into the dark tavern, stooping to pass through the low transom. Cheap candles burned inside, filling the room with the odor of tallow, but it was still difficult for him to see where he was stepping. "It doesn't look like everyone is asleep," he said, referring to the half-dozen men in the tavern and the prostitute looking to advertise her wares. "The streets were teeming with life."

Marlowe shook her head. "Just wait until dark. In a few hours, the crowds will be so thick you'll have to jostle to pass through. Let me speak to Barbara and secure a room." She moved away, leaving him to stand alone in the center of the tavern.

The prostitute was on him like a flea on a dog. "'Ello, guv." She reached out and stroked her hand over his coat. "You look like a gent what knows how to have a good time. Marge here is a very good time." She licked her lips in a way he supposed was an attempt to be lascivious, but the girl was painfully thin and younger than his sister. She looked healthier than the one Marlowe had called Cal, but not much.

"Have you eaten today?" he asked.

Marge's thin brows rose. "Hopin' a penny from you might buy me somethin' to eat, guv."

"Order whatever you like," he said. "I'll pay."

Her eyes immediately turned suspicious. "And what do I have to do in return?"

"Nothing. I'm not interested in your services. You just look hungry."

"I'm 'ungry too, guv," the man at a nearby table said.

"And I'm thirsty," a large man with a thin layer of dirt on his clothes called out. "Maybe you could buy us all a glass of Blue Ruin and a plate of meat and potatoes."

Dane saw he had made a misstep. If he refused, the men would surely not take it kindly.

"He's not buying anyone anything," Marlowe said. Somehow she was at his side again, and this time she'd brought an older woman who wore a clean dress and apron. "He's with me, and he doesn't have a cent on him. I saved him from a gang outside St. Giles, who pilfered everything but the clothes on his back."

A few of the patrons muttered curses, and Marge spit on his boots before Marlowe gave her a look that sent her running.

"What are you doing?" Marlowe hissed at him. "Are you trying to get your throat cut? We're here to meet Satin, not attract every mort and rogue in the area."

"My mistake," Dane said, spreading his hands. "Just trying to help."

"Don't."

The woman beside Marlowe cleared her throat, and Marlowe turned to her. "Lord Maxwell, this is Barbara."

Barbara made a passable curtsy. "Your lordship. I'm right honored to have you in my establishment. Marlowe says you need a room."

"I do. Do you have any available?"

"Course. I'll give you the best room in the house, I will. Just let me wake that lazy husband o' mine. Once he's up, it's all yours." And off she went.

Dane blinked. "Does she mean to give us her own room?"

Marlowe shrugged. "It's probably the best one they have. Don't worry," she said, gesturing to an empty table. "We won't be here long enough to inconvenience them, and you're paying them for it. I wouldn't chouse Barbara. She's a friend."

Dane put his hand on the table and then lifted it again, rubbing his newly sticky fingers together. "What do we do now? Wait?"

She nodded and leaned back in her chair, looking as though she was quite accustomed to waiting. With the cap covering her long dark hair, and the boys' clothing, she didn't look at all like the woman he'd danced with at the Abingdon ball just last night. Her vivid blue eyes were shadowed by her cap, and she kept them down, seeming to know they might give her away.

Had he ever thought she would make a charming countess? Perhaps he hadn't voiced the idea aloud, but the notion had crossed his mind. She was the first woman he'd ever met who aroused any interest beyond a night of fleeting pleasure. He genuinely liked her, and seeing her in this environment, he respected her. It could not have been easy to survive under these conditions, but she'd done it. She was fearless, confident, and cunning. He'd never met a woman like her, and he didn't think he ever would again.

His thoughts ended abruptly when the man covered with a fine layer of dirt and stinking of something rotten took the empty chair at their table.

Marlowe looked up. "Go away, Bentoit."

"Why? I'm just being polite. Haven't seen you around for awhile, Marlowe. Found a new game?"

"That's not your business."

"Maybe your friend can help me with my business. Maybe he has friends who need the services of a man like me." Bentoit gestured to Dane.

"No, he doesn't."

Dane cleared his throat, which itched from the smoke in the room. Finally, a man who was engaged in labor. Dane felt he should take an interest. "What sort of work do you do, Mr. Bentoit?"

His chest puffed up. "Resurrection man, my lord. The best there is."

"Resurrection man?"

"He's a grave robber," Marlowe interjected. "The worst of the worst. I don't know why Barbara allows you in here. Why don't you go to the Fortune of War with the rest of your kind?"

Bentoit sniffed. "Stinks too much."

"You stink too much," Barbara said, coming up behind them. "Off with you."

Grumbling, Bentoit shuffled off. Barbara curtsied again. "Your room is ready, my lord."

"Thank you." Grave robbers? Pickpockets? Dane felt as though he'd stepped into another world. He supposed he had. He rose and followed Marlowe and Barbara into an even darker section of the building. Barbara held a candle, or they would have been plunged into utter darkness. At the end of a long hallway, she opened a door and revealed a small room with a hastily made bed, a chair piled with clothes, and a scarred wardrobe.

"'Ere it is then," she said, looking pleased with herself. "If you need anything, just call."

Marlowe stepped inside, but Dane hesitated. "Is there a lamp?"

"No," Barbara said, "but you can 'ave me candle if you want to pay extra."

"No," Marlowe said at the same time Dane said, "Yes." He gave Marlowe a look. "Yes," he reiterated and took the candle from Barbara. She left, shutting the door behind her, and Dane held the candle aloft then quickly lowered it again. Better if he didn't see the room closely. "Do you think we might at least request clean sheets?"

Marlowe shook her head. "It's your coin."

"I don't like filth or darkness."

"Get used to them," she said. "Seven Dials has more than its fair share of both, and not much else."

"How did you live here?"

She shrugged, pushed the clothes off the chair, and sat. "It's not so hard if you don't know any better. The things you have—your food, your beds, your"—she seemed to flounder—"your carpets. I didn't know people lived like that. I'd been in houses when Satin gave me a better-racket, but they were nothing like your house. Now I wonder how I'll go back."

"You're not going back," Dane said. "After we rid the world of Satin, you're never coming back here."

She stared at him for a long time. "You mean if Lord and Lady Lyndon claim me."

No, that was not what Dane had meant at all. "I said never, and I meant never."

"Oh, really? And where will I live? With *you*?"

Dane realized he had not thought this out. He'd spoken from emotion rather than logic, which was not like him at all. "I am certain I could find you a place to live."

Her brows rose. "As your mistress? I'm no courtesan, and I'm not going to be paid to bed you or any man."

"That's not what I meant. You must know I would never suggest that."

"And you must know I have no choice but to come back here and live as I was."

Now he was annoyed. "You prefer thieving to honest work?"

"Honest work? How much do you pay your maids annually? Six pounds? Eight? I can make that in a month—in a night, if all goes well. I could make more than that as a beggar. Why do you think so many take to the streets, begging? Because honest work is hardly honest when the only one profiting is the rich man who owns the workplace."

She was right. Dane knew it, and he hated to accept it. Even if she had been a man, she had no skills, and without those, she could hardly expect to find decent employment. His opponents in Parliament had often argued as much, but he'd drowned them out or turned a deaf ear. He couldn't ignore the truth any longer.

"I have no other choice," she said, finally.

"We will find you another choice."

A soft knock sounded on the door, and Dane looked at Marlowe, who already had her dagger in hand. "Who is it?" she asked.

"A friend." It was a man's voice, which made Dane nervous. Barbara was supposed to fetch them if and when Satin or one of his cubs arrived at the public house.

Marlowe did not seem troubled. Her face broke into a beatific smile that all but stunned Dane, and she rushed to the door. She flung it open and then threw herself into the arms of the man on the other side. Dane immediately wanted to kill the swine. Perhaps the man felt some of Dane's animosity, because his gaze met Dane's. He was tall and thin, with dark hair and threadbare clothes. His skin was rather dark from either dirt or being outdoors a great deal, and he had a vicious scar across one temple, dipping into a dark eyebrow. He looked young, though not as young as Marlowe.

"Gideon, I presume," Dane said.

The man sneered at him. "What do you know about it?" Marlowe had stepped back, and he looked down at her. "Who's this gentry cove? A new bubble?"

"No." Marlowe glanced back at Dane, and he noticed she didn't move out of the other man's embrace. Dane had the urge to snatch her back. He did not like to see the other man's dirty hands on her. "I can explain, but we'd better go somewhere we can talk."

Dane gestured inside. "You can talk here."

Marlowe and Gideon shook their heads, and Dane felt heat rise to his face. "If you wish to be *alone*," he said, "I can take a walk."

"No!" Marlowe said quickly. "Half of St. Giles will descend on you. There's a door leading to an alley in the back. We'll step out there." She began to move away, but Dane grabbed her elbow and tugged her back into the room. Gideon moved forward as though to protect her, but she held up a hand, staying the lad.

Dane pulled her aside and murmured, "I don't like you going off with him."

"He's an old friend," she said, casting Gideon a glance. "There's no danger."

"He works for Satin."

She shook her head. "He has no more love for Satin than we do. We need to make certain Sir Brook received our message. I can ask Gideon to do that."

"You trust him that much?" Dane asked.

"With my life." She moved away again, but Dane had not released her arm. With a tug, he hauled her up against him.

"Be careful." He lowered his lips, and without waiting for her permission, captured her mouth with his. The kiss was long and deep and possessive. He was being an absolute idiot. He knew that, but he couldn't seem to help it. He needed to claim her.

She didn't kiss him back, but she didn't resist either, and when they parted, her cheeks were rosy and her breath short. "Why did…you do that?" she asked.

"So you wouldn't forget me. I'll be here, waiting for you." Slowly, he released her arm. She stood pressed against him for a moment longer and then stepped back and fled through the open door. Gideon stood in the doorway, and the two men's gazes locked. Finally, he moved to follow Marlowe, and Dane sat in the chair and cursed himself for a fool.

❦

"What the devil was that?" Gideon asked when they were in the dark alley. It stank more than Marlowe remembered, and was almost as dark as the window-less room, although they were outside, and there should have been light. She was careful to watch her step as she moved away from the door and turned to face Gideon.

"Nothing," she said. "Where is Satin? Tell me all the news."

"Satin? All's snug." She relaxed slightly. Gideon's mouth thinned. "With that gentry cove, it didn't look like *nothing* to me."

Marlowe blew out a breath. It hadn't felt like nothing to her, either. Her heart was still pounding. Perhaps it was Dane himself who made her ill. She had felt fine until he'd kissed her. "I don't have to explain myself. You've kissed plenty of girls."

"Girls, yes, but I ain't never kissed one of *them*."

"I don't want to talk about this."

"Oh, you don't want to talk about this," Gideon said, mocking her with an upper-class accent. "Too high and mighty for me now."

"No! I just don't see how me kissing Dane has anything to do with anything."

"Then let me explain," Gideon said, leaning close. "He's one of them. He'll use you and discard you. I seen it a 'undred times."

"I have too. Do you think I'm that stupid? I'd never fall into that trap. I'm not his ladybird."

"Then why did he kiss you?"

She shrugged. It was a question she kept asking herself. "I don't know."

"You may not want to be his ladybird, but he has other ideas."

"Then he'll be sorely disappointed."

Gideon nodded, studying her face. "You're pretty," he said finally. Marlowe felt the heat explode in her cheeks, and she ducked her head.

"Have you been drinking?" she asked.

Gideon tipped her chin up. "No. I mean, I always knew it, but now that I see you without all the dirt, I see how fine you really are. I see why he wants you."

She snorted. "*You* never did." With a gasp, she covered her mouth. She hadn't meant to say it aloud, but now she couldn't take it back. And now he knew that she'd cared for him as more than just a friend. Did she still feel that way? All she could seem to think of lately was Dane.

Gideon shook his head. "Because I was never good enough for you."

"Oh, and he's too good."

"Do you think he's going to marry you?"

"Of course not! He's an earl. He lives in Mayfair."

Gideon's eyes narrowed. "So he's the one. I thought so."

"What does that mean?"

"Satin is down. He's been watching you."

"I know. He found me in the garden at the duchess's ball." Gideon gave her an incomprehensible look, and Marlowe laughed. "I know. Can you imagine it? Me, at a ball!"

"It's not so hard, if I picture you in a dress."

"Satin found me and threatened me. He wants to crack the earl's house, and he wants my help."

"But you're in love with the earl and don't want to help."

"Don't be daft! I'm not in love with him! But I don't want to rook from him either. He's...different. And his sister is kind and sweet. I don't want to hurt them." She glanced behind her. "And I'm tired of being Satin's crony. I know a way to get rid of him."

Gideon sucked in a breath. "You're going to find yourself in an eternity box."

"I'm dead anyway," she said. "Satin will never let me go. He'd kill me before he let me go free, and if I stay with him, how long until he goes into one of his rages and kills me, like he did Sammy or Zachariah?"

Gideon's gaze lowered to the ground. They never spoke the names of the dead out loud. Never talked about what happened when one crossed Satin, but they'd all seen the boys beaten to bloody mush then dumped in the river like trash.

"I don't need to marry Dane," Marlowe said. "I have another chance. Remember that Bow Street Runner? The one who thought I was Elizabeth? He's Dane's brother. He thinks I'm the lost daughter of the Marquess of Lyndon."

"Are you?"

"I don't know, but I want the chance to find out." She paused and swallowed. "Will you row in my boat?"

Gideon took a deep breath and let it out. He pushed his hands in his pockets and toed the ground. "Tell me your game, and I'll do what I can."

She hugged him, but he didn't hug her back. Quickly, she summarized the plan, and Gideon nodded. "It might work. Will the Runner agree?"

"He's Dane's brother. We sent him a note to meet us tomorrow night. Will you see whether he received it?"

Gideon looked as though he might choke. "You want me to *look for* a Runner?"

"He can't bone you for associating with Satin." But Runners did all sorts of unscrupulous things, and Gideon knew it as well as she. She would just have to hope her instincts about Brook were not wrong.

"I'll go. Will you still be here when I get back?"

She nodded. "We rented Barbara's room."

Gideon's brows rose. "A bed and everything. You're moving up in the world." He leaned forward and kissed her gently on the cheek. Her skin tingled, but she didn't feel ill. She also didn't feel sparks.

"Keep your eyes open, Marlowe."

"I always do."

"Not just with Satin, with your gentry cove too."

She waved his advice away. "I can handle him." She started for the door back inside the public house, but Gideon stepped in front of her.

"One last thing. I don't think he's too good for you. If he won't make you his comfortable importance, then he's not good enough." And with that, he disappeared into the shadows of the alley.

❧

Gideon strolled along the familiar streets of London, hands in his pockets and head down. He wanted anyone who noticed him to see a man strolling, not looking for attention or trouble. He didn't know where this Brook might be found, but he thought the office of the Runners on Bow Street, across from the Brown Bear flash ken, a good place to start.

He wasn't looking for a racket, but it was hard not to see opportunities as he walked. There was a man who would make an easy bubble. There was a woman whose wipe he could have had without blinking an eye. But Gideon ignored the impulse to take advantage of the easy game. He wasn't a rook at heart. He'd wanted to stay alive, and he'd become a thief, but it was out of necessity, not because he loved to bilk. Most of the time he thought about his game later and hoped they didn't need the coins he'd dived for or the items he'd filched. He always felt remorse for what he'd taken. Not that he'd ever admit it. Hot coals to the bottoms of his feet wouldn't have persuaded him to admit to such a weakness.

So it wasn't hard now to ignore the opportunities to take what wasn't his. He couldn't stop himself from noticing them, but he didn't have to act. In any case, he had a mission. He'd promised Marlowe he'd find this Sir Brook. He must have been an idiot to agree to go to Bow Street's office, but it wouldn't be the first time he was an idiot for Marlowe.

He'd been in love with her since the first time he saw her. How could he not be? She had those huge blue eyes, and when she looked at him, his heart clenched in his chest. He'd taught her everything he knew about diving and the rest of the rackets. She didn't need to be told a thing twice, and after she learned all he had to teach, she taught him a few things.

He loved watching her work. Loved watching her laugh. Loved watching her sleep—that was where his idiocy came in. He'd spent many an hour when he should have been sleeping, watching her. And when she'd finally asked him to kiss her, he'd been as nervous as a corny-faced virgin. Kissing her had been everything he'd imagined—and he'd imagined it quite a lot—and more. He hadn't been able to get enough of her, though he'd made himself go slowly.

It hadn't taken more than two or three times kissing her before he realized she wasn't affected like he was. She must have found his kisses pleasant, but her cheeks weren't flushed, her heart wasn't pounding, her breath wasn't gone. He was in an agony of desire every time he was near her, but she was blissfully unaffected. So he'd told her they didn't have a spark, and ended things before they'd begun. There were other women, and he lost himself in a few of those, trying to forget Marlowe.

He almost thought he'd done it, too, until she opened Barbara's door, and Gideon had seen *him* standing there. And then all the feelings had rushed back, and Gideon had wanted to kill the nob, because Gideon could see how Marlowe looked at the swell. She was in love with him. All the things he'd wanted her to feel for him, she felt for that swell, who probably didn't deserve her. Who probably thought she was just some rook he could use and discard.

Something prevented Gideon from pointing this out to Marlowe. She wouldn't have listened anyway, that was true, but there was something else. He stopped now, a few blocks from Bow Street, and stared at an apple cart while he sorted it out.

He hadn't told her because seeing her with that nob, seeing her clean and dressed in fresh clothing, was right. He'd always known she would rise to the top if she could escape Satin. She belonged with a swell like that, not in the rookeries amidst the filth and grime.

"Apples! Fresh apples! Only a bob for an apple," the seller bellowed, and Gideon blinked. He dug in his ragged trousers and found a shilling. Tossing it to the apple seller, he picked a red apple and bit into it. It was old and a bit mealy, but Gideon had eaten worse. He tossed the core into the street when he was done and turned onto Bow Street. No matter what happened with Marlowe's swell, she'd decided to rid the world of Satin, and Gideon couldn't argue with that idea. He'd thought about doing it a thousand times, but Satin would have seen it coming immediately. He didn't trust Gideon, and he had his little rat Beezle watching Gideon all the time.

Satin would never see it coming from Marlowe. She was a girl, and Satin didn't think girls were good for much more than a tumble. Only Gideon's insistence that Marlowe was the best in the gang had kept Satin from selling her to some dirty cove for a handful of shillings. She was smart enough to keep her feminine charms covered as much as she could. She didn't want to remind Satin she was a girl any more than Satin needed to be reminded, but the older she grew, the harder it was not to see it, no matter what she did to hide it.

Her eyes were too pretty, her lips too full, her cheeks too soft. And her body. Even when she bound her breasts, there was nothing she could do about the flare of her hips or the roundness of her bottom. And so Gideon pushed down his natural reluctance to enter the Runners' office and opened the door. If Marlowe didn't get out from under Satin now, she never would.

A clerk looked up when Gideon entered, his mouth curling down in a familiar gesture of distaste. Gideon tried not to mind. He knew he was scarred, dirty, and looked like what he was—a common rook—but in his mind the Runners were a hundred times worse than him. He was an honest thief. He didn't pretend to be anything else. The Runners acted like their hands were lily-white, when they were as dirty as any cub in Seven Dials.

"What do you want?" the clerk said. Behind him, Runners moved about, going in and out of doors. The floors creaked as boots clomped over the wood. A few of the men looked up curiously then went back to their papers or their conversations. The place had a busy hum and smelled like spoiled food.

Gideon gave the man his most charming smile. "I want to see Sir Brook Derring."

The clerk, who was little more than a boy himself, laughed. "Get in line. Every female in London wants to see Sir Brook."

Gideon kept smiling, though his fist itched to knock the lad on his freckled nose. The mark he left would give the puppy's doughy face some color. "I'm not a wench. I have business with Sir Brook."

"What's your name?"

"Gideon."

The clerk shook his head. "He didn't mention a Gideon. You'd better be on your way."

"Is he here?" Gideon asked, standing rooted in place.

"What's it to you?"

Gideon moved quickly, so quickly the clerk never knew what happened. One minute the man was sitting there, feeling all safe and pretentious, and the next minute Gideon's knife was pressed to the boy's soft throat. "The question is, what's it to you?"

Gideon was aware a hush had fallen over the room, and half a dozen Runners were giving him the eye. If he so much as pricked the little clerk, his neck would be stretched in a hangman's noose before nightfall. And Gideon liked his neck just the way it was, thank you very much. Now that he had the clerk's attention, not to mention the rest of the Bow Street office, they could do business. "I want to see Sir Brook Derring," Gideon said slowly and loud enough so the other Runners could hear. "If he's not here, tell me where to find him.

"He's here," the clerk stammered, glancing up at Gideon with terror in his eyes. "He doesn't want to be disturbed."

"He'll want to be disturbed for what I have to tell him," Gideon said.

"And what do you have to tell me?" a voice said from behind Gideon. Gideon couldn't help but smile. Finally. The man himself. But he didn't remove the knife from the clerk's throat. He wanted to speak before he was hauled away. That was his only chance.

Gideon raised his eyes and searched for the man who'd spoken. He found him, a tall man with dark blond hair and cunning brown eyes. Gideon took one look at the man's eyes and knew he'd get nothing past him. Gideon made a point of glancing at the other men. "It's a private matter," he said. "This place has too many ears."

"I'm going to hang you up by the ears, if you don't start talking," Sir Brook said. He didn't move, didn't raise his voice, but the hair stood up on Gideon's neck. He'd rather die before he said Satin's name or gave anything away about Marlowe's plan. He'd long known Satin must have paid a few Runners to look past his activities beyond Seven Dials. For all Gideon knew, Satin's cronies were listening right now.

"Two words," Gideon said, pulling the knife away from the clerk's throat. "Lady Elizabeth."

As soon as the knife was gone, several Runners rushed Gideon. They grabbed his arms, and he felt their fists in his belly. He would have doubled over if they hadn't been holding him, and then suddenly he was released and almost fell flat on his face. He dropped to his knees, coughing and trying to catch his breath. A pair of highly polished black boots stood before him. "Stand up and come with me."

Gideon pushed to his feet, and ignoring the hard stares of the Runners who looked as though they'd have liked nothing better than to slit his throat, he followed Sir Brook deeper into the building.

Fourteen

DANE HAD PACED THE ROOM ENOUGH TIMES TO KNOW it was four steps across the room and four back again. His lips were still warm from where they'd touched Marlowe's, and he couldn't help but wonder if she was kissing Gideon now. She'd been gone longer than he liked.

He hated this feeling of helplessness. He wanted to go after her, but he had no idea how to find her. This was her world, and he was a visitor—and not a welcome one. He heard a creak in the hallway and turned to see the door open soundlessly. He pulled Marlowe into his arms before she had the chance to say a word. "Where the devil were you?"

She gave him a confused look. "I told you."

"Where's he?"

"He's gone to see if your brother received our note. I told you he'd help us. He has no love for Satin." She pushed out of his arms and tucked an errant lock of hair that had come loose from her cap back behind her ear.

Dane resisted the urge to pull her back into his arms. "What do we do now?"

Marlowe shrugged and moved past him. The room was so small, she couldn't help but brush up against him. "Wait. Barbara will come for us when Satin turns up."

"And you're certain he'll want to see you? Should we seek him out?"

She gave him a look that told him she thought his idea beyond the pale. "We wait for him to come to us."

She sat on the bed then stood back up again, as though the bed had burned her. Dane raised his brows. She was doing everything she could to avoid him touching her, and that only made him want to touch her more. He moved closer. "Are you concerned? You seem a bit on edge."

"I'm perfectly confident."

He moved closer, and she stepped back.

"Do I make you nervous?"

Her eyes widened. "No!"

He moved closer again. Now he could smell the sweet scent of apricot soap on her skin. "Then why do you keep moving back?"

"Because I feel ill when you're near." She closed her eyes as though shocked at her words. He was shocked as well.

"I'm sorry, but there it is," she said with her characteristic bluntness. Her cheeks were flaming now, and the longer he stood close to her, the quicker her breathing became.

"I see. Can you tell me your symptoms?"

"My…what? Can you stand back? I can't think with you standing so close."

"Interesting. What else is wrong?"

She scowled at him. "I'm hot. All over. And my skin feels tingly." She raised a brow as though she expected him to challenge her.

"Yes, your skin does look rather flushed. May I?" He lifted a hand and brushed the back of it across her cheek. "You're not warm to the touch, but your eyes…" He leaned closer, and her breath hitched.

"What's wrong with my eyes?" she asked.

"They're huge." He didn't remove his hand from her cheek, and she didn't move away this time. "What are your other symptoms?"

"My belly." She put a hand over it. "It feels like I might cast up my accounts at any moment. It's all…" She waved a hand, looking for the word. "Fluttery."

Dane could hardly keep from smiling, but he worked to keep his expression sober. "Flutters in the belly, flushed skin, large eyes. What if I do this?" He leaned down and lightly brushed his lips over hers, once, twice, three times. He pulled back, and she stared at him. It hardly seemed possible, but her eyes were even larger, and so blue as to be almost violet.

"I can't breathe," she said. She touched her chest. "The air catches here."

"Do you know what I think, Marlowe?"

"No, and I'm not sure I care. You're no doctor."

"I'm not," Dane agreed, though he doubted she would have trusted a doctor either. She'd probably never been to one. "But I don't need to be a doctor to tell when a woman is aroused."

She blinked at him.

"You want me, Marlowe. And I want you too." He didn't wait for her to deny it or to argue. Instead, he lowered his mouth to hers again, this time applying slightly more pressure as he teased her lips with his. She stepped back, and he caught her about the waist with his free hand. The other he slid up her cheek and into her hair. With a flick of the wrist, he sent her cap tumbling from her head. He threaded his hand through her thick locks until they, too, tumbled down about her shoulders.

Dane pulled back, pausing to look at her. With those violet eyes, the pretty pink in her cheeks, and the flush of red on her lips from his mouth, she was irresistible. "I do want you, Marlowe, probably more than you want me, but I'm not going to do anything you don't agree to."

He lowered his mouth to hers again, but paused just before pressing his lips to hers. His breath mingled with hers, and he brought a hand skating over her velvet cheek. His thumb pressed against the corner of her mouth. "May I?"

"I-I don't understand what you're doing."

"I want to kiss you." His thumb caressed her lips. "Here."

"Oh."

"Tell me yes."

She paused, and he feared for a moment she might say no. He feared he would have to release her, and he knew it would be anguish. He didn't think he could ever let her go. Finally, she breathed the word he wanted. "Yes."

He took her mouth with his, tasting her lips and teasing her until she opened for him. He slid inside, exploring her, stroking her, showing her with his tongue what he wanted to do with his body. She allowed the invasion for a long moment—and then she kissed him back. He almost lost control then. The tentative touch of her tongue to his, followed by longer, more erotic strokes, undid him. He groaned softly, and she pulled back. "You don't like it?"

"I love it. More." He pulled her close again but paused right before taking her mouth with his. Her head was tilted up, her eyes closed, her lips open. He could have her. He knew it, even if she didn't. But he wasn't going to take. "Do you want more, Marlowe?"

"Yes." No hesitation now. And when he kissed her, it was she who deepened the kiss, who suckled his tongue, who moaned low in her throat. Dane moved to kiss her throat, to trace the soft skin from jaw to collarbone. He wanted to strip her of her boy's clothing, but he knew he must move slowly.

"I want to touch you," he said, lips against the pulse beating rapidly just below her small ear. "Let me touch you."

"Yes," she whispered, and his hands moved to her hips, spanning her waist and then sliding under the loose shirt. Her skin was warm and smooth, her abdomen flat and hard, and he could feel her ribs. He stroked them then moved to her back, finding the gentle slope of her lower back and following it down to the curve of her buttocks under the rough trousers she wore.

"What do you feel now?" he asked.

"Like I might burst into flame. And my heart is beating so fast I'm afraid it might leap out." The look on her face was one of real concern, and Dane ducked his head to hide his smile.

"You won't burst into flame, and your heart is securely inside your chest. I excite you. I make your body react." He lifted her hand and placed it on his own chest. "Do you feel my heart? I feel the same way about you."

Her gaze lowered, and he knew she saw the hard length in his trousers. That would be what she understood of male arousal. He didn't try and hide it. "I want you," he said. "But the decision is yours."

She looked into his eyes. "You want to swive me."

"I want to lie with you," he corrected. "I want to touch you everywhere. Kiss you everywhere. I want to make you feel pleasure, make you call out in the midst of climax."

She shook her head. "You and all your words."

Dane grinned. "It comes down to this, my sweet, blunt girl. Do you want me?"

She studied him for a long moment, and he knew before she said the words her decision. The look on her face when she gazed at him slew him. He would have done anything for her in that moment—fought dragons, turned to highway robbery, done away with a thousand Satins. There was such adoration in her look, and he knew it was not something she gave lightly, if ever.

"Yes," she said simply. "I want you more than anything I've ever wanted."

❦

Marlowe knew what she was agreeing to. If it was a mistake, so be it. All of this would be over in a few days' time. They would go their separate ways. She might forever regret the consequences of what they were about to do, but she knew with a certainty that if she didn't lie with him, she would always regret it.

Dane slid his hands back under her shirt, and she shivered. Not because she was cold. His hands were warm and smooth and uncallused. They were strong and wide, and when he touched her, she never wanted him to stop. He grasped the hem of her shirt and tugged it upward. "May I?" he asked with a politeness that might have annoyed her if it didn't make her want to throw him onto the floor and kiss him.

She nodded, and he pulled the shirt over her head. She might have been cold now if his hot gaze wasn't on her. The room had no fire in the hearth, and all she wore was the strip of linen she'd fashioned to bind her bubbies. Dane's hand slid up her back and rested on the fabric. Slowly, his hand followed the linen around. When his hand brushed her nipple, she gasped, though she could hardly feel it. She remembered the sensation all too well. His fingers toyed with the knot she'd made in the center of her chest.

"Will you allow me?" he asked.

She nodded, and the way he smiled at her made her feel beautiful. Everything he did made her feel beautiful—the way he touched her as though she were fine china, the way he looked at her as though she were a delicious tea cake, the way he asked her permission…she felt like a princess. For just once, she wanted to be his princess.

She felt the knot loosen, and Dane wound the material around his hand, freeing her slowly but surely to his gaze. His eyes stayed locked on hers, and when she was free, he dropped the linen, and his hands came to rest lightly on her back again. His fingers moved over the grooves made by the tight material, soothing the irritated skin. He worked his way around, massaging her skin gently until he took her bubbies in his hand. They were sensitive, and he massaged them as well. Her nipples grew tight, and she felt a wetness between her legs as the fluttering in her stomach moved lower and grew heavier.

"May I kiss you here?" he asked, one thumb circling her nipple.

She nodded, and he lowered his lips to brush them across the aching point. She looked down at his dark hair, at her pale flesh in his hands, at the way he kissed her. He was so reverent and yet so skilled. Flutters of pleasure radiated through her body whenever he touched her. He moved to her other nipple, taking it in his mouth as well, and she couldn't stop herself from arching back, giving herself to him. He held her, kissing her rounded flesh and then moving lower to her stomach. When she didn't feel his mouth, she looked down. He was looking up at her, and he swallowed. "You are perfect. So beautiful." He stroked her again. "You should never be forced to bind these again."

His hands slid down again, coming to rest on the waist of the trousers. "How do you feel now?" he asked.

"The flutters have moved lower."

His brow rose. "Here?" He pressed her belly button.

"Lower."

"Here?" he slid his hand down two inches, and she could hardly stop from squirming.

"Lower," she whispered, and his hand moved down until he cupped her.

"Here?"

"Yes," she whispered. "But I think something is wrong. I feel…" She couldn't say it.

"Tell me." Earlier he had said her eyes were large, but his were impossibly huge now.

"I'm leaking. Down there."

His mouth quirked as though he might laugh.

She half-expected him to pull his hand away, but he didn't move. "You are not disgusted?"

"Marlowe, if your table manners didn't put me off, nothing will."

"Villain!" She pushed him, but he tugged her back into his arms.

"I am a villain," he admitted. His eyes were so dark, she could almost believe it. "If you knew the thoughts going through my mind right now, you would turn and run."

"Then the leaking is to be expected."

"It's to be desired, and it means you're ready."

"For?"

He loosened the fastening on her trousers. "For me to remove these." He slid them down onto her hips. "What are you wearing under these?"

"Nothing."

He groaned. "Please allow me to continue." He sounded as though he were in pain. She nodded, and the trousers dropped to the floor. He took her hands, and she stepped out of the garment. She was completely exposed to him now. She'd never shown her body to anyone like this. She'd barely ever glimpsed it herself, since she was always so careful to keep covered when the cubs were around. And the cubs were always around.

She should have felt shy, but the way Dane looked at her made her feel bold and stunning. He swallowed visibly, and his breath hitched when he inhaled. "I could look at you all day. All night."

She laughed. "Shall I turn around?"

"God, yes."

But when she began to turn, he put his hand on her elbow. "We'll save that temptation for another time." His hand traveled from her elbow to her hip, caressing it so softly it almost tickled. "I wish I had more light. You're so perfect that I want to see you."

"That might be tedious." After all, she had made her decision, and now she wanted to see what all the fuss was about. She knew it involved much more than looking. She'd seen enough in dark alleys and half-closed doors to have a pretty good idea what men and women did together.

"Tedious?" Dane said, brow raised. "I promise you won't find this tedious." He lifted his great coat from the end of the bed and laid it down over the bedclothes. He turned, and she thought he would invite her to sit. Instead, he swept her up and into his arms. She squealed from surprise and then sighed with pleasure when he lowered her onto the wool of the coat. It smelled like him, all leather and laundered wool. His weight came down on top of her, though he braced himself on his elbows. But he was warm and solid above her, and she wrapped her arms about his neck in invitation.

As she'd hoped, he lowered his mouth to hers and kissed her. She might have felt vulnerable and a little frightened if he hadn't kept his kisses light and teasing. There was nothing hurried in him. He acted as though they had all the time in the world. It did seem as though time had stopped somehow. Hours or days might have passed, and she didn't care, because she was in his arms. His lips skimmed her neck and down to her shoulder, and she felt more spirals of warmth spin through her. "Dane." She sighed his name, and he lifted his head.

"My name is Maxwell."

She blinked at him, her head altogether too fuzzy to make sense of his words immediately. "I can hardly call you *Maxwell*." She said his name in an accent the queen might have used.

"I doubt you'll be saying much of anything in a few moments, but if you must scream my name, you may use Max. My good friends call me that."

"You have friends?"

"Stop talking." He lowered his mouth to skim his lips down her arm, teasing the inside of her elbow, and she had no trouble obeying his order. But when he took her hard nipple into his mouth and suckled, she could not stop herself from crying out. She arched her hips, and for the first time, felt the hard length of him. It was not an unpleasant sensation, feeling it press against her intimately, and she gripped his hips and held him in place. "You are killing me," he said against her, his breath making her skin pebble. "But I am determined."

"Determined?" she asked. Her voice sounded like

it was from a dream, almost as though it belonged to someone else.

"To give you pleasure." And then his hand slid from where it cupped her bubbies down to her belly and even lower. He lifted his body, and his erection was replaced by the warmth of his hand. He cupped her, stroked her, and she could not stop herself from squirming. His fingers moved expertly over her heated skin, and she forgot to be embarrassed about where he was touching her.

"May I?" he asked. She had no idea what he wanted her permission for this time, but she nodded vigorously. His finger slid inside her, and she bucked at the invasion. She had not known that was the sensation she was looking for, but she stopped squirming and waited for what he would do next. Her body seemed to be coiling, anticipating. He slid out of her and pressed his finger up and over a most sensitive spot. She had not even known it was there, but when he circled it, she cried out.

"Max!"

"Shall I stop?"

"I'll kill you if you do."

His fingers slid into her again, this time two fingers, and his thumb worked the little nub. She should have been embarrassed that her hips would not stay still on the bed, but she did not care. There was something more she wanted. Something very, very good at the end of this. He slid in and out, his thumb never ceasing its work, until finally an intense heat crept from her belly into her legs and exploded.

Her entire body was wracked with tiny sparks of

the most delicious sensation. She threw her head back and allowed herself to enjoy it, gripping the material of his greatcoat so she might hold on to something and anchor herself. Slowly, so very slowly, the sparks faded, leaving her drowsy and heavy with pleasure.

Dane was smiling down at her. "You have the biggest grin on your face."

"Did you know about that?" she asked.

"About orgasm? Yes. You didn't?"

She shook her head. "I can see why everyone is so eager to swive, if that's how it feels."

He chuckled. "I would tell you it is not always like that, but it would be purely self-congratulatory. I hope I'm not so vain."

"Must I answer that?"

"Please don't." His face grew more serious. "I don't want to stop, but—"

She put a finger over his lips. "Then don't. Aren't you going to take any of your clothing off?"

He stood, and she watched as he tugged at his neckcloth, his coat, and finally managed to pull his shirt over his head. Now she understood why he'd wanted more light. She had seen his chest before, seen the hard, defined ridges and planes, and she wanted to see it again. Even more, she wanted to see what lay under his trousers. He sat, pulled off his boots, and she summoned the strength to sit too. She ran a hand over his back, liking the way the smooth skin felt under her fingertips. There was so much strength in him, and she bent and kissed his broad shoulders. He turned quickly, surprising her, and claimed her mouth. His kisses were no longer playful and teasing, and if she hadn't had the most wonderful—what had he called it?—orgasm earlier, she might have been afraid. But she knew what to expect now. She knew what was coming, and she kissed him back with all that she had. He groaned, and instead of retreating, he deepened the kiss, taking her breath and leaving her panting with need when he broke away.

He stood, unfastened his trousers, and slid them off. She couldn't stop herself from looking at that part of him that so fascinated her. She'd never seen one aroused, and it looked quite large and quite hard. "Can I..." She reached out a hand tentatively then looked into his face. "Can I touch it?"

"Please." His voice was low and harsh.

She extended one finger and slid it over the tip. It was smoother than she'd anticipated, and velvety. She pressed two fingers against him and ran them up and down the length of him. He was warm and alive, and he moved in her hand.

"Like this," he said, wrapping her hand around himself and showing her how to stroke him. She did as he showed her, and his breathing grew rapid. She watched his face, intrigued at the effect her strokes had on him. And then suddenly he gripped her hand. "Lie back."

He'd asked her permission for everything thus far, and the abrupt order caught her off guard. She did as he asked, though. Now would be the moment he jumped on her. But he stood looking down at her, hands clenched. And then, with deliberate slowness, he slid his body over hers. The feel of his skin against hers made every single inch of her come alive. Every part of her warmed and sparked and cried for his touch. "Yes," she murmured, running her hands up his naked back and loving the feel of his skin under her fingertips.

She could feel the hard length of him between her legs, but he didn't push into her. Instead, he kissed her again, his mouth surprisingly tender on hers. She kissed him back, eagerness and need warring within her, and he matched her passion with his own. His hands were everywhere, stroking her, arousing her, feeding her desire. And then his fingers were on that small, sensitive spot again, and she bucked up, wanting more pressure, more of him.

"I want to be inside you," he murmured against her shoulder. His fingers still played her, and now her body knew the tune. Her legs slipped open, and her hips arched. "I want to make you mine," he said, his voice husky and low, his breath warm on her skin.

"Yes. I'm yours," she said as the first stirrings of pleasure erupted where his fingers stroked her.

"Are you certain?"

"Yes!" Pleasure slammed through her, even stronger than before. The tidal wave carried her over, and just when it seemed to peak, she felt him hot and hard at her entrance. She could not help but push against him, and he slipped inside, filling her. More heat swirled within her, and she bowed back, helpless against the onslaught.

"I'm sorry," he whispered, and then he thrust into her. She felt the pain amidst the pleasure, but when she might have cried out against it, his thumb found her, and she cried out in ecstasy instead. Gingerly, he moved, filling her and retreating, and though there was pain, she was numb from the ebbing pleasure.

She opened her eyes to find him looking down at her, and what she saw in his face made what little breath she had in her lungs whoosh out. He was being so gentle with her. His jaw was tight, his face strained as he strove to control himself. He didn't want to hurt her. He cared enough about her that he wanted nothing but pleasure for her.

She tried to push away the feeling swelling within her. She tried to focus on the way he filled her or the last vestiges of pain when he moved. But despite her best efforts, she could not stop the wave of love from crashing over her. And when he came, murmuring her name in a voice so sweet and vulnerable, she closed her eyes against the sudden tears. He withdrew, spilling his seed on the bedclothes in an effort to prevent her from becoming with child. And that too made her love him. How could she not?

And then when he gathered her into his arms, whispering apologies because she was crying, the last ice around her heart melted. She gave her heart to him, completely, knowing he could not help but break it.

Fifteen

DANE HELD MARLOWE AND FELT LIKE AN ABSOLUTE arse. She was crying. He'd hurt her, and he wanted to hate himself for that. But he couldn't regret what had happened between them. He'd enjoyed it far too much, enjoyed her response too much. He was no virgin, but he'd never experienced anything like what they'd just shared. He was no libertine, so perhaps his experience was too limited. Still, he could not have ever imagined feeling the way he'd felt—the way he still felt—in Marlowe's arms. He never wanted to let her go, and God knew the bed was probably dirty and the room was dark and musty and so he should be glad to escape it. But he would have stayed here for the rest of his life, if it meant being with her.

The thought was terrifying. The strength of what he felt for her was terrifying.

He rose on his elbows and looked down at her. In the dim light of the room, it was difficult to see her expression. He could feel the wetness on his thumb when he rubbed it across her cheek. "I was too rough. Forgive me."

"Forgive you?" Her voice was steady, indicating she had probably stopped crying. "There's nothing to forgive."

"But I hurt you."

"Only a little. It was worth it for the other."

He frowned. "Then why were you crying?"

She sat, pushing herself up. He continued to hold her loosely, sitting with her. "Oh, that. Ridiculous, I know." And she shrugged. Dane doubted he would learn any more about it from her. Whatever the reason, she didn't want to say. "I won't cry next time."

Dane felt all the breath whoosh out of him. "Next time?"

"Unless you don't want to."

"Oh, I want to. I'd take you again now if I didn't think I'd hurt you." It was true. He should have had his fill of her, but his hunger for her had only increased.

She yawned. "I would not mind a nap. I had no idea swiving could be like that. It's the best thing in the world."

Dane didn't consider himself an arrogant man—or no more arrogant than the rest of his sex—but his chest puffed up at her words.

"Except tea cakes," she said.

"Tea cakes?" He frowned.

"And clotted cream. Oh, and bacon. I adore bacon. But besides those…oh, and ices! I did enjoy the ices you bought at Gunther's."

Before she could continue with her list, which he was beginning to gather was rather extensive, he rose. "I've never had to compete with food stuffs before. I suppose as long as I keep you fed, I have nothing to worry about."

"Speaking of food—"

A tap on the door interrupted her, and they both braced in surprise. "Yes?" Dane called, feeling for his clothing and pulling his trousers on.

"He's here." Barbara's whispered words floated through the door. "And he asked about you."

"Keep him here, Barbara. We'll be out in a moment." Marlowe had jumped up too and was floundering to dress. Dane was not used to dressing by himself, and she was done before him. She helped him squeeze into his tight coat and brushed his hair back from his forehead.

"Do I look like the son of a duke?"

"You don't look like one of us," she said, running a hand over the expensive material of his coat. "Let's go."

She led the way along the dark hallway and back into the public rooms. When they reached it, Dane knew immediately who Satin was. He'd never seen the man, but there was no mistaking who had the power and command of the place. The dark-haired man sat in the center of the room. He obviously felt secure enough of his power that he didn't need to put his back to the wall. He had nothing to fear.

His hair was oily and stringy, and it was difficult to tell if the mop on his head was black or simply coated with grime. His clothing was better quality than the others in the Rouge Unicorn Cellar, but it too was wrinkled and dingy with dirt. He'd been sneering at the prostitute on his lap, but when Dane entered, he looked up and swatted the girl on the bottom. The slap was hard enough to echo throughout the room. Dane felt a strange tingle creep along his spine as the crime lord surveyed him with those small eyes. No wonder Marlowe feared him. Dane would have stayed away from him, if only he had any other choice.

Marlowe started forward, and Dane followed her. Satin must have seen her coming, but he didn't take his gaze off Dane.

At the crime lord's table, Marlowe paused. "Satin."

He flicked his gaze at her and then back to Dane. "Didn't think I'd see you here. Not after our last conversation." The threat in his tone was there for all to hear.

Dane wanted to pull her behind him, protect her, but he could see she had been right to warn him not to show any affection for her. This Satin was a man who would use any and every weakness.

"We can talk about that, if you like."

His nose flared. "Oh, we'll *talk* about it plenty."

Marlowe looked unfazed by the obvious anger Satin was holding back. "But I knew you'd be interested in what Lord Maxwell has to say."

Satin's brows rose on the mention of his invented title. But it wouldn't be so easy to gain the man's cooperation. The crime lord's brows lowered, and his eyes narrowed with suspicion. Dane decided it was time he played his part.

"Am I to stand here all day like a footman?" he asked, doing his best imitation of a dandy. "I vow I haven't stood this much since the races at Ascot."

Marlowe rolled her eyes, and Dane hoped it was

part of her act. Either that or he'd just made a fool of himself. "Can we sit?" she asked Satin.

The crime lord gestured to the empty chair across from him. Dane took it, forcing Marlowe to fetch another and carry it from a nearby table. She turned it, sitting with her arms draped across the back.

"So listen, old boy," Dane said when Marlowe was seated. "This gel says you're the man to see for the business I have in mind."

"Is that so?" Satin didn't blink.

"Don't know if I trust her or you, so I'm taking an awful risk coming here." He gave the room a disdainful look. "Who knows what sorts of diseases I could catch." He withdrew his handkerchief and covered his nose.

"Must be important business for you to take such a chance."

"It is," Marlowe said. "But there are too many ears here. Maybe we should take Lord Maxwell to your personal rooms?"

"No." Satin looked around. "What does it take for a man to get a little privacy? Get out, all of ye, and I'll consider not slitting yer throats."

The few patrons still drinking grumbled, but Barbara shooed them out then disappeared herself. Dane caught Marlowe's eye, and she nodded. Apparently, she considered the fact that they were now alone with Satin a point in their favor. Dane thought it made them easier to kill. Fewer witnesses.

Satin looked at them. "You said you had business to discuss."

Dane nodded. "How do I know I can trust you?"

"I told you," Marlowe said. "If you want the job done, there's no one better."

"And how do I know he won't take all the loot for himself?" Dane didn't miss the way Satin's eyes widened at the use of *loot*.

"This some sort of better-racket?" Satin asked. "There's no one who can pull off a better-racket like me."

Dane nodded. Satin was interested now, probably far more interested than he allowed them to see. Dane made a show of looking about for eavesdroppers, then he lowered his voice. "I'm the youngest son of the Duke of Yorkshire. You know of him?"

"Course," Satin said, which was a blatant lie.

"Then you know he's one of the wealthiest men in England. Been known to loan the king a few thousand pounds when His Majesty is running low, if you know what I mean."

"A topping fellow," Satin said with a nod. "Why are you telling me this?"

"I am the youngest son. I have eight older brothers, as well as assorted sisters. My share of the fortune will be very, very small."

"Some fortune is better than none."

"True, but I have never been good at economy, and I do enjoy a night at the faro tables."

A smug smile crossed Satin's face. Dane had to keep from smiling himself, because he knew now that he had the crime lord.

"So ye've given out yer vowels."

"And I haven't the funds to back them," Dane said.

"Not very gentleman-like," Satin said with a look at Marlowe. "But then you don't strike me as a loggerhead." Satin's gaze was still on Marlowe, and Dane glanced over at her. He clenched his hands on his knees under the table, because to his eye—and most certainly to Satin's—Marlowe looked thoroughly debauched. Her lips were swollen and red, her cheeks high with color, and her throat was blotchy and red from the stubble on his chin. There was little doubt what they'd been doing before Satin arrived. If Dane had not already vowed to take her out of this place, he would have vowed it now. No telling what ideas Satin was forming as he looked at her.

"My father refuses to help me, and I've always believed God helps those who help themselves."

Satin looked back at him. "That He does. But what's all this to do with me?"

Dane looked at Marlowe, acting as though he did not want to speak of such a sordid business. Marlowe leaned forward. "Lord Maxwell has learned that the duke has some plum items waiting at a warehouse on the river."

"What sort of items?"

"Priceless antiquities," Dane added. "Coins, jewels, art from the Continent. They arrived on a merchant ship a few days ago."

"Why are they sitting in a warehouse on the docks?"

That was a good question, and one he and Marlowe had not discussed. He shot her a look, and she said, "Because the duke is not in London to claim them."

Satin frowned. "Why not? Isn't this the time of year when all the swells dress up and parade before the king and queen?"

Marlowe opened her mouth to respond, but Dane

interrupted before she sank them further. "It is the height of the Season, but none of my sisters are debutantes this year, and my father has gone to"— he remembered Lord and Lady Lyndon—"hunt in Scotland. He won't be back for another few days."

"And what am I supposed to do with jewels and art? Sell 'em to a rag-and-bones shop?"

"I know where to sell them, if you can lay hands on the items."

"This warehouse guarded?"

Dane shrugged. "Nothing you cannot handle, if what Miss Marlowe says is true."

Satin crossed his arms. "What's my cargo?"

Dane pretended to consider. "I'm prepared to give you thirty percent."

"Fifty. I'm the one risking my hide. I should get half."

"Forty, and that's my final offer. Forty percent is a fortune, I assure you."

Satin stuck out his hand, and Dane looked at it curiously. It was dark with dirt and grime, the nails long, yellow, and ragged. Keeping his gloves on, Dane shook the criminal's hand. "We act tonight," he said, standing.

"Why the hurry?" Satin asked.

"I have debts to pay. If you don't think you can be ready, I can find—"

"He'll be ready," Marlowe interjected.

"Good." Dane looked at her, waiting for her to rise, and belatedly realized she hadn't moved. Satin had a hand on her pale wrist, keeping her in place. Dane stared at that hand for a long moment, wanting to rip it off, but he gritted his teeth and lifted his eyes instead. "I'll meet you there." He gave the address. "Say midnight?"

Satin nodded. "I'll be waiting."

❧

Marlowe watched Dane walk away and wished she too could escape. Instead, she tolerated Satin's touch until Dane passed through the door, returning to Barbara's room. Then she snatched her hand away.

"Ye're a prickly one. I'm not good enough to touch the likes of you?"

"I brought you game. What more do you want?"

Satin nodded. "I always knew you would make me rich. That's why I tolerated all your sniveling when you were a brat. I could have taken in a hundred brats. Streets were full of them, but I always had a good feeling about you."

Marlowe wondered if she was supposed to thank him for abducting her. Of course, he didn't know she'd potentially uncovered the truth about who she was. And he wouldn't know until she saw him dangle in front of Newgate.

"I should have put you in skirts more often. First you bring me an earl, now the son of a duke."

"After those rackets, I'm done. I want out."

"Ye're done when I say ye're done," Satin said, leaning close and grabbing her by the back of the neck so she couldn't pull back. "You understand?"

"Yes."

He released her, pushing her head down against the table first. While she rubbed her aching forehead, he rose. She caught a flash of gold when his coat opened to reveal his shabby waistcoat. Inside, a gold chain hung from the outer pocket. Susanna's necklace. He hadn't pawned it yet. Marlowe stood, but Satin shook his head. "Where do you think ye're going?"

"To see the cubs. I figured you'd want Gideon, Beezle, and Gap working on this."

"Oh, no. Ye're not going anywhere. And if a word of this gets out, I'll make sure to personally slit your throat." He leaned close, and she tried not to breathe in the scent of stale onions. "This is me and you. That's it. You bring in Gideon or Gap, and I'll make sure this racket is their last."

Marlowe stared at him, allowing her hatred to show. How many other times had Satin cut her and the other cubs out? How many times had she gone hungry when he'd had a full belly? If she'd thought she could beat him, could kill him with her hands, she would have done it then and there. But she'd never win that way. Dane and Brook were her only hope.

"I'll see you at midnight."

Marlowe nodded and started away.

"One more thing."

She paused but didn't look back.

"If anything don't feel right, I'll gut you and leave you for dead." She heard his footsteps as he clomped out of the room, and she stood for a long moment alone, attempting to stifle the hatred coursing through her. She had to leash it for a few more hours, and then he'd be gone.

❧

Gideon looked around the small room, counting up the profit he'd have if he filched the glim-sticks, the ink blotter, and the peacock-quill pen. The rug was worth something too, but damned if he knew how to get a rug out from under the noses of the Bow Street Runners.

"Are you done with your inventory?" Sir Brook asked from behind the desk, where he sat with his feet propped on the polished surface. The desk was worth something too, but it would have taken three of the cubs to lift it, and then even if they could have maneuvered it down the stairs, what would they do with it? No one had a cart sitting around.

"For the moment," Gideon said.

"Your name?"

"Gideon."

"Do you have a surname?"

Gideon looked down. It had been so long since he'd used it. It was the last vestige of his parents he carried. "Harrow," he said then looked up. "Gideon Harrow."

"Mr. Harrow, downstairs you mentioned an interesting name. Can you repeat it now, where there aren't a dozen ears to hear?"

"I said, *Lady Elizabeth*."

Derring steepled his hands. "Why?"

"She sent me. Course I know her by another name, Marlowe." Gideon peered at Derring from under his lashes. "Maybe you know her by that name too."

"And what do you know of Lady Elizabeth?"

Gideon shrugged. "Nothing. But I know a hell of a lot about Marlowe. I know a lot about your nob brother too, and the both of them in a public house together in Seven Dials."

Derring's feet dropped to the floor. "What are you talking about?"

"She said to make sure you got the letter. You didn't get it?"

"What let—" He waved a hand, rose, and went to the door leading outside, where a thin clerk, much like the one Gideon had held a knife to, sat.

"Mr. Bowker, did you receive a letter from my brother? The Earl of Dane."

"Yes, my lord."

Gideon figured the man must have held it aloft, because Derring stormed out. He could hear their muffled voices, something about nonessential mail. A moment later, Derring strode back into the room, went to his desk, and unearthed a letter opener, breaking the seal. Gideon tilted his head. The letter opener had to be worth a fiver, at least.

"Goddamn it!" Derring swore. "What the devil is he thinking?" He looked up at Gideon. "Do you know what this says?"

"Something about a plan to nab Satin."

Derring placed the letter opener back in the drawer and closed it with a warning look at Gideon. "Do you know who Satin is?"

"I might."

"Exactly what is your association with Lady—with Marlowe?"

"I couldn't rightly say."

"You must be a friend to risk coming here in search of me."

Gideon shrugged. "I don't have anything to hide."

Derring laughed. "Oh, I doubt that very much.

You should know, Mr. Harrow, that I don't work with criminals."

"And I don't work with Runners." He put the same distasteful emphasis on the title as Derring had put on the word *criminal*. "I see you have the letter. I'll tell Marlowe you got it." He started to walk out then thought better of it. "Will you help her?"

"Do I have a choice? God knows, if I don't save my brother, I'll have to take on the earldom, and I can't imagine a worse fate."

"Good." Gideon made it to the door before Derring spoke again.

"And what about you? Will you help?"

"I did my part."

"But you'll do more. If we're both to be lurking about, perhaps we could…coordinate."

Gideon crossed his arms. "Isn't that like working together?"

"Not at all. It's much more aloof. Sit down, have a drink, and I'll explain."

Sixteen

MARLOWE HATED THIS TIME. SHE HATED THE LULL before the storm. She hated knowing the rain would pour, the streets would become muddy and impassable, and the best-laid plans would have to be set aside. The skies might be clear, but it would rain tonight, and she didn't have the luxury of setting her plans aside. She'd set the trap, and she'd have to spring it.

Marlowe stood outside the room she and Dane shared, reluctant to go inside. It wasn't that she didn't want to see him. She knew he could distract her in ways that were new and altogether quite delicious. But at the moment, she could not imagine being caged in the tiny, dark room. She was tense and edgy and needed to move. Dane must have heard her outside or begun to worry at her absence, because just as she was about to reach for the door handle, the door opened, and he stared down at her.

"What's wrong?" he asked. "Is Satin—"

"He's gone," she reassured him. "I just…I need to walk."

His brows rose. "*You* want to walk?"

She smiled. "You have corrupted me."

"I'm coming with you." He closed the door behind him.

She took a surprised step back. "No, you're not." She shook her head vehemently. "You have to stay here."

"Not a chance. Where you go, I go."

"You'll be going straight to hell when you end up with a knife in your back, lying facedown in a rank alley."

"Lovely image, but I can hold my own."

She rolled her eyes and sighed. "Fine. If you want to get yourself killed, then come along." She gave him her back, muttering to herself about idiot gentry coves.

"After you!" he called, following her. She passed through the public room, which had managed to fill up again rather quickly, considering Satin and she had been talking alone no more than a quarter hour before. Now she nodded to people she knew and eyed others warily, keenly aware that Dane was at her heels, and every man, woman, and child in the place was marking him and hoping for the chance to see exactly how deep his pockets were.

Finally, she pushed her way out into the street and squinted at the daylight. It wasn't a particularly sunny day, rather blustery and gray, but the Rouge Unicorn Cellar was so dark inside, any light took a moment to adjust to. Dane, no fool apparently, was right behind her. "I'd like to take a breath of fresh air, but I don't think it's much better out here."

"Breathe at your own risk," she advised, moving

around a large pile of rubbish just outside the public house. Her gaze was drawn to the shabby building across the street where the Covent Garden Cubs made their home. It looked like nothing other than a falling down structure, but anyone who tried to step foot inside would find out it was well guarded. Her gaze moved to the doorway, and she caught a pair of eyes peering out at her. Beezle, no doubt. He was always down. She wondered if Gap was sleeping inside and whether Joe was about.

"Do you have a flat?" Dane asked. "Family you want to visit?

"No." She nodded back at the decrepit flash ken. "The gang lives there, but they're hardly family."

Dane studied the structure for a moment. She tried to see it through his eyes, and felt her cheeks burn with shame. His home was so lovely and clean, and the flash ken was an eyesore. It listed to one side, was dark, and surrounded by rubbish. What had once been windows were now covered with haphazardly nailed boards. She felt small and ugly and unrefined showing it to him.

"I admire you," he said.

She blinked at the unexpected response. "Why?"

"Because you survived here. It couldn't have been easy. I couldn't have done it." He looked at her. "I don't think I have what it takes."

"You don't know what you can do until you have to," she said. She began to walk, wanting to be away from the flash ken and the beady eyes watching her. Watching them. Dane came after her, his long legs easily eating up the distance between them.

"So many children," he said as they passed a maimed little boy holding his hand out. Another few steps, and a girl of perhaps seven cradled a squalling infant. The mother was nowhere to be seen. Several boys about Gap's age stood with their hands in their pockets, watching her pass. She gave them a hard stare, and they quieted as she moved past them. "Where are the parents?" he asked, seemingly unaware of the boys they passed. Probably didn't see them as a threat.

"Parents? We don't have governesses and nannies here. Brats learn to survive on their own, or they don't survive."

"But surely the mother of that infant back there—"

"Probably a bawd."

"Oh." His tone was tinged with distaste.

"You can turn up your nose and give me more of your words about how the lower classes deserve their fate, but you can't tell me that innocent baby deserves to live like this." She paused and looked up at him. His gaze on her was intent, and she was surprised that he was actually listening to her. She'd thought his prejudice too deep. "I don't know that babe's mother, but I can guess her story. She was an orphan, or her family fell on hard times, and she ended up here. She met a man who bought her a meal, maybe a ribbon, maybe a glass of gin. Maybe they married. Maybe not. He took care of her for awhile, until one night he didn't come home. Or maybe he beat her, and she ran off. Now she has two or three brats to feed. The only way she can make any money is on her back."

"That can't be the only way."

Marlowe raised a brow. "Can she take that baby to a workhouse?"

Dane shook his head.

"Will you hire her to clean your fancy house? Take care of your brats? She can't speak French or play piano. She can't even read. How would she teach? Maybe she can sew a little, but with her background, what respectable shopkeeper would hire her?"

"She made a mistake," Dane said. "And now she pays the price."

"Now we all pay the price." Marlowe pointed to the children who seemed to be everywhere. "All of these children pay the price, and then you pay the price, and the city pays it too, because there's nothing for them to do but thieve and whore. While you sit in"—she changed her voice to mimic his accent—"Parliament and *discuss* the problem of the *lower classes*, the *lower classes* are just trying to survive."

He looked at the children, and she prayed he saw their hollow eyes, their dirty faces, their thin bodies.

"These people aren't a problem. They are people. Just because they weren't born in Mayfair doesn't make them any less human." She turned, giving him her back. She didn't want to hear his rhetoric at the moment.

"You're right," he said simply.

She turned back, her eyes widening. "What did you say?"

"You're right. They are humans. They deserve to live with dignity and respect. And the children—" He shook his head. "Ghastly that children should have to live this way. I should help feed them."

She blinked at him. "Are you feeling well?"

"No, not particularly. The stench is awful, I could use a good brandy, and I'm angry. Something should be done to address this."

She stared at him, unable to speak for a long, long moment.

"And if I survive until tomorrow, I will draft a bill to that point." His gaze met hers. "You've changed me, Marlowe. I look at you, and I imagine you as a little girl on these streets, and I want to protect you. I want to help you." He looked about. "I want to help all of them."

She might have kissed him in that moment. If they hadn't been in the middle of Seven Dials and her dressed as a boy, she might have done it. She loved him so much in that moment—not for how he made her feel when he looked at her or touched her or kissed her, but for who he was. She'd seen the kindness, the goodness inside him. She'd seen it in others and always thought it a weakness. But now she saw it could be a strength too. Perhaps he—they—really could affect a change.

And then she shook her head. What did she have to do with it? She didn't even know how to read more than the most basic words. He wouldn't want her help. He might have enjoyed her body, been intrigued by the differences between them, but it wasn't as though he wanted a partner, a…wife. And yet, she couldn't help but feel elated that he'd been changed by her words. That he respected her enough to listen when she spoke, to take her words to heart.

A movement behind her caught her eye, and she took his elbow. "We should keep moving."

He nodded, his walking stick thumping the ground beside them. "I think first the issue of honest work must be addressed. And wages. We can't forget that."

She was listening with only half her attention. She'd seen the boys they'd passed earlier move closer, and now that she was leading Dane away, the boys had begun to follow. That was not a good sign. On her own, she could have lost them. She could have made for the flash ken and had the whole gang at her back. But how could she lose them with Dane to look out for? The gang wouldn't fight for a swell. They'd leave him to the dogs.

"And orphanages. We need more."

"No, you need to reform those you have. Speak to Gideon on that subject."

"Your friend?" he said, slowing his steps. "He knows something about it, then?"

"Dane—"

"I suppose I could conduct an inquiry."

"Dane." Her heart thumped rapidly in her chest. She didn't dare look behind her, because she knew the moment she did, the boys would pounce. Dane was still talking, obviously completely unaware of the danger.

"But should it be an official inquiry?"

"Maxwell!"

"What on earth is wrong?"

She took his hand. "Run!"

❧

She yanked him so hard he almost protested, but that was before he heard the yell behind him. He tried to turn and see where the noise originated.

"Don't look. Run!"

And so he ran. He could not remember the last time he'd run. It had been years, and his legs were unaccustomed to the movement. But he was no stranger to exertion—whether it be on horseback or in the fencing studio—and he had no trouble keeping pace with her. He was certainly not as graceful as she. She darted around stray dogs, jumped over broken furnishings littering the streets, and deftly parted the small groups of ubiquitous beggars and children. And still the feet pounding behind them did not slow. No one offered to help. Indeed, most of Seven Dials seemed not to notice or care about the two people being chased by three young boys.

They rounded a corner, turning onto another street, and Marlowe lost her cap. She reached for it, but her nimble fingers missed for once, and it went rolling into a fetid pool of stagnant liquid. She let it go, and as Dane raced by, a child eagerly snatched it up. This street was a bit more crowded with carts and wagons, and she had to slow. She glanced over her shoulder, obviously didn't like what she saw, and cut down a narrow alley. Dane followed her into the dark passageway and glanced up at the buildings crouching above. The structures were so bowed they blocked out what little light managed to penetrate the gray clouds.

"Quick!" she said, pausing with hands on knees to catch her breath. "We can slip out the other side and lose them."

Dane was breathing too hard to speak, but he squinted his eyes down the dark alley. A pair of yellow cat eyes blinked back at him. He saw no exit through the darkness, but she knew the terrain better than he. She reached for his hand, and they linked fingers. Dane had the urge to look down at their joined hands. Hers was small and streaked with dirt. His was larger, darker, and had a few questionable smudges as well. But for the first time, he felt as though he was part of something. It was a strange feeling, one he realized he'd always sought but never found. Not at school, not at home, not in Parliament, not in the lofty gentlemen's clubs. How strange to feel it here, with her, in the middle of the slums.

But it was oddly right. The two of them together against the world—or at least their current pursuers. She tugged at him, urging him forward, and he met her gaze. With her dark hair tumbling about her shoulders, and her cheeks flushed from the run, she was breathtaking. He would have followed her anywhere. They started down the alley, startling another cat, who hissed at them then darted under a refuse pile. Behind them, he heard voices and knew their pursuers had found them.

"Almost there," Marlowe said. "These streets are like a rabbit's warren. They twist and turn. We can lose them." She rushed forward, and then came to a sliding stop.

"What the—" But Dane didn't need to ask. He saw the man step out of the shadows. He whipped his head back to look behind him, and the three boys—where had this one come from?—stood blocking the exit. They were trapped.

"Beezle?" Marlowe said, her voice incredulous. "What are you doing?"

He moved forward, and Dane had the impression of a youth of middling height. But unlike the boys behind them, this one had some brawn. His hair was dark, as were his eyes, and Dane didn't particularly like the sneer on his thin lips. "What Satin should have done a long time ago."

Dane peered behind them. The three boys had slowed to a walk now, but they were steadily advancing. Marlowe kept her gaze on the one she'd called Beezle. "If Satin didn't send you, then you'd best let us pass."

"Why? So you can lure him into yer trap? He might have fallen for your cock-and-bull story, but I won't."

"Jealous because he left you out?" Marlowe crossed her arms. She didn't appear concerned at all. The woman was quite obviously daft.

"Marlowe…"

"If you touch me," she said to Beezle, "he'll hear about it, and then they'll be fishing you out of the river."

"I'll take my chances." Beezle moved forward. "It's worth it to get rid of you."

She shrugged. "You're welcome to try."

"Or"—Dane stepped between them—"we might come to some other sort of agreement. Perhaps Marlowe and I might pay for our passage."

Beezle shook his head. "I think I'll kill you first."

"You'll have to go through me." She moved quickly, darting to the right and catching his boot with her foot. He wavered but didn't go down. She was behind him now, and Dane had three behind and Beezle in front.

"Run!" he called to her. This was her chance to escape. "I can take them."

She rolled her eyes—annoying habit, that—and jumped on Beezle's back. "Get them," Beezle ordered his cronies, and the three boys charged. Dane raised his walking stick, and the lads paused. Dane waved it about menacingly, keeping the boys at arms' length. He peered over his shoulder and saw Beezle had backed against a wall and was ramming Marlowe, who was still on his back, into it. For her part, she had her arms wrapped so tightly about his neck, his face was turning a deep shade of crimson.

"Certain you don't want to take the money?" Dane said to Beezle.

"And trust the likes of you?" he wheezed, slamming Marlowe back again. Dane winced. "Find another bubble."

Dane felt a tug on his walking stick and yanked it back, only to find one of the lads had a firm grip on it. Dane shook his head. "I didn't want to have to do this."

He pressed a small lever at the handle, and the sheath detached. The boy stumbled back, and Dane brandished his sharp rapier. One of the boys charged him, and with a deft slash, Dane cut a neat slice through the material of his shirt. Another boy came at him, and Dane lopped off a lock of his long brown hair. The boys assessed the damage, then looked at Beezle. Dane didn't take his eyes from the lads, but he could hear the sounds of struggle behind him had ceased.

"What are you waiting for?" Beezle yelled hoarsely.

"'E's got a porker!" the boy with the newly trimmed hair shouted.

"And do not doubt I know how to use it," Dane said calmly. "Years of fencing training. I can carve you like roast lamb. Or you can run away now and live. The choice is yours completely."

The boys looked at the sword then looked at Beezle, and as one, they turned and ran. Dane swung around and pointed the rapier at Beezle. He still had Marlowe pinned to the wall, and she still had her arms wrapped around his neck. "Let her go," Dane said.

"She's got me," he wheezed. Dane took a step forward, pointing the rapier's tip at the spot on Beezle's neck where Marlowe's arms intersected.

"Release him, Marlowe."

Slowly, her hands dropped away. Dane took a step back. "Now, Mr. Beezle, you move forward. One step. That's right. Another."

Marlowe slid out from behind him, and Beezle tried to grab her, but Dane pressed the sword tip against his throat, and the man ended up backing into the wall, his neck craned high. Dane cut his gaze to Marlowe. "What would you like me to do with him?"

She was staring at him, her expression unreadable. "I'd like to say skewer him."

"Very well." He dug the blade in deeper, until a trickle of blood meandered down Beezle's dirty neck.

"But," Marlowe interjected, "I'm not a miller, so maybe we tie him up and leave him here until our business tonight is done."

"Very good," Dane said. "And what should we use to tie him?"

She moved toward him, and he felt her hands at his throat. His cravat came loose and tumbled down his shirt, and she pulled it free. "You realize I haven't another with me?" he said.

"You'll have to make do without."

He sighed.

"I know," she said, shaking the fine linen out. "The horror of not being properly dressed." She motioned to Beezle. "Turn and put your hands behind you."

Dane moved the sword back a fraction of an inch, and with a look that would have melted ice, Beezle turned, pushing his face into the wall of the building. Marlowe took his hands and tied them tightly. "You'll pay for this," he said, his voice muffled. "One way or another, I'll make you pay."

"You're lucky I don't have him bloody you a bit more. I can think of a few choice appendages he might slice off."

Wisely, in Dane's opinion, Beezle didn't reply. Marlowe pushed him to his knees and moved to Dane's side. Dane nodded. "Appendages. Nice word choice."

She grinned at him. "I'm learning." She glanced up at the sky, ostensibly to check the time. Dane didn't know how she could ascertain anything, as the sky looked as gray and overcast as it had before, but she said, "We'd better go, or we'll be late to meet Satin."

Dane moved to fetch the sheath for his walking stick, fitted it back into place over his blade, and straightened his coat. "After you."

She led him out of the alley, without a backward glance for Beezle. When they were strolling on the street, past public houses rapidly filling with patrons, he said, "I'm certainly glad you didn't make me cut him. I shudder to think how Tibbs would have removed the blood from this coat."

"You're concerned about your coat?"

He didn't have to see her to know she was rolling her eyes.

"That, and I feel queasy at the sight of blood. Not a very manly thing to admit, but there it is."

She glanced at him. "Why didn't you tell me you had a tilter?"

"A rapier? You never asked."

"Is there anything else you're hiding?" She arrowed east, toward the river and the docks.

"A gentleman never tells."

Seventeen

MARLOWE COULD FEEL THE HEAT OF DANE'S BODY AS he crouched beside her behind a short wall hidden in the shadows near the dockside warehouse where they would soon meet Satin. They were close enough to the river that if she looked up, the sky was blotted out by the forest of masts on the Thames. Elsewhere, she could hear the rattle of the night coaches and the clang of a ship's bell. The River Police were apt to be patrolling nearby, and she kept her head down and her voice low. They'd been there over an hour, and the bells of St. George in the east had just rung eleven times. One more hour, and then Satin would be gone. The man who had dominated her life, dominated *her*, would be safely in prison.

If Sir Brook made an appearance. Had Gideon been able to reach the inspector, or were she and Dane shivering in the cold for no reason? Well, Dane wasn't shivering. He felt perfectly warm. She had the urge to lean into him and steal some of that warmth, but she resisted. She needed all of her wits about her now as she peered into the darkness, hoping to see Sir

Brook. All would be lost if he made an appearance at the wrong moment. And if Satin arrived early, as he very well might in order to look at the place, she did not want to be taken by surprise. Marlowe knew once she succumbed to Dane's warmth, she would forget all about the game.

It wasn't simply that she enjoyed being kissed by him, being pressed against his lovely body, or being held. It was more. Ever since she'd watched him wield that tilter in the alley, she felt that strange fluttering in her belly. Dane had said it was arousal. If that was true, she was still aroused. She hadn't known a man could look like that when holding a tilter. She hadn't known Dane could look so powerful. For once she had dropped her defenses. She'd never been able to trust another person to defend her, protect her. Of course, Gideon had saved her many times, but he'd left her to fend on her own plenty, too. She'd always taken that as a compliment. He knew she could defend herself. But was it not a compliment that Dane had defended her? And why shouldn't she desire a man who could steer her through the fanciest ball and keep her safe in the seediest alley?

She definitely desired him. She desired him more than she ought. She was still in love with him. She'd thought it was her climax that had made her mistake lust for love, but she hadn't been in the throes of passion in that alley. Why then should her heart swell and tighten in a feeling she could identify only as one she'd so very rarely felt? Love. Even now her heart soared when she caught a glimpse of Dane from the corner of her eye. He was here, with her, and she never, never wanted to be apart from him.

Dangerous thoughts, considering the two of them came from very different worlds. They had no future, even if she was Lady Elizabeth. Dane would marry a woman who could make him a respectable countess, not a woman who had been—who might still be— nothing more than a light-fingered rook.

"Something moved over there," Dane murmured close to her ear. His breath heated her skin, and she tried to ignore the shiver that radiated out from the point of contact.

"Where?" It was probably a tibby, but she could not afford not to be cautious. She peered behind her, at the drag and prancer Dane had managed to procure.

"No. This way. Two o'clock."

She glanced at him, brow furrowed in confusion. "It can't be half-eleven. I just heard the bells."

He gave her a long look. "No, the movement was at…do you know how to tell time?"

Her cheeks burned, because even though she did not clearly understand him, she understood there was yet another area where she was lacking, and he had discovered it. "I can hear the bells on the church towers. I can count."

"But you can't read a clock," he murmured. "I shall have to rectify that. Look to the right." Keeping his hand low, he gestured. "Right about there."

She followed the angle of his fingers and squinted. Nothing there, not even a cat. And then one of the shadows shifted. If she hadn't been watching, she would have missed it. The hair on the back of her neck prickled, and she took in a sharp, silent breath.

It could be anyone—Satin, Sir Brook, a constable, a

passerby. Whoever it was did not want to be seen, and that was likely a bad sign.

"Do you see it?" Dane whispered against her neck. Oh, how she wished he would stop doing things like that. She had to focus! She nodded and turned to press her lips to his ear. He smelled lovely, clean despite where they were and where they'd been.

Trying not to breathe too deeply, she murmured, "Stay here. I'll have a look." She slinked to the side, but Dane grabbed her ankle and hauled her back. She tossed him an angry look, but he bent over her, leaning close. How could she help but think of the position they were in? He was leaning over her, weight braced on his elbows, his body but inches from covering hers. She took a shaky breath. This mix of arousal and danger was distracting.

"I'll not risk you. I'll go."

She shook her head wildly. He might be good with a sword, but he was too large to move about undetected. "You'll get us both caught."

"Then we wait for the interloper to reveal himself."

She understood the gist of his message, and would have protested, if a low whistle she knew well hadn't sounded at that moment. She whistled back, and Dane hissed, "What are you doing?"

"It's Gideon," she said, pushing Dane back and sitting. She peered cautiously over the wall and saw a familiar form emerge from the darkness of the warehouse. He moved quickly into sight, and she flicked a hand so he would know where she hid. A moment later, he tumbled beside her, pressing his back to the wall where she was similarly seated.

"How dost do my buff?" he asked, giving her the familiar flash greeting.

"What are you doing here?" she whispered. Dane was crouched across from them, his arms crossed over his chest in a disapproving manner.

"And a good evening to you too," Gideon said. "I'm here to save your lovely arse."

"Watch your language," Dane said, voice low and edged with warning.

Marlowe cut her gaze to him. "Since when did you start worrying about my *virgin* ears?"

"It's not your ears he's worried about, it's your arse. He doesn't want any man but himself noticing it. That about right, cove?"

"I'm glad we understand each other."

"Oh, we understand each other," Gideon said. "And if I'd known what an arse you were, I wouldn't have gone to so much trouble." He looked at Marlowe. "I did it for her, not the likes of you."

"Then you found Sir Brook."

"I found him. Had to walk right into the offices on Bow Street, but I found him."

"And he's coming?" Dane asked.

Gideon didn't even look in the other man's direction. "He'll be here. I hope."

"You're not sure?"

Gideon shrugged. "Are you even sure Satin will be here?"

Marlowe raised a brow. "I can spout court holy water as good as any man."

"That you can." He rose on his haunches. "In that case, I'll leave you to it. When word gets out Satin's been nabbed, I want to be there for the cubs. Maybe I can keep a few of them from being gobbled up by other gangs. Not that Beezle will let them go."

"Beezle might not be as much a problem as you think," Marlowe said, peering over the wall again in the direction of the warehouse.

"Oh, really? What have you done?"

"Just kept him out of the way for a little while. If there's anything you can do for the cubs, do it. Especially Gap and Tiny."

"And if I can help, I'm more than willing," Dane said, surprising her.

Gideon scowled at him. "How would *you* help? Stick them in an orphanage? Most of us were lucky to escape."

"What if I took them on as stable boys at my country house? They'd be away from London, they'd learn a trade, and I'd even provide an education."

"Why?" Marlowe asked before Gideon could. His mouth was hanging open, and she figured it would be a moment before he shut it and was able to speak again.

Dane looked thoughtful. "It's not much. I know it's a drop in the ocean, but it's a start. I told you. I will introduce a bill in Parliament."

Gideon snorted. "You do that. You know where to find us if your lofty ideas don't fade with your lust."

Marlowe recoiled as though he'd slapped her. Was that what everyone was thinking? Dane was simply lusting after her? Had all of the changes she'd seen in him been merely pretense to woo her into his bed?

"I would call you out for that," Dane said, voice

low and menacing, "but what else should I expect? You're not a gentleman."

"And never will be," Gideon said. "I got too much honor to call myself by *that* name."

Dane lunged forward, and Gideon would have followed if Marlowe hadn't moved quickly. She'd broken up a hundred fights or more, and she had been ready when this one began to brew. She wedged herself between the two men, pushing them both sharply back to capture their attention. It was no good if they started swinging and she was in the middle. "You"— she pointed to Dane—"over there. And you"—she leveled a finger at Gideon—"it's time for you to go."

"With pleasure," Gideon said, brushing his trousers off. "But this isn't over."

"No, it's not," Dane agreed.

Marlowe gave Gideon a last threatening look, and he gave a short wave and was gone. Dane moved beside Marlowe again, and she shook her head at him before peeking over the wall. "You've now managed to make enemies with the man who was our only ally."

"It might not have been the best course of action."

She rolled her eyes. "Then why did you do it?"

He turned to look at her, and her heart thumped hard. There was something in his eyes that made her throat dry. She tried to swallow, and let out a small squeak instead. "Because you're mine," he said. Even as she shook her head, he gripped her chin lightly with two fingers. "You are. This isn't mere lust, Marlowe. I don't…I don't know what the hell it is, but I won't have your character impugned."

She squinted at him. "So you were jealous?"

He wet his lips then dipped his head to kiss her quickly. "I'd be a fool not to be."

❧

Gideon cursed under his breath as he made his way through the shadows and back toward St. Giles. He didn't know why he'd even come to the docks. They stank worse than the dirtiest hole in Seven Dials, and he had to maneuver around wharf doxies and sailors three sheets to the wind. Wouldn't they love to get ahold of him and bloody him up for sport? He must have been daft to come. As daft as Marlowe for plotting this whole racket. At least the nob she'd tapped to help her wasn't as much a coward as most of the gentry coves he knew. Gideon wouldn't have minded bloodying the man's nose. Then maybe he wouldn't look quite so pretty.

Not that it mattered at this point. Marlowe had made her choice, and it was obviously not Gideon. He should be glad. He should celebrate now that she had a chance to get away from the rookeries and start a new life, a better life. Then why did he feel so depressed to lose her? Why did his feet feel like they were cased in lead as he made his way back to the flash ken? He'd always known Marlowe would find a way out; the same as he'd known he'd live and die in Seven Dials. But maybe he could save a few of the cubs before he met his Maker.

Gideon hunched his shoulders as he spotted another group of sailors in the dim light of a tavern. The most direct path was right by them, but he didn't want to risk it, and cut behind the building, keeping to the shadows. He still had his head down when something in the dark reached out and grasped his arm. Gideon would have yelled, but he was too busy fighting off the arm around his throat, cutting off his air.

"Hold still," a familiar voice murmured in his ear. Gideon went rigid. Slowly, the pressure on his throat eased. When he could breathe again, Gideon stepped forward then brought his elbow back with enough force to cause the other man to expel a breath of air and an "oof."

Gideon bent to look in the man's eyes. "Don't ever surprise me again."

"Next time I'll just call out," Sir Brook muttered, straightening. "I'm sure that won't attract any attention."

"You're late," Gideon said.

"How would you know? You've never had a watch you haven't stolen."

"I can tell time, and you're late."

Sir Brook shrugged. "I'm here now."

"I told you to meet me by the warehouse."

"Caught sight of you headed this way and doubled back. Are Dane and Marlowe still waiting for Satin, or is it all over?"

"They're still waiting," Gideon answered.

"Then why are you over here?"

"Your brother didn't want my help."

"Then he's an idiot. I thought we went over the plan earlier."

Gideon scowled. "And I thought I made it clear I'm not working with a thief-taker."

Sir Brook didn't speak, and Gideon could feel his piercing gaze. The inspector hadn't needed to threaten

Gideon earlier, and he didn't need to now. Gideon knew the man could make his life miserable, if he so chose. He blew out a breath. "Fine. I'll show you where they are."

"Quietly now."

And that was when they heard the scream.

⚜

Marlowe heard Satin approach just after the bells tolled a quarter to twelve. He had a distinctive walk, one which she had learned to recognize. When Satin was coming toward her, she moved out of the way. She'd suffered his kicks often enough that avoidance became second nature. Now she forced herself to stand her ground. He was expecting to meet her, expecting to make enough blunt to be able to walk away from the flash ken and his old life forever. She glanced at Dane, who leaned negligently on his walking stick. She could not decide if he was playing his part or really that unconcerned. "He's here," she murmured.

Dane straightened as Satin came into view. He tipped his hat and gave the crime lord a sweeping bow. Satin looked unimpressed. "Let's get this done."

"Not much for chitchat, are you?" Dane quipped.

Marlowe would have rolled her eyes, but she was reluctant to take her gaze from Satin. Something didn't feel right. Bony fingers skittered up and down her spine, and she moved in front of Dane slightly.

"This it?" Satin asked, nodding to the warehouse just a few feet away.

"I believe so," Dane said with a nod. "We have a

horse and wagon over there. You get inside, get past my father's men, and forty percent is yours."

Satin's eyes narrowed. "It's fifty percent, or I walk right now."

Dane sighed heavily. "Fine. Fifty percent."

Satin's gaze shifted to the warehouse. "I don't see no guards."

"That doesn't mean they aren't there," Marlowe said, speaking for the first time. "They might be inside."

"Then you and I will just have to take care of them, won't we?"

Marlowe shook her head. "This is your job, Satin. I'm with Lord Maxwell."

"You're with me." He reached into his coat and pulled out a snapper with one hand while grasping Marlowe by the wrist with the other. She let out a surprised scream, but in one quick motion, Satin hauled her against his foul-smelling chest and pressed the cold pistol barrel to her forehead. Marlowe's entire body convulsed in shock. Satin had never had a snapper before. Why did he have one now? Why hadn't she seen this coming?

Satin pulled her back with him, toward the warehouse. Marlowe dragged her feet, trying to slow him even as she cut her gaze to Dane. He held his walking stick at the ready, and Marlowe wanted to shake her head. If he unsheathed the tilter now, Satin might very well kill her and bolt. Of course, if Sir Brook was waiting to apprehend Satin on the other side of the warehouse, she was also done for. Satin's hand was shaking. One false move, and she would be dead.

"Let her go, Satin," Dane ordered, moving forward but keeping his tilter sheathed.

"Why? Two work quicker than one, and you and me 'ave worked together plenty, haven't we, Marlowe?"

"Yes," she managed, her voice sounding far stronger than she felt. "Put the snapper away. If you wanted my help that badly, you only had to ask."

Marlowe hadn't prayed in years—possibly in forever—but she was praying silently now. She didn't ask God to spare her. She figured she didn't matter as much to Him. But she asked God to make sure Satin didn't have second thoughts about pilfering the warehouse. She needed Sir Brook to catch Satin in the midst of the crime. If not, Satin would go free, and she did figure God cared a bit about all the harm and misery Satin caused.

Her gaze never left Dane's, and she could feel the intensity of his stare. The night was dark and the shadows long, but the clouds that had hovered all day had cleared, and the moon shone in the sky. Dane, heedless of his position in the open, stood with his gaze locked on hers. It might have been her imagination, but she could have sworn she saw more than affection, more than simple concern in his eyes. Yes, she wanted to see evidence that his feelings mirrored hers, but if she was going to die, was it so bad to die getting what she wanted?

"If ye're feeling so helpful," Satin said near her ear, his breath reeking of onions, "then you go in first."

Marlowe's gaze cut away from Dane, and she angled her head until she could see the warehouse. It was closer than she'd realized. Her feeble efforts at

slowing Satin hadn't worked as well as she'd hoped.
Suddenly, he turned her and shoved her up against the
warehouse door. There was no one in the warehouse.
Marlowe knew that as a fact, because Dane had leased
the empty warehouse himself. Satin would see as soon
as she opened the door that this was a fob. But getting
the door open was quite another matter. Dane had
been given a key to the padlock on the door, but she
couldn't very well ask him for it. After all, if they had
the key, why would they need a thief to break in?

"Open it," Satin hissed.

Marlowe shook her head. "You know I'm a hopeless dubber. Besides, I don't have my cracking tools."

"You got a dub. You always do. And you'd better
be quiet about it. I don't want whoever's inside getting suspicious."

Marlowe fumbled in her hair for the special tool,
the dub, used to pick locks. She could count on one
hand the number of times she'd used it, but that didn't
mean she didn't keep it close. Her fingers shook as she
pulled it free from the mass of hair she'd re-pinned
tightly, and she almost dropped it on the ground.

"Easy there," Satin whispered. "What has you so
jumpy? You're not going to turn stag, are you?"

"I'm no snitch," she lied. "I'm not used to working with a pistol pressed to my head." She gripped
the dub tighter and fit it into the padlock. She'd seen
Gideon do this dozens of times. He always made it
look simple. It was far from simple, but she could do
it if she concentrated. She closed her eyes and tried to
ignore the metal of the snapper now warming against
her flesh. She blocked out the wild thumping of her

heart and the sound of the blood rushing in her ears. She turned the dub, jiggling it this way and that, until she heard one of the pins click. Now she had to manage to unlock the others without clicking that one back into place.

A bead of perspiration trickled down her neck. This was not how she wanted to spend her last moments, and these were her last moments if she opened that warehouse door and Sir Brook didn't step in to nab Satin. What was the inspector waiting for? If he was nearby and watching, he could clearly see Satin—well, she—was cracking it. Why didn't Sir Brook nab Satin now—before he decided to put a pistol ball in her brain?

Another pin clicked open, and Marlowe prayed there was just one more. Deftly, she moved the dub into place and angled her wrist. She had a feel for the lock now. She could picture its inner workings in her mind. She flicked her wrist then eased the dub up just a fraction, and the pin clicked into place. The lock opened, and Marlowe stared at the door. She reached for the handle, her hand trembling.

"Go ahead," Satin whispered. "Open it."

❧

Gideon shoved Sir Brook back into the shadows of an abandoned building and ducked back himself. "Where the devil is Marlowe?" he muttered.

"Let me take a look," Sir Brook said, edging toward the side of the building.

"I'll look," Gideon said, pushing Brook back.

"Out of my way!" Brook shoved Gideon aside

and peered out. Gideon slinked forward and squinted into the darkness. There was Lord Dane, looking tense and at attention as he stared at the warehouse he and Marlowe had targeted. But where was Marlowe?

"He has her," Sir Brook said, nodding to the warehouse.

"Who?"

"The man by the door."

Gideon narrowed his eyes at the shadows and swore under his breath.

"Is it him? Satin?"

"That's the arch rogue bastard. He has her dubbing the lock. We have to get inside. Once she opens the door, Satin is going to know he was fobbed."

Brook pointed to a high warehouse window. "If I hoist you up, can you break it silently and crawl through?"

Gideon studied it. "I can mill a glaze in my sleep. How will you get in, or are you playing the diver, and I'm supposed to drop Marlowe down to you?"

"We're not cracking a house, Mr. Harrow."

"If I was, at least I could count on my cronies. How do I know you won't turn and run once I'm inside?"

Brook shrugged. "You don't. And don't think I'm not tempted to let the lot of you rogues kill each other off."

"Then why are you here?"

Brook nodded to Lord Dane. "Because he is. Let's go."

❧

The door creaked open, and Dane wanted to shout. He'd had a dozen opportunities to run Satin through with his sword, but every time his hands itched to pull the blade free, he thought about the pistol resting against Marlowe's temple, and he held his ground.

Brook wasn't coming. That much was obvious. Dane was on his own, and as soon as Satin stepped inside the building, Marlowe was as good as dead. Dane would reach the crime lord before he could prime his pistol again, but it would be too late for Marlowe. Still, he couldn't sit back and do nothing. He couldn't lose her.

Marlowe stood and pushed the door open. Satin gave her a shove into the dark warehouse and then stepped into the darkness himself. Dane ran forward and unsheathed his sword.

✄

Marlowe stumbled inside the warehouse and immediately cut to the right. It was darker there, and Satin couldn't kill her if he couldn't see her.

"What the devil?" Satin asked as he stared at the empty warehouse. "Ye're dead, girl."

Marlowe sucked in a breath as Satin turned the pistol on her. Apparently, she wasn't as well hidden as she'd thought, because he was aiming straight for her. She ducked her head, waiting for the blast, and then heard the yell.

✄

"No!" Gideon screamed, lunging forward. He'd dropped to the floor of the warehouse just as the door swung open. He looked up, saw the way Satin's mouth turned down, the glint of the snapper, and he ran.

~∞~

Dane saw Satin raise the pistol, and he hefted his sword. He was almost to the doorway when something large and heavy slammed into him, sending him sprawling. The man was instantly on top of him. Dane managed to hold on to his sword, though the other man attempted to wrench it away. Dane swung his left hand, landing a decent blow to the man's chest, just below the throat. "Damn it, Dane!"

Dane pulled his next punch and stared at the man above him—his brother. "What the devil are you doing?"

"Saving you, you bloody idiot."

That was when they heard the roar of the pistol.

~∞~

"Gideon!" Marlowe screamed. She'd thrown her hand up at the flash of the powder, but she dropped it in time to see Gideon fall. "No!" She rose to her knees, only to be knocked back by the butt of Satin's pistol.

"You thought to bilk me?" Satin screamed. "Me? I'll smash you and then hack you into tiny pieces, you little blackguard." He raised the snapper again, but Marlowe brought her foot up, catching him in the nutmegs. It was a glancing blow, but enough to make Satin double over. Enough to buy her an extra moment to scurry out of his path. And then he was bearing down on her again. He lowered the snapper, and she rolled to the side, wincing when the pistol smashed into the floor. That was the end of the weapon, at least.

But Satin was not done with her yet. He lunged at her, landing hard and knocking the breath out of her. This was a fight she couldn't win. Satin had every advantage. But she knew how to fight dirty, and she'd inflict as much pain and damage as she could before she met Old Mr. Grim. She let out a scream and went wild, scratching, clawing, and kicking in every direction. Satin landed a shocking blow to the side of her face, and she saw stars, but she didn't stop fighting.

And then suddenly someone was yelling, and she hoped it was Satin. She hoped she'd drawn blood. But his weight fell off her, and she heard another voice from far away. It was a moment before she could convince her body to cease struggling, and then she opened her eyes, and there was Dane.

Eighteen

MARLOWE STARED AT HIM, HER EYES WILD AND UNSEE-
ing. And then she blinked and stilled and was back.
Dane moved, taking her in his arms. But she wasn't
one to be held and coddled. She pushed back.

"Where's Satin?"

Dane nodded to his brother, who was securing
Satin's wrists with iron. "We have him," Dane reassured her. "You did it."

But Marlowe shook her head and pushed to
her feet.

"Your face is bleeding, darling. You'd better rest."

"No! Gideon," she said on a sob and staggered
forward. Dane cocked his head and then made out
the shape of a man on the warehouse floor near the
window. Marlowe stumbled toward him, falling to her
knees and gathering him in her arms.

It hit Dane as hard as a hammer in the breadbox
that she loved the man. His jealousy hadn't been
misplaced. He watched, unable to move, as she
bent over the man's form and wept. Would anyone
have mourned him with so much passion? Would

his death have been anything more than a notice in *The Times*?

Dane rose and forced his legs to move across the floor, to comfort Marlowe. If Dane was second choice, then he would take it. He'd been born to be an earl. He'd always had the best of everything. But none of it mattered if he didn't have Marlowe. Nothing mattered without her.

The man on the floor shifted, and Dane caught his breath. "Marlowe." But she didn't hear him. Her face was buried in her hands as she wept. "Marlowe, he's alive."

"What?" She looked up, her tear-stained face incredulous. Slowly, Gideon turned over, groaning loudly.

"Thank God," Brook muttered behind them. "The last thing I need is a dead body to explain."

"Your concern gets me," Gideon muttered, sitting and tapping his heart with his fist. "Right here."

"Are you hurt?" Marlowe asked as Dane came to stand behind her.

"Just my pride. I hit my head on the floor when I ducked. I don't think I have a slug in me." He looked down at his chest, seemed to be checking if everything was in its right spot. Marlowe didn't wait for him to complete his inspection; she fell into his arms. It was the hardest thing he'd ever done, but Dane clenched his hands and didn't interfere. He glanced at his brother, who was hauling Satin away. The sympathetic look his brother sent him was far from welcome. Dane had never been the object of pity before.

Marlowe helped Gideon to his feet, and Dane followed them out of the warehouse.

"Don't suppose any of you could lend me a hand with this thief," Brook said. "I caught him rifling this warehouse." He winked.

"I'll kill you!" Satin yelled. "I'll kill the whole lot of you."

"I'll help," Marlowe said. She stepped forward, pulled her arm back, and hit Satin across the face. She might be small, but she had a good arm. Satin's head snapped back. He didn't lose consciousness, but she shut him up. She stepped closer to him. "That's for all the times you beat on people smaller than you. I hope you think of me when you drop from that scaffold at Newgate. I can't wait to see your neck stretched."

"Why, you—"

Brook stepped in front of Satin. "I'll take it from here."

"Will he hang?" Dane asked.

"With everything we know about him? We'd hang him twice if we could."

Dane heard Marlowe let out a sigh, and he could see her shoulders slump. It was over for her now. She was finally free.

"I'll go with you," Gideon said. "I'd like to make sure he doesn't escape."

Brook raised a brow. "You'd voluntarily enter a prison?"

"I didn't say I'd enter, but I'll see you get there."

"Let's go, then."

The two of them started away, and Dane cleared his throat. "Brook?"

His brother turned back.

"Thank you. We couldn't have done it without you."

Brook smiled. "I know that must have hurt. Sometimes it's not so bad having a hero for a brother." With a tip of his hat, Brook walked on.

Marlowe looked up at Dane. "I see why you don't like him."

"He has his uses."

"That he does."

Dane glanced down at her hand. She held a gold chain in it. "What's that?"

She smiled. "My last dive."

All her flash talk was making his head spin. "I have a horse and wagon to return. And then, Miss Marlowe, how would you like to spend your first night free of Satin?"

She shook her head, and Dane resisted taking her face in his hands to have a closer look at the welt on her cheek. She'd have a bruise tomorrow, and her head must be aching right now. "Would you believe me if I said I wanted a bath?"

"No."

"Well, believe it. You really have corrupted me, Lord Dane."

Dane took her hand. "That's only the start."

He ordered her a bath when they arrived back at the town house, and one for himself as well. He had work, details to see to, but it could wait until after he was clean. When he'd bathed and shaved, he dressed in trousers and a linen shirt and made his way to the library, where Crawford waited for him. Dane spent the next hour giving orders and writing missives to his solicitor. He was bleary-eyed and ready for his bed when Brook opened the library door. "Thought I'd find you here."

"Is Satin in prison?"

"He's under lock and key," Brook said, going to a small tray where Dane kept several decanters of spirits. He poured a brandy and sipped it.

"Good. And Gideon?"

"He's gone back to"—Brook gestured vaguely—"wherever it is he goes."

Dane shook his head. "It's a hovel. You should see how they live. Tomorrow I'm for Seven Dials and hiring Marlowe's friends. They can start as grooms or tigers."

Brook lifted a brow. "We'll be robbed three times over."

Dane shrugged. "I have to give them a chance."

"What has gotten into you?" Brook asked. "You were never one for charity or benevolence. What was it you once said? For the poor always ye have with you?"

Dane glowered at his brother. "That was Christ. I said—well, never mind what I said. I was wrong."

Brook started. "Pardon? Could you repeat that? I didn't hear you."

"You heard me. I was an idiot before—"

"Go on. I'm listening." He grinned.

"—but I've changed."

"I suppose I don't have to ask why. Is she here?"

Dane looked at the ceiling. "She's upstairs. Asleep, I imagine."

Brook sipped his brandy. "And are you going to ask her to marry you?"

Now it was Dane's turn to register shock. "Are you mad? I can't marry her."

"Even if she is Lady Elizabeth?"

"Even so. Her life before…the scandal…the past Earls of Dane would rise up from their graves."

"I never thought you were the sort of man who cared what anyone said about him. But, come to think of it, you've never done anything that would cause anyone to talk. You've been the perfect heir to the earldom. Until Marlowe. I think she's good for you."

Dane made a face. "She is not good for me."

"You're right. She's bad for you, and that's just what you need. Why, for the last few years, I've worried every time you gave a speech in Parliament that you might start an epidemic of yawning."

"I hope you are amusing yourself."

"I always do." He raised a finger. "But I have a feeling that whatever happens in the next few days, no one will be yawning."

Dane pushed past his brother. "I am for bed."

"One last thing, Brother," Brook said, causing Dane to pause at the door. "I received word this evening that Lord and Lady Lyndon have returned to Town."

Dane turned. "That was quick."

"Apparently, they were already en route to London but hurried their journey to arrive as soon as possible. I imagine they will call in the morning."

"I'll tell Marlowe."

"You'd better do more than that," Brook called after him, "or you will lose her."

And just what the devil did that mean? Dane wondered as he climbed the stairs, candle held aloft to light his way. He'd almost lost Marlowe tonight, and he wouldn't risk it again. Dane pushed the door to his bedchamber open, momentarily surprised when Tibbs didn't greet him. But, of course, he'd told the man to go to bed. Tibbs had made certain the fire burned in the hearth and set out a glass—no, two glasses of wine—for him. Two glasses?

Dane's gaze traveled to his large crimson-and-gold-draped bed, and he sucked in a breath. Reclining on her side with her elbow propping up her head, was Marlowe. Her hair was down about her shoulders, a rich swirl of chocolate against the white of her linen chemise. Her thin linen chemise. He could see the faintest hints of her skin through the fabric.

"I thought you were never coming to bed," she said, smiling at him.

"How did you get in here?"

She raised a brow. "I opened the door."

"Of course." He was having a bit of trouble thinking with her so close and looking so utterly alluring. "And why did you come?"

"Isn't that obvious?"

"Yes, and thank God." He crossed to the bed, and before he reached her, she sat and opened her arms to him. He pulled her to him, the heat of her body seeping into him, making him realize how cold he'd been. She smelled of apricot, and her hair was slightly damp from the bath she'd taken. His lips found hers, and she returned his kiss with eagerness. In fact, he found himself struggling to reject the urge to push her onto her back and thrust into her right then and there.

She broke the kiss and looked up at him, her hands pushing his hair back from his forehead. "Do you know how long I've been wanting to kiss you?"

"I had no idea, or I would have come to bed much, much sooner." He bent to take her mouth again, but she placed a finger over his lips.

"It was when you pulled that tilter—that sword— from your walking stick and brandished it at those three boys." She giggled. "The looks on their faces! And you, with one hand on your hip, one leg before the other, as though you were ready to duel."

Dane nodded. "In hindsight, I probably did not need to assume proper fencing stance."

"No, you did not, but I am glad you did." Her voice lowered a fraction, and Dane's breath caught in his throat.

"Why is that?"

"Because watching you made me feel incredibly ill."

Dane's eyes narrowed. "That was not the answer I was expecting."

She laughed. "But, as you pointed out, what I think is illness is actually arousal. Watching you, I was incredibly aroused."

"Were you?"

Her eyes darkened to a deep sapphire. "I still am."

"What shall we do about your…condition?"

"There's only one thing to do."

"What's that?"

She rose, leaning close to his ear, and whispered in vulgar, quite descriptive terms exactly what she wanted. Dane had never heard a lady speak like that, and at the moment he was quite thrilled that Marlowe was no lady. When she was done, his throat was dry, and he could not seem to speak. Instead, he nodded, then digging his hands in her hair, brought her mouth to his. Her hands fisted in his shirt, and she kissed him hard, dipping her tongue into his mouth so he could taste her. She tasted of the wine and of Marlowe.

His hands found the hem of her chemise, and he ran his fingers along the warm, sleek skin of her thighs as he raised the material to her waist and then to her shoulders. She lifted her arms, and he stripped the garment away, dropping it on the floor and inhaling sharply.

The room at the public house had been dark, too dark for him to appreciate what he saw now. She was lovely. Her legs were long and slender, her hips slim but sweetly curved. Her waist was small. He placed his hands on either side of it and moved them upward to cup her breasts. They were full and heavy, the nipples a dark rose and hard with arousal. He brushed a finger over one, and her head rolled back. He repeated the motion, and she moaned.

She'd told him to take her quickly, but he was not in the habit of following orders—even if said orders were most agreeable. Instead, he lowered his lips to her hardened peak and feathered kisses over the tender skin, making it pebble. He teased her with his tongue, lightly at first, and then flicking her until her back arched. One hand slid behind her, holding her where he wanted her, holding her against him, while the other explored the swell of her hips and bottom, trailing over her skin until he cupped her sex. She was warm, and he took her nipple into his mouth. He sucked gently and felt her grow wet.

His finger slid easily inside the moist heat of her, and he stroked in and out, teasing that small nub at the center of her. Her body moved to match the rhythm he set, and her breathing sped up, punctuated by small cries of pleasure. His own member was hardening. The more he aroused her, the more aroused he became. And yet he could have pleasured her all night and taken nothing in return. This was for her. He wanted to give her everything she desired and more.

Dane slipped another finger inside her, and she cried out again, "Yes. Oh, yes."

He slicked his fingers over her center again, and she began to tremble. She was close, so close he could feel the first tremors of her climax rippling through her. But he wanted to give her more. He wanted pleasure to crash through her until she was so stunned she could not even think. He wanted her to feel as he did every single time he laid eyes on her. And so at the last moment, he pushed her down on the bed, spread her legs wide, and took her with his mouth. She bowed up, crying out as he teased and sucked and stroked her until she was shaking and pleading that she could stand no more.

He rose on his knees, loosed the fall of his trousers, and her eyes opened. They were half-lidded with pleasure, but she reached out and stroked his hard member. "That's what I've been waiting for. Hard and fast."

"If that's what you want." In one move, he turned her onto her stomach then came down on top of her. She turned her head to the side to look up at him, and he murmured in her ear, "Do you want this?" His tongue teased the delicate skin behind and below her ears, and she squirmed against him. He prayed she agreed, because he had never wanted a woman—never wanted anything—as much as he wanted this.

"Yes."

His hands gripped her hips, raising them. He kicked her legs apart and opened her. On her elbows, her head turned so she could see him, she smiled. He would have driven into her, but he was no brute. He would not risk hurting her. Instead, he entered her slowly, inching inside until he filled her. She moaned, and he moved, stroking her. Taking her hips in his hands, he thrust in and out, holding his own pleasure back as long as he could. When he felt it mounting, he reached for that small, tender nub at her center and stroked it.

"Dane," she cried as she tensed around him.

"My name, Marlowe."

"Maxwell," she breathed as she gripped him in the throes of passion. With her climax, his own came, and they both tumbled over into darkness.

❧

Several hours later, Marlowe lay weak and sated in Dane's bed. The curtains had been drawn, but she could see the light from the sun beginning to seep through in slim slivers of gold. Beside her, Maxwell lay sleeping. He'd taken her—and she'd taken him—several more times that night, and she felt sore and achy and thoroughly pleased.

He was a man with many sides. He could be tender and sweet, and rough and demanding. No matter what side he showed, he always made her heart pound. If she didn't think it would kill both of them, she would have taken him again right there. Maybe next time he could strap on his tilter and do a few of his fencing stances—naked. She giggled at the thought, and then sobered when she heard the sound of footsteps outside the door.

The servants were awake, and that meant the mopsqueezers would be in soon to see to the fire and the linens. His valet would arrive to dress him. Cook would have breakfast ready for them. How easy it would be for her to settle into a life like this. Her every need would be seen to. Her every desire catered to. How easy to forget where she had come from and the squalor she left behind. If she were Dane's countess, there was so much she could do to help those trapped in rookeries like Seven Dials. But that was false confidence. She was in his bed, and assumed she was in his heart. But for a man like Dane, it was a long path from lover to wife, especially when the lover was nothing more than a common thief. He'd never take her as his wife, and she didn't expect him to.

Except for the small fact that she was in love with him. Desperately, madly, completely in love with him. A few days ago, she would have laughed at the very idea she would ever marry the Earl of Dane. Now she was not laughing. She wanted him to be hers, in the same way she was already his. A few days ago, she might have been persuaded to accept the role of his mistress, but that was before she'd fallen in love with him. That was before the idea of him looking at another woman, touching another woman, sleeping with another woman made her so angry she could hit someone or something.

Marlowe elbowed Dane roughly. He mumbled then opened his eyes. "What's wrong?"

"Nothing. Yet."

He frowned at her then reached over and pulled her into his arms. "Go back to sleep," he murmured against her neck. She almost complied. It would be lovely to snuggle up to him, press her cheek against his warm, solid chest, and sleep. He smelled of sleepy man and clean linen, and there was a hint of her own scent on him too. She liked that, knowing he was hers, if only for a few hours. But he was not hers, and she couldn't go back to sleep.

She pushed back and sat, pulling the sheet up to her neck. "The staff is awake. The maids and your valet will be here soon."

"I don't care."

"I do. I don't want them to see me here."

One eye opened. "Because it's improper?"

She nodded. "I don't want everyone whispering about me any more than they do. I'm not a bawd."

He sat and faced her. "No one would ever think that of you. You don't think that's my opinion of you?"

She wanted to ask what his opinion of her really was, but she had too much pride. She hopped off the bed and found her chemise. After she pulled it over her head, she said, "I should go."

"Back to your room?"

She shook her head. "No. Back..." Seven Dials was hardly a home. "Back to where I came from."

Now Dane rose and grabbed her arm. He was apparently unconcerned about his nudity, but Marlowe was quite aware of it. "No. I told you. You're not going back there."

"I have nowhere else to go. And you know where to find me if Lord and Lady Lyndon are still interested in meeting me when they return from Scotland."

"They can find you right here."

She shook her head. "This is your home, not mine. My presence here has forced your mother and sister to leave, and caused you to risk your life. I thank you for your help. I do. I can't say how much it meant to me, but I don't belong here."

"You don't know that. If you are Lady Elizabeth, this is exactly where you belong."

She leveled a look at him, and she watched as the realization of what he'd just said dawned on him. He opened his mouth but didn't correct his statement. Marlowe supposed she had no choice but to put her pride aside. "Are you saying that if I'm Lady Elizabeth you want to marry me? That's the only way I could truly belong here."

He looked away. She didn't even need to wait for the words, because she knew what he would say now. He didn't want to marry her. Of course he didn't. What man of any means or character would want to marry her? She was such a fool for even suggesting it. She'd known he would never marry her, known that a night or two was all they would have, and she had wanted it to be enough. But her heart had other ideas. Her heart wanted it all.

"Marlowe, I care about you, but marriage is—"

She shook her head. "I do not want to hear your explanations of what marriage is. It's not something you want from me, and I knew that. I don't know why I even mentioned it, because I know you would never become leg-shackled to me. It's just I had to be an idiot and go and fall in love with you."

He released her and stepped back, a look of pure shock on his face. "What did you say?"

"Nothing. Go back to your life, Dane, and I'll return to mine. I can see myself out."

She found her wrapper and pulled it on, cinching it tightly at the waist. All the while, he stood completely frozen, as though he was still reeling from her revelation. She practically ran to the door and had it open when he finally spoke. "You can't leave yet."

"You can't stop me."

"That's not what I meant."

She looked back and met his gaze.

"Your—Lord and Lady Lyndon are in Town. They want to see you this morning. Here."

Nineteen

MARLOWE'S LEGS GAVE OUT AT HIS WORDS. SHE DIDN'T think she could have possibly heard him correctly. Lord and Lady Lyndon were in Scotland.

"Brook told me last night," Dane said, still standing naked as a new babe in the middle of his bedchamber. "They were en route to London and made haste when they received his missive."

"And you didn't tell me last night?"

He had the grace to look ashamed. "When I saw you…it slipped my mind. I apologize. You will stay to meet them?"

She nodded. "Yes, and then…" She did not know what would happen next. "And then I'll be out of your way. If you don't mind, I'll make use of the dress Susanna lent me. I'll return it when I can."

Dane shook his head. "Keep it."

"No. I'm not a thief any longer." She closed the door on him and walked quickly back to her room, ignoring the servants she passed. She didn't want to see their looks of curiosity, and she didn't want them to see the weak tears welling in her eyes. He was well and truly done with her. He hadn't even asked her to stay. He hadn't even tried to make her change her mind. He was giving her the dress and dismissing her. He hadn't wanted her to feel like a bawd, but she felt like one now.

When she reached her room, she had enough time to wash and begin dressing before Jane knocked on her door. For once, Marlowe gratefully accepted her assistance dressing, but she wouldn't allow the maid to do more than pull her hair back in a tail. "I don't want to look like a rum mort," she said. "This is who I am."

Finally, she was ready, and she took a last look at the room she'd inhabited for so short a time. This had been the first room she'd called her own. The first bed she had slept in—well, the second. She'd been a different person when she first entered this room. Now she was free of Satin. Now her heart was broken.

She made her way downstairs and heard the clink of silver on plate. She peered in the dining room and found Brook sitting there, sipping from a cup. Behind him, Crawford stood with his back against the wall and his eyes fixed forward. When Brook saw her, he rose. "There you are," he said with a smile. "Did you sleep well?"

She scowled at him. "Is that supposed to be amusing?" Was there anyone who didn't know she'd spent the night with Dane?

His brows rose. "It was supposed to be a polite morning greeting."

Perhaps he didn't know. "Oh. Then yes."

"Where is Dane?"

"How should I know?"

Brook held up his hands. "I seem to be saying all of the wrong things this morning. Let us start again. Good morning, Marlowe. Would you like tea?" He gestured to Crawford.

"No." She swallowed. "Thank you."

Brook crossed to a chair and pulled it out. "May I offer you a seat?"

She sighed. "Fine." She took the chair, and he took his, and they looked at each other for a long moment. Marlowe looked away. When would Lord and Lady Lyndon be here? She wanted away from this place.

"Would you like me to make you a plate?" Brook asked. "At breakfast, we generally serve ourselves from the sideboard."

"I know what the proper thing to do is. I'm just not hungry."

"That's something I never expected to hear you say," Dane said from the doorway. She hadn't even heard him come down the stairs. He stood tall and handsome in charcoal-gray breeches and coat. His riding boots were polished until they gleamed, and his cravat was snowy white against the dark red of his waistcoat. She had to make herself look away.

"Did you tell her?" Brook asked.

Dane entered and crossed to a seat opposite her. "About her parents? Yes."

Brook nodded and smiled at her. "Then perhaps it's just nerves."

"When will they be here?" Marlowe asked suddenly. "I don't have all day."

"Ah, yes, your pressing business in Seven Dials," Dane said. "If you don't object, I might go with you."

"What?"

"I said—"

"*Why?*" She didn't want Dane going with her. She was trying to get away from him.

"I thought I might see if any of your gang would like honest work. I could always use a new groom, and Lloyd could train a new footman."

Crawford made a noise that sounded suspiciously like something an injured animal might make, but when she looked at him, he appeared unfazed. "Why would you do that?" Marlowe asked.

"Because I want to help those less fortunate than myself. This seemed as good a start as any."

"Well, they won't take you up on it. Who would want to be a slavey when he can make more diving?" She looked at Crawford. "No offense."

"I assure you, miss, none taken."

"Because you're not likely to have your neck stretched in service," Brook pointed out.

"Or face transportation," Dane added. "I cannot force them to accept my offer, but I can make it, can I not?"

He was right, and who was she to stand in the way of Gap or Tiny or Stub finding honest work? She didn't want to see any of the cubs dance upon nothing at the gallows. If Dane hired them, it was a better future than what was in store for her. She didn't know what she would do tonight or tomorrow or the week after. She just knew she couldn't stay here.

Dane asked for tea, and the three sat in silence as the men sipped from their cups. Marlowe wondered how long she would have to sit here. How long she would have to wait until she knew who she really was? Still, when the knock came, she was unprepared.

"Who would be calling at this hour?" Crawford murmured, leaving his post, but not before Lloyd, the head footman, took his place.

"If it is Lord and Lady Lyndon, show them to the drawing room," Dane said casually, but his gaze was on Marlowe. She could feel him watching her. She hoped he could not see how she trembled. She hadn't known how she would feel when this moment came, but she'd hoped she would be able to pretend as though she didn't care. As though whether these people accepted her or not meant nothing to her. She didn't need them. She didn't care if they wanted her or not.

But now she feared she wouldn't be able to pretend. She was too nervous, too scared the Lyndons would not know her. And she was equally afraid they would. What would she do if she was Lady Elizabeth? Could she accept that her whole life was about to change?

As if in a dream, Crawford returned. He must have said the visitors were Lord and Lady Lyndon, because Brook and Dane rose and gestured for her to follow. Her body obeyed, but she seemed to have no control over its actions. She followed Brook up the stairs, wishing now that she had allowed Jane to style her hair more artfully. She felt so plain and so utterly not like a *lady* must feel.

Dane was behind her, and he was saying something. From the tone of his voice, it seemed designed to put her at ease, but she couldn't hear him. There was a rushing sound in her ears that blocked everything else out. And then before she knew it, she was standing outside the drawing-room doors and Crawford swung them open and she stood face-to-face with an older, distinguished-looking man. She stared at him, willed herself to recognize him, but he wasn't familiar at all. He looked like every other swell she knew. He was dressed in fine clothing, albeit a bit wrinkled from his journey. His hair was dark brown with streaks of gray. He was short and stocky, and he looked at her with narrowed eyes.

Dane exchanged some sort of greeting with the man, and Brook did as well. All three of the men spoke, but Lyndon did not take his gaze from her. Neither could she pull hers from him. Finally, she closed her eyes, swallowed, and when she opened them again, she heard him say, "Is this her, then?"

"Yes." That was Dane. "This is Marlowe. Sir Brook can explain where and how he came to conclude she might be the…person you are looking for."

"Where did you find her?" Lyndon asked. Brook had acted as though the man was desperate to see her, but he obviously wasn't pleased with what he saw. He sounded hard and cold, and Marlowe began to wish she could find a means of escape. This was wrong. She wasn't Lady Elizabeth after all.

"She was living in Seven Dials, part of a group of criminals," Brook said. "I believe the leader, Satin, abducted her as a child. I've taken him into custody, and when I questioned him about it, he all but admitted as much."

Marlowe's gaze snapped to Brook. When had he questioned Satin? Had Satin told the truth, or said what the inspector wanted to hear in order to buy himself an easier punishment?

"That doesn't mean she's mine," Lyndon said. He looked at Marlowe again. "What is your name, gel?"

"I—" Her voice wouldn't seem to work, and she cleared her throat and tried again. "I'm called Marlowe."

"And have you ever been called anything else?"

"No, my lord," she said. "Not so as I remember." There were those memories of being called Elizabeth, but she didn't even know if they were real memories or just her imaginings. And if she told this man she remembered the name, wouldn't he think she was lying because she wanted to be his daughter? She was a thief. No one thought she did anything because it was right, only if it was for profit. And so she didn't mention the memory. She realized she was biting the pad of her thumb and hastily lowered her hand to her side.

"Do you remember anything about your childhood?" Lord Lyndon asked. "Did this Satin tell you where you came from?"

"He said I was a bawd's by-blow," she told him. "She didn't want me, and he took me in."

Lord Lyndon's mouth turned down in distaste, and he gave Sir Brook a look that indicated this had been a waste of time. "I paid you to find my daughter, not the bastard of some whore."

Dane stepped forward. "You will watch what you say about her, sir. Whether or not she is your daughter, you will treat her with respect."

Lyndon inclined his head. "Of course. My apologies, Lord Dane." He addressed Brook again. "We will speak soon. Thank you for your efforts, but she is not my daughter." He turned. "I will see myself out."

The drawing-room doors opened and closed, and Marlowe felt her legs give way. A dainty chair was nearby, and she clawed for it, sitting heavily. Dane was beside her immediately. "I am so sorry, Marlowe. I honestly thought——"

She held up a hand. "You don't have to apologize. I told you all along I wasn't any swell's daughter."

"He's wrong," Brook said. "I searched for months to find you. Everything about you tells me you are Lady Elizabeth—your history, your appearance, even Satin admitted as much."

"He lied," Marlowe said. "And I don't care. I've had enough." Her legs felt suddenly stronger, and she rose.

"What are you doing?" Dane asked.

"Leaving." She started for the doors.

"I'll fetch my walking stick and accompany you."

"No." She turned to face him. "I don't want to see you ever again. I"—her voice broke—"I cannot take any more."

"Marlowe."

She waved her hand, dismissing him, and practically ran to the drawing-room doors. They were still open, and she rushed through them and down the stairs. At the front door, Crawford stood guard. "Out of my way, pantler."

"With pleasure, miss." He stepped aside, and Marlowe reached for the door.

❧

She was leaving, Dane thought. She was leaving, and she was not coming back. He should let her go. That was the right thing to do. The proper thing. He was an earl, and she was a common thief. Even if Lord Lyndon had acknowledged her, she would still be a thief. She was not the sort of woman he could marry. He had a duty to the past and future Earls of Dane, and he had always done his duty.

But she was leaving, and devil take him if he had anticipated how much her departure would pain him. It was as though his heart was being ripped from his body and dragged through the street with each step she took.

"Will you allow her to go?" Brook asked with what sounded like passing interest. How could his brother be so nonchalant when Dane felt as though a piece of him had been torn out and stomped on?

"You love her, you know," Brook added.

Dane turned to his brother. That was it. That was the feeling. He *loved* her. Dane didn't think he'd ever loved anyone or anything like this before. And he knew he never would again.

"I love her," he said, his voice sounding as though it came from someone else. It was full of wonder and awe. But of course he loved her. He must have loved her for days, if not almost since the beginning. Why else would he have gone with her to Seven Dials, allowed her to stay under his roof, decided to write that bill to help the poor? What else but love could have changed his mind about the lower classes, could have made him see them as people and not simply criminals? His father would turn in his grave, and

Dane did not care. He loved Marlowe, and she loved him back. She'd told him so. "I love her," he repeated.

"And?" Brook asked.

"And I love her!" Dane shouted. "I really do love her."

"Will you do anything about it?"

Dane frowned at him. "Do…?"

Brook raised a brow. "Stop her, for instance?"

"Stop?" Oh, yes. She was leaving. No, he couldn't let her leave, not without telling her how he felt. Not without begging her to forgive him, to marry him, to say—again—she loved him back. Why hadn't he told her this morning? Why hadn't he realized he could not lose her? She was everything.

Dane sprinted toward the stairs, taking them two at a time and almost falling and breaking his fool neck. But he didn't care. He didn't care about anything but reaching her.

"Stop her!" he yelled to Crawford when he saw the butler step aside and allow her to reach for the front door.

She turned to face him, her mouth dropping open at the wild display he must be making. Dane started to laugh. He must look like a madman, and he didn't care. It didn't matter. To hell with decorum and duty and all the rest. *He loved her!*

He skidded to a stop before her, and her eyes went wide. She looked up at him, clearly at a loss for words.

"You cannot leave," Dane said, panting. "Do not leave, I beg you." He grasped her hand, holding her in place.

"Why not?" she said finally, looking down at his hand holding hers.

"Because"—Dane glanced up at Crawford, who made no attempt to hide the fact that he was staring. Dane looked over at Lloyd, peeking out of the dining room. He peered up at Brook, slowly descending the stairs. And he didn't care if he had an audience. He wanted to shout it from the rooftops—"because I love you." He sank to one knee. Crawford made a pained sound, but Dane ignored him. "Because I want to marry you. Please, Marlowe. Will you do me the *great honor* of becoming my wife?"

She looked at him for a long moment, so long he thought perhaps she hadn't heard him. He knew he'd spoken the words, because Crawford's eyes were shut and his face contorted in pain. And then she opened her mouth, closed it, opened it again, and said, "No."

Dane felt as though his world was spiraling down, down, down into oblivion. His vision dimmed, and everything around him save her seemed to grow dark and shadowy. She'd said *no*. He'd lost her. He *could not* lose her. Fortunately, he was a man accustomed to winning, and he would win her. She was worth every effort.

"If you think that means I'm giving up, think again." He rose and grasped her hand to keep her from bolting. "I'll ask you every day. I'll prove to you how much you mean to me. I'll never give up, Marlowe."

She shook her head. "You have to. Don't you see? I'm nothing. I'm no one. You cannot marry me. What kind of countess would I make?"

She was right. She was perfectly correct. It was a prime mésalliance. If it had been another man, Dane would have been shocked and appalled. He would have commented that the other man had married far beneath him. But something had changed in Dane the day he met Marlowe. He'd seen her as less than human before. He'd seen all of the poor as less than human. And now, he saw that he had been the one who'd been inhuman. He had cared more for himself than his fellow humans, and in that way been more like an animal than he wanted to admit.

"At one time I would have been bothered by your position," Dane admitted. "But now it doesn't matter to me in the least. *You* are not a class. You are a person. You're my Marlowe. I need you." He gestured to the house and the servants. "Don't you see that none of this means anything to me if I don't have you? You are my *everything*." It was so appallingly true. Nothing mattered without her.

She tried to pull her hand from his, but he wouldn't release her. "But I don't know how to be a countess. I don't know how to behave in your world."

"Then we'll live in your world."

Her eyes widened in shock. "You don't mean that."

"Oh, yes, I do. I'll walk away now if you but say the word."

"Max, no." She was calling him Max. That, at least, was a good sign.

"Or we'll make our own world, Marlowe. I don't care where we live or what we do, as long as I live with you. I love you, Marlowe. I have never loved anyone, not like this. And I will spend the rest of my days, the rest of my hours, the rest of my minutes, doing everything I possibly can to make you happy. All you need to do is say yes."

She shook her head, but he saw the emotion in her

eyes. He saw the sparkle of tears and the tremble of her lips. "Allow me to make you happy, Marlowe."

"I—"

A quiet rap interrupted the weighted silence in the vestibule. Dane swore, Marlowe jumped with surprise, and Crawford cleared his throat and moved, with all the dignity he seemed to be able to muster, to answer the knock. Dane stared as Crawford revealed Lady Lyndon on the stoop. "Lady Lyndon," he said in surprise. "Won't you come in?"

Marlowe's hand tightened almost painfully on his. Lady Lyndon's eyes flicked to Marlowe, and she nodded and entered. "I am sorry to interrupt."

"You just missed your husband, my lady," Dane told her.

The marchioness's mouth turned down, and Dane blinked. The expression was exactly the same one he had seen Marlowe make on occasion when she was annoyed. "No, I did not. He is waiting in the coach." She looked down. "I had been waiting there earlier, but I could not leave without meeting her." She glanced up at Marlowe again. "Is this she?"

Marlowe spoke. "I'm Marlowe, my lady. I'm sorry about your daughter and sorry you came all this way only to be disappointed."

Brook came forward then. "Are you disappointed, Lady Lyndon? As I mentioned in my note, I investigated your daughter's abduction, and Marlowe's background thoroughly. I do believe she is Lady Elizabeth."

Dane could believe it too. One look at mother and daughter, and it was impossible not to see the resemblance. Both had the same thick dark hair, the

same large eyes—though Lady Lyndon's were lighter
blue—the same nose and determined set of the jaw.

Lady Lyndon had not torn her gaze from Marlowe.
"Do you…do you remember me?"

Marlowe looked at Brook and then Dane, and then
shook her head.

⁓

It pained her more than she wanted to admit to shake
her head. The white-haired woman seemed kind and
genuine and in deep pain. But Marlowe did not recognize her. She had always thought when—*if*—she ever
saw her mother again, she would know her face, her
voice, her scent. But this woman was a stranger to her.
If her heart had cracked a little at Lord Lyndon's rejec-
tion, it absolutely ripped in half when she had to deny
this woman. She'd allowed herself to hope, which was
a dangerous and futile thing in Seven Dials. Now she
would suffer the heartache for her foolishness.

The woman smiled sadly and stepped back. "Then
I won't take up any more of your time. Thank you."
She turned, and Crawford, who had barely closed the
door behind her, reached for it again. But before he
had it open, Lady Lyndon looked back again. "I have
one question, and I cannot leave without asking it."

"I'll answer if I can, my lady."

"Do you remember your mother, Marlowe?"

Marlowe shook her head and then slowly changed
her mind and nodded. She had never told anyone
save Gideon of these memories. She had been too
frightened to even mention them. Some of the fear
still lingered, but Satin was gone now. He could never

hurt her again. She squeezed Max's hand tightly and then released it. She needed to do this on her own. "I do remember a little."

Lady Lyndon stepped closer. "Tell me what you remember."

Marlowe closed her eyes and tried to picture that time so long ago. The pain in her chest when she thought of it was sharp and still fresh, but it could be no worse than the ache she would feel when this woman walked away. "I remember she was always laughing. She was so happy. And she had fancy clothes." She smiled slightly. "At least they seemed so to me." There was more, but she had never told anyone this part. It was the last thing that was truly hers and hers alone. She swallowed. "I…I remember I liked it when Mama did bedtime and not Nanny. Mama always sang to me."

"What song did she sing?" a feminine voice asked.

"I don't—" But she did remember. When she thought back very hard, she did remember. "Elizabeth's true, dilly, dilly," she sang quietly. "Elizabeth's sweet." She could not remember the rest of the words. They hung just beyond memory. "A…kiss…will…" she began tentatively.

"A kiss I will give, dilly, dilly," Lady Lyndon sang with her. "When next we meet."

They sang the last together, and when it was done, Marlowe heard not a sound, not even breathing. She opened her eyes, and the first thing she saw was a woman's gloves gripping her hand. Lady Lyndon had taken Marlowe's hand in both of hers. And then she looked up and stared into the woman's eyes. Tears streamed down her face.

"You know the song," Marlowe said.

Lady Lyndon nodded. "I used to sing it to my daughter, Elizabeth. I used to sing it to you. And that"—she motioned to Marlowe's mouth, where the pad of one thumb was lodged—"I used to scold you for that."

Marlowe nodded, but she was still unwilling—unable—to allow herself to hope again. And then Lady Lyndon—her mother—pulled her into her arms. Marlowe stiffened, and then she caught the scent of the woman, the feel of her arms around her, and she knew she was home. She knew this was exactly where she had always longed to be.

Twenty

"I STILL DON'T UNDERSTAND WHY I HAD TO WAIT A fortnight before you would give me an answer," Max said, sounding surly and a bit melodramatic. Marlowe didn't think he was too upset, considering he was currently stroking her bare abdomen.

"Will you stop that?" she said, pretending annoyance. She lifted the volume he had been teaching her from earlier. It was not Shakespeare. Max promised they would read that soon, but this book was a bit easier for her to understand at the moment. "I am trying to read." She squinted, attempting to sound out a word she did not know.

"Are you, now?" His hand moved higher, tracing her breast until her nipple hardened.

She swallowed. "Yes."

"I will soon have a bluestocking for a wife," he said, his hand dropping back to her abdomen and then inching lower. She couldn't read a word with him distracting her like that. She lowered the book, and Max took advantage of her inattention, closed the volume, and tossed it on the floor beside his bed.

"Would you like a bluestocking wife?" Marlowe asked.

"If she is you," Max said, making her shiver with the feather-light touches of his fingers. "Why did you make me wait so long for your answer?"

She rolled her eyes. Back to his marriage proposal. "I was busy, you know. I was becoming reacquainted with my parents. And then there was Gideon and the cubs to think of. I was hardly thinking about marriage."

"You could have at least said yes. You know Susanna was happy to plan all the details."

"I do adore Susanna," Marlowe said, "but I don't think your mother will ever forgive you or tolerate me."

"She will," Max said with confidence. "If you give her grandchildren."

The dowager countess did not seem at all the type to welcome children. And yet, Marlowe thought that maybe there was more to her. Maybe given time…

Max's hand moved again, and she forgot all about his mother.

"She will be satisfied when I have an heir," he whispered. "We should probably start to make an effort."

"Start?" she laughed. "We have been married all of ten days, and all you have done is make an effort to swell my belly."

He moved over her, and she sighed with pleasure.

"Shall I leave you to your reading?" he asked.

She wrapped her arms about his neck, keeping him in place. "Absolutely not."

He bent and kissed her, his mouth tender and unhurried. "That's not all I've done," he said when they parted for breath. Marlowe's breath was quite shallow now, and she had to take several quick gulps of air. "I've been to Parliament with my bill to aid the poor, and consulted with my solicitor in order to allocate funds to open a soup kitchen. And I made certain Gap and Tiny are settling in to their new positions at my country house."

"Thank you for that," she said. He put a finger on her lips.

"It's not for you. It's the very least I can do, and far less than I should do. But I will remedy that."

She had no doubt he would, and a small part of her could not help but think it was her fault more of the cubs had not left Seven Dials. After she had been reunited with her parents, it had taken several days before she'd returned to the old flash ken. By then Beezle had the gang under his control. He was the new arch rogue, having taken Satin's place. She'd managed to speak to Gideon and begged him to leave with her, but he'd refused. Where would he go? To be her servant? He wasn't cut out for the life of a slavey. Besides, he felt responsible for the cubs. He wanted to protect them from whatever plans Beezle was making.

She'd told him Dane was willing to offer the boys honest work at his country estate, far from London, and Gideon had managed to convince Gap and Tiny to leave the gang. She'd hoped it would be more, but at least two of the boys were away from Beezle. Dane's country house was a half-day's ride, but he'd been twice to check on the boys, and said they were doing well. They'd put on weight, and the country air seemed to agree with them. He had promised to take her to visit in a few days' time. Marlowe looked forward to seeing the boys again, but she was loath to spend any time with the dowager countess, who was currently protesting her son's marriage by staying in the country. Marlowe felt horrible for Susanna, who was stuck with her mother.

And she felt incredibly fortunate to have found her own mother. Lady Lyndon—she was even beginning to think of her as Mama—was kind and sweet and could not seem to stop hugging Marlowe. It had been awkward for Marlowe initially. She was not used to affection, but between Dane and her mother, she was becoming used to being loved. Even her father had softened. He was not at all as he'd appeared when she first met him. Then he'd had all of his defenses raised against disappointment. But now that he'd accepted her as his daughter, he could not stop smiling. And he was thrilled with her marriage to Dane, although he would have preferred she wait to marry and spend more time with him.

But Dane was not to be put off. He'd acquired a special license and was quite insistent upon marrying her sooner rather than later. It didn't seem to matter that his friends and most of his family were appalled. Dane said in three- or four-dozen years, no one would care anyway. Marlowe could only marvel at the changes in him. She could only marvel at the changes in her own life. For years, no one had wanted her. And now she had more love than she knew what to do with.

"What are you thinking about?" Dane asked, and Marlowe realized she'd been quiet for several minutes.

She looked into his eyes. "Love."

"Ah. My favorite subject." He kissed her nose, then her cheeks, then her lips.

"I love you, Maxwell," she murmured against his lips.

"I love you, Marlowe Elizabeth Grafton Derring, Countess of Dane. Now." He kissed her lips. "Tomorrow." He kissed her again.

"It *is* tomorrow," she pointed out.

"Forever." He pulled her close into the warmth, safety, and love of his arms.

Acknowledgments

Thank you to my fabulous agents, Joanna MacKenzie, Danielle Egan-Miller, and Abby Saul for their support and feedback on this novel and the series. I am so, so fortunate to work with you.

Thanks to my longtime friend and critique partner Tera Lynn Childs for reading the draft of this book and giving me suggestions and feedback. Thanks to Tera as well for the title of this book.

Thanks to my awesome, fabulous, wonderful friend and assistant Gayle Cochrane. You are a sanity saver. I would not get any sleep without you. Thanks also to my friends, the Shananigans, for all your support. That's you Sarah, Sue, Susan, Flora, Misty, Ruth, Patti, Barbara, Nicole, Lisa, Connie, and Kristy!

I'm blessed to be a member of the West Houston RWA chapter. The members are so supportive, especially my friends Jo Anne Banker, Kay Hudson, Mary Lindsey, Sophie Jordan, Lily Dalton, Nicole Flockton, Vicky Dreiling, Colleen Thompson, and Lark Howard. I'm also grateful to the Beau Monde chapter for their help with all those research questions I can't find the answers to on my own.

Thanks to the Brainstorm Troopers—Robyn DeHart, Anne Mallory, Emily McKay, and especially Margo Maguire, who sparked the idea for this series.

Thank you to my editor Deb Werksman; my publicist Danielle Dresser, to whom this book is dedicated; and all the wonderful professionals I'm privileged to work with at Sourcebooks.

Most importantly, thank you to my husband and my daughter for all your patience and love. Princess Galen, in particular, has been waiting to see the real copy (not the ARC) of the "red book."

About the Author

Shana Galen is the bestselling author of fast-paced, adventurous Regency historicals, including the RT Reviewers' Choice *The Making of a Gentleman*. *Booklist* says "Galen expertly entwines espionage-flavored intrigue with sizzling passion," and *RT Book Reviews* calls her "a grand mistress of the action/adventure subgenre." She taught English at the middle and high school level off and on for eleven years. Most of those years were spent working in Houston's inner city. Now she writes full time. She's happily married and has a daughter who is most definitely a romance heroine in the making. Shana loves to hear from readers, so send her an email or see what she's up to daily on Facebook and Twitter.

"Sit up straight," the Dowager Countess of Dane hissed at her daughter before turning back to their hostess and smiling stiffly as the marchioness prattled on about bonnet styles this season.

Lady Susanna straightened in her uncomfortable chair and tried to appear interested in the discussion. She was wilting in the heat all the ladies had already remarked upon as being unseasonably warm for June. Susanna fluttered her fan and tried to take an interest in the conversation, but she didn't care about hats. She didn't care about garden parties. She didn't care about finding a husband. If her mother ever *heard* Susanna admit husband-hunting was not her favorite pursuit, she would lock Susanna in her room for days.

Susanna did not mind being locked in her room as much as her mother seemed to think. In her room, she could lose herself in her drawing. She could bring out pencil or watercolors and sketch until her hand cramped. Sketching was infinitely preferable to spending hours embroidering in the drawing room, listening to her mother's lectures on decorum and etiquette.

Susanna did not need to be told how to behave. She had been raised to be a perfectly proper young lady. She was the daughter of an earl. She knew what was expected of her.

One: She must marry well.

Two: She must *at all times* exhibit good *ton*.

Three: She must be accomplished, beautiful, fashionable, and witty.

That third expectation was daunting, indeed.

Susanna had spent two decades playing the perfect earl's daughter. She'd had little choice. If she rebelled, even minutely, her mother quickly put her back in her place. At the moment, Susanna wished her place anywhere but here. She sympathized with her failed sketches, feeling as though it were she tossed in the hearth and browning in the fire. She burned slowly, torturously, gasping for her last breath.

Could no one see she was dying inside? Around her, ladies smiled and laughed and sipped tea. Susanna would not survive much longer.

And no one cared.

Ladies of the *ton* were far too concerned with themselves—what were they speaking of now? Haberdashery?—to notice she was smothering under the weight of the heat, the endless cups of tea, the tinny politeness of the ladies' laughs, and the interminable talk of buttons. If she were to sketch her life, she would draw a single horizontal line extending into forever.

Susanna stifled the rising scream—afraid she might wail aloud for once, rather than shriek silently and endlessly. Before she could second-guess herself, she gained her feet. She wobbled, shaking with uncertainty and fear, but she must escape or go quietly mad.

Lady Dane cut her a look pointed as a sharpened blade. "Do sit down, Susanna."

"E-excuse me," Susanna murmured.

"What are you doing?"

Susanna staggered under the weight of the stares from the half-dozen women in their circle. She had not thought it possible to feel any heavier, but the addition of the women's cool gazes on her made her back bow.

"Excuse me. I need to find—"

"Oh, do cease mumbling." Lady Dane sounded remarkably like a dog barking when she issued orders. "You know I hate it when you mumble."

"I'm sorry. I need to—"

"Go ahead, my dear," their hostess said. "One of the footmen will show you the way."

Susanna's burst of freedom was short-lived. She'd no more than moved away from her chair, when her mother rose to join her. Susanna choked back a small sob. There really was no escape.

"Could you not at least wait until we had finished our conversation?" Lady Dane complained, as though Susanna's physical needs were the most inconvenient thing in the world.

"I'm sorry, Mama."

"Why don't you stay, Lady Dane?" the marchioness asked. "Surely, Lady Susanna can find her way to the retiring room by herself."

Susanna's gaze locked on her mother's. Inside, she squirmed like one of the insects her brothers used to pin for their collections. Lady Dane would most certainly defy the marchioness. She would never let her disappointing daughter out of her sight.

Susanna had one glimmer of hope. Her brother's scandalous marriage a few weeks ago had noticeably thinned the pile of invitations the Danes received. The family was not shunned, exactly, but they had spent more nights at home than the debutante daughter of an earl should.

Her mother patted Susanna on the arm, the stinging pinch delivered under cover of affection.

"Do not dawdle."

Susanna need not be told twice. She practically ran for the house.

"She is perfectly safe here." The marchioness's voice carried across the lawn. "I understand why you play the hawk. She must make a good match, and the sooner the better."

The sooner she escaped this garden party, the better. Every group of ladies she passed bestowed snake-like smiles before raising their fans and whispering. Sometimes the whispers weren't even whispered.

"Dane introduced a bill to establish a central police force! What next? *Gendarmes?*"

A few steps more.

"I heard her brother began a soup kitchen."

Almost there.

"St. Giles! Can you imagine?"

Susanna ducked into the cool darkness of the town house and flattened herself against the wall. She closed her eyes, swiping at the stinging tears. *Breathe, breathe.* Free from the whispers-that-were-not-whispers and the stares and, best of all, her mother. She slouched in smug rebellion.

"May I be of assistance, my lady?"

Susanna's spine went rigid, and she opened her eyes. A footman bestowed a bemused smile on her. She imagined it was not every day a lady ran away from the marchioness's garden party and collapsed in relief.

"The ladies' retiring room. Could you direct me?"

"This way, Lady Susanna."

She followed him through well-appointed though cold, impersonal rooms until she reached a small room filled with plants, several chairs, two small hand mirrors on stands, a pitcher of fresh water and basin, and screens for privacy. Susanna stepped inside and closed the door. Finally alone. She straightened her white muslin gown and adjusted the blue sash at the high waist. Her hat sported matching ribbons. She might have removed it would it not been so much trouble to pin in place again. At the basin, she splashed water into the bowl and dabbed at her face. One look in the mirror showed her cheeks flushed and her brown eyes too bright. She had the coloring typical of a strawberry blond, and her pale skin reddened easily.

In the mirror, she spotted something move and a woman in a large, elaborately plumed hat emerged from behind the screen. Susanna's heart sank.

She willed the woman to return to the party quickly and leave Susanna to her solitude. The screens provided a convenient shield.

"You are Lady Susanna, are you not?"

There would be no hiding—but she was the daughter of an earl. Susanna pushed her shoulders back.

"Yes, I am. I'm sorry. I don't believe we've met."

The woman patted her perfect coiffure, which was tucked neatly under her hat, and poured water from the ewer over her hands. "I am Lady Winthorpe."

"*Oh.*"

In the mirror, the countess's face brightened with amusement. "I see you have heard of me. Do not worry. All of my children have married now." She bent, baring her teeth in the mirror and examining them closely. "I cannot tell you what a relief it is not to have to push them at every titled man or woman in Town. I imagine your poor mother is at her wits' end."

Heat rushed into Susanna's face, and in the mirror her cheeks reddened most unbecomingly. Dane's marriage was indeed scandalous, and because it was, no one ever mentioned it to her.

"I…" Her tongue lay thick and clumsy in her mouth.

"What came over the earl?" the countess asked, patting the yellow and white plumes of her hat, which matched her gown. "Why would he make such a poor match?"

The countess turned to stare directly at Susanna. In the mirror behind the countess, the red-faced girl shrank.

"Lady Elizabeth is the daughter of the Marquess of Lyndon." She'd said it so often it had become a chant.

The countess flicked open her fan and wafted it. Painted on the fan was an image of a peacock with its feather spread. "*Lady* Elizabeth was raised in a rookery as a thief. Even being the daughter of a marquess cannot redeem her."

She would not shrink. Susanna forced iron into her spine. "My brother loves her. That is enough for me."

"Love. How sweet."

The fan snapped closed and the countess tapped Susanna's arm with it. "What does your mother think of this profession of love?"

"I—" Susanna had no idea. She'd never once heard her mother speak the word *love*, although she railed against her eldest son's mésalliance often enough.

"She was in love once. Did she ever tell you that?"

Susanna dared not open her mouth for fear she would only emit babble. Were they still speaking of the Dowager Countess of Dane? Surely, she had never been in love. Her mother did not know the meaning of the word. But perhaps Lady Winthorpe spoke of her late father. He had not exactly doted on his children either, especially not on her. But the countess might have mistaken the late earl's marriage for a love match.

"My father and mother—"

The countess waved the fan, narrowly missing Susanna's chin.

"I do not refer to your mother's marriage. She married him for the title and the money, I imagine. Your mother is no fool. But there were days, in our youth, when I thought she might choose another course." The woman's blue eyes had become so unfocused as to look gray. "Handsome young beaux. Picnics in Hyde Park. Nights at Vauxhall Gardens. Long, dark nights." She winked at Susanna, and Susanna flinched with shock.

The implication…or was it an insinuation…or an intimation…?

The countess was not to be believed.

"I don't know what you mean."

"No, I see that you don't. In any case, your mother made her choice." The woman's eyes, blue again, narrowed. Once again, Susanna was reminded of the exposed and vulnerable insects pinned to her brother's boards. Of course, the insects were dead, and she was still alive.

Barely.

The countess stared at her so intently, Susanna actually took a step back.

The countess tapped her chin with the edge of the fan. "I wonder…"

Susanna held her breath, leaning forward to hear each and every syllable. All for naught. The woman didn't continue. The long silence, coupled with her curiosity, compelled Susanna to prompt Lady Winthorpe.

"You wonder?"

Voices rose and fell outside the door, and Susanna emitted a weak cry of protest. The door opened, revealing two young women speaking quietly to each other. One look at Susanna and their conversation ceased. The girls shared a look before they disappeared behind the screen and dissolved into giggles. Susanna toed the pale pink carpet with her slipper.

"Good day to you," the countess said, opening the door and stepping out into the music room.

Susanna stood rooted in place with the giggles behind her and questions swirling like dust motes in her mind. She should not pry further, but she was always doing as she ought. Her slipper dug into the rug, attacking the threads viciously. She caught the

door before it could close all the way. The countess whirled when Susanna emerged behind her, and
Susanna took advantage of the woman's surprise.

"I cannot help but ask, my lady. What do you
wonder?"

"I think I had better not answer that." She spoke
slowly, enunciating every word. Weighing each one
against her tongue before speaking it. "Your mother
would not thank me."

And there was that look again—the pitiful look one
gave a pinned insect.

"But I see you, Lady Susanna, with that hair and
that nose, and I do wonder." She sauntered across the
music room. "Yes, I do."

Susanna touched her hair and her nose. What of
them? Did the countess mean to confuse her?

She crumpled onto the piano stool. Chasing the
countess was not an option, least of all because it
would mean returning to the garden party.

Neither did she wish to return to the retiring room.

She wandered to a harp and plucked at one of the
strings. She'd always wanted to play the harp, but her
mother had not allowed her to learn. Sitting with the
instrument between her legs was unseemly. Susanna
plucked another string, enjoying the light, airy sound
of it.

What had the Countess of Winthorpe meant about
her mother being in love? Had her mother fallen in
love with a man before she met Susanna's father?

She plucked the strings, feeling the thick wires
vibrate through her gloves.

A man her mother met at Hyde Park...no, not

Hyde Park. Hyde Park was fashionable, the place to see and be seen. The sunny breezes of Hyde Park chased any scandal away.

But dark, sensuous Vauxhall Gardens…

Susanna had never been. Her mother would not permit it. Her brothers had undoubtedly visited, but Susanna did not possess their freedom.

She plucked another string. She should ask her mother what Lady Winthorpe meant. Her mother's reaction might provide some clue. Of course, her mother might also tell her it was none of her concern, but Susanna was twenty now and would certainly marry in the next year. Lady Dane might relish the opportunity to share stories of her own days as a young debutante.

Susanna had only to muster the courage to ask. A dissonant note sounded on the harp.

It would require quite a lot of courage.

❧

Gideon stood in the Golden Gallery in the dome of St. Paul's Cathedral. All of London sprawled before him. The sun set on the River Thames, clogged with ships of all sizes and shapes. The forest of masts jutted from the foul murky water like dead tree branches in winter. Just beyond, the soot-blackened buildings of London were crammed together as though huddled in fear. The day was hot and the streets clogged with short-tempered people jostling their way through the throngs. Peddlers pushed carts, children chased dogs, and horses pulled rattlers. The noise on the streets deafened him at times.

High above it all, blissful silence reigned. The wind whooshed in his ears and ruffled his hair.

But even up here he found only temporary escape from the world below.

Beezle stood just behind him, his gaze as dark as the dirt under his fingernails.

"I could get used to a view like this," Gideon said, spreading his arms like a king surveying his kingdom. He breathed deeply for effect, as the air up here wasn't much cleaner than that below. "Smell that fresh air. The wind in my hair. This is the life."

"You do the trick, and you can have any life you want," Beezle said quietly. With Satin dead, Beezle was the new arch rogue of the Covent Garden Cubs. Gideon had tried to distance himself from the gang, but old habits were hard to break. That, and Beezle was none too willing to allow one of his best rooks to walk away.

Reluctantly, Gideon abandoned the indigo and orange skies of London. "I pinch the necklace, and I never have to see your ugly mug again?"

"And here I thought it was the blunt you were after. A hundred yellow boys will make you rick as a gentry cove."

"The necklace is worth ten times that."

"The necklace is mine, and I choose to let you in on the game. Do we row in the same boat, Gideon?"

Gideon rocked back on his heels, imitating the swells who had all the money and time in the world.

Beezle waited. His expression remained hooded, but Gideon would have bet a shilling—if he'd had one—the rogue chafed at being made to wait. They were of a similar height—he and Beezle—and both had dark hair. That was where the similarities ended. Beezle had a narrow, bird-like face perpetually twisted into a malevolent expression. Gideon liked to think of himself as a rum duke. He bore no one ill-will and was generally good-natured.

He didn't want to row in Beezle's boat. Hell, he didn't want to be in the same ocean with him, but this was his chance. The blunt from this job would allow him to walk away from rooking. He could be his own man, start over in a new place with a new name. Be whomever he wanted.

He'd never make it out of London without first lining his pockets. It took guineas to start over, and that's where Beezle came in.

Gideon held out a hand, offering it to the devil.

Beezle's icy fingers wrapped around his flesh, and Gideon's belly clenched in revulsion.

"Let's do the trick," Gideon said.